KOMAROV'S CONSPIRACY

DAVID STUART BLACK

For Bobby
With my best wishes
from
David
21/11/15

Komarov's Conspiracy

This is a work of fiction. Names, characters, places and incidents either are the product of the author's imagination or are used fictitiously. Any resemblance to actual persons, living or dead, events or locales is entirely coincidental.

Copyright © David Stuart Black 2014

All rights reserved. Except as provided by the Copyright, Designs and Patents Act 1988. No part of this publication may be reproduced, stored in a retrieval system, or transmitted, in any form or by any means without the written permission of the publisher.

ISBN-13 : 978-1519430915
ISBN-10 : 1519430914

1

7.30am, Thursday, 2 April 2015
Makati City, Manila, Philippines

The instructions to the SWAT team were explicit. They were to take their target alive - there was much vital information to get out of him. Sergeant Aquino, the leader of the team crept forward silently along the muddy narrow alley. Carefully he counted down the numbers on the doors. Just as he and the team were reaching the address they'd been given by the anonymous tip-off, a short but large Filipino woman burst through the beaded curtain that served as her front door and into the alley in front of them. Brazenly, she crossed her arms over her ample chest, her feet firmly planted on the ground, intent on blocking their way.

'What you doin' in my alley?' She gave Aquino one of her matriarchal stares.

Aquino halted the team and, as silence was an absolute requirement of the raid, he resisted the risky option of forcing her aside. Instead, he stepped quickly forward, towering over her, his chin just inches above her head, Slowly she tilted her face up towards his, her expression still defiant.

'National Security,' he whispered – as harshly and loudly as he dared. 'If you don't want to spend the rest of your miserable life in jail, you'll get back to where you came from right now, do you understand?'

Apparently she did understand. This close to him, she could see the discrete label on his left shoulder: the initials SAF – the Special Action Force. Obviously she had heard of them – the Tagaligtas. Their reputation was enough for her; she dropped her arms and went back into her house.

Above them, in the first floor apartment that had been rented for him for the duration of the job, Antonio Ramos caught a slight echo of this exchange. He frowned; strange for there to be any activity in the alley at such an early hour. Rising from the trestle table where he was working, he tip-toed as silently as a cat across the bare floorboards to the half-open window above the alley. He winced and pulled a face as he stepped on a squeaky board; his presence here was supposed to remain unknown. On reaching the window he used just one finger to move the curtains apart a couple of inches. Peering down, he could now see the five of them – charcoal-grey helmet tops, gun muzzles, bulky body armour - and was just in time to see his neighbour Imelda going back into her house. He felt his pulse rate rise swiftly; sixty, one hundred, a hundred and twenty, and, suddenly, there it was, throbbing in his throat.

He had known there were risks working for 'the foreigners' - as his partner called them - but the money had been too good to let caution decide. What worried him at this moment was how they had located him. The foreigners had rented this place for him, equipped it, bought the sparse furnishings - and all of it in supposedly absolute secrecy. Still, no time to think about that now; he knew instinctively, that the squad had come for him.

Letting the curtain drop, he ran back across the room to the front door. On his way he pulled his mobile phone from his pocket, and, despite fumbling fingers, managed to press a speed-dial number.

Whilst it was ringing out, he reached the door, turned the heavy key in the old lock and grimaced again at the noise this made. Reaching up, he threw the heavy bolt across the top of the door. Neither of these actions would stop the squad, of course, but they might give him an extra minute or so to make his escape.

The mobile was answered as he ran from the door back to the trestle table,

'Don't talk,' he whispered. 'There's an SAF hit squad on their way up here to get me – not sure if they'll try to take me in or shoot to kill,'

There was a babble of noise from the mobile,

'Don't have time for any of that, gotta go. You know where all the money is... no, no the money the foreigners paid me...'

More babble from the phone,

'Yes, take the lot, get the hell out of Manila, get down to Uncle Paolo's in Boracay, I'll meet you there.' He slammed the clam mobile shut and thrust it into his pocket. On reaching the trestle table, he tried to work his feet into sandals with their straps still done up, while, at the same time, pressing down on the power buttons of the two laptops he had been working on – no time to shut them down properly but vital to turn them off, to give the authorities the trouble of having to crack the passwords and the special defences he had installed on both of them.

'Come on, come on.' He waited for what seemed like an age for the machines to die – though, in fact, they did so in just four seconds. With a flicker of a relieved smile, he shut their lids and gave each a tap as though to reinforce his defences. As he bent down to kiss one of them, he whispered, *'Think they'll get my secrets from you easily do they? You'll hold out, won't you, my clever little babes?'*

This was no sooner said than he heard the faint creak of a board on the stairway. Jolted back into action, he looked around;

snatching up an old green canvas shopping bag, he picked a bulky Toshiba laptop from amongst other brand-new machines, and forced it into the bag. Next, hurriedly but carefully, he pushed a printer to one side to make more room on the top of the flimsy trestle table, and with the help of a chair, climbed up onto it. It creaked and moved a couple of inches to the left but, to his relief, it seemed to steady and settle.

Just then the silence of the apartment was shattered by an explosion of noise from the door behind him, and a blow from something metallic which left a ringing echo. In a frenzy now, he reached forward, undid the latch of the window and threw it open as far as it would go. Putting the straps of the canvas shopping bag around his neck, he cradled the bag itself into his lap, bent double, and began to squeeze through the window frame. As he desperately forced himself through it, a second blow landed on the door, showering the room with splinters of wood and screws. The old-fashioned lock sagged, lopsidedly, now held to the door by just one screw.

The corrugated roof of an outhouse was only five feet below the window sill and Ramos jumped just as a third blow burst open the door behind him.

On the far side of the door, the young squaddie had thrown the third blow of the two-handled battering ram in a wide arc above his head. It had torn the bolt from the catch on the door-frame and burst the door wide. The squaddie stepped back to allow Aquino to squeeze past and enter the apartment first.

Aquino, gun held out in front of him at shoulder level, was just in time to see the silhouette of Ramos as he jumped. His first shot hit Ramos in the leg, disabling him as intended. But the strap of one of his sandals had caught in the long arm of the window stay, turning Ramos's jump into a fall. By the time Aquino fired his second shot, Ramos's body was horizontal. The bullet entered his groin, tore through his vital organs and exited at his neck, slicing through his carotid artery. He was dead as his body hit the corrugated iron roof below.

Aquino rushed forward, leant over the trestle table as far he could and peered down at Ramos. The young man lay sprawled like a rag doll, the straps of the shopping bag entwined round his neck. A trickle of blood had oozed from his mouth and his nose, and his eyes looking up, unseeingly, at the blue Manila sky.

'Shit,' said Aquino. 'Bloody hell,'

He backed away from the table, to the VHF from its clasp on his shoulder and rang into Control.

'Stormboy here,' he said as soon as he was through to them. 'Mission completed though I'm afraid the target was killed trying to escape.'

The squaddie standing next to him could hear the torrent of

Control's verbal abuse crackling from the VHF.

'Of course I knew he was to be taken alive,' said Aquino as soon as there was a break in the din from the other end. 'Yeah, yeah, I knew we needed to get information out of him. But, Hell, he was already halfway out the window! Seconds later he'd have been gone, never to be seen again in all the maze of alleyways round these parts.'

More ranting came from the VHF. Aquino was acutely aware that his boss's boss – those and above him even – had got involved in this incident. Although he didn't know why, he knew that this was being treated as more than just the apprehension of another young hacker. When he spoke again, he was more subdued.

'I'll do that right away. He fled with something obviously important in a canvas shopping bag. I'll get one of the lads to secure it right now. There are two laptops up here. He must have been working on them; they're switched off but still warm. I'll get them and anything else back to you as soon as possible. We'll need a van to the end of the lane, and there's the hacker's body to pick up too.'

There was more 'talk from the VHF and when it stopped, Aquino said, 'Okay, I understand the rush, so the sooner the van gets here, the sooner you'll have the laptops.' He clicked the VHF off and returned it to its clip.

'Right, two of you get down and secure the body and the shopping bag till the van gets here,' said Aquino to the two of his men behind him. 'And you Felipe,' he continued to the squaddie beside him, 'help me collect up all the stuff in the apartment. We need everything - the laptops, the printer, mobiles, the answerphone, the lot, all right?'

The two of them set about collecting the machines to the end of the table and then rifled through empty boxes pieces of paper, collecting up invoices and delivery notes - anything that might help identify the young man's employers. In their search, Aquino spotted a new fibre optic internet cable, snaking in through the lower corner of the window frame, almost hidden by the curtain. Outside, he could see that it was but one of a tangle of wires strung along poles running here and there through the maze of alleys and shanty houses —wires used by the locals to steal electricity and cable TV. Tracing the internet cable back would be difficult but, with Ramos now dead, it might still need to be done in order to find out who was behind him and more of what they were planning.

The tip-off they had received in the early hours of the morning had proved to be right both about this address and about Ramos, '*the way he had tried to escape proved that,*' thought Aquino. But they still needed to know what the tip-off had meant by 'the big one'. The caller had said that the recent spate of cyber–attacks on Manila's smaller banks had just been practice for the 'big one' but, as yet, no one knew what it was, nor where or when it would happen.

* * * * *

A specially convened meeting of the Association of the Asian Bankers of Manila had been called to discuss a number of recent cyber-attacks on small banks in and around the City. Understandably, the attacks were unnerving for the Association's members. The blinds in the conference room were half down to cut the glare from the sun outside. The atmosphere was the perfect blend of temperature and humidity; the only two sounds were those of the speaker and the faintest whirring from the air-conditioning unit. Those attending were seated round a large oval mahogany table and all were focused on one of their number who was demanding to know what the authorities were doing about these attacks. The Chairman was sweating despite the cool of the room; he appeared anxious, and was fidgeting, for the truth of the matter was that the police had but one lead – one that had come in that very morning about which he still had no details.

'So, Mr Chairman, I hope, that, with this new lead, you have some good news for us – perhaps the cyber police are making some progress at last?'

A bank messenger entered the room just as the speaker finished asking this question.

'One minute if you please.' The Chairman turned towards the messenger, 'I hope this is urgent as…'

But the messenger merely bowed and, as though he were mute, pointed to the far side of the table.

'Very well, carry on,' said the Chairman and the messenger went round the table, all eyes following him until he stopped beside the chair of Zhang Wei, Chief Executive Officer of the Manila Beijing Bank. Bending low, he whispered his message into the other's ear. What little colour there was in Zhang's face drained away and he put a hand up to his forehead, hiding his eyes from the others. The messenger backed slowly away from Zhang, straightened up gave another shallow bow, and hurried from the room. Zhang looked up and, avoiding eye contact with the others, turned to the Chairman.

The message could hardly have been worse or come at a more embarrassing time and he made his first decision on the crisis that had just struck his bank – unable to save face by telling his fellow bankers the truth, he lied.

'My wife's been involved in a serious motor accident' he said, 'and is now on her way to St Luke's Hospital in Global City. I beg that I may be excused to go and be with her.'

'I'm sorry to hear that,' said the Chairman, 'I'm sure we all wish her well - of course you must be excused to be with her.'

Zhang rose, collected his papers and stuffed them into his briefcase. Then, with downcast eyes, he hurried from the room.

In the lobby outside, waiting for the lift, he shifted his weight back and forth from one foot to the other, his gaze fixed on the lighted box above the lift doors telling him of the lift's dilatory progress towards his floor. The lift arrived after what seemed an age; he continued to fret the whole way down to the lobby, desperate to get out of the building before someone stopped him and asked what he had just been told. On reaching the marble lobby he half-ran out into the bright sunlight and the wall of heat and going down a couple of the wide marble steps, he stood for a moment, peering left and right for a taxi. Looking alternately left and right, at last he spotted one coming down the street. As it got closer he could see that it was for hire, and he ran down the last few steps, using his briefcase as a weapon to barge through the crowds, hailing the taxi with his free hand as he went. To his relief the car pulled over. He struggled for a second or two with the reluctant door handle, finally won, and clambered in.

'The Manila Beijing Bank, Paseo de Roxas,' he said, in a demanding, abrupt tone.

Spurred on by the promise of double the fare, the driver pressed the taxi whenever the traffic allowed, the faster parts of the journey exposing both the age of the car and its weaknesses. The bodywork shook as though one half of it were a different vehicle to the other; passing over some of the more severe bumps, the rattling box gave the impression that it might come apart at any moment. Throughout the journey Zhang thought about the message. It had merely said *'Bank forced to close its doors - you must come back.'*

As the taxi was approached his head office building, up ahead he could see a large gathering of people pressing towards and against the thick glass doors. From their gestures it was clear that they were in a state of collective agitation and as the taxi drew closer, he could hear the shouting too. He made his second decision of the crisis. He sat up, leant forward and told the driver to pass on by the bank's front entrance and take the first left. As soon as they were out of sight of the crowds, he had the taxi stop, got out and paid. Crossing the narrow street to a small door, he took out a bunch of keys, he selected one and let himself in. He found himself in a narrow passageway with a short flights of steps at the end of it. As he hurried along, sweat held his fine, sparse hair to his whitened forehead. He soon emerged into a narrow hallway with two service lifts; as one of these lifts was at the ground floor, he quickly entered, closed the metal gates and pressed the button for the top floor. After an unsteady ride, the lift ground to a noisy halt on the top floor. Hurrying out, around a couple of corners, and through another set of swing doors, he came at last into the main lobby of the executive suites.

As soon as he appeared, the crowds of whispering people, gathered in small groups, drifted apart to allow him through to his office which, like the hallway, was a melee of anxious people. They stopped speaking and most sidled away out of the room as he entered. He went round his desk and slumped into his chair. He glanced at the little gold-plated carriage clock on his desk - it was just coming up to eleven-thirty. The remaining people in his room dispersed and, soon his most senior manager, Guan, and one other short darkish man were all that were left of the earlier crowd.

As soon as he appeared to have regained some composure, Guan cleared his throat, stepped nearer the desk and introduced the short dark man.

'This is Emilio Gonzales, head of Manila's cyber police unit,' he said.

Gonzales took a step forward and held out his hand. Zhang, remembering his manners, got to his feet, bowed slightly and shook hands. With a sweep of his hand he indicated that all three of them should sit.

'I'm afraid that whilst you were out at your meeting, we suffered a major cyber- attack,' said Manager Guan. 'We lost all our current customer records, names, account numbers, transactions, balances...'

'Our databases; – were they just destroyed or have they been stolen to be put to some other use?' asked Zhang.

'Destroyed, we think,' replied Guan, 'but Mr Gonzales is here because this attack is apparently just the tip of an iceberg – perhaps he should take over now and explain that to you.' Guan made a small gesture with his hand towards the other man.

'We had an anonymous telephone tip-off early this morning' said Gonzales. 'When we followed it up, we raided a young computer hacker in the Pasay City area of Manila. I'm afraid he was killed trying to escape but we've seized his equipment, including a couple of laptops he'd been working on. We're still trying to crack the passwords on those two. We found it easy, however, to get into a third machine he took with him as he fled. From this, even in the short time available, we've been able to get quite a lot of useful information and I can tell you already that the main reason for the attack on your bank was not to damage the bank itself, but was just a trial run for something much bigger.'

'Something much bigger?' repeated Zhang, 'I don't understand.'

'Let me explain,' said Gonzales, 'We believe that the Toshiba laptop he took when he fled was his personal machine. Strange, but when we managed to get a tricky catch open, we found that it was just an empty shell and hidden inside it was a small brand-new

Russian-built machine – we're guessing that this ruse was to make it less likely that anyone would steal it. The information on it was limited, though the emails he regularly sent his associates were in English and often had bits of computer software attached to them which he had developed or rewritten for them. From other information on it, we're now confident that these associates were his financial backers and they also directed his hacking efforts.'

'Aha, so presumably you managed to trace these associates through the email address?' Zhang's face muscles relaxed almost as far as a smile.

'We're working on that,' replied Gonzales, 'even though the email account and all particulars of it were terminated last night. We also know from this little Russian machine, that Ramos was practising hacking into just one particular type of computer defence system - one that's produced by a British software company called CSL. It appears that he was perfecting attack software for what the tip-off had also called "the big one". Through the Toshiba, we've now established that this "big one" is almost certainly an attack due to take place on a bank which is protected by CSL software and that it's scheduled to take place in London tomorrow.'

'But you say that the young hacker was killed early this morning, so who was it who attacked my bank this morning?' asked Zhang.

'We are almost certain it was his associates – the people paying him for all this hacking and software writing. They probably used the latest software he'd developed and written for them.'

'So you're telling me that his associates got Ramos to risk being caught hacking into these banks, improving or refining their attacking software for them, and they then tipped *you* off to dispose of him as soon as he'd served his purpose ?' asked Zhang.

'Yes, looks like that,'

'Bastards,' said Zhang. 'But here's another thing I don't understand. If you're going to '*do*' a bank, why the tip-off about it? Doesn't make sense.'

'At the moment, it doesn't make sense to us either,' said Gonzales, 'and we're still working on that. In the meantime we've warned our counterparts in London of a threatened attack. It's still only seven-thirty in the morning there but we'll certainly let you know of any developments later.'

Gonzales left soon after that. In the silence that followed all the turmoil of the past hour or so it suddenly struck Zhang. In the drama of the morning's events he had entirely forgotten the one person who was even more important to him, than his career – his daughter Meiling. Just last week she had rung him to say how excited she was that her UK immigration papers had been approved. At last she and her partner were safe to go ahead and buy a place of their own in London. But now Zhang wondered: how safe would that be?

If the threatened attack tomorrow in London was carried out on a big bank, almost all the experts agreed that with all the inter-bank loans, deals, and contracts, it could quite possibly lead to a general collapse of all of them. Like a falling house of cards, the City of London, then Wall Street – and maybe the World. Even with some of the banks running continuity sites, replicating their operations, such an attack could give rise to panic and how safe would buying a place be for Meiling be then?

He agonised over what to do. Should he ring her and warn her of what he had just heard? But what if it came to nothing? What if there was no collapse? Would he not just worry her needlessly? On the other hand, if he failed to ring and financial turmoil ensued, would she ever forgive him if she had locked herself into something impossible to get out of? He would give it an hour and decide then.

2

Thursday, 8am

Home Office, Whitehall, London

The news of the Manila cyber-attacks and the threat of an attack on a big bank in the City of London tomorrow, came first to Sandy Scale. As the head of the City of London's Cyber Crime Unit, Scale was responsible for monitoring and countering all cyber threats to the City. He was Emilio Gonzales's counterpart in this respect and the two had met a couple of times as part of the international network dealing with the growing incidences of bank cyber-attacks. Although there was no real detail yet to Gonzales's news, Scale was taking no chances; he rang the Home Secretary, Peter Forsyth, at his London home at about the time he guessed he would be having his breakfast.

'You did the right thing ringing me this early,' said Forsyth after Scale had told him all that he knew so far. 'I'll ring the PM and the Chancellor personally; I'm pretty sure the PM will want a Cobra Meeting as soon as everyone can be got hold of. While I do that, will you ring Bill Fisher at the Bank of England? I don't know if you've met him yet; he's the Governor's recently appointed advisor on all cyber warfare matters. Fix up a meeting with him. Give him all the information you can and, if necessary, pursue matters further with your contacts in Manila. I'll expect the two of you to take a lead in this and keep us all advised of developments.'

'Certainly, Home Secretary, I have actually met Fisher and I'll ring him right away,' replied Scale. This conversation over, he looked up Fisher's number and rang it. As he waited for a reply, he thought about Fisher and about the present threat. By reputation, Fisher was a smart operator, someone good to have on your side in an emergency. The Manila news was the first time they had been given an advance warning of something of this kind, the first time it was necessary to worry about what was coming before it arrived. He was looking forward to having someone as good as Fisher with whom to share this burden.

'Sandy, you're early; – does that mean that something's up?' said Fisher as soon as he heard who was calling,

'Yes, afraid so.' Scale, went on to give Fisher a quick resume of Gonzales's news and finishing by saying, 'so the Home Secretary suggested we meet right away and see what more we can get from Manila or any other sources,'

'Okay,' replied Fisher, 'but as my boss, the Governor, will be sure to be called to attend the Cobra Meeting and will want to meet you before that, could you come here to my office in the Bank of England?'

Though Scale probably outranked Fisher, he had yet to meet the Governor of the Bank of England, so he agreed.

'Good, I'll warn security to look out for you,' said Fisher

Scale took some time to get to the Bank of England as, even at eight in the morning, traffic was heavy. When he eventually arrived, Fisher had organised coffee for the two of them and poured some as Scale seated himself and got some papers out of his briefcase.

'Thanks for your early morning call about the threat from Manila,' said Fisher

'You know, coming here close just near to each other and an appalling thought occurred to me. If this threatened Manila attack succeeds, chances are that those two, along with all the other banks throughout the country will close. I just pictured them, queues of people snaking away from their firmly shut doors, all of 'em waiting in vain to get their money out. Our analysis at the office is that, unlike 2008, an attack on a big bank would turn very quickly into the closure of them all – ATMs turned off, cash drying up, credit cards useless: a nightmare. Before you could say it, there'd be bloody anarchy in the streets... In terms of security, which is our remit, it could turn into an absolute disaster.'

'Yes, - except none of that's going to happen,' said Fisher,

There was a silence for a moment as Scale looked back at him, his cup halfway to his mouth,

'I don't understand,' he said. 'What do you mean, *"none of that's going happen"*?'

'You've been invited to the conference here at the Bank of England tomorrow, haven't you?' asked Fisher.

'Yes, I'll be there,' replied Scale. Then, the thought suddenly struck him, he added, 'Ah, yes, the cyber defence software you're introducing to the financial world at the conference.'

'That's it,' said Fisher. 'We're introducing Athena. That's why a bank collapse isn't going to happen,'

'Damn, I should apologise to you,' said Scale, 'although you've invited me, I confess I haven't read all the literature your people sent about the conference or... er Athena – thought I'd learn all about it when I got there. So what is Athena exactly?'

'Named after the ancient Greek goddess of strategic warfare. The man who came up with the original idea that later led on to Athena was Sir Jeremy Towneley, head of the Towncley Bank - you'll have heard of him?'

'Oh, yeah, everyone knows of Sir Jeremey, the Towneley Foundation, his philanthropy, the acceptable face of banking...'

'Quite,' confirmed Fisher. 'Well a year or more ago he and a couple of others at the top of world finance, people like Warren Buffet and Isiah Feldman, said that, in their view, the greatest danger to the stability of the world's financial systems was a cyber-attack on a big bank. They agreed that the collapse of one big bank these days could bring all the others down too. Sir Jeremy was damned if *his* bank's three-hundred and fifty years of history was going to go down the tubes with the rest of them. But, unlike the others in the financial world – who still spend huge sums of money on cyber defences - Sir Jeremy decided to go on the offensive - that *counter-attack* was a better strategy. With me so far?'

Scale just nodded, as he was sipping his coffee at that moment.

'So he put together a unique team to develop counter-attacking software,' Fisher went on. 'He also acquired computers powerful enough to deliver really effective retaliatory blow to hackers. I'm afraid that Sir Jeremy contracted terminal cancer not long ago, so he passed the project over to his nephew, Ranald MacCrammond…'

'Ranald?' repeated Scale, as though he had misheard,

'Yes, real Scottish Highland name, indeed Ranald moved the team to his father's remote island up there, Craithe…' Fisher quickly put his clenched hand up to his mouth as soon as he had said the island's name, 'damn, shouldn't have said that last bit.'

'What bit?' Scale, put down his cup.

'The bit about moving it all up to the island of Craithe, that's a closely guarded secret. Still, seeing it's you, no harm's done – but keep that to yourself. Anyway, as I was saying, the island's way up off the west coast of Scotland – ideal from a security point of view. He also went into partnership with a large, secretive conglomerate, leaders in the new quantum computing technologies.'

'Why secretive?' asked Scale. 'Do *you* know who they are?'

'Not sure,' replied Fisher. 'Maybe the research and production of weapons of cyber warfare doesn't fit in with the image of their other businesses. Anyway, the point is, between this conglomerate and the team on Craithe, they're now reputedly ahead even of Microsoft, Google and the Wall Street Bankers Goldman Sacks in their development of quantum computing technologies. The team on Craithe have come up with a way of synergising quantum and digital technologies to produce what Sir Jeremy first wanted, the ultimate cyber warfare weapon – one that can both counter-attack and attack.'

Scale became more attentive at this, leaning forward and taking up his pen which had been lying on the table till then. 'As head of City cyber security I should have heard of this.'

Fisher was not sure if this was a regret or a rebuke. 'It's been top secret till now, and we need to keep it that way,'

'I understand,' said Scale,

'I happen to know from talking to Ranald MacCrammond, that this was the one thing he most feared when he took over his uncle's project.'

'And what was that?'

'He desperately wants the project to succeed – being his uncle's legacy so to speak; he's put everything into it, and I think there's as personal, family thing driving him on as well.'

'Well, that's very laudable,' said Scale, 'but what's there to fear in that? And what's the family thing? You've got me hooked on this story now.'

'Sorry I didn't explain fully,' said Fisher, 'It's true that soon after its's official launch tomorrow, the Athena attack warning system will have been installed in most major institutions in the City of London – and soon after that Wall Street, then Tokyo followed eventually by the rest of the world. In no time at all bank hackers will discover that the warning system will trigger a millisecond response from Athena which will effectively destroy any of their equipment connected to their attack. Before long, Sir Jeremy's dream will have been fulfilled when the world of bank hackers will have reached the conclusion that hacking banks is simply not worth the cost and the trouble.'

'Well, that's great isn't it?' said Scale. 'Job done. So, again, where's this fear you mentioned?'

'A fear that's become a reality. The fear that the team might come up with more than just bank hacker software.'

He stopped for a moment and topped up their coffee.

'And I'm afraid that they have,' he continued, 'their research and development ran on at such a pace that they did indeed produce the monster Ranald had always feared might be developed.'

'Monster,' repeated Scale sitting up straight. 'Isn't that a bit over the top?'

'Not really. What they developed is so powerful that the Craithe team labelled it cyber warfare's first nuclear device.'

'Come on; – nuclear device? Now that must be an exaggeration,' said Scale smiling

'You're right, it is a bit much,' said Fisher, 'because of course it's not a bomb. Having said that, in military terms, Athena takes cyber warfare from bows and arrows straight to missiles. Thanks to its quantum computing elements, it can slice through any known present-day computer defences as though they simply weren't there, and once inside a target's core operating system, it can either take complete control, paralyse it or destroy it.'

'That much of a difference from other current weapons? Extraordinary that I had no inkling such a thing was possible, let alone that it now exists.'

'Yes, as it can master any computer system there is and, there's absolutely no defence against it for the foreseeable future.

Just as the first atomic bomb was what our American friends call a 'game changer', so Athena is a revolution to cyber warfare.'

'What you say about mastering any existing computer system…' said Scale. 'You mean this Athena could take down an air traffic control system, a power grid, or a rail network?'

'Yes, right. So perhaps you can now see. What Ranald feared has actually arrived - a cyber weapon without which any state-backed hacker team would lag disastrously behind all the others. And as for any self-respecting organised crime syndicate or mafia organisation, just imagine what they could extort if holding a power grid to ransom?'

'It hardly bears thinking about, does it? So how did you come by all of this secret information about Craithe anyway?'

'Almost by accident, really,' replied Fisher. 'The two of us had been attending a small elite cyber warfare conference here at the Bank of England, and after dinner at an hotel in the West End for all the delegates, the two of us got on really well. He's one of the most personable people you could ever meet.'

Fisher took another long sip of his coffee but already seemed to be remembering the evening as though it had been yesterday.

'After the dinner, as we were both staying at the hotel,' he continued, 'and we retired to comfortable chairs in the bar. I no longer remember how we got onto the subject, but obviously Ranald's no great drinker and the more we drank, the more he poured out his soul. – I got the impression that he had never wanted to burden anyone else with his fears or demons but the drinks loosened his inhibitions and so he got things off his chest,'

'Sounds like a hell of a security breach to me,'

'Not really, after all I am head of the Bank of England's cyber- crime. But I really felt sorry for the guy,' continued Fisher, 'not only does he take responsibility for the team developing such a world threatening suite of software as Athena, but he spoke quite a lot about this family thing constantly nagging at him,' Fisher seemed to have drifted off down some vague memory lane. He finished off his cup of coffee, still gazing, unblinking, out of the window, but without appearing even to seeing the City skyline. He shook his head,

'Yeah, absolutely driven.' Then, in an instant, his manner changed and reaching across, gave Scale a mock-punch on the shoulder. 'Hey, we shouldn't get depressed about this. When you meet Ranald you'd never know any of this. He's bright and optimistic on just about everything. So just keep all of this to yourself will you.'

'Of course,' said Scale,

'Now that you've got the Manila incident in this fuller, different context what do you think?'

'On the one hand relieved that Athena can deal with the threat,' said Scale, 'yet, on the other hand the Manila seems part of some conspiracy – can't quite put my finger on that yet,'

'But the tip-off?' queried Fisher. 'Does that make more sense to you now?'

'It does. Firstly only a nutter or an anarchist would want to take down a bank if financial chaos ensued and, secondly, if you were going to take down a bank, why would you give a tip-off about it? But as we've kind-of agreed that it's about Athena and not a bank, yeah, makes sense. If I'm right and they are planning to steal Athena, they first have to discover where it's located.'

'How are they going to do that?'

'Tracing it might be done electronically,' said Fisher. 'During an attack perhaps. But knowing of it electronically, wouldn't be enough, to steal it they need to know where it's located – one of the reasons it was hidden away up on Craithe'.

'Yes of course,' said Scale. 'Does Ranald and his Craithe team, know yet about this threat coming from Manila?' asked Scale,

'No, I left off ringing him till you were here – needed to give you the wider context to everything and bounce my theory off you before telling Ranald'

'I see,' said Scale. 'One thing still puzzles me. When you say Athena will defend the bank, doesn't their being way up there in the wilds of Scotland hamper their response – I mean the distance, broadband speed, things like that?' asked Scale,

'Funny, I asked the same thing,' replied Fisher, 'and I got a mind-bogglingly technical answer. I know you're technically clued up, but, for my sake, do you mind if I give you the answer in layman's language?'

'Not at all, explain it any way you like,' said Scale

Fisher looked up for a moment, as though for inspiration. 'You know that Traders on the London and New York Stock Exchanges are constantly trying to get ever faster transmissions for their deals, beat their competition on a trade?' he said,

'I do,'

'Well Athena's software and mainframes – especially the quantum one - are faster than any of the traders' software or computers,' said Fisher, 'they have a response time which, in simplest terms, means fast enough to do fifteen or so round trips between London and New York in just one second,'

Scale looked back at Fisher and grinned. 'Now you're having me on,' he said, 'London - New York, each round trip some seven thousand miles, and they can do fifteen of those in just one second?'

'Yup, that's for real,' replied Fisher, 'so you can see that being on that remote island still within the UK is no problem to dealing with an attack in London,'

'God, you *are* serious,' said Scale. 'Quite a feat though, counter-attacking *and* knocking out the attacker's equipment all virtually instantaneously',

'It is,' agreed Fisher, 'but we still need to ring Ranald to warn him that he's going to have to use Athena for real for the first time tomorrow. He also needs to know that, in our opinion, the people intent on stealing it are intent on discovering its location at the same time – God knows what happens if they learn about Craithe.'

'This meeting's certainly been an eye-opener,' said Scale. 'When I got the Manila news I thought that we might be heading for another banking collapse and yet another recession or worse,'

'Thanks to Athena,' said Fisher, 'although it's yet to be tested in a live situation, all the trials indicate that it can stop a bank collapsing from a cyber-attack. To make the defence of a bank tomorrow that much more certain, it would help if we can find out as fast as we can who the backers of the young Manila hacker are. Most likely to be behind this are a team of State-sponsored hackers but there are also a number of mafia or organised crime people who are big enough and have the resources to conspire together for something as desirable as Athena.'

'Does it make much difference which it is, I mean state-backed, mafia, or organised crime?'

'Not sure of the answer to that,' replied Fisher, 'state-backed people might well have a quantum computing capability even if it's a limited. A mafia organisation much less likely. That's where your contacts in Manila might help us out.'

'Sure,' said Scale. 'Want my help with that?'

'Yes. You told me the young hacker in Manila's had two laptops and that they've not yet managed to get into them, is that right?'

Scale nodded.

'Using Athena, the Craithe Team should be able to crack them in no time. Could you help get Craithe and Manila talking to each other as soon as possible – maybe we could get the backer organisation's identity from one of them.'

'Of course, we can do that as soon as we speak to Ranald. 'You were going to that now anyway weren't you?'

'Yes,' said Fisher, 'so let's do that now and get this thing underway'.

3

Thursday morning,

The Towneley Vassilov Bank, Isle of Man

Ranald MacCrammond stood looking out of the half-open window, his six-foot two frame motionless, his dark grey banker's suit strangely at odds with the wild sweep of the hills and countryside he was viewing. But even though he had set up the joint venture Towneley Vassilov Bank in the countryside outside the Isle of Man's capital town, Douglas, he always dressed as one would expect of a banker – something which all the bank's staff noticed but – naturally – did not comment upon.

He now stood, entranced by the sound of the skylarks' songs above the gorse, watching the swirling morning mists that chased each other around the island's highest mountain, Snaefell Peak. His silent reverie was cut short by a knock on the door and the entrance of his secretary-cum-PA Kim Bradley. She breezed into the room, a flurry of print dress and bobbing brown curls – her pretty face dominated by large green eyes and a wide smile.

'Sorry, Boss,' she said as he turned to face her. 'Didn't mean to interrupt one of your daydreams'. She had called him Boss almost from day one of her employment and Ranald was never quite sure if the was not an element of tease to it.

'One of my daydreams - was it that obvious?' he replied, smiling and crossing back to his high-backed swivel chair with the slightest of limp – a legacy of an incident a few years back.

'Well, for a moment you looked a thousand miles away,' she said, moving forward and sitting down on one of a pair of comfortable brocade-covered arm chairs the other side of the desk from Ranald. 'Hope I'm not getting personal, Boss but as you invited me up to Craithe this weekend,' said Kim, her voice quieter than usual; almost coaxing. 'I'm going to be meeting many of your family – some of them for the first time. I've tried to keep out of what's not my business, but in the two years I've now been almost joined at the hip with the bank here, there's some unspoken family thing isn't there? Perhaps something I should know about if I'm not to put my foot in it? I just wondered if...'

'You're right Kim,' interrupted Ranald getting up out of his chair. 'You've become indispensable here and it's time I told you the truth about this family thing as you call it– and, yes, someone's quite likely to allude to it over the weekend anyway,'

He walked back over to the window and, raising his arms, clasped his hands behind his head and stretched, pulling arm against arm.

'Just where to start,' he said. Dropping them to his sides, and shaking his head slowly from side to side, he turned to face Kim. She was shocked. In just seconds his handsome face had transformed into a picture of misery, his eyes half-closed.

'My Uncle, Sir Jeremy, had a son, Tommy,' he began. He turned back to look out of the window again, then, raising his voice he continued, 'Tommy was two years older than me. First cousin of course. I had played with him since childhood. More like an older brother.' He gave the faintest of gasps as though for want of air but then went on. 'I hero worshipped him, he kind-of broke the ice for me, led the way. At Prep school, at public school and on to University, through all of my life he took me under his wing, look after me,' He gave another sigh and a part of Kim began to wish she'd never asked,

'He was such a brilliant man, Tommy, always top of his class, always excelling at any sport he took on. Though, I'll concede, he could be his own worst enemy. Many said he was just a show-off, too bloody pleased with himself, but I think he just had to challenge himself all the time – and, yes, some of his stunts were downright dangerous. Come to think of it, that was his undoing,'

'His undoing?' Kim almost whispered it,

Ranald turned round and faced her again, his face still a picture of sadness. 'It was while we were both still at University. A whole bunch of us went up to Craithe for the Easter weekend – this weekend will be a ghastly anniversary of it, might even be mentioned,'

'Anniversary?' repeated Kim to keep him focussed on his tale.

'Yeah. Typical of Tommy. We'd been through the Corryvreckan to get to Craithe of course. He and the other friends up for the weekend were told all about it – could see it for themselves too. One of them – don't care to remember who – challenged Tommy to show off his legendary water-skiing prowess by water-skiing round the outside of the great whirlpools. Utter madness. Anyway to cut a long story short…' He sighed another deep sigh, and then taking in a couple of gulps of air went on, 'Tommy being Tommy took up the challenge, I think a stupid bet was placed. Crazy. I was the local lad so I was to drive the boat. The others were to follow Tommy doing his daredevil skiing, taking pictures of the escapade. Hardly need to tell you how it turned out do I?' He looked directly back at Kim,

'If it's not too painful, do you mind just finishing the story, I'd like to know why it seems to haunt everything still.'

'He wore a wetsuit of course; the waters were freezing after a long winter. Knowing about the Corryvreckan, Tommy wasn't that foolhardy, we were only going to take him skiing round the outer edges of the maelstrom and the others following in the other boat would be able to pick him up almost instantly if he fell. Because Tommy was Tommy there was not question of him being filmed wearing a life jacket, even a slim-line safety vest or belt.' Ranald stopped, and shook his head. 'As you'll have guessed, even though there was no question of his being allowed the ultimate show-off of going onto one ski, he did fall, the following boat was up to where he fell in no time at all but, inexplicably, he was never seen again. I mean not even his body has ever been seen again.'

'Oh my God,' whispered Kim.

'As you may imagine,' went on Ranald, turning back to the window again, 'the repercussions of the loss of Tommy were, well, horrendous. I won't go into any of that but, as you will have guessed, that's why I had to step into his shoes. There's always been a Towneley as head of the Towneley Bank and with Tommy gone and me a half-Towneley through my mother, well...'

'But that's, terrible. Didn't you have any say?'

'Not a question of having a say or not,' said Ranald over his shoulder, 'I had only the vaguest idea of how I was going to spend my life. Mostly this consisted of looking after the estate on Craithe, the other islands, that sort of thing – but nothing worked out in any detail. It was obvious, I'd have to step into Tommy's shoes. Hell, I had no excuse not to. But there was more to it than that, of course. Naturally, I was devastated, but seeing the effect his loss had on my aunt and uncle was more than I could bear. In a flash I just knew I had to do whatever it took to try and become a substitute son for them – to fulfil my uncle's dream of having family follow him on and run the bank. My parents were very supportive – especially my mother, of course as she was a Towneley.'

'I thought there was something, but I had no idea it was such a tragedy,' said Kim's eyes welled up at the thought of Ranald's life completely reshaped in a moment of what appeared to be a folly of bravado.

'That's why I wear a suit all the time,' said Ranald, turning round again and smiling down at her. 'Never had even an inkling I'd have to become a banker. So I thought to myself that if I *played* the part, wore the trappings, the banking mentality would get into me. And, as you can see, it worked.' He was now smiling broadly and Kim squirmed in her chair, torn between dropping the dreadful subject they'd been talking about and what now appeared to be Ranald back into his usual light-hearted mode. She chose the latter.

'So you're saying that as a clown dons a clown's outfit in a circus and so becomes one, you put on a banker's suit and…'

'Exactly,' cut in Ranald, 'and it worked, didn't it. Got a job at the prestigious Towneley Bank, soon got seconded to the Vassilov Kapital Bank in Moscow, sought you out for your amazing talents and ability to speak Russian, dreamed up the idea of an off-shore joint venture bank here on the Isle of Man – what more evidence do you need – wearing the suit has worked,' Unable to carry on with the charade, he laughed watching Kim staring back at him, her mouth slightly open, disbelief on her face,

'You're having me on,' she said at last breaking into a mixture of a laugh and a splutter.

'Of course I am – though, when I first began in the City of London I naturally had to wear the banker's uniform and rough gear are my clothes of choice and the mountains of Craithe natural habitat, as I forced myself to wear a suit, and in doing so, I mentally pulled on what I considered to be a banker's mind-set. I felt had to do something similar when my uncle did me the ultimate honour of passing his last project over to me – what has become Athena. And now I need you too, to learn as much as possible about *that* world and become my right-hand in that just as you have in the bank.'

'I'm honoured of course – thrilled,' Kim added, blushing slightly as she spoke which was most unlike her. 'Although I'm quite computer-literate, as you know, I'm afraid I might get lost when it gets into the technical bits,'

'So did I, to start with,' said Ranald. 'But I really need you more on the people side – especially as we're about to launch Athena on the world at large,' He smiled, and the earlier misery seemed to have lifted from him like a mist and his face had now lost its sorrow. 'Anyway, despite that sad background, I for one will still be looking forward to the holiday weekend - seeing Tatty and little Jerry again. Ridiculous how time flies, they've been in Moscow with Mikhail three weeks now,' he said

'I'm looking forward to getting to know them better over the weekend,' said Kim, 'and, despite what you've told me, thanks for inviting me to join you all.'

'Part of your transition shall we say,' said Ranald, 'and as we have very little banking business to deal with before the helicopter comes for us after lunch, what aspects of Athena would you like me to go over for you?'

'The team first I think, I've spoken to most of them over the past year but it would be useful to have a bit more background before I meet them all,'

'Okay, but before I deal with individuals, let me just tell you the aims I had as I changed the team when I took it over.' Ranald came back from the window and easing himself into his swivel chair. He tilted it back for a moment, looking up at the ceiling and then lowered it again and leant across the desk towards Kim. 'My uncle's decision to tackle bank hackers by counter-attacking them instead of just defending against them was crucial to all the successes since. So the team we decided to build was probably different to everyone else's. We needed the very latest technology, that's where Professor Hapsley came in with our secretive conglomerate partners. We needed the very best hackers we could find – on the basis of set a thief to catch a thief. Perry and Marty fitted in there and we needed extras such as the quite amazing mathematical genius of Johnno, and the 'outside the box' thinking of philosopher Pete. The result is the Craithe team's got way beyond any other like team in the world and way beyond our own dreams as well.'

Kim was leaning forward on the desk as Ranald seemed to be about to do some serious digging into the subject when the telephone rang. She got up quickly and answered the call, nodding a couple of times. Then she passed the phone over the desk to Ranald. 'It's Mr Fisher from the Bank of England.'

'Better listen in to this' whispered Ranald taking the phone from her and switching on the speaker with the other hand. 'Unexpected call from you, Bill, something about the conference?'

'I'm afraid not,' replied Fisher, going on to give a full account of the events in Manila and his conversations with Scale.

'Sandy Scale and I think this looks more like an attempt to find Athena than it does about bringing down a bank,' said Fisher

Kim watched Ranald intently as the tale unfolded. She let out a little sigh as she watched his reactions to Fisher's story. His face had gradually taken on its former saddened look, his eyes half-closing, though his jaw muscles had tightened.

'Does the fact that Athena is now being asked to defend a bank and still keep its location hidden give you any extra problems?' asked Fisher,

Suddenly Ranald sat upright in his chair. He looked across at Kim and, to her surprise, he winked at her. 'Nothing we can't handle. I'll get onto the team right now but you don't worry about any of that, all right?'

'It's not just me,' said Fisher, 'it's all the people who'll be going to the Cobra Meeting which the Secretary to the Cabinet is organising. Only one or two of them know about Athena, though some others have heard that we have developed some super computer 'something', though this last lot know little of what it is.'

'So, what you're saying is that those going the Cobra meeting need to know that Athena's going to save the day, yes?' said Ranald.

32

'Exactly that,' replied Fisher, 'and the Chancellor of the Exchequer, who said he was an old friend of yours, was asking for some sort of update on Athena's current capabilities, for his eyes only, so that he has that in his hands for the meeting. Is that a problem?'

'No, Freddy Briston is indeed and old friend of mine and I'll deal with him personally.'

'I'm afraid I already told the head of the City's cyber security unit that Athena will see that there's no problem with this attack and that there's not going to be any banking collapse – I hope I didn't overstate that?' A note of doubt in Fisher's voice came over the telephone.

'As I said, Bill,' replied Ranald, 'don't you worry about a thing, just ooze confidence, say you've spoken to me and got all the reassurance you needed. Now, pass that message back to all the quivering politicians and I'll get on with seeing if it's true or not.'

'Oh God, tell me you're joking,' said Fisher,

'I'm joking, so off you go and do your bit,'

As soon as Ranald had put the telephone down and switched off the speaker, he smiled at Kim. But, she, uncertain whether he had or had not been joking with Fisher, leant forward across the desk.

'Come on, you can tell me,' she said. 'Can Athena defend the bank and keep its location a secret?'

'Let's find out,' said Ranald. 'In theory the answer's yes of course it can – that's what it's been designed to do - but, in practice it depends if the bank they attack is one which has installed our bank-attack warning software.'

'You mean there are some who are still relying on their old standard digital defence systems?'

'Afraid so,' replied Ranald, 'though the demonstration this afternoon should fix that.'

'The demonstration?'

'Yes I'll tell you about that later,' said Ranald. 'It's key to getting Athena's protection into the companies that need it most. But, right now, we need to do something I've been meaning to do for some time. I've been relying for its security on Athena being hidden away up on Craithe, but, with this news, that's not going to be enough. The solution lies with my old friend Borislav Boreyev, in Moscow. I've spoken to him before since you joined the bank, haven't I?'

'You have,' answered Kim. 'Want me to get him for you now?' She began to rise from her chair,

'Yes, please, and he can be pretty elusive sometimes, so keep at it till you find him, will you?'

'Of course,' said Kim getting up and hastening out of the room.

Ranald thought for a moment while Kim tracked down Boreyev. From its earliest days after the move to Craithe, the team had used sophisticated technology to keep its location invisible to the state-backed and mafia hackers hunting for it. That situation might change, as Ranald guessed that defending a bank might open up an electronic pathway and allow a would-be cyber-thief to find Athena. If this were to happen, the Athena team's location on Craithe would be out in the open. The time had come to protect both the team and the coveted software products they had produced. Ranald had always had the solution to this problem at the back of his mind; he picked up his pen and wrote just the one word – Boreyev. Just looking at the name, brought memories instantly flooding in on him like some pent nightmare, lurking there to catch and overwhelm him whenever it could. Like many dreams, the whole event now ran through his mind in full, like some dread video, but in just a few seconds of real time.

That nightmare incident had been in the third year of his time with the Vassilov Bank in Moscow. Seconded there from the Towneley Bank, he had blended quickly into Russian life and his command of the language had rapidly become excellent. Most importantly, he had struck up a great rapport with 'The Boss', Mikhail Vassilov. This rapport between the two of them had matured such that he had been invited several times to join Vassilov's family for weekends at their Dacha in the Crimea. The incident which now flooded his senses had happened the second time he had been invited down there.

They were all having evening drinks on the veranda under the striped awning after a blisteringly hot day; Mikhail and his wife Olga, their beautiful but distant daughter, Tatiana, Borislav Boreyev and himself, the young Scots seconded to Mikhail's bank. All laughed and chatted; Ranald was even aware, by then, of some of the idioms of the language. Even Tatiana seemed to have warmed to him. This was an exciting development for him. It was not that she was aloof or cold, just that she had a permanently distant look in her dark eyes – holding perhaps memories of the difficult route her father had chosen in becoming an oligarch. Whatever the reasons, at that time she was still 'out of bounds' to Ranald.

Three gunmen, wearing thick black woollen balaclavas, had suddenly appeared up over the balustrade and bushes round the far edge of the large patio. They must have scaled the cliffs from the beaches of the Black Sea three hundred feet below. They were no more than six long paces away from the happy group as they vaulted over onto the flagstones. Running forward, slightly crouched, the lead assailant fired after just two paces. Olga Dmitrievna Vassilov, Tatiana's mother, was killed instantly by the first shot. She had half-risen in her panic and fell back on top of her husband as they both crashed to the ground. Her deadweight body somehow enveloping him; the assailant's next two shots went into her rather than him.

The intricate filigree cast iron table, the chairs and cushions, all of them scattered as the other three fell backwards onto the ground, trying to shelter themselves behind the flimsy cover. Glasses, bottles, a small plate of sliced lemons, a water jug, and some snacks on plates, all exploded into the air and began to crash onto the stone floor around and between them.

Borislav Boreyev had thrown Ranald a heavy Yarygin Viking automatic pistol. The safety catch must have already been pushed to 'off' and it fired before it was properly in Ranald's hand. It gave him a violent kick on the ball of his thumb but no more than a second later he had loosed off two shots into the chest of the man towering directly above Tatiana. He then felt a sudden searing pain in his left shoulder and another near his left knee as a couple of bullets struck him, fired by another of the gang. Before he could even turn on this assailant, the huge black hulk of a man was felled by Boreyev. More shots rattled round in the frantic fracas.

By the end of the attack, Olga lay dead. Mikhail Vassilov, Boreyev and Ranald had been wounded − though none seriously. Tatiana was the only one of them unscathed − physically at least. She finished up on the ground, like the others, but enveloped in Ranald's arms and spattered slightly by blood from a bullet-graze wound on his left temple which, if it had been but millimetres further to the left, would have killed him. Both of the injuries were to be with him for ever − the slightest limp from his damaged left knee and an unconscious gesture of swiping away an imaginary fly from the tiny scar above his left eye, something he did involuntarily in times of stress.

After it was over, it proved almost impossible for any of the small group to recall how many shots had been fired, by whom, or how quickly. It was seemingly over as soon as it had started. Death, wounding and terror - all in mere seconds.

All three of their assailants had been killed. Sometime later Ranald and Boreyev discussed the incident and came to the conclusion that whoever was behind the assault had not picked the best of attackers, for had the three of them been real professionals the outcome would undoubtedly have been much worse,

The Dacha incident had pulled all of them together in a bond of shared trauma. It had probably precipitated Ranald and Tatiana's engagement and later marriage – perhaps saving her life at last qualifying him for more attention. The whole family had since seen much of Boreyev and from that time had all been enveloped in a cosy cocoon of warm friendship.

The telecom buzzed. It brought Ranald back to the present with a jolt.

'Mr Boreyev's in a meeting but I told his secretary it was urgent' said Kim. 'She promised he'd ring back as soon as he comes out of the meeting'.

'Thanks,' replied Ranald, and thought again about the new security problem he would discuss as soon as his old friend rang back. It seemed to him that a state-backed team intent on the theft of Athena would not do anything too openly to get at it – such as an invading group – much more likely would be the stuff of films, a James Bond-like approach perhaps. Either China or Russia would have no shortage of people capable of theft in that manner, and Boreyev's people would be ideal for protection against such an approach – his security company being one of the best equipped in Europe. Ranald knew that Boreyev's people had been used to deal with Russian upheavals in several of the countries round the fringes of the Russian Federation, and they would do well now in providing for Craithe's defence.

The telephone rang, and Kim announced that it was Boreyev on the line.

'Hello, my old friend, how are you doing?' said Ranald in Russian.

'Fine except for the bloody President's people, following me, listening in on all of my telephone calls - pain in the arse,' replied Boreyev, getting his current whinge off his chest right away,

'What did you do to get all this? I thought you and the President were pals.'

'We were, we were. Stupid of me, I suppose, I took three of my elite men down to the Crimea and Eastern Ukraine, checking security on Mikhail's place and some other clients' places. You know our illustrious President is up to his elbows in the Crimean secession and the nonsense in Ukraine, and is ultra-sensitive about any criticism, especially criticism at home.'

'Yes, it's made its way into the media here,' said Ranald,

'As a result, the people around him are also paranoid about anyone who's been anywhere near that part of the world - hence the tailing me and my people all the time,'

'Last time we spoke you said you'd had lunch with Tatty and Mikhail and you apparently told them something about getting away from Moscow for a bit.'

'I did, you're right,' said Boreyev. 'Just haven't done anything about it yet. Though this is becoming a more attractive idea as each day passes.'

'What about doing just that, come away right now to Scotland? You'd be doing me a favour at the same time.'

'A favour? What kind of favour?'

'Could a few of your elite do a spell of protection for me? - I'd pay of course,'

'Tutch! No need to pay, well certainly not my usual fees – perhaps a few of the expenses,' replied Boreyev. 'But yes, of course, I could bring some over. What sort of problem do you have? You don't have riots on the west coast of Scotland, on your islands of Craithe or Man do you? So what would you need us to do?'

'Haven't worked out the detail yet. It's the island off the Scottish coast that needs protecting, or rather a team of people working on a secret project there – they need to be kept safe. You'd need small arms, maybe crowd control stuff. There are only two ways onto the island, boat or helicopter, – so, to keep them and the secret stuff in the Lab' safe? I don't know you're the expert...' His voice tailed off as he realised how ridiculous and ill-thought-out this must sound in Moscow. There was a silence at the other end, but just as he was about to ask if Boreyev was still there, his friend replied,

'Sorry, just thinking about some numbers', he said. 'Me and five of my best, – I call them my elites – that should do. I was also thinking, at short notice, even with a small amount of equipment we couldn't fly commercial. I'd need to see if I can borrow a plane off Mikhail, your father-in-law, maybe. Trouble is, with the kinds of equipment I'd be bringing, I would need to unload direct from a plane into a van of some kind – not the kind of stuff you can put through usual customs channels, if you get my meaning. Could you fix that? Diplomatic bag perhaps? Couldn't be doing with prying customs people and awkward questions.'

'I'm sure I could arrange something along those lines,' replied Ranald with no present notion of how he might arrange it, 'and if Mikhail can lend you his plane, how soon could you put all this together and get yourselves in to Glasgow?'

'Assuming Mikhail's got a plane lying idle, could get there tomorrow morning,'

'That would be great. Let me have details later and I'll organise a van, customs, and a marked map to get you to Crinan, We'll pick you all up there and take you to the island. I'll sort out a place to stay for your five elites. You, yourself, must stay with us up at the Castle.'

'Okay, I'll ring Mikhail and get back to you shortly,' said Boreyev.

'I look forward to getting your arrival details in due course, then, it will be great to see you again,'

'Likewise.' said Boreyev. 'Made my day, as you say in the West. One minute I'm stuck here with the President breathing down my neck, the next I'm on holiday in Scotland.' He laughed, his deep guttural chuckles sounding reassuring to Ranald.

Under the word 'Boreyev' written on his pad, Ranald had added a few notes. There were reminders to contact others, a question around diplomatic immunity, the right kind of vehicle to hire for the six of them and their equipment, accommodation for the five elites at the Derby Arms Hotel in Stanleytoun. He would deal with each of these shortly.

Putting down his pen and leaning back in his chair, he reflected, he must be losing his grip on reality. He had just arranged for a mini-army to fly in from Moscow tomorrow morning. To do what? As yet there was no known adversary; maybe there wasn't even a real physical threat. He consoled himself – at the least, Boreyev's small group would allay any concerns the team might have for the continued safety of Athena.

After his call to Boreyev, Ranald dealt with the last banking matters before leaving for the Easter weekend and was surprised when Kim buzzed though to him to say that, after a space of less than an hour, Mr Boreyev was on the line again from Moscow. He confirmed that he had indeed managed to borrow Mikhail Vassilov's Hawker 800 private jet and had even lodged a provisional flight plan to get them from Moscow to Glasgow, arriving at around 9am tomorrow.

'The other reason I rang, is I'm worried about what's just been happening to me. I don't believe in coincidences and strange things have been going on since I lodged a flight plan for my trip tomorrow.'

'I don't understand,' replied Ranald. 'Have you been having more bother from the President's people again?'

'Maybe, maybe not – though I suspect so. If I tell you what happened, will you see if you can help me out?'

'Of course.'

'As I told you, got my people to lodge the flight plan,' said Boreyev, 'and was cleaning everything up in case I'm away for a bit, so I began to gather in some of my money from here and there. The first, the largest, was to move ten million Euro's from a small bank I use in Spain for my businesses in the Middle East. I used to use Cyprus for this, but so many of my dubious Russian compatriots use Cyprus for laundering money, I changed that a year ago.'

'I hope you're going to swear on your mother's grave that this is all clean money, Borislav,' said Ranald,

'Kneeling by her grave itself, I promise. It's all legit, most of it out of my Israeli businesses - you know how many Israelis are originally from Russia.'

This at least sounded genuine to Ranald.

'You said you tried to move the money,'

'Yes, I did as I always do. But my UK bank recently split in two, and suddenly the people I had always dealt with are gone. With ten million involved, these new people talk about 'looking further into this' or 'looking into that'. For Christ's sake I don't want people looking further into *anything,* do I? − even though it's all completely above board.'

'So?' asked Ranald.

'So I got onto my man in Spain, Victor Seryogin - he's based in the little town of Mijas on the Costa Brava where my Mediterranean operations bank is.'

'Yup.' Ranald was now jotting a note on his pad.

'Suddenly, as soon as he's in the bank and trying the transfer, Victor hears rumours. Talk of it closing the doors, bomb scare or something. But this is before I can get my money out. What the hell am I to do? Ten million for Christ's sake. And then I think. All of this happened within minutes of my lodging my flight plan, and I don't believe in coincidences'

'As they're watching your every move, didn't you think to lodge the flight plan in Mikhail's name?' asked Ranald

'I did, but Mikhail had said that with Tatiana and his grandson flying to Scotland today, him lodging a flight plan to follow them at the same time wouldn't look, er…?'

'I get his point,' replied Ranald, 'So, in short, you'd like me to get your ten million out of Spain and into my bank here on the Isle of Man — have I got that right?'

'Exactly, can you do that for me? — I don't want this to come back and hit you though. Do you have ways of doing this secretly so no one else knows?'

'There are ways, yes.' Ranald knew that Perry, the Craithe Team's top hacker, would manage it. 'My problem, however is that I'm a banker and, even in an off-shore operation like ours, international rules apply especially if there's even a whiff of money-laundering. So my problem is not whether I can do this — which I can — but whether, as you say, it could come back to bite me later.'

'Of course,' said Boreyev.

Ranald thought for a moment, no one would ever know about the transfer — with Perry's expertise even a sum of this size would simply be there one minute and gone the next.'

'Consider it done,' he said,

'So how will I know when it's been done?' asked Boreyev

'Give me your bank details now and telephone numbers for your man Victor in Mijas and I'll get this done. I'll send you a text message confirming it's done and you can just reply with your estimated arrival time in Glasgow, Okay? I'll give you the details of your new account here when I see you,'

Boreyev gave Ranald the details he had asked for and as soon as he had written them down, he simply said, 'Promise me you'll not say a word about this to anyone except to warn Victor that I may be in touch with him in Spain?'

'Right and thank you my old friend'.

'See you tomorrow in Crinan,' said Ranald.

Of course Perry did manage it, he had been moving other people's money since he was twelve. Equally as important as moving the money was the fact that, thanks to his unique software, it was done without leaving any electronic traces of his visit to the Mijas bank or where the money had gone.

4

Thursday lunchtime.

Nikol'skaya Street, Moscow

For Igor Komarov, life was a constant juggling of many balls in the air at the same time. Not only did his boss, the President, suffer from acute paranoia, he himself was driven by an insatiable lust for power and money – *'a volatile conflict of competing interests'* as one of his few friends had once said of him – referring, of course, to need to keep his power-base by tending to the needs of the President and looking after his own interests at the same time. In the project dominating his life at present, where these two interests were incompatible and his own were about to take precedence.

His long job title, printed in ostentatious gold on his business cards, could be understood in more than one way, but in practice, he was probably the foremost of the President's 'fixers'. Both he and his principal aide, Pavel Rostov, had started their working lives alongside the President in the KGB in St Petersburg. But whereas Komarov and Rostov grew closer over the years, working together, the President had greater ambitions and gradually distanced himself from his two colleagues as he climbed faster than them towards the pinnacle of power. Some speculated that the two left working in the KGB, (and later the FSB), held some secrets about the former threesome's times in St Petersburg and Moscow. For, diligent and as ruthless as they needed to be in the pursuit of their craft, they lacked the President's killer instincts yet both remained close to each other and closer than most others to the President.

Befitting a couple so close personally to the President, they had complete access to all of the powerful tools of the Russian Federation's many espionage networks. The office suite that the two of them and their teams shared, was conveniently situated almost exactly halfway between the Kremlin and their old KGB offices in Lubyanka Square – now occupied, of course, by the KGB's successor, the FSB.

Whether or not the comparative sizes of the two men had anything to do with their comparative status, was a subject of whispered speculation in the office, for whereas Komarov was a giant of a man, nicknamed the Russian Bear by the staff - but never called that to his face – Rostov had more the look of a weasel, small, furtive, ever watchful. And although an unfair assessment, Komarov was credited as being someone you could trust, whereas Rostov was not. For these and perhaps some reasons unknown to the staff, Komarov was the Boss and Rostov his number two.

Rostov, who had specialised in surveillance in his early KGB, and, later his FSB days, was in charge of all this equipment and, along with two dedicated members of staff. He was an invaluable support to Komarov's power base – *knowledge of others* being the power behind the power in today's Federation.

This Thursday, approaching lunchtime, the two of them had been in what could have been described as 'panic mode'. Both were well used to the President's sudden bursts of ice-cold temper but, first thing this morning, his fury had caused more than usual concern. Both were acutely aware of the Federation's current problems – both the collapse of the world oil price and the West's sanctions were ruining the Federation's economy and it was the job of the President's minions, especially the two of them, to come up with suggestions on how to alleviate these problems, and to keep the full extent of the truth from the public at the same time – another factor calling on Komarov's juggling skills.

The drop in the international price of oil by more than half, had already reduced the country's annual income by the colossal sum of 850 trillion roubles – over two hundred billion dollars – and was still dropping. Clearly there was nothing that Komarov and his team could do about that, but the US and European Union sanctions? – Well, that was quite another matter.

Komarov had rashly suggested that he might have a way of retaliating against these and for some weeks the President had been asking for more details of this retaliation.

Although Komarov would no doubt fail any formal examination paper on psychology, he had a very good understanding of himself and therefore of others. He would have hesitated to ascribe the word 'revenge' to the President's present feelings towards the West – the man always boasted of his detached, logical and subjective approach to matters as important as foreign affairs. Whereas to some of the sycophants around the seat of power this might appear to be a valid boast, Komarov knew better. The President's whole view of foreign affairs was dominated by the burning desire to return the Federation to the days of Russia's past greatness. This would include surrounding herself once again with 'buffer' states or countries to keep her secure from the perennial enemy, the West. Whether or not this view made any sense in today's world was irrelevant – it was the President's view and that was that.

Working around the President's strong and personal motive of revenge, was something that Komarov had more or less mastered, but at present almost every day, he was being asked if he had come up with a solution not just to the West's sanctions, but also if he'd made progress in regaining the Federation's control of the small Baltic Sea countries. The urge to take revenge for these sanctions and for the West's meddling in his need to rebuild the buffers around the Federation were building almost daily. The good thing was that Komarov was almost certain that he had found the solution to these pressing problems; the bad thing was that he did not yet have his hands on it. Worse still, with no solution, he might lose his position at the heart of power.

This solution was, of course, the much-rumoured existence of a new weapon, which could dominate the dark world of cyber warfare. And although the State and its various agencies had very serviceable cyber weaponry and excellent hackers, the rumour hinted at this new weapon had the ability to cut through the defences of almost any known digital encryption – almost as though the Allies had had the power of today's super computers to crack the famous Enigma codes during the second World War. And Komarov knew, in theory at least, that this ability could indeed exist if someone had got the next generation computer technology - quantum computing – to work alongside the digital.

So although Komarov was virtually certain of its existence – he had also gathered far too much circumstantial evidence for it to be just a fantasy – he still needed to find it and then steal it.

Once in his hands, well then, of course, the ability to begin taking control of, say a power grid here, or an air traffic control system there could absolutely transform the President's power for revenge on the West.

'We simply cannot go on bluffing,' said Komarov, 'The President's feeling of the pressure on him builds every day and we still have no concrete proof that we're about to solve his problems for him. Where the hell is this thing – this new weapon? Where have we got to with that searches for it?'

'Right, I'll give you the negative results first,' replied Rostov. 'No progress on the quantum computer manufacturers in Canada, nor the ones in Silicon Valley in the US, and no progress on either the Google or the Microsoft research teams though we keep our tabs on them night and day. Our two people in China sound as though there might be a breakthrough soon, though there's nothing to report as yet. On the positive side, however, our little investment in the Philippines has gone well. The young hacker did his job well and our team is now back in Moscow. The software the young Manila hacker developed for us looks about right now – the practices went well. It will be interesting to see that when we use it at the Bank of England's conference in London tomorrow.'

'You think that the Bank of England will use what we're looking for against our attack?' asked Komarov. 'If they've got one, that is,' he added as an afterthought.

'Our contact in London tells me he's sure that what they're going to unveil at the conference is just that,' replied Rostov, 'And he says he has it on the highest authority that they're going to use it - so we'll see, won't we. But, just in case they *don't*, we're not risking bringing down a big bank. The last thing we need is another bloody recession, and our London contact will be nominating a smaller target while he's actually at the conference,'

'Good,' said Komarov, 'but I want you personally to monitor the choice of target to ensure no mistakes are made like taking down something that will cause ripples.'

'Got it,' said Rostov, 'I'll make doubly certain of that.'

'Our second main focus at present,' said Komarov, 'is the anti-Crimea dissidents. The President's determined to get back control of countries like the Ukraine and we simply have to silence the internal dissent on this vital policy of his. How are we doing there?'

'Funny you should mention that,' said Rostov. 'You know the automatic warning system we have when anyone on the dissident list tries to move money or assets?'

'Yes.'

'Just minutes ago one of them, an old pal of the President's, tried to move a large sum out of Spain and into the UK', said Rostov, 'it came up on our private link with the Sluzhba Vneshney Razvedki or SVR for short,' Komarov was particularly pleased that not only did he have a private link to the Russian Federations *foreign* intelligence he also had virtually the exclusive services of one of its most dedicated operatives, Danil Morozov.'

Komarov glanced at his watch and gave a small sigh of relief, Danil Morozov would not be on duty at the moment – for what he now had in mind, he needed anonymity for once.

'Do we have the SVR's report on that yet?' asked Komarov, 'their 24/7 surveillance of all foreign internet and email traffic is sure to have logged it as well as spotting it.'

'Yes, that's where the SVR's I believe better than the UK's GCHQ, we keep everything but I believe that in their great democracy, they're not allowed to keep everything without getting permission from their Courts. Can you imagine anything so ridiculous? So, yes, to answer your question, the SVR will be sending it through shortly,' replied Rostov, 'though I know the outline of it now, if you're interested,'

'No, no, I can wait for the fuller report itself.'

'Well, if that's all for now, I thought I'd get off to lunch,' said Rostov, 'you coming too?'

'No, I've got a couple of things to deal with, I'll see you later' said Komarov.

As soon as Rostov had left, Komarov picked up the direct line to the SVR. He read off the code of the operative who had sent the most recent report and asked to speak to him. After that it was just routine investigative stuff and half an hour later he had the information he needed – a substantially enhanced report on what had happened after Boreyev had tried to move his money from the bank in Mijas. The SVR's standard practice of putting a bomb-scare down to a bank to close it if a dissident who was trying to move money, had been automatically triggered. But when that was followed minutes later by Boreyev's money vanishing without trace *after* the bomb threat, well, that was not only unique but of considerable personal interest to Komarov.

An important addition in the new report was further information on Ranald MacCrammond. This was brief but thorough. It covered MacCrammond's career with the Towneley Bank, his secondment to the Vassilov Kapital Bank in Moscow and then his setting up of the joint-venture investment Towneley-Vassilov Bank on the Isle of Man. On the personal side, it also noted that he had married the daughter of the oligarch, Mikhail Vassilov. All the other standard checks on both him and the new Isle of Man bank were strongly positive.

Komarov was delighted with these findings and put a call through to the said Ranald MacCrammond.

'Mr MacCrammond, this is Igor Komarov here; you don't know me but I'm a friend of your father-in-law Mikhail Vassilov', he said in Russian – although his English was very good.

'Yes Mr Komarov,' replied Ranald in English, 'what can I do for you?'

'I am aware that you will be about to leave for the weekend, so I'll be brief. I was most impressed with the way you were able to move your friend Mr Boreyev's money for him from the bank in…'

'Mr Komarov, I'm sorry to cut you off there, but I'm afraid that…'

'My turn to interrupt *you* Mr MacCrammond, I'm on your side. I have it in my power to do you a great favour if you will just hear me out…please,' said Komarov in a suitably conciliatory manner, and in English,

'Very well, but my time is short,' Ranald could be heard tapping the desk with his pen in irritation.

'Because of his recent visits to both the Crimea and to Eastern Ukraine, Mr Boreyev - and by implication your father-in-law Mikhial

Vassilov, have automatically got themselves onto a dissidents list. This you probably know. The President does not like our citizens openly opposing democratically chosen policies; so they will remain on that list for the foreseeable future. This will effect movements of assets of any kind, and lead to restrictions in travel, very irksome stuff for them as I'm sure you'll agree - just as your EU sanctions are irksome to me, an innocent bystander in these international games,'

'I'm not sure the West would call them games, Mr Komarov,' said Ranald,

'We're both men of the world, Mr MacCrammond,' replied Komarov, 'I have it within my power to have your friend Mr Boreyev and also Mikhail taken off the dissidents list in the flick of a finger, setting them free of all restrictions as quickly as computers can be updated. In return, I would be grateful if you could move some of my monies into your bank on the Isle of Men. You could manage that for me, could you not?'

Ranald had but seconds to make a decision. A combination of much chess-playing when in Russia and an acquired banker's need to make rapid assessments, helped him at this moment. 'How much money are we talking about, Mr Komarov?' he asked.

'Forty-two million US Dollars,' replied Komarov 'and I know you might think it strange that I want to pull monies in from various sources and finish up putting such a huge sum in one place, but our intelligence tells us that the West's sanctions are about to tighten and so my first priority is to sidestep those.'

'Very well, if that's what you wish to do. If you will now give me all the details of where you monies are deposited at present, plus passwords and so on I will do that for you. 'Just one thing – how will I know if you have taken my two friends off your dissidents list?'

'First I need to speak with the President,' said Komarov, 'then I will ring both of them and tell them how they may check that they've been taken off the list for themselves. Both of them can then ring and tell you, simple as that.'

'It will take me some time to move your money,' said Ranald, 'I shall expect calls from Mr Boreyev no later than one p.m. GMT today. You realise also, don't you, that you will not be able to access your money until after the bank holiday weekend. Though it will be safely here by around one p.m. and I can send you an email giving you a way you can check the balance online,'

'That's fine, Mr MacCrammond. I have no need of the money right now, I just need it to be beyond the reach of the sanctions now and accessible for the future,'

'Good, so if you can now give me all the details I need I'll get going with my end of the deal right away and I'll expect their calls to me in due course,'

It took a few minutes for Komarov to tell Ranald the various places where he kept his money, and the bank details involved.

It was less than forty minutes later that Ranald had a call from Boreyev.

'I don't know what you and Igor Komarov have been up to,' said Boreyev, ' but after a series of strange telephone instructions and calls it would appear that neither Mikhail nor I are any longer persons of interest to the FSB. Mikhail says hello to you but won't ring as he's just seeing Tatiana, Jerry and Anastasia off to Glasgow. Look forward to seeing you tomorrow,'

'Likewise,' said Ranald. Just before he picked up his cross pen, he unconsciously brushed the tiny scar on his left temple. He then jotted a note on his pad; it read *'Ring Mikhail and get more info on Igor Komarov.'*

5

Thursday, late morning

Towneley Vassilov Bank, Isle of Man

Had City Traders discovered that the main cyber defence systems of all the largest City institutions were to be replaced by new generation technology, it might have made some them jittery. Were to learn more, that some organisations were objecting to being told what to do in cyber defence matters, it might have upset them even more. The launch of Athena to the City of London had therefore been planned to take place during the long Bank Holiday weekend while the markets were closed – this would also allow for any early difficulties to be ironed out.

The time had come to tie up the loose ends before leaving for Craithe and Ranald buzzed on the intercom for Kim to come through. Moments later she breezed into his office, yet, despite the verve with which she did everything, she closed the door silently and turned to Ranald, 'Going to finish off telling me about the team and Athena?'

'Yes I was going to do that, wasn't I – interrupted by our need to get hold of Boreyev,' said Ranald,

'Have we the time to do it now? I'm intrigued; such a small team – and however well-funded – being ahead of the likes of Microsoft and Google in research,'

'A good reason,' said Ranald, 'is the unusual mix of people. First there's Professor Henry Hapsley, formerly Emeritus Professor of Computer studies at Cambridge University – probably the world's leading expert in the new quantum computing technologies. My uncle financed some of his research when university funding took a dive after the 2008 crash. Our secretive conglomerate partners wanted only him for their quantum research and so joined us as well.'

'Quite a catch, then,' said Kim

'Yes and Perry's opposite. Our young genius hacker, Perry, was deserted by his father when he was twelve; he had to support his alcoholic mother with large quantities of booze, pay for the food, the house-hold bills, all the jobs of a head of the family, I wonder what would you or I have done in his shoes?'

'No idea,' said Kim, 'get odd-jobs? It's hard to see how that would be enough though – a problem too, if you're too young to claim benefits and your mother's too drunk to do anything about them. What a hole to find oneself in.' She gave a faint shudder and frowned; 'so what did he do?'

'Short answer's that he found he was a natural at learning from the internet,' replied Ranald, 'taught himself everything, improved all the time, upgraded his equipment regularly; by the time he was twenty he had a substantial income from syphoning money from the accounts of Organised Crime syndicates and the Mafia – chose them as he guessed that they'd never create a fuss over the money – all of it stolen, of course. To get away with this he developed unique computer software to cover his tracks – no one could see who he was or where he'd been – the Craithe Team uses the same technology to this day.'

'He seems quite difficult to talk to sometimes,' said Kim, 'I don't know if that's just me or…'

'No he has a touch of Asperger's syndrome, makes him shy, even distant to some,' said Ranald, 'but he's fine with people he knows,'

'I see. Unusual name too – Perry,'

'Yes, it was a compliment to my uncle. He provided Perry with a QC at his hacking trial, got him a mere community service sentence. Got it in exchange for valuable information on the mafia and organised crime syndicates. To avoid mafia reprisals, however, he needed new names. He chose Fraser for his surname and wanted to choose Jeremy as a first name. My uncle suggested Perry might be better; Peregrine in full, it had been a recurring Towneley Christian name for centuries. Intrigued by this, he learned also that it was the name of the fastest bird in the animal kingdom – the peregrine falcon – that clinched it, and that's how we have the abbreviated Perry today.'

'Well, it suits him,' said Kim, 'I'll be meeting all of the team won't I? What about some of the others?'

'There's the other hacker, Marty, there's the brilliant mathematicians, Johnno and Sam and not forgetting Morag and Jennie – you probably speak to Morag quite often – the one who keeps the whole team in order and looks after the mini-telephone exchange.'

'Yes. Anything else I should know about Athena as we're on the subject?'

'Perhaps a quick word about our first priority this weekend' replied Ranald, 'the demonstration this afternoon,'

'The demonstration, I've heard it mentioned, but what is it exactly?'

'It's an important part of Athena's launch,' said Ranald, 'let me explain why. To protect the City of London institutions, we need to install our own cyber-attack warning system onto the computer systems of any organisation likely to be attacked – Banks in particular. The moment an attack is detected, that warning system triggers a retaliatory counter-attack from Athena and the attackers have their equipment immobilised – effectively made useless. All right so far?' Kim nodded her head.

55

'Unfortunately, a few organisations are refusing to install Athena's warning software; without that installed and nothing to trigger an Athena counter-attack, they'll just have to rely on their own defences – and we all know how inadequate some of those are,'

'Don't know where I heard it,' said Kim, 'but I thought the aim was to have Athena just about everywhere in the City of London and that it would then be installed progressively throughout the world after that. Wasn't the idea that hackers would eventually give up attacking financial targets. So, does it give you a problem if some don't join in?'

'Afraid it does,' replied Ranald. He flicked an imaginary fly from a scar on his left temple and looked out of the window for a moment. 'I just want to do justice to my uncle's last project and ideally that does mean everyone installing. It would be Sod's Law if the one that didn't install, was the same one to be brought down wouldn't it. Trouble is it might affect everyone else,'

'But why on earth won't they all install?'

'Most of them have agreed the installation with their Boards of Directors, but some waverers still talk of Bank of England "intrusion" – bullying them to putting our software onto their systems. They say that they know how to run their businesses, and have perfectly adequate and extremely expensive defences already.'

'Well, they do have their own defences, don't they?'

'Yes, but not *counter-attacking* defences; I'm trying to fix this problem, however, by putting on the demonstration this afternoon and hoping that it will shock the waverers into changing their minds,' continued Ranald, 'It'll show them what a cyber-attack could do to their businesses, how they could lose everything without Athena. It's being televised on ITV as part of a documentary on the London Stock Exchange. When they see how Athena had achieved the almost impossible feat of hacking into a Hedge Fund who are known to be paranoid about their defences and then altered its secret trading algorithms . . . '

'Its *what*?' repeated Kim,

'Its trading algorithms. They're computer programmes, consist of software instructions which run all their market trades automatically. It means they can do without expensive human traders with their huge bonuses. Anyway, the authorities told us which hedge fund to use for the demonstration, and we then rewrote a section of their trading programmes. The result of this is that, for just one minute, the company will trade with all its safety restrictions removed, upper and lower trading limits for example; we also switched off the hedging function as well.'

'You lost me there, what does all that mean, in layman's language?' asked Kim,

'In layman's language, let me see. In effect it will be like a bookie at a race course taking bets on the horses without limiting the size of the bets. Imagine what would happen if he also didn't bother hedging those bets, that's to say spread his risk by laying those bets off and with other bookies?'

'He'd risk going bankrupt, wouldn't he?'

'Exactly that,' said Ranald, 'so we're hoping that the waverers will understand that if Athena can hack its way into such a well-protected hedge fund, and force it to trade wildly out of control, that they'll have the sense to see what it could do to them too. We hope that having thought again, they'll allow us to install our software onto their systems,'

'Right,' said Kim nodding her head, 'one other thing – so that I've got the whole picture – why restrict the wild trading to just one minute?'

'To limit potential losses,' replied Ranald. 'Although the Bank of England is picking up any of this Hedge Fund's losses, they still want to keep these to a minimum. For example when high frequency trading on Wall Street ran out of control not long ago, in just three or four minutes of chaotic trading, the Dow Jones Index

57

dropped some fifteen percent – that was *billions of dollars of losses,* in just minutes.'

'So let's hope the demonstration message gets across to these waverers,'

'Yes, fingers crossed,'

'Just so as I understand the actual process,' said Kim, 'you install the Athena warning system and then what happens?'

'As soon as an attack comes in, virtually instantaneously, it triggers Athena's counter attack which disables the attacker,' replied Ranald, 'their equipment will be rendered useless.'

'Right,' said Kim. 'Is there anything to do with Athena or the weekend that I can help with before we go up to Craithe?'

'Maybe,' replied Ranald. 'We've been asked to get the latest information we have on Athena over to my old friend Freddy Briston for the Cobra Meeting that's about to take place,'

'Freddy Briston, the Chancellor?'

'Yes, he's asked for the Athena update for the meeting and he's about the only person I'd trust sending it to and we need to do that right away.' said Ranald.

'What could I do to help with that?' asked Kim,

'Ring Perry if you will,' replied Ranald. 'Perry or just about anyone else in the team knows what to do. At short notice – which it is in this case - the safest way to send secret documents is to put them onto a special computer memory stick. Just tell whoever you speak to, to use this usual method send what's known as the update file to Freddy at Number 11 Downing Street by Towneley Bank courier,'

'If the Athena stuff is so secret, isn't that a risk, a little memory stick?'

'Not memory sticks we use,' said Ranald, 'they all have a self-defence programme on them. Anyone intercepting it and trying to get into it to see what's there will simply have their equipment locked down unless they've first used a complex password,'

'So completely safe,' asked Kim

'Yes, always worked very well when we've used them to date, so if you ring Perry he'll tell you what to do.'

During the next half hour or so, Kim got Perry to deal with Briston's request and she typed up a couple of letters which closed off all the banking issues for the weekend. She then returned to Ranald's office.

'As you're now going to be involved in Craithe's business,' said Ranald, 'I'll put this call on speaker so that you learn more as we go along,'

'Thanks,' replied Kim as she sat opposite Ranald again.

Perry had already been in contact with the Manila Police and had successfully got through Ramos's special defences and into the first of the two laptops. He said he would get into the second machine shortly. He also told them that the professor had 'awoken' the demonstration software planted two days earlier on the hedge fund's computer system – like a sleeper spy – and said that it would come into action at three thirty this afternoon as planned. And, lastly, he confirmed that all preparations for tomorrow were done.

'A little while back,' said Kim, 'I asked you if Athena could cope with both the launch and an attack at the same time, and you said something to the effect of I hope so – why the doubt?'

A smile flickered across Ranald's face for a moment and was quickly gone again. 'Up till now we've only been able to practice on mock adversaries. But tomorrow the attack will be from a real live hacker – one who has been practicing for their attack in Manila. We won't know if they've learned some new tricks until they attack.'

'Is that a worry?' she said, managing a weak smile.

'Don't know really. Mainly for my uncle's sake – but others' too I suppose – Athena's just got to succeed. And whereas the Craithe team's probably among the best in the world – probably as good as anything of the NSA's – we won't know just how good we are when faced for the first time by the real thing,'

'I see,' said Kim quietly, 'quite a burden of responsibility for you. I'm sorry I hadn't really appreciated that before.' She gave Ranald a wisp of a smile and went back to her office to get ready for the trip north.

Ranald was beginning his tidying up to leave when the telephone rang.

'Yes Perry,' said Ranald, 'is this about something that can't wait? The helicopter taking us up to meet the others at Glasgow Airport is due shortly and I'm just finishing up here,'

'Though I haven't quite finished my searches of Ramos's two laptops in Manila,' said Perry, 'I've done some quick scans and thought you'd like to know who his associates are, especially before you leave the office,'

'Yes, I would.'

'Two names keep coming up,' continued Perry, 'they're Silayev and Komarov. This Komarov is the same Igor Komarov whose money you asked me to move to your bank earlier today. I'll need more time to look further into Anton Silayev'

For a moment there was silence.

'You did the right thing catching me before I left for Scotland,' said Ranald, 'see what more you can get on both of these two and we'll have a chat when I get to Craithe,'

As soon as he had put the telephone down, he pressed a couple of numbers on the intercom. As soon as he was through to Peter Fleming, his General Manager he spoke urgently. 'Pete, do us a favour, will you.'

'Of course.'

'The new account I opened for a Mr Komarov and transferred money into this morning, remember?' said Ranald,

'Mr Igor Komarov, yes, I remember.'

'Make sure that account is blocked immediately will you. Until further notice, no one but me is to be allowed to access that account, got that?'

'Got it,' said Fleming.

6

Thursday, lunchtime,

Number 11 Downing Street, London

Whilst Ranald had been involved with Igor Komarov's money moving operations, Freddie Briston, the Chancellor had rung to speak to him. It was urgent. He was soon to attend a Cobra Meeting, and the Athena update he had been promised earlier had not yet arrived. Kim told him that, as it was eleven-thirty, the information should be arriving as they spoke. Even while they were still on the phone, The Chancellor had checked, found that to be correct, and thanked all for their efficiency. Cape, his chief legal aide at Number 11, got down into the hall just as the Towneley Bank courier arrived with the package. It underwent the standard safety checks – for such as explosives or anthrax – and Cape then took it to his office.

As many Government computers have their usb memory stick drives disabled, Craithe had also verified that Cape would use his own laptop into which he could plug the memory stick. Cape now back in his office, plugged the security-cleared stick into his laptop followed by the password given to him earlier by Perry. On opening the files on the stick, he first read through the schedule to be sure he was up to date with Athena's launch programme:

Today, 3.35pm to 4.15pm, ITV's programme 'A Day on the London Stock Exchange'

3.50pm Demonstration of Hedge Fund's erratic trades for exactly one minute. Presenter of this sponsored programme to focus on this erratic trading. (Programme available thereafter on iPlayer for one week).

Good Friday, 9am to midday, Bank of England Cyber Defences Convention. By invitation only. Repeat of the attack sequence from the televised demonstration.

Installation of Athena's attack detection software on any mainframes still not protected by it. Questions and Answers on Athena.

Conference to be warned that, at any time during the conference, there might be a cyber-attack on one of the companies attending.

Athena software on client's machines to detect the attack and from its base, Athena to counter-attack and eliminate the attacker.

Cape looked through the contents of the memory stick a second time and chose a few documents which he thought would help the Chancellor at the Cobra Meeting. These he copied into a new folder on the machine's desktop and named it "for printing". He then called for his secretary, Mina, to come in quickly as there was an urgent print job to be done.

'Mina, the Chancellor's going to a Cobra Meeting shortly, and he needs some documents for that,' he said,

'What's a Cobra Meeting?' asked Mina,

'Look, I know you're always asking questions because you want to get better at the job,' said Cape, 'but we're in a hurry right now'. Mina put on her little pouting face for a second, and, as usual, Cape relented, 'All right then; Cobra meetings are named after the initials of 'Cabinet Office Briefing Room',' he said, 'they're emergency meetings for when a threatening incident would benefit from a get-together of the PM, senior ministers and advisors. There, that's all I'm saying on that, so please do the printing now. I've put the documents the Chancellor needs in a file on the desktop and named it 'for printing'. I've got more to look through on the memory stick when you finished and as I don't want to have to re-enter the long password, just leave the memory stick in the machine while you do the print job. Okay?'

Mina was aware that the memory stick might shut down on a time lock if not used for a while. She needed Cape to keep it 'awake' when she took it for printing. 'Could you just check you put everything you want me to print into that folder?'

'All right,' said Cape. He quickly looked through the files once more. 'No, that's all I need. Get them printed now as quickly as possible, will you?'

'Of course, quick as can. But I have to go the photocopying room with this as the printer in my office is not working,' she said putting on her 'cute' accent – the one she had used when they had first met.

'Very well, if you must. But careful with the memory stick, now that I've opened it with the long password, anyone could read what's on it,'

'Yes, of course,' replied Mina and she hurried out holding the Laptop carefully, as though it was made of porcelain. She hoped he would not check that there was nothing wrong with her printer. For what she needed to do, she needed to be out of sight of him. She hurried along the corridor to the photocopying room. She saw no one on the way - many staff having already been allowed to go off early for the long holiday weekend. Although this was Cape's own laptop, it was already set-up for use on one of the wifi-enabled printing machines there.

She clicked for it to print off copies of the documents in Cape's 'for printing' folder, and whilst the machine gently whirred and clicked its way through them, she went over to the door and peered along the corridor in both directions. There was no one in sight.

Hurrying back to the printer and laptop, she reached into the top of her bra and pulled out a small computer memory stick of her own. This she plugged it into one of the laptop's spare usb ports. She then carefully selected Ranald's memory stick which was still 'open' on the desktop. *She then copied much of its contents onto hers.* She was careful not copy the entire contents, in case the Craithe Team had software on it that would detect a *complete* transfer and see it as theft. Clearly well used to this kind of operation, she then extracted her own memory stick and snuck it back into the top of her bra with many of Craithe's and Athena's secrets now on it.

As soon as all the printing was finished, she collected it up, stacked it on top of the closed laptop with Ranald's memory stick still firmly in place and hurried back to Cape's office. During the entire operation she had seen no one.

'All done, want to cheek?' she beamed as she carefully laid the laptop and pile of papers down on his desk.

'Check,' he corrected, 'it's check not cheek.' She smiled, though, out of sight under the desk, her left foot tapped with irritation. Looking through the copies and checking them off against his list, Cape finally said, 'Great, you're getting quite good at all this now, aren't you?'

'Yes, I hope,' she smiled yet again.

Checks completed, Cape looked at his watch. No time left for looking at other material on the stick right now, so he removed it from the laptop and put it into his small wall safe. Shutting the door firmly, he twiddled the locking wheels and then tested that it was properly secured for it was not just the instructions that had come with the memory stick that made him nervous about its security – what little he had read convinced him that its contents should be kept limited to as few people as possible.

'If you meeting with the Chancellor for some time, shall I take quick lunch now?' asked Mina, 'That way I'm ready help you when you finished meeting with him?' She gave Cape one of her coy looks.

'Good thinking,' replied Cape and, glancing at his watch again, suggested that she be back by two thirty - rather over an hour from now. Then, with his thoughts focused on how he would brief the Chancellor, he hurried from his office, head bent low, small quick steps, concentration on 'high'.

* * * * *

As soon as he was gone, Mina half-ran from his office back to her desk. She collected up her large floppy leather bag, put on her coat and a Cossack style mock-fur hat, rushed downstairs and out of Number Eleven. Leaving Downing Street, she gave a broad, little-girl grin to the policemen on the gates, turned left and headed up Whitehall towards Trafalgar Square. As soon as she was out of sight of the Downing Street Gates, she got out her mobile phone and rang another mobile number. A phone told her the number was in use.

She smiled. The information of the memory stick was hopefully going to be worth a good deal of money to her - enough perhaps for some celebrations in Italy. She would also be able to give her other branch of 'the family' what they were looking for. She would try the mobile again in a minute. She tried twice. In her eagerness, she nearly dropped the phone – trying to use it a third time whilst threading her way through the lunchtime crowds. It was still some distance to the small Internet Café she often used, so she stopped in Trafalgar Square and sat on a step there. She rang the number a fourth time. Eventually it was answered.

'Wheeler' said a firm voice,

'It's me, Mina,'

'Mina, nice to hear from you - something for me?'

'Yes, very big, I'd say it's "hot stuff" - you'll be most surprised I think' she said, now speaking without a trace of accent, in quick, fluent English.

'Hot, you say?' Wheeler sounded cautious.

'Yes, hot', she repeated. 'I have a memory stick with some secret information on it. I'm on my way to the Internet Café I usually send you this kind of secret information from – I'll be there in five, six minutes. I'll email some of it to you - all of it will be too much, might make the internet café owner suspicious. We'll have to meet some time for me to give you the memory stick itself, Okay?'

'Well, yes if that's what you need to do with it. In the meantime, can you tell me a bit more about what you've got?'

'Could tell you a bit more I suppose,' she said, 'but I *also* need to talk to you about a special bonus for this lot.'

'We'll talk about bonuses when I see what you've sent,' replied Wheeler, 'but give me a hint anyway.'

Mina explained as briefly as she could the events of the morning - the way she had copied the contents of the memory stick and what she had been able to overhear from Cape's various telephone conversations. She had only been able to look a few of the files on the stick, but could tell Wheeler what had been on the pages she had printed off for Cape. When she finished her tale, there was a coughing sound from the other mobile.

'Let me see if I've got this straight,' said Wheeler, his voice now hoarse. 'There's going to be a demonstration this afternoon to show off the power of Athena's internet hacking capabilities? Who the hell is Athena?'

'It's apparently the next generation of computer software,' she said, 'Mr Cape was saying to someone on the phone that it will take over from all the present computer systems which he said were like kid's stuff by comparison,'

'It's going to be easier for me to understand once I've actually seen what you're sending me and what's on the memory stick,' said Wheeler. He was intrigued. Why would the Chancellor be interested in a new generation of computer software? Why the secrecy? Why hold a Cobra Meeting – such meetings were usually only convened when there was a perceived threat to the nation.

'Anyway,' she added, 'as I already said, this information should mean a really big bonus?'

'Okay, Okay,' replied Wheeler, now irritated with her usual harping on about money – even though he acknowledged to himself that her payments, her bonuses as she called them were probably her entire motivation for risking so much passing on information to him. And with two of the world's giant accountancy firms as clients, her information was one of the main reasons he had manoeuvred her into the job there.

After a pause in the haggling he conceded 'If what you've got there is as good as it sounds, you'll be very well rewarded, believe me'.

'That's better,' said Mina, 'we can talk about that when I hand over the stick with the rest of the materials on it. I'll go to the internet café now and send you what I printed out for Mr Cape - it still has everything about the demonstration, the hedge fund being used for it, the agenda for Athena's launch tomorrow. I'm going to pretend I'm sending something very personal so I don't make the café manager suspicious, I'll think of something', she said as she got to her feet to continue her journey, still holding the mobile to her ear.

'Just send me what you can and meet me tonight at the Antelope Pub in Eaton Terrace,' he said 'be there at seven o'clock if you can make it by then. I'll bring my laptop and I promise I'll bring plenty of money in case your information's worth it.'

She ended the call and hurried on towards the Globespan Internet Café.

At the café, knowing that most booths had just a keyboard and screen, she went straight to the manager's counter and smiled her usual blend of lost little girl and coquette. The young customer services manager behind the desk recognised her from earlier visits, gave her a broad grin and came out with the usual 'can I help you?'

'I have to email with my employment details for a new job - my CV,' she said looking directly into his eyes, 'but unfortunately they're here on this memory stick; is there somewhere I can plug it in to send it as an attachment to an email ?' She had put the foreign accent back on, to help with the plea.

'Sure, do it from here,' he said as he lifted the section of the counter and beckoned her through.

She quickly sat down at one of the Café's admin screens, pulled out the little memory stick, and inserted it into the desktop's tower drive down by her left knee. Next, carefully checking Wheeler's email address, she opened an email form on the screen. She wrote a covering email to ensure that he did not forget to bring plenty of cash to the Antelope. In it she boasted again about the importance of the information she was sending - the demonstration, Athena's new software and the preparations to counter a cyber-attack on a bank tomorrow. She then attached three files off the stick and pressed send.

This done, she took a second little memory stick out of her bag, plugged it into the tower of the desktop and copied the entire contents of the first stick onto the second. Taking both sticks out of the tower, she put one back into her bag and the other into an envelope she had already addressed to what she called "her other family" in the east end of London.

Her clandestine work successfully completed, she got up and hurried out. In a flurry of confidence in the value of this information, she left far more cash on the counter than was needed for the time she had spent on their machine - she even hummed a favourite Italian song to herself as she headed for a very quick pub lunch before going back to Number Eleven.

Strange that she had ignored some of her training from Wheeler whilst in the café. She had allowed her excitement at what she was sending to overcome her trained caution. In writing her long email, she had forgotten that the ever-watchful eyes of the world's surveillance teams would be on the lookout for a number of words that she had used in it – not least "cyber-weapons" and "Athena".

7

Thursday, mid - afternoon,

The SVR, Yesenevo, Moscow

Igor Komarov had taken great care when setting up his personal links to the Federation's various intelligence services. The arrangement meant that his assistant, Pavel Rostov, looked after all matters connected with internal affairs. This meant mainly keeping a close watch on the President's list of dissidents. Until Ranald MacCrammond had moved Komarov's money this morning, both Boreyev and Mikhail Vassilov, had been on this long list of dissidents. Naturally, Komarov said nothing to anyone in the office about his financial dealings with MacCrammond, but hinted that it was the President's wish that the two of them be removed from the list because of some personal rapprochement. Apart from this one instance of personal intervention, Komarov left the boring dissident matters to Pavel.

The exciting activity, and potentially that from which the glory would come, was the hunt for the new cyber weapon and this Komarov took for himself. This hunt was almost exclusively handled by his own personally fostered connection with Danil Morozov in the SVR.

Much of the strength of the link between Morozov and "mentor Komarov", rested on Morozov's near hero-worship of Komarov's close connections to the President and, in his own mind, lifted Morozov above the rest of his co-workers. Indeed, by inference, Komarov allowed Morozov to feel that he was but a step and a half from the President himself. Thus, whereas many on electronic stake-out duties might easily have allowed the hours boredom to take the edge off vigilance, Morozov's dedication on his mentor's behalf was devoted and meticulous.

Danil Morozov's main areas of his expertise were the monitoring of all foreign communications - emails, telephony – both landline and mobile. His computer surveillance programmes were also set up to keep a watch on social media sites such as Facebook and Twitter. All of his work had recently been greatly enhanced with yet another reorganisation of the SVR's capabilities and was now supposedly able to match those of any of his counterparts in the UK's GCHQ or the US at Langley and the NSA.

Morozov's search programmes – sophisticated algorithms - were capable of spotting words or phrases which "popped up" in emails, documents, or telephone conversations almost anywhere on the internet or over the airwaves – that is to say, anywhere in the world. It was therefore of considerable excitement when, just after three in the afternoon, a small red-light alarm went off when one of his key search words, "Athena" had been picked up more than once in an email that had just been sent in the UK. Morozov quickly focussed more machine power on this UK search which had found this first occurrence. Soon more of his key words and phrases began to appear. By looking through not just emails, but databases on the laptops and computers involved in the first email – Mina's to Wheeler - more and more data came flowing into Morozov's files where his internal systems began to sort and organise them.

To make even greater use of information, Morozov was able to ask other machines to expand on new names as they appeared. It was the fruits of these expanded searches that got Morozov's pulse to quicken, for he soon found that Mina was listed as working for the office of the Chancellor of the Exchequer of the United Kingdom and the recipient as being the partner of a London PR company. Further searches through the contents of attachments of Mina's email seemed to indicate that this "Athena" could well be the new generation software Komarov had been trying to hunt down for the past year.

His usual method of working with Komarov was to put his findings into documentary form and email them twice a day. Now, with this exciting breakthrough, he picked up the telephone in the hope that Komarov too would be excited by the news and would not want to wait for one of the usual emails late that evening. To his disappointment, Komarov was out of the office and not expected back till much later. Morozov's excitement prevented him from just leaving matters at that and asked the junior in Komarov's office if he could leave a message.

'It's Morozov here from the SVR,' he said, 'could you alert him the moment he gets in to look at an email and attachments I've just sent him. It is of great importance and also urgent.'

8

Thursday Lunchtime

Struthers & Wheeler & Co, The Strand, London

As Max Wheeler was due to receive Mina's email, he told his secretary that he was not to be disturbed and did not want any calls put through to him till further notice. He wanted to study what Mina was sending him before telling his partner, John Struthers - for a start, his partner was not even aware of Mina's existence.

Although all of his informants were financed through the company, the funding was carefully hidden from Struthers and Wheeler wished to keep it that way. He had found Mina in the Italian immigrant community. As had been the case with some of the others he had recruited into his small group of informants, he and Mina had met casually chatting in a pub.

They had met again a couple of times and he had also got her an introduction to Cape at a party given specifically for that purpose. Spiked drinks combined with Mina's charms were all that were needed and Mina eventually got the job at Number 11. Mina was delighted. Though she had learned well how to manipulate Cape so as to get information needed by Wheeler, she had also learned how to manipulate Wheeler who was still under the impression that the bonuses she got from him were important to her impoverished family in southern Italy and were also her entire motivation. This background story she enhanced each time she and Wheeler communicated and she always bargained for more than he offered. She even went as far as giving Wheeler her boyfriend's address as being hers, whereas she lived nearby in a very comfortable furnished apartment within a security-guarded block of flats. Her boyfriend's apartment was in an insalubrious old block and when Wheeler was initially vetting her this was one aspect of her life that convinced him he could maintain a strong hold on her. Mina had soon come to understand the cynical ways in which Wheeler used her and it amused her that he still believed that he had recruited her – though, of course, it was the other way round as she had her own very good reasons for seeking out Wheeler to use his expertise to get her into Number 11. It was working well as the other side of her "family" frequently told her.

The information that Wheeler got from his team of informers varied considerably - as might be expected. In Mina's case, it was for her to get advance information on the government's intentions in world of finance and finance law, as this would be invaluable to two of his company's largest clients – both amongst the largest global accountancy firms. Whereas his army of spies were not always good judges of the importance or indeed the relevance if the information they were passing on and sometimes, without telling them, their offerings went straight into the bin. On many other occasions – as with this one of Mina's – the information from Cape's memory stick and conversations was sure to be of direct relevance to several of Wheeler's clients.

Advance and secret information on a new kind of software and its launch at a Bank of England conference was interesting enough, but her specific mention of hedge funds had caught his attention and he now settled himself comfortably at his desk and opened Mina's newly arrived email. As he read, he jotted notes. Struthers & Wheeler had two hedge funds as clients, three companies involved in internet security and the contents of the email could well impinge on any or all these. It was as he was reading through that he suddenly dropped his pen. He read the sentence a second time.

"The demonstration on the Matthews Finch Hedge Fund this afternoon will show beyond any doubt Athena's mastery of the internet and its unique ability to hack right into the core programmes of organisations, however well protected they may think they are from cyber-attack."

As he got his handkerchief out of his pocket to wipe his forehead, he noticed to his horror that his hand was trembling. Fine beads of sweat had formed round his pale, freckled forehead, just beneath his close-cropped red hair. The Matthews Finch account was one of their star clients and any adverse publicity on them – such as this – could reflect badly on him as well. He quickly read on the end of the email and its attachments. To make sure that he had not misunderstood what was happening, he read through the passage a second time and then picked up the telephone and asked for John Struthers.

As one of their clients put it, "if you want good press coverage, a reliable job well done or a well-managed launch event, go to John Struthers, but if it's flair you need or someone on your side in a scandal, Max Wheeler's your man". Although Struthers did not mind this widely accepted view of the two of them, he was wary of Wheeler's sometimes unconventional methods - already this year he had need to step in to sort out a mess that Max had got the company and a client into. So when he got an excited Max asking for an urgent meeting, he was already on the defensive.

Wheeler's account of the email, "from a reliable source" was hurried and emotional and Struthers sat back nodding his head, not entirely sure why Wheeler was so hyped-up over some new software, cyber-attacks, or a Bank of England's conference the next day. But he sat up and leant forward across the desk at Wheeler's next part of the tale,

'This demonstration this afternoon is using Matthews Finch as a guinea pig to show off this new software,' Wheeler said, 'quite how the Bank of England has come to be endorsing illegal computer-hacking is beyond me and I hope to learn more when I meet my source this evening,'

'Maybe Nat Matthews or Paul Finch personally authorised this tampering with their trading software?' suggested Struthers, 'Perhaps they offered their company for demonstration purposes, in exchange for something we don't know about?'

'Never, not a chance,' replied Wheeler, 'Nat Matthews is paranoid about anyone getting anywhere near his unique trading software, he'd never let that happen – besides, what could they offer him to make him agree to break that principle?'

'Well, in that case, the whole thing's quite extraordinary,' said Struthers, 'so we'd better get in touch with Matthews. I happen to know that Paul Finch was in New York this week and going down after that to Florida for the long weekend, so he'll be virtually impossible to contact,'

'I'll try and get hold of Nat Matthews then,' said Wheeler, 'as usual around this time of year, he's staying at the Palace Hotel in St Moritz for his annual skiing holiday,'

'When you make contact with him, why not ask him about stopping this demonstration,' said Struthers, 'I mean shutting down the company's trading at the time of this demonstration is due to start,'

'Wouldn't doing that look worse to his clients and the markets than allowing the demonstration to go ahead?' said Wheeler, 'Let's face it, any major unscheduled interruption to trading is going to get people asking questions. Anyway, it's getting hold of him that's going to be the problem. From past experience, I know that he bans all communications with him whilst he's on holiday. Still, leave that with me – I'll get hold of him somehow.'

* * * * *

Wheeler knew that Matthews did not spend that much of his now very substantial earnings on himself - unless, that is, you were to include his Turbo Bentley, his Quattroporte Maserati and his house in Wilton Crescent. His only other personal extravagances were his two holidays each year. On these, he always went alone - St Moritz usually around Easter, and Italy - usually Tuscany followed by Rome in the late summer. The cognoscenti might not consider the skiing facilities in St Moritz as being the best in Switzerland, but it had the Cresta Run, the horse racing on the lake, and, above all, the cachet of being one of the oldest and grandest ski resorts in the world. It was that aspect of it that appealed the most to Nat Matthews. When possible, he always stayed in the same room at the Palace Hotel. He liked familiarity and had come to regard it, with its wonderful views out over the lake and across the mountains the far side of the valley, as though he owned it.

Wheeler considered himself to be outside Matthews's embargo on communications from the office, since he was neither a partner nor staff. He also considered that he had a special relationship with Matthews. As his PR advisor, he had managed to extricate Matthews more than once from one indiscretion or another - he had even once managed to put his errant client in a good light after a tawdry tale involving a lady of the night and a nightclub of poor repute. For these 'extra' services, Matthews was always genuinely grateful.

Having done his duty by briefing his partner, Wheeler got back to his own office and set about contacting Matthews. Naturally he tried the obvious first. He telephoned him at the Palace Hotel. As he had anticipated, Matthews was out skiing and not expected back till after dark. He was also told that Mr Matthews usually left skiing back down to the last safe moments, just as the pistes were beginning to ice up and that, on getting back down into St. Moritz, before returning to the Palace Hotel, he nearly always went to Hanselmann's for its ridiculously rich but delicious cakes and tea.

Failing the easy approach, Wheeler then sent him a text message *"ring Wheeler immediately, business threatening situation"*. From reports of his previous holidays in St Moritz, Wheeler also knew that Gustave, the concierge, was the epitome of a great fixer and looked after Matthews every outlandish whim - so he also sent a message to Gustave, urging him to get Matthews to contact Mr Wheeler urgently.

This second message eventually had the desired effect, and Matthews rang him back shortly after three. Gustave had managed to track him down to the Corviglia Club half way up the mountain and Matthews had responded immediately, taking the funicular down to St Moritz rather that skiing back down.

'This had better be bloody important,' said Matthews as soon as he spoke to Wheeler from his Palace Hotel room, 'I've cut short my usual afternoon programme to respond to the text message you sent to Gustave – so what's this all about?'

Wheeler recounted the whole thing, Mina's emails, what she had told him she had overheard from telephone conversations - even including the connection between Athena, Sir Jeremy Towneley and his nephew now running the team that had hacked into his company.

Wheeler finished by saying, 'John Struthers and I didn't do anything to stop the demonstration, because we felt sure that either you or Paul must have agreed to it - I mean we assumed that . . .'

'Of course I didn't bloody agree to it,' shouted Matthews, 'do you think I'd suddenly go mad enough to agree to such a hare-brained idea? Christ, you weren't joking when you texted the words "business threatening". Don't you realise that if we aren't trading completely normally on Tuesday morning when the Stock Exchange reopens, we could lose all our bloody clients - millions draining out of the company like a severed bloody artery.'

'Look, as soon as we've finished this conversation,' he continued, his voice calmer, 'I'm going to get myself back to London the fastest way that Gustave can arrange it for me. As soon as I am away from St Moritz, I'll have him to text you the time I'm expected to get home - by then I'll probably be in an effing helicopter arriving in Zurich. But, here's the important bit, by the time I get back home, I want you, Struthers, the office, my lawyers, the wholly bloody lot of you to have started on a plan to get me free of bloody computer clutches of Jeremy Towneley and his effing nephew. I also expect you to have found a way which allows me to tell all our clients, first thing Easter Tuesday morning, that whatever happened this afternoon was just a hiccup. They need to hear that our trading is entirely under our complete control again. Is all of that crystal clear?'

'Crystal clear,' repeated Wheeler as he heard the telephone click dead the other end of the line.

The message was stark. Get the company shot of the influence of MacCrammond's lot or there would be no company - legal redress or recompense could wait for another day, but no one could postpone the arrival of Tuesday.

Wheeler bit his lower lip and for just a few seconds wrestled with his duty to tell Struthers of a plan that was forming in his mind. A moment's further thought persuaded him that Struthers's innate caution would scupper his emerging plan. There would be time enough to inform him later; right now he decided to get on with what he needed to do. His excuse for not telling Struthers everything right now, would be to tell a white lie and use the excuse that he was still having difficulty reaching Matthews.

He looked up a number on his mobile phone, having decided there was just one person ideally suited to meet Matthews's demands; he rang, but his man was out.

He left a message, '*Max Wheeler calling, need you and your unusual contact's special skills urgently. Ring me back on this mobile as soon as you can, thanks'*. Whether or not the recipient of this message would come up with a *legal* way of helping mattered far less than that he should be available. It would be a difficult wait till he got an answer to this.

9

Thursday, evening

Nikol'skaya Street, Moscow

    Igor Komarov had spent an uncomfortable afternoon. He had been kept waiting by the President for several hours and although there was an apology of sorts when they eventually met, Komarov had a dread feeling that his standing with the President was slipping. His recent few years as an indispensable 'fixer' had allowed him to amass a considerable fortune, so, becoming *dispensable* might leave him with that fortune, but losing his source of power was not something he wanted even to contemplate.

    On arriving back at the office just as everyone was leaving made matters worse, there would be no one on whom to vent his frustration and his fears for his future. His heart lifted, however, when the last remaining office junior told him there was an urgent message for him from Morozov of the SVR.

    He felt a tickle of sweat at the back of his neck as he hurried through the office. Morozov only ever sent reports, not messages. He read the email and then almost tore the paper as he snatched up the printed out attachments. As he read these, he loosened his tie and reached for the remains of a cup of cold coffee from lunchtime which no one had yet bothered to clear away. As soon as he had finished reading, he looked at his watch and calculated the time difference. It was 3.32pm in London and he immediately realised that the UK TV programme had already started.

Fumbling, he picked up the telephone and dialled a number he would not like the President know was on his quick-dial list.

Anton Silayev had done up his apartment in Tverskaya Street in a manner that would have done just fine as a high class brothel in Paris in the nineteen-thirties. A mass of heavy red brocade curtains swathed the windows, gold fittings glinted on the doors, the curtain stays and on much of the heavy rococo furniture. Silayev for all his amassed fortune, had not yet acquired a degree of modesty in either his manners or his style of living. Still, being an important direct link between Komarov and what the outside world refer to as the Russian Mafia, Silayev's appalling appetites were tolerated – it was his contacts that Komarov needed and over the years they had built between them profitable businesses converting Komarov's close connection to the seat of power into profits and capital for onward investment.

As the telephone rang, Silayev was sprawled in a comfortable chair behind a massive, ornate desk. A half empty bottle of vodka stood near the telephone and when it rang out, he topped up his glass even before he reached for the handset. Having spent the afternoon commiserating with a couple of friends on a dubious business deal that had gone wrong, when he did pick up the telephone, he was about to dismiss the caller with some rude excuse, until he realised that it was Komarov ringing him.

Instantly he sat up in the chair, and waved at his two companions to leave the room and shut the door,

'Igor, sorry to keep you waiting,' he said, sobering up with the shock of a call from his vital link to real power as opposed to his own brute variety. 'Just getting rid of some old friends who had been commiserating with me . . .' he added.

'Business friends?' asked Komarov,

'Good heavens, no,' lied Silayev, 'death in the family of one of them, known them for years . . .'

'This is important and time is of the essence,' said Komarov, 'if you haven't been drinking too much at the wake, are you in good enough shape to do something important for me?'

'I am fine, what's up?'

Komarov told him of the SVR's surveillance report - how it had picked up Mina's email to Wheeler and enough of what it contained to give Silayev a good idea of how important this was,

'Do you have RT TV?' he said as he finished,

'I do,' replied Silayev,

'And can you get hold of your top IT people right away, I mean *right now*?'

'Yes, I could,' said Silayev, 'but as you know I'm pretty clued up myself on most . . .'

'I know that Anton,' said Komarov, 'but we need someone highly technical to watch a UK television programme that's already started,'

'One of the people with me before you rang was my IT technical director, Ivolgin, a friend of the deceased,' replied Silayev, 'he's just in the next room.'

'Get him back right away, I need you to watch this UK programme called "A day on the London Stock Exchange". At precisely 3.50 GMT – that's 6.50 here of course.' said Komarov, 'I need you to be watching some trading on a Bloomberg screen on that TV programme. There is going to be one minute of trading that is supposedly going to show what happens when the trading algorithms of the hedge fund have been re-engineered. Do you understand what

I'm saying? We might be looking at the work of elusive cyber warfare programme we've been searching for.'

Silayev slammed his glass down on the desk, stretched out and grabbed a small pad, at the same time he pressed a button on his intercom and held it down. On the pad he then wrote the name of the programme and the timings. The intercom answered,

'Get Ivolgin back in here, *now*,' he shouted into the machine,

Moments later Ivolgin and a girl who looked more like a call-girl than a secretary came back into the room,

'I'll get onto this right away,' he said back down the phone to Komarov, 'I'll watch it with my IT man and ring you back after the programme' He replaced the receiver and gave the instructions to Ivolgin and the girl. Despite her inappropriate dress, she acted with efficiency, pulling a large widescreen television in front of some chairs near the fireplace, switching the machine on and finding the foreign programme on RT TV.

Silayev and Ivolgin moved to the chairs in front of the television in time to catch the last twenty minutes of ITV's "A Day on the London Stock Exchange". Just after 3.45 London time, Ivolgin sat forward and pressed 'record' on the TV remote. They then watched in complete silence. At 3.49 precisely, the programme presenter turned to the TV audience,

'And now we're going to see a typical Bloomberg trading screen. On it you will be able to see how the graph moves as trades are done,' he said,

As the television camera focused on a trading screen viewers could see the graph fluctuating up and down gently with small boxes round the main central picture showing numbers and symbols incomprehensible to a layman but which Ivolgin watched closely. At 3.50, as though someone had pressed a 'fast forward' button on a recording, the graph seemed to go out of control, fluctuating wildly from top to bottom of the screen whilst the figures in the small boxes also went into the same fast forward mode. Exactly one minute later the graph returned to the way it had been running earlier. The ITV presenter moved the programme onto other matters and Silayev turned the television off.

Silayev turned to Ivolgin,

'Apparently, that the wild trading we just saw was the result of someone hacking into the hedge fund over the internet and re-engineering its trading algorithms, what did you think of that?' he said as he watched Ivolgin's reactions closely. Ivolgin switched the television on again, re-wound the recording and watched the demonstration a second time. When it was finished, he shook his head slowly from side to side.

'Not possible with any technology that I know of,' he said, 'quite apart from hacking into the company itself, and presumably getting past some quite sophisticated defences, . . . ' he paused for a moment working things out in his mind as he spoke. Then went on, 'having got past the defences – no mean feat with today's encrypted versions – you say they re-engineered the trading algorithms? As I said before, and I'll repeat it with complete confidence, that's not possible with any technology I know of. My guess is that those watching that TV programme have been subjected to a very clever hoax - very clever, but a hoax nevertheless,'

Silayev immediately rang Komarov back, and passed on Ivolgin's views.

'And you're sure Ivolgin is as good as we've got anywhere in the Federation?' asked Komarov

'Without a doubt,' replied Silayev, 'you know that, Igor, how the hell could we do what we do without him being the best? – he does all our special IT stuff'.

'Okay, that's fine, I believe you,' said Komarov, 'it's just that the people who did what your man is calling a hoax, are the same people who will be defending the bank in London against our attack tomorrow.'

This was met with complete silence as the implications of what he was saying sank in.

'So, as you've probably worked out by now,' continued Komarov, 'it looks as though we have indeed found the software and though we weren't ready to believe him, our contact in London was right after all. We'd better meet even earlier than planned - tomorrow morning - so that we can discuss how we might use our attack on the bank to get our hands on this Athena software.'

10

Thursday early afternoon

The lawns of the Towneley Vassilov Bank

The Agusta helicopter was on time arriving on the lawns of the Towneley Vassilov Bank. Kim and Ranald were ready and as soon as bank staff had stowed their luggage, they climbed aboard. On take-off, the helicopter rose swiftly and swung right, north, for Glasgow International Airport. Depending on air traffic control, they should touch down on the charter company's apron in about an hour's time. As the helicopter climbed, so did their spirits. For Ranald, there was the imminent prospect of the long weekend with the family and, for Kim there was the excitement of a trip up to the remote island she had seen only in photographs, and learned about only when talking to the members of the Craithe team.

The agreed rendezvous for all the family was the airport's main concourse and the first to arrive was the helicopter with Ranald and Kim aboard. His Uncle, Sir Jeremy Towneley, who had chartered a Cessna TTX from the City of London Airport arrived less than twenty minutes later. As the two of them met up and greeted each other, it was with an emotional embrace, for it was evident to Ranald from his uncle's appearance, that his illness was having a serious effect on him and that he maybe had not long left with them all. Until recently still well over six foot tall, with an abundance of white hair, he now had a slight stoop and had clearly lost yet more weight since Ranald had seen him last, only a month earlier.

The KLM flight in from Moscow was on time and Tatiana seemed tired though young Jerry was irrepressible, insisting his father swing him round by his arms as though he were on a fairground ride. It was only when this was finished - with Jerry in fits of giggles - that Tatiana was allowed to give her husband a hug, and, after that a fond kiss; she then buried her head in his shoulder and let out a deep sigh. Young Anastasia, the au pair, was introduced by Ranald to Sir Jeremy and, to the latter's surprise and delight, she gave a hint of a courtesy as she took his hand. She was then introduced to Kim and was visibly pleased when Kim exchanged greetings with her and asked her about the flight in fluent Russian.

They all followed Ranald out to the helicopter hire company's tarmac apron and were shown up into the Agusta's comfortable leather seats for the brief flight up to Craithe. Little Jerry was thrilled and bouncy as he and Anastasia peered out of the window. As soon as all their luggage had been stowed aboard, the helicopter rose out over the west end of Glasgow and flew slightly north of west following the south shore of the River Clyde. On leaving the river where it turned south, they continued straight on, climbing up over wild, rugged moorland and mountain terrain. Anastasia occasionally pointed out to Jerry the small herds of Red Deer and of sheep that scattered from the noise of the helicopter, galloping off across the new spring heather. Kim too, was already enjoying the views and the start to the long weekend.

It took less than a quarter of an hour for the Agusta to reach and to pass over the small town of Lochgilphead on Loch Fyne and soon after that, the coastal town of Crinan. Over the deadened sound of the engines and rotor-blades, Ranald leant across to Kim and pointed out the turbulent waters of the Gulf of Corryvreckan between the islands of Jura and Scarba.

'The Corryvreckan sometimes makes it near impossible for most craft to get to or from Craithe,' he said, 'that's why we had to buy a retired Lifeboat to get us back and forth when the weather's bad'. Kim looked down at the narrow channel between the two islands and could see that, in contrast to the calm, dark seas either side of the gulf, the Corryvreckan was quite white with breaking waves,

Almost immediately after passing between the two islands, the pilot swung the helicopter round in a wide arc round Craithe Castle. Neither Kim nor Anastasia had ever seen anything quite like it. Sixty to eighty foot walls of granite, punctuated here and there with windows of many different sizes, cut into the great walls of stone in apparently random patterns. On the eastern corners of the main central block of the castle and its south west, there were three massive towers, each of the over a hundred feet in height. Later, awed by the sheer size of the south west tower, Anastasia asked what was this hundred feet in her more familiar metres - 'well over thirty', she was told.

The sixty-five mile trip had taken just under half an hour and the Agusta landed in one of the few spots possible, the top of a sweep of three terraced lawns running some two hundred yards down from the front of the castle to the cliff tops above the sea. Formally planted terraces of box hedges and decorative flower beds covered the few flat areas and, at the far western end where the forests of pine started, there was a large walled garden full of produce grown for the castle inhabitants. Like many great houses in Scotland, there was also a fifty foot tall circular dovecote, with a conical roof. In times gone by, young pigeons were bred in it for consumption in the castle.

As soon as the engines had been switched off and the rotors had stopped, they all got out and Anastasia, having jumped down first, twirled in delight as she marvelled at the daunting yet thrilling sight of the massive walls of the Castle - great sweeps of sheer granite, yet pretty, she thought, with its pinkish-grey colouring.

Ranald's father and mother had been waiting for them at the massive fifteen foot front doors, great thick barriers of oak. These were firmly shut with a more normal seven-foot door cut through one of them in Victorian times stood open. Ranald's mother, Florence, was standing by it and greeted her brother Jeremy fondly; it was the first time she had seen him since he had been diagnosed with terminal cancer and she took him by the arm to lead him into the castle.

Everyone else followed these two across the large outer entrance hall with a gallery above it at the top of the wide sweep of the stairs. From the outer hall, they turned right and into a truly enormous room, known as the Great Hall. Little Jerry was being carried by Tatiana so Anastasia was able to stop on her own as soon as she was though the doors. There she just stood in awe looking about her. Kim, too, who had known in general terms of Ranald's privileged background and had seen one or two photographs of the place, was still quite taken aback by the sheer size of the place now seen live. The two of them stood next to each other gazing round. The vaulted ceilings above them and the room itself might have accommodated the entirety of Anastasia's parents little country house, her home, some sixty miles outside Moscow and as soon as they were into the room, they swung away from the group and slowly wandered around. Nowadays The Great Hall served as the Castle's main Drawing Room so, despite its seventy foot length, fifty foot width and thirty foot vaulted ceilings, it was surprisingly warm and comfortable. This was largely due to the eight foot square fireplace and massive mantelpiece dominating the end of the room which, on Florence's insistence, was almost always alight with blazing wood fire most months of the year.

The Great Hall itself must have been part of the original castle and, in mediaeval times would have been very cold. The walls were now covered a fine, beige coloured harling giving it a strange giant's sandpaper effect. These were hung about with an assortment of ancient weaponry, stags heads, and hanging tapestries with, at regular intervals, poking their heads through all of these, portraits of long departed MacCrammonds. Beneath one of the larger portraits, the label proclaimed that it was of Charles James Stuart, Bonnie Prince Charlie, and the Young Pretender to the Stuart Throne. It was only the sheer size of the hall that allowed for this disparate mass of wall ornament to blend into a pleasing kind of giant montage, so that the overall impression was that it was not even cluttered. Anastasia and Kim continued to walk slowly round peering occasionally at the names below the portraits and Kim wondered what these ancestors would have been like to meet and to talk to.

Ranald saw the two of them wandering around together and went over to them.

'All these weapons and the pictures of all this fighting', said Anastasia in Russian.

'Yes, but it's always been that way most places in the world hasn't it?' he replied, also in Russian. 'It's always been easier to take one's neighbour's hard earned treasure than go out to earn it oneself - easier to steal from his grain store than grow one's own.' She laughed as this brought to mind the Russian tribal wars of over the centuries.

'And these wars and skirmishes had been happening between the Clans since Viking times', continued Ranald - and he led them both over to a table behind one of the sofas on which sat a large, ancient looking leather-bound book. It was entitled "The MacCrammnonds of Craithe, a Family History" - a book of the type many old Scottish families had compiled for themselves. The page size was nearly twice that of a standard glossy magazine and overall was a good nine inches thick, its buff coloured leather smooth and shiny with much handling and beautifully engraved in gold lettering with its title and description.

Ranald opened it and went straight to the back of it where there were a number of appendices. He quickly found what he was looking for - a much abbreviated history of Craithe - so abbreviated that it fitted onto one page.

'You can read English, can you?' he asked Anastasia, still in Russian, as Kim looked on beside her,

'Oh yes, top grades at Uni', she replied in English, 'why you show me this?' she added as he pointed to the short history.

'Because after all these centuries, my father and I have just changed it - we've given it a new ending.'

'Is that the joining of Craithe to the Isle of Man Crown Dependency, the negotiations you were busy completing last year?' asked Kim, also speaking in Russian,

'It is indeed, re-joining Craithe to the Isle of Man to bring it back to the old Viking Empire; so, yes, it's now part of that Crown Dependency,"

'And that's good?' asked Anastasia

'It is indeed,' he said, 'like the castle, it gives us extra protection,'

He then let them read down the page through the history:-

Craithe - Chronology & notes:

- 795 to 1266 Viking / Norse West Coast 'Kingdom of Man & the Isles' .Stretched from the Island of Lewis in the north, included all the Hebridean Islands along with strips of the Mainland south, down as far as and including the Isle of Man. Many years of debilitating fighting and the strain on resources eventually led the Vikings to sell the Kingdom.

- 1266, Treaty of Perth, 'The Kingdom' sold by King Magnus V of Norway to King Edward I of England. This kingdom then used by several successive English Kings as a special reward for outstanding service to the Crown.

- 1485, Title and Tenure of 'The Isle of Man and the Isles' given to John Stanley, first Earl of Derby, as a reward for his key role

in crowning Henry VII on the battlefield at Bosworth upon the death there of Richard III

- 1642, Craithe and the Isles passed by James Stanley, 7th Earl of Derby to his second daughter Louisa as her Dowry on her marriage to James MacCrammond, Laird of Craithe, (Written Permission for this transfer given by King Charles the First, in a letter dated 12 June 1642)

- 1828, Isle of Man sold by Dukes of Atholl to the Crown, ('The Isles' retained in the ownership of the Lairds of Craithe, in feu to the Crown).

'This Crown Dependency?' asked Kim in Russian so that Anastasia would feel included, 'am I right in thinking that means they, like the Isle of Man, Craithe is now outside the laws of both the United Kingdom and the European Union?'

'It does indeed,' replied Ranald, 'very useful for what the team are doing here'.

'Aha, your own sovereign state just like the Federation of Russia,' cried Anastasia, smiling as though she now understood the significance of what she had just been told.

'Yes, smaller version,' said Ranald. All three laughed.

During this short dissertation on history, Kim had been leafing through an earlier bit of the book and had come across an extensive family tree with dozens of pretty, ornate coats of arms on it representing the many families of Ranald's ancestors.

'Good heavens,' she cried, 'look at all of these.' She continued to look in greater detail at some of the names under each shield. 'A lot of very grand Earls and a Duke here,' she went on, 'and here's a Stuart – a relation of Bonnie Prince Charlie by any chance?'

'Well yes actually, and I have the Stuart name in mine to acknowledge that,' said Ranald, 'but they're not all grand, look here.

There's Maria daughter of the bad, Jack Black, notorious pirate and general scoundrel – eventually caught and hanged. His daughter inherited his huge quantities of ill-gotten gains. She was a very feisty lady herself and you can tell how beautiful she was you'll find her portrait in the dining room and her father's name too is in mine.'

'Ah that's better,' said Kim, 'I like the thought of a banker having pirate's blood in his ancestry – very appropriate,'

'Are you mocking me by any chance?' asked Ranald,

'Heaven forbid I should ever mock you, Boss,' replied Kim grinning back at him.

The far end of the room, the Laird beckoned them and Ranald took them back over to join the others. As they got to the main group, it was clear that little Jerry was both tired and hungry and as soon as Anastasia had taken him from Tatiana, Ranald took the two of them upstairs to the old nursery suite where he had played as a child. It had been cleaned out for the long weekend but was much the same as it had been in Ranald's childhood. Helen McGovern, head of castle's female staff and what used to be called Housekeeper, took charge of Anastasia and the boy - something she had been looking forward to these past few weeks.

When Ranald returned down to the Great Hall - he was anxious to talk to Sir Jeremy. He found him on his own, seated in a comfortable chair, sipping a glass of whisky, he was looking out of one of east-facing windows, relaxing in the view of the islands of Scarba and Jura and the mainland beyond. His eyes were half closed in peaceful contemplation of the shimmering seas, the islands and the pale blue of the evening spring sky. A small pot of pills lay on a delicate little Georgian side table beside him and Ranald could see that the earlier pain had gone and that he was now enjoying being here in this tranquil world. Ranald helped himself to a small glass of whisky from a table of drinks in the corner of the room and went over to join him.

'How're you feeling?' said Ranald as he drew up a comfortable arm chair next to the other.

'I'm fine, though I found the helicopter a bit difficult after such a long day', he smiled a wisp of shadow leaving it as he looked back at his nephew. His illness meant that he had little to do with the project from day to day, but as it was to be his last project and his legacy, he liked to be kept informed of developments.

'You'll have heard that Athena gets launched tomorrow,' said Ranald,

'Yes, you've done wonders getting it as far as you have,' replied Sir Jeremy, 'and I can't thank you enough – yet again - for taking over the burden of developing it for me. You may not know this, but I was very aware of the sacrifice you made when you gave in to my pleading and joined the Towneley Bank when Tommy died. Believe it or not, I was aware that you had inclinations to do other things with your life and I'm truly grateful you gave those up for a career in banking.'

Ranald seemed about to say something to all of this but Sir Jeremy held up his hand to stop him, and continued. 'When your still in your prime, things like 'family history' and 'heritage' don't mean a great deal and it must have been difficult for you to understand why, when Tommy died, the dying out of the male line of the Towneleys mattered to me so much. As you're half a Towneley, I hope one day that you'll thank me for press-ganging you into all of this against your wishes and I thank you for doing so – especially as family, lineage, and all that are regarded as a bit of an anachronism, not just by you but by most people these days.'

'It's kind of you to say all that,' replied Ranald, 'but I've come to see that you gave me something really worthwhile to do with my life and as we complete the first objective of your project with its launch tomorrow, the financial world will quickly begin to become a safer and more stable place ,'

'I gather there's a threat of an attack on one of the banks expected tomorrow, can the project, I mean the team you've built up, can they cope with that?'

'Yes, we will' said Ranald, 'the only thing to stop that will be if the attackers go for one of the banks which has not yet installed our software,'

'I'm still not clear why this matters quite so much now,' said Sir Jeremy

'Mainly because without our own cyber-attack detection software on a system, when an attack comes in, Athena won't be triggered to counter-attack. I'm afraid we know, that those just relying on proprietary defence systems are going to fail and suffer the consequences. Still, after the demonstration this afternoon and a repeat of the crucial bit of it at the conference tomorrow morning, we hope that the rest of them will allow us to install,'

'That'll be good,' said Sir Jeremy, 'everything else under control?'

'I'm sure it will all go just fine,' replied Ranald smiling back down at his uncle.

'You're *sure*?' repeated Sir Jeremy, 'I've often found that when people use the phrase "*I'm sure*" they often actually mean "I hope". But there's no shame in hoping and I too naturally hope you'll all succeed.'

'You're right, of course,' replied Ranald, 'there was no way in which even Athena can *guarantee* to deal with the incoming cyber-attack, depends somewhat whether or not cyber-attack teams had learned any new tricks for which Athena has not been prepared.' Just after he had said this, he flicked the tiny scar above his left eyebrow as though there had been a fly there.

Sir Jeremy seemed to be about to doze off after his medication so Ranald quietly left him and went up to see how Perry was getting on with his researches into the software brokerage company, Silayev

& Komarov. All that was known so far was that Komarov was close to the President - did that mean that the attacking team were state-backed or was it perhaps a team belonging to the less-known character Silayev? Ranald wondered when they would discover the full truth behind the Komarov Silayev twosome. Was Komarov acting with the Silayev mafia or was the real power behind the two of them the Kremlin? It was going to be interesting to see how it was going to play out – well interesting, but also, even in Ranald's mind, a touch daunting.

11

Thursday late afternoon,

Eaton Square, London W1

Jed and Maisie Butters had been looking forward to the long Easter weekend for some time. Not because they needed the rest - working for Sir Jeremy and the late Lady Towneley was hardly demanding - even less so since her death last year. They were excited, because their daughter and grandchildren were coming up to London to visit them for a week or so.

These days, Butters was more of a caretaker and general handyman than his earlier role as full-time butler. Maisie was hardly overworked as part-time cook either, for as often as not, if there was to be a dinner or luncheon party, Mortillas were called in to bring and serve the whole meal, right up to and including the coffee. The days of entertaining, however, had all but ended after Lady Towneley had died and Sir Jeremy became ill.

Butters used to worry that the Towneleys thought he and his wife too old for the job, but whether or not that was true, nowadays, the current arrangements seemed to work well and they were down in their sitting room watching a game show on the television, relaxing whilst they had the opportunity to do so before the grandchildren arrived and turned the whole place into a fairground. As Sir Jeremy had gone to Scotland, the other two members of staff had been given the long weekend off and so the two of them had the whole place to themselves.

It surprised the couple when the front doorbell rang. Not knowing if it might be a friend of the Towneley Family who were not aware that they were away, Butters quickly tidied himself as he went up to answer the front door. The bell rang a third time as he reached the door but, just before opening it, he peered through the peep hole in the door. There was a young police couple at the door, both probably constables. Considering the recent spate of burglaries, in this, probably the most expensive and tempting area of London, it was nice to see the two of them on the beat again.

He undid the chains, unbolted the door but, as he opened it, was shocked to be thrust aside as the two police barged past him into the house and, turning quickly, slammed the door shut behind them. This was immediately followed by the young male constable thrusting a gun up into Butter's throat.

'Not a squeak.' he said, and then he added, 'how many in the house?'

'Just myself and my wife,' replied Butters, his voice quaking,

'And where is she?'

'Downstairs in our sitting room, watching television',

The policeman nodded to the police girl who left the two of them in the hallway and went off downstairs to find her. In the small, snug sitting room she went over to Maisie Butters, put a gentle hand on her shoulder, and smiled down at her.

'No need to disturb your viewing,' she said bending down close to the old lady. 'Constable Smithers and I are just upstairs with your husband - we're just checking out the alarm systems and windows, can't be too careful these days.' Maisie looked back up at her, smiled and nodded her head in agreement.

The young police woman then pretended to check the windows whilst looking round the room. Surreptitiously, she pocketed up a mobile telephone on the side table and, with Maisie once again intent on the television, she wound the telephone wire round her hand a couple of times and, with a sharp pull, yanked the connection out of the wall socket. She smiled broadly again at Maisie, gave a little wave and left the room to search the rest of the large downstairs area. She pulled out the telephone wires of one other extension and also pocketed a second mobile phone she found in the kitchen.

She then returned upstairs, to join the other two. Smithers had got Butters to give him the full layout of the upstairs rooms and the three of them then proceeded together on a thorough search of the house for telephones and a safe. They did a quick search of the ground floor rooms, disconnecting two telephones, one in the hall and the other in a back store-room. One floor up, the young police woman searched the drawing room while Butters took the constable into Sir Jeremy's study. Here he was asked to open the safe, which he did with a key from the desk. He was then told to stand by the curtained window whilst the constable searched for files or notes or, more importantly, a laptop computer or tablet. This he did slowly and methodically, disturbing as little as possible, and, after a while, he found what he was looking for - hidden under some papers in one of the leather-topped desk's side-drawers, there was a small laptop with its charging lead. The constable gathered these up and put them into a small cloth bag he took from his pocket.

Together, all three went round the rest of the upstairs, pulling out telephone connections wherever they found them. Butters, trembling by now, swore on his children's lives that they had disabled all the telephones in the house and that there were no more mobile telephones either. He was taken downstairs told to sit and watch the television and constable Smithers then used the key to their sitting room which Butters had taken off a large key-ring and locked the two of them in. The two police then left the house, and hurried round to a side street where they had parked their car.

The young police couple, had they not been on a tight schedule, might have done more to ensure that Butters and his wife could not give them away for many hours. After a few minutes had passed, however, Butters explained as gently as he could to Maisie what had happened upstairs and then quietly, as though the young police might still be in the house, rose from the sofa, and went over a tall dresser against the wall near the door. Here he scrummaged around in the back of one of its drawers, and soon found what he was looking for - a spare master key for the downstairs rooms. Unlocking their sitting room door, he crept back upstairs, and crossed the hall towards the dining room. Just to the left of the dining-room door, tucked away out of sight for discretion, behind a heavy curtain, there was another telephone. He rang both the real police and then Sir Jeremy Towneley at Craithe.

* * * * *

Wheeler arrived at the Antelope pub in Eaton Terrace, and no sooner had he settled into his usual seat in the small snug bar at the back of the pub, than his mobile telephone rang.

'Hello, Max,' said the voice the other end, 'we've made a good start on your project and I've already got some interesting information for you - when can we meet?'

'Ah, good, Jock,' replied Wheeler, 'I've a short meeting with someone in a few minutes, immediately after which my client gets back from Switzerland and I'm seeing him at his place. Why don't we get together after those two meetings? I can then see what you've got for me. Shall we say nine at the Antelope Pub in Eaton Terrace?'

'Okay, see you there at nine,'

Wheeler took a sip of the pint that had been put on his table while he was on the phone. His mind turned to Jock Hunter's call. He was pleased with such a quick response for he had first contacted the Major only a few hours ago – soon after his call to Nat Matthews in St Moritz. His urgent need to get on with Matthews's insistence on sorting matters out by Monday night had left him with little choice but seek out Jock – or, rather the Major as he liked to be known. He thought about him for a moment. Over time Wheeler had discovered that Jock Hunter was not really a major at all. Maybe he had been a senior warrant officer, a sergeant-major perhaps. Chameleon-like, Jock Hunter had picked up many officer traits along the way which now allowed him now to play the part. He had also trained briefly with the SAS before being rejected on fitness grounds, but was thus also able pass himself off as ex-SAS officer. Wheeler had noticed on a couple of occasions, however, that Jock was careful not to do so in any company that included ex-military - no need to wilfully expose himself to 'discovery'. Still, right now, choosing the Major seemed to confirm that he had been right to pick him - already having some 'interesting information' for him.

Whilst waiting for Mina, he looked about him, the reassuring familiarity of the Antelope a peaceful counter to the new anxieties of the current situation. The pub had been allowed to remain unchanged in its decor for over sixty years, though the yellow-ocre patina of years of smoke haze had been painted out soon after the smoking ban was introduced in pubs. About the only thing that had changed was that a number of the older pub regulars had moved on to celestial bars, replaced by the likes of Wheeler. He had been coming here, his 'local' ever since an unexpected inheritance had helped him to buy a two floor flat in one Cliveden Place's extremely expensive houses round the corner from here. He knew both the faces and names of some of the regulars. None were his friends however, as he used this as an extension of his house, as a kind of extra office rather than for leisure. Most of the regulars knew that Wheeler used the quiet comfort of the panelled room this way – no one listened in to his conversations, no one asked questions, some of them used the place for the same reasons.

Mina was prompt as always, and as soon as Wheeler spotted her coming through from the front bar, he caught Harry the barman's attention. With nothing said, Harry poured a large glass of Chardonnay and Mina collected it from the bar on her way over to join Wheeler – a procedure seemingly well-practiced between the three of them.

She was in a good mood. Not only did Wheeler owe her for the information she had emailed to him earlier, she still had the memory stick with her. Though she was now well practiced in pretending to Wheeler that she was only a part of his team of informants because of the money she could send to her supposedly impoverished family, she quickly reminded herself to maintain the charade as she reached his table.

There was no small talk, no time wasted on 'catching up'. They got straight down to business. As soon as she was seated next to Wheeler, she delved into her large floppy leather bag and, after a moment of rummaging around, brought her hand out with the tiny memory stick in it. Wheeler held his hand out for it but instead of handing it over to him she said,

'How much for the email and for this as I've more even than those two?' Unlike her demeanour with Cape, there was no trace of an accent when dealing with Wheeler and a stranger overhearing her might have thought her a native Londoner.

'Five hundred for the email,' said Wheeler, 'same again depending on what's on the memory stick. After that, we'll see what your other information is worth to me',

At five hundred pounds, she handed over the memory stick.

Wheeler pulled out a small laptop from behind him, opened it and plugged Mina's little stick into it. He opened the files and began working through them. Twice he said 'shit' as he read through the files. Whilst he did this, Mina pretended to be looking round the photographs on the panelled walls and she amused herself by wondering just how much each use of the word 'shit' was going to be worth in money for her.

As she was getting near to the end of her glass of Chardonnay, he snapped the laptop shut and put it to one side taking the memory stick out of it and putting it in his pocket. He then picked up his half-finished pint and downed the rest of it.

'Another?' he asked. Mina just nodded.

On returning with the drinks, instead of his usual bargaining stance he simply said, 'You've done well, Mina'.

She was quite shocked. All they usually discussed was money, but this comment of his sounded close to praise. She smiled – and, come to think of it, the smile was probably the first she had ever given him since her recruitment.

'So that's five-hundred for the email,' he said, returning her smile, 'and five hundred for the memory stick. What else have you got for me?'

'Mr Cape thinks I'm stupid. I don't understand that 'cos he's a clever lawyer - how come he thinks I'm stupid?'

'Two good reasons,' replied Wheeler, 'One, I'll bet all the money I'm giving you right now, that you use a really cute little Italian accent with him, am I right?' Mina grinned back.

'Secondly,' he continued, 'some men, even clever men, have difficulties when it comes to dealing with other people. They just can't read their fellow human beings. Your Mr Cape's probably one of these. Anyway, before we got onto the subject of his stupidity, what were you going to tell me?'

'Ah, yes,' said Mina, 'Mr Cape said that Sir Jeremy or Mr MacCrammond would keep in touch with him over the weekend as things developed. What did he mean by *'developed'*?'

'Because there's a lot of things going to be happening between now and Tuesday morning, and much of cannot be predicted right now, matters are likely to *develop* in unpredictable ways – that's what he means.' Wheeler paused, rubbed the side of his nose, as a thought occurred to him,

'Tell you what, I'll give you another five hundred, if you'll keep an eye on Mr Cape over the weekend… Can you manage that or do you have other plans?'

She smiled back at him. 'No other plans, but I'm already going to a conference with Mr Cape tomorrow morning - something to do with the launch of this Athena,'

'That's good. So fifteen hundred it is,' said Wheeler, 'and, for that, I need you to ring or contact me by email or text the moment anything significant happens, can you do that?'

'I manage,' she replied in a rare lapse of English grammar.

Wheeler handed her an envelope, one of two he had filled before leaving the office, for he had decided how much to give her long before this meeting or what transpired during it. Mina took the envelope, got up, smiled gratefully down at him and, after promising to keep in touch, left the Antelope.

12

Thursday evening,

Wilton Crescent, London W1

As with most things organised by Gustave at the Palace Hotel, Nat Matthews's journey home was faultless. It was both fast and comfortable, and took just over three hours in all. From the Helipad near the hotel he was whisked in a Eurocopter to Zurich's Engadin Airport. There a chartered Cessna six-seater jet flew him direct to London's City Airport and he alighted from his taxi at Wilton Crescent at seven twenty five. The journey, pampered all the way, also put new fight into him to deal with the potential demise of his company.

At exactly eight o'clock, Wheeler rang the doorbell at Matthews's house. It was opened to him by a butler who welcomed him in and took his coat. Although Wheeler had extricated Matthews out of some embarrassing situations, and regarded himself to being as close to Matthews as anyone, it was his first visit here. He liked to think of himself as 'a man about town' and that there was therefore little that would surprise or shock him. He was wrong about that. As he looked about him in the hall and up the elegant unsupported spiral Georgian stairway of this classical house, he let out an involuntary gasp; never before seen such an extravagant, outlandish display of wealth. Gone were the staid furnishings and understated simplicity of its previous aristocratic owner's taste in decoration. In its place, there was now a profusion of both pictures and furniture and as much gold leaf as might have rivalled an Austrian Baroque church.

'Well, you'd better come up here, then'. Matthews's voice from beyond the top of the stairs had a sharp edge to it. The Butler laid Wheeler's coat temporarily on a small chair near the front door, led him up the stairs and ushered him into the Drawing-room. This bright forty by twenty foot room, with three tall windows looking out onto Wilton Crescent, was, like the rest that Wheeler had seen, over-furnished and decorated. There was an incongruous mix of classic Dutch School still life paintings next to minimalist modern works in garish colours; it had an un-lived-in air, and it made Wheeler feel even more uncomfortable than still. Matthews himself had already crossed the room and seated himself in a large wing chair to the left of an ornate white marble fireplace.

'Have a seat,' he said, indicating a similar chair to his own the opposite side of the fireplace. Wheeler sat down on the front edge of it and looked back at Matthews with a degree of trepidation. He had witnessed the other's temper before.

Matthews's face was blotchily red and his small pale blue eyes darted here and there, agitated; his close-cropped hair glistened slightly – with sweat, Wheeler surmised. Sweating, darting eyes, red face, danger-signs Wheeler knew well. He quickly rehearsed again the opening lines he had practiced earlier.

'I'm sorry to have dragged you away from your holiday, but, as I told you on the 'phone, I thought…'

Matthews cut his sentence short. 'If I properly understood your call to me in St. Moritz, the Matthews Finch Hedge Fund has been hacked into over the internet and my unique trading algorithms have been illegally tampered with. Have I got that right?'

Wheeler had barely time to open his mouth to reply than Matthews continued, at pace. 'This effing hacking team's mucking about with the company's trading may have lost us millions already;

I'll be checking that in detail in due course. Those losses, however, pall into insignificance against what will happen as soon as any of my clients discover that the money they have invested with the Fund is no longer under our complete control. Am I right in that too?'

'I'm afraid that's also true, but... '

'And I told you over the telephone I needed two things right away. The first I said I needed a top PR storyline to be held in readiness in case this hacking story gets out. The second thing was for you and all your fancy contacts to make a start on getting this fixed. As you've had more than four hours since we spoke, where are we with those?'

Wheeler put up his hand as might a child in class; this time Matthews allowed him to speak,

'First John Struthers and I felt that we needed to look at *all* the options open to us,' he replied, pausing so that Matthews might get the point that rushing into immediate, frenzied action might not be the best way forward. 'Would you like me to run through the options which we considered?'

'I suppose so.' Matthews let out a grunt of irritation. 'But make it brief – all I want to know what you decided to actually **do** about this...this outrage,'

'Okay,' replied Wheeler, clearing his throat. 'To start with, as this hacking operation seems to be under the auspices of the Bank of England, we ruled out trying to do anything like getting an injunction or mounting a legal challenge. We also thought these pointless as we felt we'd never get anything done along legal lines with the holiday weekend upon us. Next, bearing in mind the over-riding need to be trading normally come Tuesday morning, we decided that whatever we decided to do, it should be as under-cover or secret as possible,'

'That sounds good to me,' said Matthews. 'So what exactly does that translate into?'

'You'll be pleased to hear, I think, that I've already got the first lot of people on board with this. I'm confident that they and another group I'm contacting shortly will have everything back to normal - as though nothing had happened - by Monday night.'

'Well that sounds better.' Matthews's eyes closed for a moment as though he was lost in thought. 'But that's not very specific is it? Who are these people and what exactly are they going to do? If you can give me the outcome – it can't be that difficult to tell me how they're going to get there, can it?'

'That brings me to one of only two conditions I need in all of this,' replied Wheeler

'Conditions?' Matthews face instantly reddened further and Wheeler noticed his hands go from a loose clasp to tight fists. Wheeler reacted to this apparent escalation in Matthews's state of agitation. He reacted swiftly by getting to his feet and going over to stand in front of the fireplace. From this vantage, he looked back down at Matthews. 'You'll recall that last year I got you out of that mess in Budapest and also dealt with the fiasco in Siena the year before that...?'

Matthews said nothing, struck silent by this unexpected turn in the conversation.

'What you probably don't realise,' continued Wheeler, 'is that I have sometimes have to do things to get clients out of trouble which it's far better the clients know nothing about, do you understand what I'm saying ?'

'Yes, I understand, and I appreciate what you've done for me in the past. Are you now saying that it would be better I don't know what people you take on or what they might have to get up to?'

'That's exactly what I'm saying,' replied Wheeler 'You're a notable City figure and a partner in a well-known company; not only must you not be involved in any way with what now needs to be done, but it will also be much better for you if you know nothing of what we may need to get up to.'

'I understand,' said Matthews. He looked down at his hands which were now just loosely clasped in his lap.

'All you really need to know is of a satisfactory outcome once it's all over, don't you think?'

. Matthews gave a nod, his face now expressionless, though at least he now looked relaxed for the first time and some of the heightened colour had gone from his face.

'I can't tell you more for a further reason,' continued Wheeler. 'Because of the time-constraints, we're going to have to use what I might call a gloves-off approach, a way which I believe this situation requires. Do you understand what I'm saying?'

'Gloves off? That's fine by me' said Matthews. 'A moment ago you said you had *two* conditions, one is that I don't ask any questions about what you're doing, what's the other one?'

'Money,' said Wheeler but then quickly added, 'to get the results we both want, I'm going to be using only the best of people, those with proven track records. You'll just have to steel yourself to the fact that if you want to get your company back safe within this tight time-frame, is going to cost you. Do you need to talk to Paul Finch, about that?'

Matthews had not thought about his partner Paul Finch until this moment. Whereas Paul was an accountant at heart, Matthews saw himself as the vitality of the partnership, the one who had seen the future in algorithmic trading. Paul provided the gravitas of someone known throughout the City, and respected even by the City's more traditional bankers. He did not mind being called 'flash' by some of Paul's more staid friends, for, despite marked differences between the two of them, it had evolved into an ideal partnership.

At this moment, Paul was on business in New York and, was probably already in Florida for the rest of the weekend; it suited Wheeler that it would be nigh impossible to track him down there for a consultation.

'No, I don't need to talk to Paul,' said Matthews, as though reading Wheeler's mind. 'This situation comes under operations, my side of the business anyway,'

'Good, so let's get the money side agreed and out of the way, shall we?'

'Right, so what do want of me?' said Matthews

'Can you transfer one hundred thousand into my account straight away? That will allow me to make a starter payment to the first of my contacts who have already started on the problem. Everything needs to be done in cash – we don't want any pieces of paper leading back either to me or to you.'

'Right, a hundred thousand and no paper-trails. Done.'

'After that, we'll just see how it goes,' said Wheeler. 'But I guess that if we're going to secure a future of Matthews Finch, we'll need to be prepared to spend whatever's needed, won't we?'

Matthews thought about this for a couple of seconds and simply replied, 'Of course'. Going over to a small delicately inlaid chest of drawers, he took out an iPad. On it he logged into one of Matthews Finch's accounts, the operations account.

'If you give me your bank details, I can transfer the money to you right now,' he said.

Wheeler read these details off from his smartphone and Matthews tapped them into the iPad; within a minute, the money had been transferred into Wheeler's account.

As he completed this simple electronic task, Matthews seemed to brighten up, he even smiled a wan smile as though relief came in some liquid form and had somehow suffused right through him. By handing over of the problem to someone he now hoped could put it all back the way it had been before the hacking, he appeared to have gone from irritated and angry to the calm and rational. He went over to a drinks tray in the corner of the room and poured himself a brandy.

He looked across to Wheeler and, by gesturing, asked him if he would like one. Wheeler accepted. Returning, he handed Wheeler his drink, went back into his fireside chair, sank into it with a deep sigh and took a large swill from the glass.

The same wan smile lingered on his face as he seemed to be looking into the distance. Strange thoughts scampered across his mind, helped maybe by the brandy. He had instantly liked Wheeler's use of the phrase 'gloves off'. It had suddenly reminded him of his father's excited stories of *his* father, Nat's old grandad. Back in the great depression of the nineteen-thirties, almost any form of income could mean the difference between having a meal or not. He had been enthralled by tales of his grandfather's involvement in the illegal bare-knuckle fights just off the East India Docks; tales of lookouts to warn of the police, of quickly snatched winnings, and of the hurrying of the young fighter back home to tend the hands for another fight another day. Yes, gloves off, they would show young Ranald MacCrammond he could not play around with another's business with impunity.

Whilst Matthews had apparently retreated into this mild trance, Wheeler too, relaxed somewhat. He was growing in confidence as his barely mapped-out plan matured in his mind; as soon as he had finished his drink, it was time to begin implementing it for, to meet the inexorable deadline of Monday night, he and the Major needed to get on with it. Their combined ideas and contacts would have to translate this sketchy plan into action and then implement it – fast.

He finished his coffee and rose to leave. Matthews got up too, came over to him, and facing him, put his hands on Wheeler's shoulders. Looking into Wheeler's eyes, he said, 'Come to think about it, I don't care what this costs. I'm putting my trust in you to get my company back for me by Monday night. Everything I've built up over these past few years is at stake here, so, for God's sake, don't let me down.'

'I won't. You're safe to put your trust in me. I know the right people to get everything back to normal - sooner than you think.'

They parted and on leaving Matthews house, Wheeler headed down into Belgrave Square and through the darkening streets towards Sloane Square. Walking at a brisk pace, he reckoned it would be about a ten minute walk from Wilton Crescent to Sloane Square - just in nice time for his meeting with the Major at the Antelope pub. Not only was he looking forward to hearing what the 'interesting information' was that the Major had found for him, he was also looking forward to hearing if the Major had acquired the people needed for the outline plan in his mind - time to turn it into a reality.

13

Thursday, late evening

The Antelope, Eaton Terrace

Wheeler arrived back at the Antelope in good time for his meeting with the Major. He was pleased to find the pub was nearly empty, the commuter crowd having gone home. His usual table was empty and soon after he had got himself a pint of best bitter and settled comfortably by the fire; he spotted the Major coming through the main bar towards the snug.

The two of them greeted each other with an embrace of camaraderie. Wheeler got him a pint the same as his own and they sat for a while catching up on what each had been doing since they had last met. After twenty minutes or so, Wheeler could hold back no longer from asking what the Major had for him.

'Well, as soon as I got your call,' said the Major, 'I set about following your instructions - to find out as much as I could about Sir Jeremy Towneley and his connection to Athena. I had to improvise pretty quickly. Luckily for you, I still had contact with a young couple who had recently done a job for me and still had all the gear. They just had to get back into their police uniforms and they were ready to go. As you'd suggested, they were to look for a laptop belonging to Sir Jeremy and I think that, in that regard, we've done pretty well for you.' He leant down, pulled up a bulky leather briefcase he had brought in with him, and, after fiddling about for a moment unlocking it, eventually took out of it a small laptop.

'Christ,' whispered Wheeler, 'you can't use a stolen laptop here in the pub, suppose the burglary's been called in'.

'My young couple told me that wouldn't happen for some time,' said the Major, 'still I suppose you're right.' He quickly put it back into the briefcase.

'We'd better take that back to my flat, it's round the corner from here,' said Wheeler, 'see if it's got on it what we're looking for,'

'Looking for something in particular?' asked the Major

'I'll tell you when we get back to my place,' replied Wheeler. They rose and downing their drinks, collected up their briefcases and hurried out of the pub. Turning right at the end Eaton Terrace into Cleveden Place, they walked for some fifty yards towards Sloane Square, crossed the street and approached Wheeler's house. Letting themselves in, they made their way upstairs to Wheeler's first floor sitting room where Wheeler hurriedly crossed the room and drew the heavy curtains; he gestured for the Major to sit on the sofa. The place had clearly been decorated by a woman for a bachelor in his mid-forties like Wheeler would never have chosen on their own, the floral chintz and pastel colours. With his barrel-roll walk and the build of a one-time wrestler, Wheeler looked somehow out of place in it – even though it was his home.

'Like a coffee or something?' asked Wheeler

'Thanks, a coffee would be fine',

Wheeler trundled out to make the drinks as the Major, who had already got Sir Jeremy's laptop out of the briefcase, started it up. When the machine asked him for a password, the Major got a small memory stick out of his briefcase, stuck it into the side of laptop and the small light on it flickered away as it cracked the password.

Wheeler returned with a tray and some biscuits.

'So what exactly are we looking for?' asked the Major

'First I want confirmation that Athena is run from Sir Jeremy's nephew's place – or rather, his father's place – Craithe Castle,' said Wheeler,

The Major used the laptop's general search facility to find the word Craithe on the computer. Numerous instances were immediately found. There were files detailing equipment which Sir Jeremy had been involved in purchasing for 'the Lab' up in Craithe Castle, and more information confirming that Craithe was indeed Athena's base. They also got a good idea of some pieces of highly advanced computer equipment there, including a quantum computer from suppliers in Canada. Other files told of a spur had been taken off the new Oban fibre optic internet cable and run from the mainland out to the island. This particular file showed that Ranald MacCrammond had gone to great lengths – and considerable expense – to hide exactly where on the mainland that spur was located. Although none of the emails or notes named the conglomerate that was working with the Craithe team, there was much to look at later detailing the advances in merging quantum and digital computing technologies.

Neither Wheeler nor the Major fully understood some of the technical phrases in both the files and emails, but it was clear nevertheless that they had stumbled onto much more than just a hacking team. It became clear that the team were indeed responsible for hacking into the Matthews Finch Hedge Fund, but files and documents also showed that Craithe was home to much more than just that – a subject of more searching later. For now they had reached their first objective. They had confirmed beyond doubt Athena's base and thus the location of the Matthews Finch Hedge Fund's woes. They could now safely base their plans on that certainty.

Wheeler was so delighted with this that, taking over the Towneley laptop from the Major, he wrote an email to Nat Matthews to update him on the project.

'*Pleased to be able to tell you,*' it read, '*good progress in tracking the Matthews Finch tormentor's location. Software called Athena, responsible for your troubles, and steps to end their control of your company now well in hand. Will report more soon.*' He signed it Wheeler and sent it.

The two of them then sat for a while discussing the options for their next move.

'When we first discussed your clients problem I to the liberty of talking to of my most reliable contacts,' said the Major, 'and, with what we've had confirmed to us just now from the laptop, I think they'll prove to be the answer to our problem'

'Tell me more,' said Wheeler,

'With this MacCrammond and his family all together on the island for the Easter weekend,' said the Major, 'it struck me that a pretty straightforward way of sorting out your mess would be to kidnap MacCrammond's wife. These contacts I've just mentioned are experts in that field, having used it on behalf of the UK Government during 'the Troubles' in Northern Ireland in the nineteen-nineties.'

'You reckon that if we were to take his wife hostage and hold her in captivity till they complied, MacCrammond would respond to our demands concerning the hedge fund?' asked Wheeler,

'Of course he would, it's not as though he was ever trained in the army or Special Forces to cope with the pressure we could put on him that way. Anyway, what else could he do if we were holding his wife? With the Easter weekend making any kind of retaliation virtually impossible? My contacts grab her, remove her to Northern Ireland and then we make our demands – remove their team's control of Matthews Finch's trading software, maybe even give us this Athena software, we could be onto a real winner here.'

'Right, so who exactly are these contacts of yours?' asked Wheeler.

The Major went on to explain about Mick Rollo and his team of ex-coverts. 'The Coverts' were not even supposed to have existed. Indeed, anyone making enquiries about them through the Ministry of Defence, The Irish Office, or trying to conduct internet detective work on the Northern Ireland Troubles, would soon come to information cul-de-sacs. Even though the coverts had played a key role in establishing the peace in the troubled provinces, it was impossible to find anything about them even on infinite data sources of the world- wide web.

The reason 'the Coverts' had been needed in those times, explained the Major, was that individuals or small groups of renegades on both sides of 'the Troubles', posed serious threats of violence but could not be stopped through the normal processes of the Law. In such cases, successive UK Governments used small, highly trained teams of 'Coverts' to remove such renegades from the conflict. The Coverts became masters at kidnapping and delivering these undesirables to the authorities – though what happened to them after they had been delivered, no one seemed to know – or care. All the Coverts operations were carried out on a 'deniable' basis; if a mission became exposed or failed, the coverts were on their own. It was not a job for the faint of heart, but it was well paid and it had a special kudos to it as well.

These days, following the success of Northern Ireland peace process, most of 'the Coverts' had become redundant. They had mostly left the army and some fell by the wayside - like many soldiers do as they try to return to civilian life. A few had used their savings and skills to carve out new lives for themselves – some of them in illegal activities. One such surviving group was assembled over a period of time by Mick Rollo, the Major's ruthless, highly organised ex- sergeant major friend. These two had known each other back during those times and had remained in contact since. As Rollo trained his growing team, the Major found work for them. He brokered three mercenary jobs for them in Africa, two in Bosnia and one recently in the Ukraine. Indeed, wherever trouble flared up one would be likely to find the Major sniffing around for business to pass on to Rollo and his team.

The Major assured Wheeler that not only would Rollo and his team be perfect for what, for them, would be the simple job of kidnapping someone on a remote Scottish island, they would also be adept at dealing with resistance, should they come up against any.

'Well, they sound the right people,' said Wheeler as he poured them each another coffee. 'Do you think they'll be available at such short notice?' and, bringing the deadline date forward, added, 'I gave my word to Nat Matthews that we'd have fixed his problem by Saturday or Sunday night,'

'As I told you,' replied the Major, 'I took the liberty of contacting them as soon as you'd outlined the Matthews problem to me. Naturally I didn't tell them any details or anything about you, so all they know at the moment is that it's a kidnap job somewhere in the UK. I'm pleased to tell you, however, that, for the right money, they could have their best men available any time you give the go-ahead.'

'That's a relief, what sort of money are we talking about?'

'I've used Rollo and his coverts before,' replied the Major, 'and I think around seventy-five thousand for a two or three day job of this kind would be about right,'

'Good, let's give him a ring,' said Wheeler, 'get the job confirmed and get it under way,'

Even though it was by now getting on for ten o'clock, the Major picked up the telephone and rang Mick Rollo's number in Northern Ireland. With business in the offing from the Major's earlier contact, Rollo had been waiting for the call.

Wheeler sat back in his chair relaxing - though listening in on the telephone conversation next to him. The Major now gave Rollo a résumé of the Matthews Finch Hedge Fund's problem and the outline plan to kidnap MacCrammond's wife from the Castle on Craithe and holding her hostage until their demands had been met. Rollo had a few questions - not the least of them being about the money for the job. Wheeler pulled a face when the Major said that 'money was no object', though he admitted to himself that he had used the same phrase when recruiting the Major.

The upshot of the conversation between the two of them was that the Major was to be on the flight out of Stanstead about seven tomorrow morning and that he would be picked up at Londonderry airport. There was only one final stipulation, Rollo did ask for an email confirming the outline plan and non-refundable retainer fee. The Major sent his confirming email from the stolen Towneley laptop lying on the table in front of him.

* * * * *

Danil Morozov had gone off duty at seven Moscow time, four in the afternoon in London. His first coup at spotting the exchanges between Wheeler and Mina and of the existence of Athena had kept him working late. As it was now well beyond the end of his shift and he had to go, he was confident that if he was especially careful setting all the parameters of his searches, that, after he had gone off duty, his machines would still catch anything that mentioned Athena again or any of his other key words and phrases. He made sure - for a second time – that all the recording systems would also capture and retain in a file, whatever the searches came up with. He then packed up his daily belongings and, reluctantly, left his machines to do their job.

What the Wheeler and the Major did *not* know was that Morozov's search engines began to pick up everything that happened on the stolen Towneley laptop from the moment that Wheeler had tapped the word 'Craithe' into his search for information on Athena's location. Morozov's machines had begun to record everything that followed on the laptop, the emails, their searches, everything they had been done on it. Most significantly, it had recorded Wheeler's email to Matthews and the Major's email to Rollo.

Morozov also knew that it was practically certain that GCHQ, the NSA and others would also have picked up the same information. Whether or not they paid any attention to it would depend if they were focusing on such matters at present or had other priorities. None of this occurred to Wheeler or the Major, of course, but what the two of them in Cleveden Crescent had thought would be a neat, simple kidnapping affair had just about to get one hell of a lot more complicated.

14

Good Friday, early morning

The SVR, Yesenevo, Moscow

Danil Morozov was back into the office early the next morning. He was so excited to see what his machines might have recorded overnight, that he rushed through the offices to get to them. He threw off his heavy coat as hastened across his room towards his desk, casting onto a chair on the way. As he bent his tall, thin and angular body, reaching over the top of his chair to the keyboard. He brought his computer from standby and into life and typed at speed to bring up the pages which would show him what the bank of machines had found and recorded for him.

His heart skipped a beat as he saw the volume of data that his keywords and phrases harvested and scrambling round the chair, he sat down and spent the next twenty minutes sorting all the information into more easily readable form. He then took a further twenty minutes or so to explore what had been added to trawl of information he had received. He followed one particular file – that on Rollo – and found that, using UK and US databases in addition to those of the SVR, he was able to find many of Rollo's personal history. Along with information on his exploits in The Ukraine, Bosnia and Nigeria, there accounts of many of his nefarious business operations back and forth across the Northern Ireland border with the

Republic. Similar history was there on how the Towneley project, Athena, had passed from the Towneley Foundation to Ranald MacCrammond and had then been moved to Craithe. In fact, the amount of information that Morozov's searches had come up with had made it the most detailed and telling digital portraits of anyone's anywhere of the key players related in some way to Athena.

He read through the entire package and report once more, becoming so excited in the process that, as he sent it off to Komarov, he sent a separate email to ensure that he dealt with as soon as it arrived. On the basis that 'knowledge is power', even a minion like Morozov could see what he had amassed would be of considerable value to Komarov.

* * * * *

Komarov also arrived early at the office to prepare for the monitoring of the Bank of England's Conference and to be sure that Morozov was ready to carry out full surveillance of the event. He was surprised to find that his young SVR genius had already sent him two emails – the second urging him to look at the first one right away. Intrigued – as this was so unlike Morozov - he got himself a large breakfast-sized cup of coffee, settled into his chair and began to read the long first email and its attachments. He had got about half way down the second page when he sat up with a jolt in his chair, spilling some of his coffee onto his lap. Cursing, he jumped to his feet and brushing the hot coffee off his trousers, rushed across the office to grab some paper towelling near to the coffee machine and mop himself down.

Back at his desk, still wet and muttering to himself about his clumsiness, he pushed the now empty cup to one side, sat back down, picked up Morozov's report again. He read again the couple of sentences that had caused the spilt coffee mishap. There was no mistaking it. The man, MacCrammond, to whom he had just entrusted much of his UK and European money, was the same man as was in charge of the Athena programme.

His mouth remained open, as he was by now panting slightly, his breath coming in little gasps. How could he have been so careless? He ran back over the events in his mind, trying to see how he had come to make such an elementary mistake.

Was his faltering relationship with the President to blame for his undue haste? Maybe. Was his need to secure his home base better to blame? Maybe. Urgently needing to get his money out of the clutches of the West's sanctions before they tightened further? Yes, definitely. But witnessing the clever money moving exercise which MacCrammond had used for Boreyev's money? That should never have been the basis for a decision to do the same for himself. Even the research he had done on MacCrammond's Bank and the man's personal credentials – he could see now that should never have allowed him to make this beginner's error.

He laid the report down on the desk and, after a while, a solution of sorts began to form in his mind. He sat up, reached across his desk, picked up the telephone and rang Anton Silayev.

'I don't know about you,' he said as soon as Silayev answered, 'but I've got one hell of a morning ahead of me and it's been made even more difficult by something that came to my attention a few minutes ago. I'm sorry but, on account of this discovery, I need you to drop everything and meet me right away, can you do that?'

'Yes, I could manage that,' said Silayev, 'where do you want to meet?'

'The café on Nikol'skaya, the one near to my office,' said Komarov, 'I've something I need to discuss with you urgently,'

'Right,' said Silayev.

As soon as Komarov had put the phone down, he gathered up the sheets of Morozov's report and stuffed them into a neat green leather pouch along with an A4 pad, a couple of pencils and a slim file labelled "Athena".

The Café next to the office was large and busy with commuters from out of town snatching a quick breakfast. He found that his usual table by the window, somewhat apart from others, had just been vacated and sat down at it quickly before it had even been cleared. While waiting for Silayev, he gave some more thought to his dilemma.

Naturally, he would keep his financial folly to himself just as he would keep from the President Silayev's imminent involvement in his plans. He had begun to consider how to proceed, making full use of the mass of information Morozov had found for him. Firstly, Wheeler's plan to kidnap MacCrammond's wife might suit his own needs very well – provided, of course, that he introduced some form of control into it.

Just before nine o'clock the café emptied as people had to get to work and shortly after that Silayev arrived. The two of them ordered croissants and coffee. Komarov began by outlining the Major's and Rollo's plan to kidnap MacCrammond's wife but soon Silayev had to stop him.

'Do you mind if I write down the names of the people involved,' said Silayev, 'I'm not so good with English names and it will be easier for me to remember them if I've first written them down in a list with a note on each too, maybe,' He got a small pad out of his briefcase and as soon a she was ready, Komarov began, spelling them out phonetically for Silayev to translate into Cyrillic form; *Matthews* a partner of the *Matthews Finch Hedge Fund*, tampered with by *MacCrammond*, head of the *Athena* team on the *Island of Craithe*. He brought him up to date with *Wheeler*'s recruitment of *Major Jock Hunter*, referred to in emails as just 'the Major' and that they had both just recruited a *Mick Rollo* in Northern Ireland, leader of a bunch of mercenaries referred to as the *'Coverts'*. And, finally, their plan to kidnap MacCrammond's wife.'

'All right so far?' asked Komarov,

'Yeah, much easier for me,'

'So it struck me that we could join this mission of theirs to our advantage,' said Komarov,

'What exactly do you have in mind?'

'Firstly, I know from experience, that he President will want this done covertly. He won't want anyone castigating the Russian Federation for being involved in openly stealing business rights from another foreign power. So all of what we do needs to be done in the name of our partnership. Incidentally, of course, this gives us a great chance to cream off business and profits for ourselves. I know this might look a little bit like some dark conspiracy, but I assure you it's the best way of doing it.'

Silayev looked doubtful, rubbing his chin, frowning.

'It's not difficult. We use Silayev & Komarov LLC as the front.' Continued Komarov, 'that way they can look up the partnership website on the internet. They should be duly impressed by our mythical list of collaborators and by the deals we're supposed to have done in around the world.'

'But what if they check in depth on some of those?'

'Come on,' replied Komarov, 'they all stand up to as much scrutiny as is likely to be brought to bear on them - for goodness sake, these people are hardly likely to be able to check the degree of the President's involvement with our front company or any of its claims, are they?'

'No, suppose not,' conceded Silayev.

'So, what I propose,' went on Komarov, 'is to allow us to join forces with them by sending this imaginary employee of our company and while they do their kidnapping, our man steals Athena, simple as that,'

Silayev nodded his head slowly for a moment as he considered this then asked, 'And what are we going to offer them as an incentive? I mean so that they allow their plans to be complicated by our arrival - foreigners, even enemies, you might say?'

'I propose to get round that by offering a three things. One of course is the threat of exposing their plan to MacCrammond or even the authorities, another is something which transcends artificial boundaries of friends and enemies,' replied Komarov, 'that's to say money and lots of it'. As soon as he said this Silayev looked back at him in surprise.

'Whose money?' he said, 'we don't want to be using our resources when we're going to be handing Athena over to the President, we'll get nothing out of it ourselves' and he sat back in his chair and folded his arms - as though this was an serious objection to the plans,

'Of course we don't use our own money,' said Komarov, 'but we can promise substantial sums in the form of a commission percentage on our sales of Athena round the world, can't we?'

'But we're not going to sell Athena surely?' Silayev looked even more perplexed,

'No of course we're not,' replied Komarov, 'but, dealing with this chap Wheeler, what does he know? We can still offer him commission on sales, and deal with that lie later. For goodness sake, our website is chock-a-block with examples of software sales and customer computer solutions or whatever the garbage is that we've got written there,'

'So how are you going to reconcile this with your promises to the President of delivering him the new cyber weapon?

Komarov gave a broad smile, reached over and struck Silayev playfully on the shoulder,

'Don't you worry about my handling of the President,' he said, 'I've being doing that in my sleep for years now. The real clincher to allow us to join their expedition, however, is I'm going to offer them the use of a helicopter for the full duration of the operation.

I'll get the London Embassy to charter a UK registered machine so that there are no unnecessary questions raised – they'll quickly realise what a boon this will be to their plans.'

'Sounds good, I like that,' said Silayev,

By the time they had finished their breakfasts, they had covered much of the finer detail needed to implement the plan. Silayev left the café on the promise that Komarov would speak to him as soon as he had monitored the Bank of England's Conference. Komarov said he would pay the breakfast bill and held back until Silayev had left. It was still only a quarter to seven in the UK, so he stayed on and drank some more coffee as he began to work out in more detail how he would benefit the two of them before passing Athena over to the President. When he left some time later, he had a good idea how he would manage this and went back to his apartment full of renewed confidence. By the time he had got back there and freshened up, it would be time to ring Wheeler with his proposition.

* * * * *

Komarov had just a couple of hours or so to wait before he could ring Wheeler and put the time to good use jotting down, in English, Wheeler's possible objections to allowing a Russian to join their mission and also wrote down answers to each of these objections. At eleven thirty sharp, Moscow time, he rang the telephone number Morozov had given him as Wheeler's. Wheeler, just getting his breakfast organised, and wondered who it might be ringing him this early. Irritated by such an early call, yet intrigued when the caller display told him that the call was 'international', he answered it.

'Mr Wheeler, we haven't yet met,' said Komarov in perfect yet heavily accented English, 'my name is Igor Komarov and I am speaking to you from Moscow. I need to talk to you urgently about your proposed project with Mr Rollo,'

Wheeler had a sudden urge to sit down and shuffling a couple of feet to his left, he felt with his hand for one of the high stools round the eating island in the kitchen, and edged himself onto it,

'I'm afraid I don't know what you're talking about Mr . . . er, Mr . . .' said Wheeler

'Igor Komarov, my name's Igor Komarov, and before you risk yourself and colleagues the inestimable damage of not hearing me out, I suggest listen to what I have to say,'

Wheeler wondered what 'inestimable damage' might mean, but anyone who seemed to know about secret matters not more than a few hours old, might just be capable of doing just that, damage. His thoughts raced. Moscow. Plans overheard? Internet Surveillance – the Towneley laptop. Christ, was this man KGB or whatever they were called these days? Better hear him out,

'I'm listening, Mr Komarov.'

'Firstly may I say that, though you don't know it, we're on the same side. We both have business to do with Mr MacCrammond,'

'I'm still listening,' said Wheeler, a gripe-like pain now circling below his rib-cage.

'If I understand Mr Matthews's company's problem correctly,' continued Komarov, 'if he does not have control back of its software by, say, Monday night, and his clients find out what happened with yesterday's demonstration…'

This appalled Wheeler further. How the hell could someone in Moscow know much detail? Definitely KGB, he concluded, but why would they be interested in MacCrammond?

'So?'

'So, as I was about to say,' continued Komarov, 'if Mr Matthews clients find out that they're with a fund that can be manipulated by someone else, are they not likely to take their money out of that fund faster than you can say John Robinson?'

'It's Jack Robinson,' said Wheeler, 'the English idiom is Jack Robinson, not John,' said Wheeler

'Thank you for that, Mr Wheeler,' said Komarov with a deep chuckle, 'but you get my meaning, I expect,'

By now Wheeler had given up any hope of pretence, and needed to get to the point - however uncomfortable that might turn out to be.

'I do, so where's this getting us?'

'You will be pleased to hear, Mr Wheeler,' continued Komarov, 'that I have no intention, at present, of telling Mr MacCrammond of your project - he'd be horrified to learn of the possibility of someone close or dear to him being kidnapped, don't you think?'

Wheeler said nothing, he was now sure that this nightmare was going to play out irrespective of anything he might say.

'No, I'm not going to tell him,' continued Komarov, 'because, as I said earlier, we are on the same side. I have a couple of things I need from Mr MacCrammond, and as it so happens it would suit myself and my colleagues if you allowed us to add just one person to your project – your trip to the Island of Craithe. His presence will not interfere with your plans, he would go about his business whilst you go about yours. As a gesture of my good faith and so that you feel that you have something to gain from a man of mine joining your expedition, I am happy to facilitate and speed this whole project up by offering you the unlimited use of a UK registered eight seater helicopter for the time that it takes for us to do what we have planned.'

Wheeler suppressed what otherwise would have been a sharp intake of breath.

'For both of us to do what is required on the Island of Craithe might take a day or two, yes? You need to get your hostage back to Northern Ireland although my man's work, acquiring Athena, can be done in an hour or so. What if I say we will provide the helicopter for three days? How does that sound to you?'

By now, Wheeler was finding bit difficult to keep pace with this Russian, and he just managed to say, 'Fine.'

'And that's not the end of it, Mr Wheeler,' continued Komarov, 'if you visit our website you will see that we have much success selling computer solutions, software and so on. My partner and I would be happy to pay to a commission on all of our international sales of Athena. Naturally you will want to check us out and discuss all of this with your colleagues. So, if you have a paper and pen near you, I give you our website name. If you go to it, you will find most of the answers to the many questions you would still like to ask me. Anything else you wish to know, you can ask me when next we speak, how about that?'

Wheeler got up went over to where the telephone base sat, got a pad and pen there and sat again ready to write down the name of the website.

'Yes, on you go, the website's name?' he said,

'It's "silayevkomarov.com.ru" and, for the international computer software solutions marketplace, you'll find a version of it in English. I have some other business I need to attend to this morning, but I will telephone to you after that. This will be in an hour or two from now and I shall ring you again at this same number of yours - unless you wish to give me your mobile number perhaps. I hope that this will give you time to consult with your various colleagues - Mr Matthews, Major Hunter, Mr Rollo. Unlike you, I have no time problem with what I need from Mr MacCrammond but you must decide if you will accept my proposal by the time I telephone back, yes? If you and friends have not decided, I make alternative plans and I would need to think again about keeping your little secret...'

'I'll have an answer for you by then,' said Wheeler quickly and then heard the click of the telephone the other end.

Getting off the stool, he went over to one of the many fitted cupboards, opened it and took out a half bottle of cooking brandy and pouring a large slug of it into a tumbler, drank almost all of it straight down. He immediately coughed and spluttered but, recovering, drank the rest of it and poured another.

When he spoke to each of the other three in turn, it hardly surprised him that none of them - Matthews, the Major nor Rollo - believed him, at least not to start with. Eventually, however, the detail with which he was able to back up his story of this unlikely call from Moscow was sufficient for each of them in turn to take it seriously. Wheeler had also had the website checked out by an IT expert he knew well and whose judgement he trusted. After around half an hour's reflection time, during which Matthews had rung Wheeler back and told him he would just leave all of this matter to him, it was ten o'clock. Wheeler rang the Major and Rollo on a conference telephone call.

'I'll summarise the situation, first, then you can each have your final say on this matter,' said Wheeler. 'Our number one priority is to get Nat's hedge fund clear of any influence from the bunch up on Craithe,' he continued, 'after all that's what he's paying us for. I think we've all agreed already that, in view of the short time frame, kidnapping MacCrammond's wife is the only way to achieve that objective. Are you both still of that opinion?'

'Yes, I am,' said the Major, 'but what about Nat Matthews's view on this?'

'I've had him re-affirm that he'll go along with anything we three agree,' replied Wheeler,

'That's fine then, you're running the show, so I'll go along with that,' said the Major,

'Okay by me too, 'said Rollo,

'Next, referring to my telephone conversation with this Russian, Komarov,' continued Wheeler, 'I've had him checked out as best I can and I'll say a couple of things on that. Firstly he's close to the Russian President but also appears to have a legitimate computer software business. What seems clear to me is that he has some kind of access to the Russian intelligence community, so his veiled threat that he tell MacCrammond of our plans to kidnap his wife are too real to ignore - in fact, I believe that if we don't allow him in to complete his mission alongside ourselves, there's a risk of his blowing our best chance of doing the right thing for Nat. So, in summary, I vote we accept his offer of the helicopter and just keep a close watch throughout the whole operation on the man he sends on the mission with us. What do the two of you think about that aspect?'

'Makes sense to me,' said the Major, 'and, hell, if we have two or three of Mick Rollo's top men alongside just one of him, what harm can it do? So, I say accept his offer,'

'Speaking purely operationally,' said Rollo, 'I think the helicopter would make the whole thing much easier and, as the Major says, my lads can easily keep an eye on the Russian - don't care even if he's a bloody KGB James Bond superstar,'

'They're called the FSB nowadays, not the KGB,' said Wheeler, 'but I agree with Mick so let's go for it. In addition this, Komarov suggested we could benefit from a commission on the sales of Athena and the Craithe lot's software which he's going to acquire – whatever that means. My own thought is that there's plenty of time to look into that later on, isn't there?'

Both of the other two agreed and Wheeler told them he would go ahead with Komarov.

'It's up to them to organise this James Bond figure they're sending with the helicopter,' he added finally, 'and I'll let both of you know as soon as they give me the details.'

* * * * *

Guiseppe Lupo, stood at the large floor to ceiling window of his New York apartment looking out at his favourite view over Central Park. He had been deep in thought for the past few minutes. His short thin and wiry frame swayed very slowly from side to side and he hummed a little tune to himself, one of Dean Martin's Italian 'hits'. He brushed a hand through his hair, once jet black, now flecked here and there with grey and white. Turning from the window, he came back into the centre of the room and sat down on the sofa next to Rocco his computer boffin, business manager, and general right-hand-man.

Rocco had been updating 'the Boss' on the latest news on their hunt for the rumoured new cyber weapon, and told him of the Bank of England Conference today and what the Boss's cousin in London had said about the situation. For some minutes the Boss had been looking out over Central Park assessing what he had just learned.

'So you're sure there's something on the move at last with Komarov?' asked Lupo as he crossed the room and sat down on the sofa next to Rocco.

'Practically certain. No, I'll go further than that, I'll bet my life on it,' replied Rocco, swivelling his round shiny head to peer back at his Boss, 'yeah, I'll say it again, that's what one of our contacts in London has said too,'

'You think Komarov's found what he's been looking for, then?'

'And what we've been looking for too,' added Rocco,

'Okay, I know we've been getting him to do all our work for us, using his vast resources, but you think this is it?' Lupo looked back at Rocco and smiled - this might be coming to the culmination of over a year's highly risky shadowing of Komarov.'

'Look, he did all that very poorly disguised work in Manila, gets himself all prepared now for the Conference today,' said Rocco leaning forward towards his Boss, 'then, suddenly there's this flurry of activity with a new group of people in London' he said. 'Must be that his SVR people have found something? We also know he's been in touch with the Russian Embassy in London and that his partner has an operative hidden there. As I say, I'll bet my life on it, they're about to make a move. So much so that I've booked us rooms at the Dorchester Hotel in London, and got digs for the men.'

'You know I rely on your judgement,' said Lupo, 'let's just hope you're right about this,'

'I am right, you'll see, and sooner than you think,' said Rocco. Lupo just smiled. For some time now he had been dreaming of the effect of finally acquiring this new weapon would have on his standing within the fraternity, plenty to smile about, indeed.

15

Good Friday morning, 3 April

Conference, Bank of England, London

From soon after eight in the morning, the doors were opened to Bank of England's conference. Both of the Bank's supervisory bodies, the Financial Conduct Authority and the Prudential Regulation Authority had sent personal invitations to senior personnel in organisations under their supervision. Excuses for non-attendance would not be accepted – though, in exceptional circumstances, an alternative attendee could be sent in place of the person named on the invitation. As a result, by eight-thirty the conference room was nearly full – a mix of chief executive officers, senior IT personnel, and senior partners of hedge funds – most of them irritated at being forced to be here after the start of the Easter Bank Holiday weekend, but resigned to attending. In short, the top seventy-five companies represented were those most likely to suffer a cyber-attack and whose demise might also effect the City rather than just themselves. Naturally, all of those UK companies whose collapse might threaten the stability of the world's financial system had been forced to install Athena's warning software, though, for smaller companies it was still voluntary. Over a period of a number of months, many foreign banks were secretly told all about Athena and most, keen on the latest technologies, had installed Athena's software. Fisher, watching this process wondered if, by any chance, the US banks' keenness in particular gave a clue that Athena's other backer – the secretive conglomerate partner – just might be an American company. He never did get an answer to this speculation.

Bill Fisher was due to make his welcoming address to the conference at nine-thirty, but, just before nine, the unobtrusive red warning lights behind the scenes, installed at the Craithe Team's request, began to flash on and off rapidly. The light was switched off and, as had been agreed, Fisher immediately rang Craithe.

* * * * *

In the cyber team's rooms at Komarov's offices, he and Silayev had arrived well before the Bank of England conference was due to start. Ever since Morozov had found out about Athena, the team had been looking to select the best organisation for their attack. As the objective of the attack was merely to confirm for them that Athena was indeed the rumoured super cyber weapon, they did not want to attack a bank that was big enough to cause ripples. Thus, the job for their 'mole' currently attending the conference was simply to help them pick a suitable target. It needed to be defended by CSL, and have Athena installed so that they could easily break through the main defences and be sure to trigger a defensive response from Athena.

In due course, the mole had managed to speak to the chairman of CSL who had been happy to boast of his company's extensive client list and had got his secretary to email him the list. The mole emailed Komarov with the name of the ideal target, a smallish investment bank by the name of Greystone & Frobisher.

All eagerly gathered around the machines, Komarov gave a nod and the young operative hacked into it and delivered the cyber-attack. He and an assistant were ready to note carefully the sequence of events the moment he pressed the key initiating the attack and a stand-by machine had also been set up to record all events. They were shocked, however, at the practically instantaneous response from Athena – it seemed to come at almost the same moment they hit the key for the attack. It was followed by the machine they had used to make the attack being shut down. The second machine monitoring it, picked up the fact that it was indeed Athena doing the counter-attack but was too slow to record the sequence of events or exactly which files Athena had hit to kill the attacking machine. Thus, in effect, the purpose of the exercise, to find ways to steal Athena over the internet had been a complete failure.

'Christ, that was fast,' said Komarov, 'hope to God you were quick enough switching off our second machine here – the last thing we need is MacCrammond knowing our real identity or location. Still, we now know we've found our new weapon and, at last we can give the President the good news. So let's get on with the details of our plan with Mr Rollo's group.'

'We could use a man of mine who recently had an assignment in London,' said Silayev, 'he's still sitting there waiting for a suitable moment to get back here to Moscow' said Silayev, 'and he's well up to this job on Craithe.'

'A hell of a lot hangs on this,' said Komarov, 'are you sure he's right for it – we could still get an SVR operative to Northern Ireland in time?'

'Well he may not be trained up quite as much as your fancy KGB, FSB, or SVR operatives, but he's done good work for me,' replied Silayev. Anyway what can be so difficult about stealing a load of software? More importantly, he has the advantage of being ready to go over to Rollo's place right now. His name's Dmitri Zaytsev,'

'Well as you're vouching for his competence,' said Komarov, 'the fact that he's already in the UK, does make things easier.'

He stopped for a minute, rubbing his chin. 'The other factor of course is that the President's losing patience with me over this whole bloody thing. So right then, I'll take your word on him. I'll get the Embassy to organise a helicopter for the weekend; is this Zaytsev man of yours trained on Eurocopters like most of our people?'

'I'll double check that when I contact him. Want me to do that now?'

'Yes,' replied Komarov, 'you have all the details? Rollo's location, everything else you need to brief him for this project?'

'I can brief him fully, he'll be ready later today,' said Silayev.

'Good. We've just taken the first steps to an exceedingly lucrative business,' said Komarov, 'with Athena's capabilities, this could be the biggest thing that anyone in the brotherhood has ever pulled off. The Wheeler lot using MacCrammond's wife as a hostage will be like a children's tea party compared to the infrastructure hostages we'll be able to take once we've got Athena. Just imagine, a whole power station as held to ransom – even a regional grid,'

'Okay, Okay, less gloating, we haven't got it yet,' said Komarov 'let's get all the loose ends tied up. First thing is to organise Zaytsev and the helicopter,'

'I'll also ring Wheeler once we've done those two' said Komarov, 'this is beginning to look good.'

* * * * *

The telephone up in the Lab at Craithe had been busy when Fisher rang – no doubt connected to the attack, but when he got through, it was the professor who answered.

'Our alarms went off down here,' said Fisher, 'was that a false alarm or for real?'

'For real,' confirmed the Prof, 'good to have been prepared. It was a small investment bank called Greystone & Frobisher. As expected, it had originally been protected by CSL and we only installed the Athena warning software last week. All went to plan and the attacker was duly shut down. We're in the process right now of trying to get more information on the attackers, but I can tell you already that they're Moscow-based, and traces indicate they are the same lot as the Manila attackers. Anyway, all's well, nothing more to worry about and we'll ring you when we know more.'

Fisher thanked him, much relieved that, when it had come to the first real cyber-attack of this kind, and that the Athena programme had worked so well.

At nine-thirty, Bill Fisher came to the lectern on the podium and called for order. By now all the attendees had found themselves seats and most seemed intent on making the best of a tiresome duty – many also intrigued about what the Bank of England would say about the demonstration all had been mandated to watch on Thursday afternoon. Some were also looking forward to an explanation of the hacking into a hedge fund's operations for the demonstration. He welcomed everyone, laid down some 'housekeeping rules', and reminded them that the purpose of the conference was to ensure that everyone was fully aware of the current threat levels of cyber-attacks and that all should have Athena's warning software installed.

'Most of you here will not be at all interested in computer software nor in computer defence systems', he continued after the initial welcome, 'and I'm sure many of you think you spend quite enough money on cyber defences as it is,' There was a subdued noise all round of muttered agreement to this.

'That is not how Mr Zhang Wei, Chief Executive Officer of the Manila Beijing Bank felt yesterday, however,' he continued. 'The cyber-attack on his bank destroyed all his customer account data forcing him to shut the bank, all its branches and ATMs. Briefly, it caused a run on his bank. The attack, the third of its kind in Manila in the past week or so, could have bankrupted the bank. He got over this by restoring his customer data from the previous night's backups, which, of course were out of date. He therefore had many complaints of wrong transactions and balances, but his bank survived - just.'

'The Manila Beijing Bank and two other banks raided earlier,' continued Fisher, 'were all defended by one of our best known and respected cyber defence providers, CSL. The hackers had been practicing on CSL defence software and they have warned us through a tip-off that a large bank, probably one also using CSL defences would be attacked whilst we are here at this conference this morning. I have to tell you that, soon after nine this morning, a small investment bank was attacked, here in London,' he said,

There was a short spate of coughing and throat-clearing as Fisher paused for a moment and some exchanged glances with their neighbours.

'I'm happy to tell you that, wisely, it had installed Athena detection software and as soon as it was attacked Athena counter-attacked and disabled the attacker's equipment. We now know that the attacker was from the same organisation that was responsible for the attacks in Manila though we are still trying to establish their full identity. So, what I'm saying to you is this, the threat levels are as high as they can get, and will remain like that until every attack is countered by Athena. It vindicates the Bank of England sponsored demonstration to try and get this message across to all of you and I trust that a combination of that demonstration and the attacks this morning will persuade the rest of you to see sense and install Athena later today or over the weekend. I know that installations of this kind can be complex and sometimes need to deal with compatibility issues, but all our many Athena users are relieved that they took the decision to install it.'

The conference ended around midday. It was deemed by the Bank of England and the regulatory bodies to have been a success as, by the end, all the waverers had signed up for Athena and had booked times for the software to be installed. Sir Jeremy's dream of the world's financial stability being protected by a substantial mass of counter-attacking companies seemed near at hand, with London and some of the US and German Banks leading the way. Full reports of the day's events began to be circulated around the world's other financial centres and, already, many who had been appraised of Athena's capabilities now began to request Athena installations.

Cape had been there with Mina from before the conference began, getting her to take notes as the morning progressed. Mina said she needed to go out for a smoke break from time to time and twice she found Sandy Scale out in the street, ostensibly for the same reason. They chatted during these breaks, Scale asking Mina how she found working Cape in Number 11 Downing Street.

Up on Craithe, the Professor, Perry and the team were at work still trying to get the full identity of the conference attacker. Without Komarov's resources – especially Danil Morozov – they still had no idea of the existence of Mina, or Wheeler or of the plans to turn their world upside down.

* * * * *

After Wheeler had had the time to get over the shock of Komarov's appearance on the scene and the transformation of their plans, his discussions with Komarov's were almost cordial – though the cordiality was helped somewhat by the provision of the helicopter, as mounting the kidnapping operation using only power-boats would have been both more difficult and risky.

On discussing what had now become their *joint plans*, it became clear that the Major's trip out to Londonderry would be immensely easier if he hitched a lift in this helicopter with Zaytsev.

The Major was quickly alerted to this and rushed back to his place, packed and got himself down to the London Heliport by lunchtime. He found Zaytsev already there, with the Embassy-chartered machine and was waiting to go. While the helicopter was given a last check-over, he sized up Zaytsev.

The man's appearance was everything one would expect – the perfect embodiment of a one man mission, just right for one of such importance. His spoken English was faultless if a touch accented, and his manner and physical bearing inspired immediate confidence. As the Major walked with him towards the machine, he felt relaxed and in good hands and the uncomfortable rush to get there for a lift to Rollo's place well worth the effort. Once strapped in aboard the Eurocopter, the pilot ran quickly through the pre-flight checks and then they were off, rising quickly over the Thames and heading west along the river – a good start to what promised to be adventuresome project. The Major glanced across to Zaytsev and smiled. The smile was not returned and, on reflection, the Major thought this more in keeping with the seriousness of the mission that was to follow and thereafter he just admired the views as they sped up the river at a mere couple of thousand feet.

16

Friday Morning

Norbally House, Portrush

Northern Ireland

As instructed, the Pilot took the helicopter in near Belfast to top it up with fuel. It had been explained to the charter company that there might need to be a number of trips between Northern Ireland and the West Coast of Scotland over the weekend, and that further refuelling visits should just be debited to their account which would be settled at the end of the charter; as the charterer was the Russian Embassy, this was readily accepted. From Belfast there it was just another twenty minutes further flight time to Portrush and Norbally House on the north coast.

Only a few years earlier, Norbally House had been almost derelict - a large Northern Ireland mansion in the Georgian style with a home farm adjacent. During 'The Troubles,' whilst the Irish Economy was in poor shape, it had been put up for sale though, for years, no one seemed interested. Eventually an anonymous buyer appeared, and though the offer they made for the place was low, the sellers, keen to get it off their hands, accepted.

For some time afterwards, the buyer's identity remained unknown. Much work on it and its grounds could be seen by the locals, including large new wrought iron gates and over six miles of tall, electrified wire-mesh fencing. It was only after this work appeared to be complete did the new owner moved in and his name was eventually discovered to be Mick Rollo.

There was some local speculation about his origins and the nearest anyone got to the truth was that he had once been in the British Army's Special Forces. This was thought possible as it was also rumoured that, with a name like Rollo, he was originally from Scotland. He was soon joined at by a team of six or seven fit, military-looking young men. Some of these occasionally came down to the pub not far from the main gates, though they always kept to themselves. Eventually it became known that this team had all once been members of 'the Coverts' and as everyone in Northern Ireland knew, the coverts were best left to themselves.

As soon as the pilot had landed the helicopter on Norbally's large front lawns, Mick Rollo came out of the house and stood, arms folded, waiting for them by the front door. As soon as the Major had jumped down from the helicopter and come across the lawn, Rollo greeted him with an embrace and mutual back-slapping. He was then introduced to Zaytsev.

As soon as they got to the large Drawing room, Rollo summonsed three of his coverts - Flaxman, Bookie and Tulloch and introductions were made. They then moved to Rollo's study where there was a large whiteboard standing on an easel. He had already written up on it the names of the four members of the mission. They all seated themselves and Rollo went up to the Whiteboard.

'This initial briefing won't take long,' he said, 'as the Major will go into more detail when you get up to the Inn where you're staying tonight. Your two jobs are quite straightforward.'

'Greg,' he said, turning to look at Flaxman, 'you'll take Bookie with you and the two of you will be responsible for kidnapping MacCrammond's wife. Shaun,' he continued turning slightly and looking at Tulloch, 'you'll be with Mr Zaytsev here . . .'

'Dmitri, please, my name's Dmitri,' interrupted Zaytsev,

'You'll be with, er, Dmitri whose job it is to acquire the Craithe Team's software suite they call Athena. We've booked in for an indefinite time at an old Inn called the Galley of Lorne. The owner there, Hamish Munro, is very obliging. It seems that he has a liking for the bottle and so, conveniently, I've found him nicely talkative. He should be a good source of local knowledge. Shaun, I picked you because you're a keen photographer, I've already told this Hamish Munro that you've photographed Castles all over Europe – an extra cover should we need access to areas of the Castle not open to the public. Dimitri, you can pretend to be Shaun's European cousin, interested in comparing castles in whichever country you choose to come from,'

'The Ukraine,' said Zaytsev, 'we have many beautiful fortresses and old castles in the Ukraine,'

'Good, the Ukraine it is,' repeated Rollo. 'Munro is hiring a boat for us for just as long as it takes us to complete our two missions. Munro vouches for this boat captain as being the best there is. The Major and I have discussed all of this and we feel confident that our success will be down to surprise and to small, unobtrusive two-man teams. Once we're settled in there this afternoon, the Major will discuss individually with each of you, the details of the two mission. Any questions on any of that?'

There were no questions asked, but a few lesser points were covered - for example a hire SUV would arrive from Oban at the Galley of Lorne soon after their arrival at the Inn. It would be used principally to find a rendezvous point for the boats and the helicopter after the kidnapping and the theft of Athena. Then there was the Major's hope that, as a backup to stealing Athena, he might be able to find and sever the Island of Craithe's Internet cable. He had already booked an appointment in Oban with one of the engineers who had installed this fibre optic cable. The four carrying out the two operations would have the rest of the afternoon to familiarise themselves with the castle layout. This they were to do from the internet and from the castle's own brochure and from these studies they could work up the fine details of their plans.

The Meeting concluded with the four participants suitably 'fired up' for the tasks ahead. But, just before they went out to the helicopter, Zaytsev asked what facilities Rollo had for the kidnapped prisoners once they had been brought back to Norbally house. In particular, he asked what had they by way of rooms which might be used to get information from people who were not immediately willing to impart it. Rollo was surprised at the question, as the kidnapping was nothing to do with him, but, keen to show off his facilities, he simply said 'come with me'.

Zaytsev followed Rollo to the back of the house and then into a dimly lit room.

'Wait here and look at that large mirror there,' he said as he pointed to it taking up much of the room on one wall. Rollo then left and a moment later lights came on beyond the mirror, showing it to be a two-way window into what was obviously an interrogation room. From the room Rollo flicked a couple of switches and then asked, through a speaker system,

'Does that answer your question, Dmitri?'

'Yes, but how do you have a facility like this?' asked Zaytsev

'It was put in and used by the previous owners,' replied Rollo, 'probably used in the very difficult times of in Ireland known as the Troubles,'

'Ah, yes the times of the bombs,' said Zaytsev

They walked back through the house, picked up the three coverts' overnight bags and equipment lying in the hall and went on out to the helicopter. As soon as all were aboard, the pilot started up the Eurocopter and they climbed off the front lawn and immediately swung north over the shore nearby. They headed towards the Mull of Kintyre which had become clearly visible as soon as they had gained height over Norbally House and, with a distance of just 75 miles to the Galley of Lorne, the trip was going to take them around half an hour. Despite his training with the SAS all those years ago, as this was the first time that the Major had joined in on one of the missions he had brokered, he was both surprised and slightly embarrassed to feel that his stomach was churning at the thought of how things might go from here.

17

Friday Mid-morning

Glasgow International Airport

Borislav Boreyev and his team of five had arrived at Glasgow International Airport about a couple of hours later than planned, about eleven o'clock. The flight in Mikhail Vassilov's Hawker 800 jet had been delayed for take-off - some confusion over the flight plan.

With some assistance from his friend Freddy Briston, who had spoken at the Cobra Meeting to his Cabinet colleague, the Home Secretary, Ranald had got the flight diplomatic status and on arrival at Glasgow, the jet was directed to a private tarmac apron which would give access to private customs clearance and the hired vehicle organised by Ranald.

No sooner were the doors opened and the steps let down, than a UK customs officer, accompanied by a smart young man in a well-tailored suit entered the aircraft.

'Mr Boreyev?' enquired the young man in the suit,

'Yes, I'm Borislav Boreyev,' he replied as he unstrapped himself and rose from his seat.

'My name's Geoffrey Plumstead. The Home Secretary has sent me to convey our welcome to the United Kingdom to you and your group. As a diplomatic gesture all your baggage and belongings will be loaded directly into the minibus which has been hired for you by Mr MacCrammond. Chief Customs Officer Smalley is here with me to ensure your smooth passage through the documentary formalities and then to speed you on your way. Is there anything else I can do for you?'

'No, thank you, and please convey our thanks to the Home Secretary,' replied Boreyev,

'I will indeed, Mr Boreyev, and welcome again to the UK.' With that, he turned about and left the plane. Chief Customs Officer Smalley stayed behind, examined the passports and asked Boreyev to sign a couple of documents. After that, he too was gone.

A minibus with a large luggage space behind the seats had arrived next to the plane. As soon as Boreyev and the other five were down on the tarmac, they watched as their baggage and equipment were loaded. Just as this was being completed, there was the sound of a mobile telephone ringing from the driver's seat inside the minibus. It had been put there on Ranald's instructions and its number had been passed back to him by the minibus rental company. One of the baggage handlers picked it up, answered it and brought it over to Boreyev.

'I think this'll be for you,' he said as he handed it over,

'Borislav, you arrived safe and sound?' said Ranald

'We have, yes, Ranald, many thanks for the welcoming party,' he said in Russian, 'this was really most kind; I'd have hated trying to explain my equipment going through normal customs channels,'

'You're welcome,' replied Ranald, 'In addition to this mobile, I asked the van rental people to get a map for you and to mark it with your route from the airport to Crinan. Tatty and I will be waiting for you there. There's no hurry but I've booked a table for lunch for all of us at the Crinan Hotel, as we have to wait for slack tides to get us through the Corryvreckan.'

'The what?' repeated Boreyev,

'The Corryvreckan,' replied Ranald, 'I'll explain about that when we meet,'

As he had been speaking, Boreyev had found the map, and half-opened it to see Crinan highlighted on the map.

'The marked map looks good, how long will it take us to drive up to Crinan?'

'As you're not familiar with driving on the left, and on account of some of the winding roads, it will probably take you about a couple of hours, or so'

'Good, we'll see you in Crinan for lunch then,' said Boreyev and they rang off.

The map showed them the way across the River Clyde from the Airport, along its north bank and then, turning north, up the west side of Loch Lomond. They motored on good, well sign-posted motorway at a steady pace, slow enough to take in the beautiful surroundings firstly the River Clyde below them and, after turning north near Dumbarton, on up above Loch Lomond. Some stretches of the road were high above the loch and the views of it and Ben Lomond on the far side of it were spectacular. Cameras and smartphones clicked as they drove through the magnificent scenery.

Near the head of the loch, at the tiny hamlet of Tarbet, they turned away from the Loch Lomond and the road now took them over wild mountain passes, down into the deep valleys, round the heads of a couple of sea lochs until, at last, they arrived at Inveraray. Cameras clicked again to record the magnificent Castle, its four grey slate-roofed towers glistening after a brief April shower.

The last leg of the journey, from Inveraray to Crinan was short and on arriving in Crinan, they saw their rendezvous with the MacCrammonds, the large white building of the Crinan Hotel. After parking the van in the hotel car park, they sauntered down to the loch's edge to admire the views, stretch their legs and draw in the fresh sea air. Looking west, straight out from where they stood on the high quay, the horizon west was dominated by the bulk of the Island of Jura and, to its right, the slightly smaller Island of Scarba. Through the gap between these two islands, they could also just see the towering mountains of the Island of Craithe.

'There you are,' came a voice in Russian from behind them - it was Ranald MacCrammond coming down from the hotel, with the beautiful Tatiana by his side, and Kim Bradley following behind. Boreyev turned and walked briskly over, first to Tatiana who he engulfed in his arms and then kissed on both cheeks and then to Ranald who he also enveloped in an all-enveloping embrace.

'How beautiful a place you bring us to,' he said in his deep Russian voice, as he released Ranald. He then spotted the slight figure of Kim Bradley, standing a few yards back towards the hotel. He suddenly felt a pang of he did not know what, seeing the shy-looking, frail figure standing there, awkwardly, he thought. Ranald saw him looking towards her and quickly introduced her.

'Boris, this is my invaluable Secretary cum personal assistant and all-in-all wonder, Kim Bradley,

'Delighted to meet you at last,' said Kim, in fluent Russian, stepping forward confidently with her hand outstretched before her. Boreyev's impression of her underwent an instant transformation, thanks, of course both to Ranald's introduction and to Kim's change in demeanour for, as she looked back up at him confident, smiling, she took his hand in both of hers.

'Miss… er…Bradley,' he said, in English, taken aback by her immediate closeness and familiarity,

'I've spoken to you so often,' she replied in Russian, beaming back up at him, 'that I feel I've known you for ages, Mr Boreyev, and, anyway my name's Kim'

'In that case, I insist that you call me Boris,' he said. They kept smiling back at each other and, had there been some newly-invented gauge which could detect human ESP, it would have bounced up off the top end of its activity scale for several seconds.

'Right all of you,' said Ranald in Russian, 'lunch is ready,' and taking Tatiana by the hand, added, 'follow me,'

As the group, all conversing in Russian entered the hotel, the staff were waiting to look after one as locally important as the son of Sir James MacCrammond, Laird of Craithe. Most of them knowing him well - but having no knowledge of his years spent in Moscow - were astounded to hear him also conversing in fluent Russian.

The group sat at a large table with wide panoramic views out west towards the islands. Ranald explained the geography of this part of the world and went from there to tell them why he had called on their services, and the babble of conversation was replaced by attentive listening.

'As your boss, Boreyev knows,' said Ranald, 'We have on the island where you'll be staying for a while, a team of computer scientists. They've developed valuable software and we have reason to believe that there are some who would want to steal it. Your job will be to protect the team and the software from theft. Borislav will tell you what this will entail for each of you when we get to the island, In the meantime I welcome you all to Scotland and hope you enjoy your stay in addition to the protection work.'

He looked round the table and all seemed quite content with the short briefing. He then raised his glass,

'So, I give you a toast, to a happy stay on the island of Craithe.' Everyone raised there glasses in the toast, and, as soon as they had drunk to it, Ranald added, 'Just one other thing, if you have reason to speak to my father, just call him simply Sir James and if you're speaking to others about him you might just refer to him as The Laird,'

'We have no titles in Russia any more,' said Boreyev, suddenly switching his attention back to where it should have been these past minutes, 'so what is all this about - Sir James and the Laird?'

'Sir James is just a hereditary Baronetcy, so when he dies I become Sir Ranald – but don't worry about it it's becoming a bit of an anachronism in this age. And as for *the Laird* that isn't even a title at all. It derives from the English word "Lord" and is usually said of any large landowner of standing; it's just a mark of respect though that doesn't stop some west highlands crofters trying to hide some of the Laird's sheep amongst his own when it comes to Market time,'

A ripple of laughter ran round the group which now seemed relaxed about the weekend ahead and the threat of software hunters somehow diminished.

'Anyway, we won't need to have a session on security until you've settled in properly,' he concluded, ' and we'll probably do that tomorrow morning,'

When lunch was finished and Ranald knew that the slack tide was due, one of the group went and collected the mini-bus, the others, eased down with holiday quantities of vodka, made their way down to the Laird's boat.

The boat itself was an Arun class lifeboat, not long retired from RNLI service - the finest sea-going boat for the sometimes treacherous waters in these parts. The Laird had been on the point of getting something different but just as he was making his choice, a young couple had lost their lives in the wild seas of the Corryvreckan. The thought that a lifeboat might have saved their lives prompted him to look into the possibility of buying one no longer in service. He found the Louisa and, on committing to allow her to be used as a backup to the Oban lifesaving boat, he bought her at a substantial discount off the one million pound price tag. Even this discounted price was high but Ranald, returning from Russia to start the new joint-venture bank, offered to pay a substantial part of its purchase and running costs and the conglomerate's almost bottomless pockets also made a contribution.

Her skipper, Sandy Grieg, a large man in his late forties had been chosen from many candidates, all of whom had to undergo interviews both with the Laird himself and the Lifeboat service. A local man, Sandy was one of those people that instil instant confidence and soon became known along the coast as one who had saved a number of lives since then, as the Louisa's services had been called upon help out the Oban RNLI boat in particularly stormy conditions of the previous year.

Once all the Boreyev group's equipment had been transferred from the minibus into the Louisa, the bus itself was parked back in the Hotel carpark, and, with all aboard, Sandy made ready for the return to Craithe. He had some difficulty initially in starting one of the two large diesel engines. He had to do some quick tinkering with that engine's fuel injection system but after a few minutes was able to start them both with deep powerful grumbles from the 1500 horse power between the two them. He then shouted for the willing helpers ashore and as soon as she was cast off, he nudged her out into Loch Crinan.

Once clear of the many yachts and small boats anchored near the quay, he gently pushed the throttles forward for more speed. The growls became muted roars and even in the choppy passage of sea known as the Dorus Mhor, with its seven or eight knot tide rips sweeping past the boat, the Louisa just bobbed in the powerful cross currents and sliced her way through them. Soon, even above the noise of the engines, they could all hear the roar of the straits of the Corryvreckan ahead them and, a short while later, they were in the midst of churning and standing waves – these where seas, coming at each other from different directions, clashed and stood against each other as though in a test of strength. The Louisa's exceptionally wide beam of some seventeen feet made her comfortably stable and despite the violence of the waters all around them, she just gently rolled a few degrees, first this way then that, as she powered at nearly twenty knots straight through the middle of the maelstrom. Ranald pointed out the Great Whirlpool itself as they passed within a hundred yards of it – a great, wide depression in the sea, some fifty yards across filled with waves tumbling over each other and circulating in a macabre marine dance.

As soon as they were through the straits and past the islands of Jura and Scarba on either side of the gulf, the island Craithe loomed really large ahead of them; its massive castle and jagged mountains beyond it quite awed even the hardened Boreyev elites. As they approached the entrance to the old walled-in harbour of Stanleytoun, Sandy Grieg eased the power off and the Louisa settled down into a slow gurgling approach towards her own permanent berth. It was at this point that an intermittent coughing sound could be heard coming from the same engine that had initially refused to start. Grieg exchanged glances with Ranald.

'If Borislav or anyone else needs her over the weekend,' said Ranald, 'she's got to be in full working condition – full power, total reliability. She doesn't sound quite that at the moment, does she?'

'No she does not, sounding a wee bit wheezy,' replied Grieg,

'Can you get her a hundred percent by the end of the afternoon?'

'Oh Aye, I can tell without even looking that it's nothing serious, but the worst that could happen would be making do with just the one engine,' he said

'No, no, that won't do, see if you can get it fixed properly at Brown's and let me know up at the Castle when that's been done, will you', said Ranald

'Aye, I'll do that'.

Grieg nudged her gently towards her berth and as they came near the quayside, people appeared as from nowhere to help tie up the Laird's boat. These same people then helped with getting the baggage and Boreyev's equipment up on to quayside. Two Land rovers had been driven down to near the Louisa. One of them had a game cart attached to the back of it and soon all had been loaded. With the Louisa's enclosed cabin then safely locked, they all made their way along the quay to the Derby Arms Hotel.

This had once just been just a good pub and restaurant with a dozen rooms and just a couple of bathrooms. Recently, with the tourist trade quadrupling over just a few years, a large extension had been added and it now boasted a fine panoramic view restaurant, eight more bedrooms, most of them with their own bathrooms. Boreyev's five were to stay here in the rooms that Ranald had managed to book for them and once they had been happily installed in the hotel and given a fair number of notes for pocket money, Ranald, Tatiana and Kim took Borislav up to the castle. Ranald seemed relaxed about the threat of any intruders, but Boreyev was keen to learn about the layout of the Castle right away as, in his experience, it was never wise to be over-confident in security matters. Ranald gave him a quick guided tour both inside and outside the castle. As they went, Boreyev made notes and did little sketches, already, almost intuitively, planning a defence strategy. Whatever Ranald might think the chances were of an attempt to steal Athena, Boreyev was going to make damned sure it would not be an easy task for anyone attempting it.

18

Friday lunchtime,

Galley of Lorne Inn,

Ardfern, Argyllshire

Hamish Munro at the Galley of Lorne Inn, had told the Major at the time he had made the booking that he would put out a large white cross of sheets on the best level spot near the Inn to show where the helicopter should land. After passing Crinan, the pilot slowed the Eurocopter as the white cross came into view up ahead. He landed, let his passengers off, and, as the helicopter would not be needed here again till tomorrow afternoon, took off again and swung south back to Ireland.

The five of them quickly settled into the comfortable Inn and after a quick lunch, each of them had research to do for their missions.

The Major's first job was to check on something he had asked Wheeler to do for him while he was getting from London up here via Norbally House, and he went to his room to make the call.

'I've arrived at the Galley of Lorne Inn with Rollo's team and the Russian,' he said, 'One interesting development, in his eagerness to look after our every wish, the owner of the inn here, has already told us that his cousin, Geordie Munro, is odd-job man at Craithe

Castle and occasionally acts as a special guide for guests of the Galley of Lorne.'

'That sounds good,' said Wheeler,

'It does,' said the Major, 'and Rollo's head man, Flaxman, is going to talk to both the owner here at the inn and his cousin - might find a way to make our jobs just that much easier. Talking of making things easier, did you find out anything for me about exactly where they took a spur off the Oban fibre-optic internet cable for the Craithe Castle line?'

'No, afraid not. I've searched the internet and asked around, but nothing to be of any help to you,' replied Wheeler, 'So you'll need that interview with the engineer tomorrow morning and I'll text you his name and the time and place I've arranged for you to meet him,'

'Good, I look forward to that,' said the Major, 'in the meantime, I'll get on with looking for a good rendezvous for the boats after the jobs have been done and I'll ring you tomorrow with a progress report – hopefully to tell you that both missions went off without a hitch,'

'Good luck,' said Wheeler, and rang off.

Greg Flaxman had become a master in the art of kidnapping, but in his days with the Coverts his targets had usually been snatched from some housing estate in cities such as Belfast or Derry or from a lonely cottage in the countryside. The time factor to this mission, however, meant that he and Bookie needed to seize MacCrammond's wife from the security of the huge castle and, to this even more difficult, it had to be done at the earliest opportunity, which meant it would most likely have to be carried out in broad daylight.

After Munro's gesture of hospitality – offering to get his cousin Geordie to act a special guide for the modest extra fee of twenty-five pounds – a neat plan suddenly occurred to Flaxman. He decided to put this to Munro when they met, as agreed, after lunch.

Flaxman arrived at two-thirty in the bar, and found the large red cheeked Munro pouring himself a significant slug of whisky.

'Would you like one of these yourself, Mr Flaxman – on the house?' asked Munro, 'I find it helps the digestion,'

'No thanks,' replied Flaxman, 'too many of my former comrades turned to the bottle in a big way on returning from Afghanistan, so I don't touch the stuff myself,'

Munro did not appear to notice this reference to his over-indulgence of the bottle and, anyway, by now had already taken a large swig from the glass. Flaxman had already noticed this weakness in him, and mentally stored it as something that he might be able to exploit if the need occurred.

The two of them settled into a long bench-seat in the bow window at the end of the bar and Flaxman leant forward towards the other. 'I need your advice,' he said,

'Happy to help in any way I can,' replied Munro,

'I'm an old friend of Ranald MacCrammond's and what I'd really like is to give him a nice surprise when I get over to the Castle tomorrow,' said Flaxman,

'Well, what a small world,' said Munro, 'where did you know him?'

His fabrication well prepared, Flaxman, leant back smiling,

'Moscow,' he said, 'my Russian cousin Dmitri Zaytsev who's with us on this trip, he also met Ranald in Moscow – both of us also met his lovely wife Tatiana, she's from Moscow, did you know? So, any ideas on how we might get up close to him and Tatiana? It'd be such fun to suddenly confront him – completely unexpected,'

'I see what you mean,' said Munro, pausing for a moment and looking out at the view of the loch below them for inspiration. 'I should think that Geordie could find out what his and Tatiana's movements will be tomorrow, though he might not be able to get those till the morning. Why don't we ring him now, let him in on our little secret, and we can get that answer from him by ringing again before you set off in the boat?'

'Perfect, let's do that' replied Flaxman, 'and you can confirm if you will that we'd like Geordie to act as a special guide for us tomorrow. Tell him we'd like to double his fee to fifty quid as we're also asking him to keep our little secret,'

Munro beamed with delight at the plan. Geordie was always pleased when Galley of Lorne guests were directed towards him for guide work of this kind. Munro went back over to the bar whilst Flaxman leaned on the bay window and looked out at the view. He listened carefully, however, as Munro talked to Geordie, after initial difficulties finding him.

After the call, Munro returned to the bench seat smiling,

'Geordie's delighted with the whole idea,' he said, 'and he's sworn to secrecy – loves a secret, Geordie. And don't be fooled by his appearance tomorrow, he's a little backward, if you know what I mean, but absolutely ideal for a prank such as this,'

'Good,' said Flaxman getting up to leave, 'so after breakfast and before the boat gets here I'll come to your office and we can ring Geordie again? Did he think there will be any problem finding out what Ranald and Tatiana will be doing tomorrow?'

'I don't know if you overheard me ask him that very question,' replied Munro, 'but he said it would be no problem at all, and I reminded him to be careful not to give our little secret away when he was trying to find out about their movements,'

'And what did he say?' asked Flaxman

'He told me that he often asks Ranald if there's anything he would like done for him,' replied Munro, 'so asking him won't seem unusual at all.'

'Excellent,' said Flaxman, 'looking forward to tomorrow morning then,' as he rose, gave a wave and left the bar.

The rest of the afternoon was spent learning as much as they could of the castle and its layout. This meant studying the visitor's brochure for Craithe Castle, a large scale map they had brought with them; The Inn also had other booklets about the West Coast of Scotland, and the islands here just south of Oban. They found it both interesting and informative and both the kidnapping and software theft were beginning to look much easier than either Flaxman or Zaytsev had initially feared. There was just one thing they came across in the local guide that concerned them and the effect it might have on their plans. The booklet explained that, on account of the very sparse population and the mountainous terrain, mobile telephone and satellite services ranged from very poor to non-existent. This meant that once any distance from the mobile relay masts on the mainland, mobile telephone connections were either out of range or the signal could be blocked by intervening mountains. It was too late now to get a hold of satellite mobiles or radios. They would need to be careful to bear this in mind when setting up the rendezvous tomorrow.

As they all met in the bar that evening for a drink before dinner, they agreed that, apart from the late discovery of communications difficulties in this remote part of the world, tomorrow's missions were now looking much easier than they had once feared.

19

Friday afternoon

Craithe Castle

During Friday morning, Ranald had been speaking to a number of people about the results of conference. The Bank of England team had been delighted with the way it had all gone - especially Athena's successful counter attack on a small bank. It was not until the afternoon that Ranald got round to meeting up with Boreyev to discuss plans for protecting the Athena team and the banks of machines holding all their work.

When Ranald had taken over his uncle's project and gone into partnership with the conglomerate to further develop Athena, it had become clear that security could to become an issue. Even early discussions on the effects of marrying quantum computing technologies with the best of today's digital, it became obvious that the team were likely to produce some revolutionary software. It occurred to Ranald that his father's castle off the west coast would be the perfect place to hide the team and the Laird was happy to let him have the whole of the massive south east tower and some rooms in the east of the main castle were also assigned to the team.

To entice members of the team to move to such remote location, everything had to be of the best. Though none of them were on the new Athena project for the money, the conglomerate insisted that they should be paid at least as well as the very best of their other research people in Cambridge. The south east tower was almost gutted and every modern facility for their comfort was installed both in the tower itself and the main castle block – bedrooms, bathrooms, a large sitting-room, a smaller television room, and a restaurant with its own kitchens and staff. The Laboratory – the 'Lab' to the team – was equipped to the very highest standards with a rare, latest version of a quantum computer, making it at least as well equipped as any research facility of its kind in the world.

The security of the whole operation would be child's play compared to such a set-up had it been in or even near London. For a start, the castle itself had never been breached, even under Cromwell's principle commander, General Monck – its entrances were few and easily monitored.

The main security risk was from would-be software thieves posing as tourists. A large-scale forcible attack to steal Athena could only get onto the island by boat or by helicopter, and, as in times past, would be easy to rebuff. Due to the islands mountainous terrain and few level areas, there were but few large enough for a helicopter to land and an attack by sea would be likely to succeed only under cover of darkness.

Boreyev had taken a long look round the castle and grounds on Friday afternoon while Ranald was busy so, when he was eventually able to meet up with him in the evening, Ranald agreed to go round the castle both inside and out and listen to his thoughts on how best to use the Russian team.

'I know I got you over here to do some protection work,' said Ranald as they went out of the castle's main front door, 'but I think that your stay here is going to be more of a holiday than anything else. For starters, I don't think anyone knows yet that the Athena team is based here on the island and for some time now Perry has had in place a software decoy programme which entices those looking for Athena to search the west end of London or Cambridge. And funnily enough, we've had a number of people trying to hack into those false locations.'

'You may be right,' replied Boreyev, 'but as I'm here now and you just launched Athena to God knows how many people in London. I'm happy to tell you that I've done a rota system with my men that should keep everyone safe – even if no one turns up to steal your software.'

The two of them toured to castle both inside and out, with Boreyev pointing out where and how his people would deal with people passing certain critical points, With many tourists going round the castle, following guides, a new system had also been put in place to gently shepherd any strays away for potential access to the south east area of the castle.

'You've done a great job, Boris,' said Ranald, 'and if there are any would-be software thieves on their way here, it seems they won't get past your lot.'

'That's as maybe,' replied Boreyev, 'but, to start off with, over a week or so after the launch of your main software, I'm going to put one of my men on watch by the one entrance to the south east tower and the Lab'. When that watch finishes at 4a.m I'll take over and my man can get a few hours' sleep in my room.'

'Are you sure?' said Ranald, 'isn't that taking things a bit far, I mean . . . '

'Just a precaution,' said Boreyev, interrupting him, 'If I were the software thief, I reckon I'd come onto the island as a tourist, mingle with all the other tourists, hide myself in the castle somewhere and attempt the theft under the cover of darkness,'

'Well, you're the expert,' said Ranald, 'so of course you must do whatever you think is best. If you need any extra assistance, please, you must let me know,'

'No need for anything extra for now,' said Boreyev, 'but we can review that as we go along. In the meantime, starting tonight, I'll get a man in place on watch and relieve him myself at four,'

They chatted a bit more about other matters and Ranald then left Boreyev who continued off around the castle familiarising himself with its many rooms, corridors and small passageways.

* * * * *

Although Tatiana had been to Craithe a couple of times and Ranald's parents had been to Moscow also on two occasions - not least her wedding of course - she had spent little time with the Laird. On Ranald's advice she had 'booked' him for a chat for, although she guessed he was in his late-sixties, he seemed to be constantly busy. The two of them had agreed to meet in the Great Hall after lunch and she purposely made sure to get there early.

She now sat sipping the cup of coffee she had brought with her from after lunch, and looked about the great room. This, and so much more about Ranald were in such sharp contrast to herself. Both had been born in the late seventies but whereas Ranald's birth-right was one of privilege, stability and a way of life centuries old, Tatiana's was not. Her father, Mikhail Vassilov was one of a number of bright, adventuresome people who began to take advantage of the spontaneous privatisation that took place in President Gorbachev's time and whilst he rose to become one of the Oligarchs, his position was always tenuous and her youth was spent in a state of permanent uncertainty, sometimes of fear too. The climb to the status of Oligarch had also made many of these titans of business a number of enemies and the Dacha incident in which her mother had been killed was just a particularly violent outbreak of something always lurking in their lives.

The arrival of the handsome, carefree young man from Scotland and the City of London, seconded to her father's bank, had brought her a glimpse of his very different world and, after the Dacha incident when he had saved her life, she had embraced both Ranald and his way of life.

She was always intrigued to learn more of his background, if only to better understand him and the source of his striking self-confidence and she hoped that meeting his father this morning might further that.

As she looked round the Great Hall with its portraits and the history of the MacCrammonds, around its walls, she felt both daunted and yet proud that her little Jerry would one day be master of all of this, and this connection though her son gave a surge of confidence even as she looked round about her.

Her thoughts were interrupted by the noise of the heavy main door opening. The tall, but slightly stooped, wiry frame of the Laird breezed into the hall, bustling with energy and looking ready to be quizzed by his daughter in law. As always he was dressed in an old yet well-tailored tweed jacket and a kilt so old and faded that it could easily have been handed straight down to him from one of his ancestors pictured on the walls above them.

'My dear Tatty,' he said using Ranald's pet name for her, 'I do hope you haven't been waiting too long for me - I'm running a bit late I'm afraid.'

'Not at all,' she replied in her perfect English. Her time at St Andrews University had given her an excellent command of English and, although this command was faultless, as is so often amongst foreigners, it was delightfully tainted with that deep plumy accent that all Russians seem to have - whichever language they speak in.

'When I think back over my little life to date,' she said to the Laird as they sat down near the fire, 'I just find it so *difficult* to understand all the centuries of history here in this room - it seems to come out of the very walls. And although, as you know, History was my subject at St Andrews, all of this is almost overpowering. Doesn't it daunt you and Ranald a bit to be part of all of this?'

'Not really,' replied the Laird, 'all of it here in this room just reminds us of how we fit into its history. All of these people', he continued with a sweep of an arm, 'they were all just like you and me. All had their time for tears and for their joys as well. Their struggles were different in the sense that the world moves faster these days, but theirs was often bloodier. But, anyway, you didn't come here for a history lesson. I wasn't allowed to choose my parents and nor were you, we all just have to make the best of what we've been given, don't we. I don't think it was much different for them either'.

'And Ranald?' she asked, 'is doing all right - making the best of what he was given, do you think?'

'He's doing more than just that, in my view,' replied the Laird, 'When he got a good first degree from Oxford, the world might have been his oyster but, when his cousin Tommy was drowned, he bowed to his Uncle Jeremy's plea to go into the Towneley Bank. I believe it was about the last thing he had wanted to do with his life, still in our family as in many others, duty comes before one's own wishes.'

Tatiana gave a little grimace, 'He doesn't seem to resent that choice now',

'Of course not,' replied the Laird, 'look how it's turned out, eh? He was seconded to your father's bank, met you, married and then little Jerry came along, what could be more wonderful than all of that - resent it ? I should say not indeed,' He gave a bellow of a laugh at the thought of it.

She was looking back up at him again, smiling though he had become more serious.

'Why the frowning?' she asked,

'Jeremy's latest project is fraught with difficulties - the one Ranald's taken over from him,' he said, 'They may have come up with a brilliant way to further protect the City of London's financial systems - but in developing something lots of other people seem to want, I worry that they may have invited more attention to the island of Craithe than they've bargained for,'

Tatiana moved even further forward in her chair, she had not heard speak of Ranald's work like this before,

'Ranald makes a point of never boring me with his work' she said, ' He's told me before that, with my father in banking too, I must be fed up with it the financial world, so he doesn't like to risk boring me and never talks of it,'

'Maybe I shouldn't have spoken about it then,' said the Laird

'Oh no, I'm glad you did. I won't use your words to bully him but it gives me a chance to ask him more about that now that I know',

'Bully me?' said Ranald from the door into the Great Hall. The two of them had been so intent on their chat that neither of them had heard him come in.

'I was just saying to Tatty that I think yours and Jeremy's ways of shaking up the international financial world to protect it may be brilliant but dangerous,' said the Laird,

'Well only a little dangerous,' conceded Ranald as he came over to the fire. He bent down and gave his wife a little peck on the cheek though they had seen each other less than a couple of hours before.

'Why dangerous?' she insisted,

'No point in worrying you about what might never happen,' he said drawing himself up to his full height and resting an arm against the fireplace. 'What we're doing right now is certainly ruffling a few feathers in the City of London and on Wall Street but that's to be expected. But I will admit that we've now got here something others would like to get their hands on but that's always been a hazard of life, hasn't it? I heard the other day that a hedge fund billionaire was giving away most of his money to charities because his family had been threatened with kidnap for ransom.'

'What you mean we're at risk the same way as a billionaire?' asked Tatiana

'I very much doubt that,' said Ranald smiling down at her, 'for a start I don't think anyone knows where we and our programmes are,' and then added after a slight pause, 'and anyway, that's why I got Borislav and his men over from Moscow to protect us. There's really nothing to worry about'.

* * * * *

Throughout the rest of Friday life within the castle took on the air of a family on Holiday - worries of Athena, thieves, and dangers were put aside. Ranald took one of the Land Rovers and drove Tatiana, Jerry, Anastasia and Kim around the island. The three women, chatted away in Russian, admiring the spectacular scenery, the mountains, the cliffs the wildlife while little Jerry, sitting in the front seat next to his father, played on a small, mock steering wheel as though he were the driver. Exhausted by his day, Jerry was off to bed early and even the grown-ups retired to bed soon after dinner, tired too after a long day.

As planned, Boreyev posted one of his men, Ivan, near the entrance to the south west tower for the first watch. Ivan was told he could make himself a hot drink if he wished in the restaurant's kitchens but, naturally, was to remain vigilant at all times.

Earlier, during the afternoon, Boreyev had paced out a few critical points in the castle. Now, on his way back to his room, he counted his steps at some of these critical points – indeed he was so busy counting that, in the near-darkness, coming round the corner of the tower corridor onto the Gallery landing, he ran smack into Kim coming the other way.

They quickly disentangled themselves and Boreyev, with a mixture of embarrassment and sudden excitement, could only blurt out, 'you shouldn't be out alone in dark,'

'But, I'm not alone,' she replied and smiled broadly back at him. There was just enough light for him to see this but, for a fateful moment he hesitated. Then, regaining his self-control he said, 'Though we've no reason as yet to suppose anyone is going to come here to the castle to steal Athena, my men will be jumpy about people moving about the Castle after dark',

'I'm sorry, that never occurred to me', she said,

'Well, from now on, better to think about that,' he said. She nodded and she went on towards her room with a whispered 'good night' over her shoulder.

Boreyev too continued his walk round the gallery but he gave more thought to the incident. He had twice now said he thought after dark would be good for an attempted theft. A good would-be thief might think the same. That meant, maybe, that the opposite was the more likely – a bold attempt in broad daylight by someone posing as a lost tourist. He made a mental note to act on this new assumption in the morning.

20

Easter Saturday morning,

Crinan, Argyllshire

    Starting the new season, this particular year Neil McKinnon was in good spirits. This was the first time he would be taking out his gleaming Mitchell 31 touring boat, Calistra, with the thirty-five thousand pound loan on her paid off. For the first time she was truly his. Her sleek black hull, reflecting mirror-like the waters of the loch, her beige decks, the white cabin, the large open space in the stern, she was the perfect craft for touring around this, one of the most beautiful coastlines in Britain.

    He felt that the omens for business were good. Most unusually, he had a choice of three bookings for this first day. Two of them had been for full boatloads of ten, one out of his home port, Crinan, the other out of Ardune, just up the coast - but he had chosen the third. It was for four young men. They had wanted the boat to themselves for the whole day and were prepared to pay the full amount of a boatload of ten. This third choice seemed the obvious one to pick, same money, less trouble, no over-boisterous young, and no elderly to complain about the roughness of the seas or the ride.

    The booking had been made for them by Hamish Munro, owner of the Galley of Lorne Inn. Most of the hotels and B&Bs and some of the caravan parks along the coast had leaflets extolling the delights of trips aboard the Calistra. McKinnon took bookings from the owners or managers of these outlets in return for a small commission. But, rather than the commission, it was his reputation for giving everyone a great day out that kept up a steady flow of business coming his way. Of all of his business providers, Hamish and his Galley of Lorne Inn was his preferred source.

At the last minute, only an hour before McKinnon was due to pick up the four, the time of departure was put back by a couple of hours to eleven o'clock - something about a fifth gentleman, maybe joining the four but delayed in getting back from Oban.

Despite the tiresome change of plan, McKinnon made sure he left Crinan to be at the Galley of Lorne in good time. Young locals helped him to cast Calistra off from the quay and he motored north across Loch Crinan and up Loch Craignish, arriving at the Galley of Lorne's private jetty just before eleven - the amended time. A young lad who had been fishing off the end of it jumped to his feet and helped to tie Calistra up alongside. McKinnon thanked the lad and then climbed out of boat and stood on the jetty next to her bows, his battered white-topped captain's hat tucked under his arm.

There he waited for his four customers. They were late. After McKinnon had been standing there for some twenty minutes, and was just about to go back aboard Calistra to get his mobile telephone and try ringing Munro – a kind of lucky dip activity, mobile phones, even here on the mainland. He had the mobile in his hand when he spotted the four leaving the Inn up the hill above him. He put the mobile away and waited until they appeared round the corner of the path leading down to the jetty. As soon as they reappeared, he immediately guessed that they were of the military – all of them tall, straight-backed, in step, one behind another. He guessed that they were either still serving or just ex'; perhaps they were on well-deserved leave form the hell of Afghanistan or Iraq. When they got to the jetty, the leader introduced himself as Greg Flaxman and, waving his hand to indicate the other three behind him, he mumbled their names as though they were of little account. This and the lack of an apology for their lateness irked McKinnon. Used to years of assessing his customers, he decided that this was not a nice man, nor a leader to have to follow either.

They had also brought with them an old-fashioned wicker picnic basket which, as soon as they were aboard, Flaxman put down carefully in the stern of the boat. They then stood near the basket as McKinnon did his usual introduction to the boat and told them a few things on safety at sea.

'You're welcome to use the wee cabin below decks – you'll find it up front in the bows if you feel at all queasy, you might want to lie down there on one of the bunks,' he said, 'though I recommend staying out in the fresh air if you've not found your sea legs yet. There's a toilet, known as the heads here on board, it's just aft of the cabin and opposite it there's a wee galley for making tea or a meal if you wish. If it's a snack you're after there are biscuits an' things in the cupboards, just help yourselves. Steps from down there lead up into the main cabin in front of us here and if it gets rough or it turns to rain that's the spot for you. But I find that most of my guests like it best out here in the open of the stern, plenty of seating as you can see and good for all round views.'

'When we get out into the open sea, especially near the Gulf, I'll need to use the microphone and address system on account of the noise of the waves and the engine, but I'll tell you more about that later when we get out there. Any questions at all?'

None of them spoke. McKinnon sensed that this might be a difficult day, but he smiled at the end of his little speech – perhaps they all had weightier matters on their minds.

He started up the engine and, helped by the same young boy, cast off and headed Calistra south, back down Loch Craignish. At the end of the loch they turned right, to the west. The two younger members of the foursome sat on the seats in the stern, Flaxman and the equally large man who seemed to shadow him everywhere, both came up and stood next to McKinnon who had now settled up onto his skipper's high white leather swivel chair behind the wheel.

'How long to get out to Craithe?' asked Flaxman,

'On a calm day like this, about an hour an' a half' he replied, 'depending, of course how much time any of you wish to spend looking round and photographing the famous Corryvreckan,'

'What's that exactly, the Corryvreckan? Someone was talking about it in the bar last night but I wasn't really listening,' said Flaxman,

'Third largest whirlpool system in the world,' replied McKinnon, 'quite safe on a day like today and the present state of the tides. But when the seas are rough, it can become impassable to almost any craft, except maybe the lifeboats. Today, because of the tides and the afternoon weather forecast, we'll need to be coming back through the gulf by four o'clock, will you remember that?' he said

'Four o'clock, yes I'll remember that,' said Flaxman. Then, on hearing for the first time that this whirlpool system might affect the timing of their return he added, 'so why the whirlpools, what causes them?' There was sharp irritation in his voice.

'The waves an' the swell come a-rolling some two an' a half thousand miles across the Atlantic; as often as not they're driven on by the westerly winds, an' the first thing that they hit on arriving here are the three or four hundred foot underwater cliffs of Scarba. That island up ahead there, to the right.' He pointed it out to Flaxman. 'Anyway, as I was saying, the waves smash into the underwater cliffs and with a ragged sea floor and a great underwater stack of rock, the seas are thrown up all o'er the place - causes the waters to turn an' turn about themselves - you'll see what I mean quite soon.'

By now, the seas were already tumbling over themselves on the surface, as he had described,

'And you say this becomes impassable?' asked Flaxman peering ahead,

'Oh aye, the waves can get up to ten, fifteen feet or more, too much for this poor wee boat,' replied Mckinnon.

'Not today, I hope,' said Flaxman, looking even more intently at the churning waters,

'Not unless the weather turns more than expected. They say there are to be a squall or two later on, but here on the west coast that can happen at any time, especially this time o' year. I always keep an eye on the weather, though,' he added, 'only once in all the years I was not able to get my customers back home on time.'

Flaxman fell silent, not sure if this meant he need not worry about getting back today or not.

As they got nearer to the narrow point of the gulf, McKinnon pointed out to them some of currents in the waters coming in against them from the Atlantic Ocean. Flaxman could see the bubbles and spent spray on the surface of the sea flowing past them like a rivulets in a fast stream. Already there was a roar from the sea ahead of them and McKinnon leant forward and switched on the small speaker system. About half way through the gulf they came towards the Corryvreckan itself. McKinnon, spoke to them through a microphone.

'If you'll look on ahead, on the starboard side of the boat - that's on the right - you'll see the whirlpool of the Corryvreckan,' he said. The speakers were loud but not offensively so - just enough to be heard over the roar of the cascading waves some of these now higher than Calistra's decks. The four guests each raised their binoculars and looked out of the right-hand side of the boat at the larger, white-topped waves coming into view. As they drew closer they marvelled at the huge bowl-like depression of rotating waves of the whirlpool itself. The bowl must have been many times the size of Calistra, maybe a hundred yards across.

'Nice to see her so peaceful,' said McKinnon over the speakers.

The four of them looked on in silence as they passed on by. None of them could have imagined the speed of the currents sweeping past nor the occasional six-foot standing waves. This show of the power in nature was accompanied by a roaring sound that was like a combination of huge ocean rollers crashing onto a beach and some mighty waterfall.

Even past the Corryvreckan itself, the constantly breaking waves caused the Calistra to wallow and yaw in her progress. Flaxman's two companions looked as though their arrival at the small town of Stanleytoun on Craithe could not come soon enough, both of them pale and clearly not enjoying the boat's lurching progress.

As they drew closer to the island, McKinnon could tell that none of them had seen before anything quite like the castle. They all looked up at it and two of them scanned its massive walls, towers and French-style blue-grey slate rooves with their binoculars. Its position and size meant that it dominated everything around it and it seemed to echo the grandeur the craggy mountain peaks behind it. Beneath it, the little town of Stanleytoun was a tourist's dream of charm, with its walled-in harbour, steeple church and neat, granite-built waterside houses.

As they were still some minutes or so out from the harbour walls, McKinnon, following his usual routine, gave them his standard brief history of the town and the Castle. This little discourse always got favourable comments from his customers - though he was not be expecting much response from these four. Out of habit, he gave it anyway.

'You'll see a lot of the look of a French Chateau in the look of the castle,' he said, 'the wife of John Stanley, seventh Earl of Derby was French. That was about 370 years ago in the 1640s. She spent some time here when Oliver Cromwell was rampaging about the countryside down south. His daughter Louisa Stanley married the young MacCrammond, son of the Laird of Craithe of the time. The Stanleys were amongst the richest families in England in those days, hence the magnificence of the castle here compared to some other castles in Scotland. In addition to the fortifications against the Clan Wars in these parts, the Stanleys also strengthened them to keep Cromwell out when he extended his military campaigns to Scotland in 1650. In fact Cromwell's main field commander, General Monck, had a go at taking over the castle but failed. It's never been breached by anyone,' he concluded with almost proprietary pride in his voice.

Shortly after McKinnon had finished his short tale, Calistra passed through the narrow entrance to the harbour and as they glided slowly to the quay side where there were many willing hands to help tie her up. Charming as the views of the town might be, all four of them were off the boat and onto dry land as soon as she was tied up, and whether psychological or not, the colour returned to their faces.

'We've no plans' said Flaxman to McKinnon as he climbed ashore behind the other three. This, as McKinnon would later discover, was a lie, but what he said next did have some truth to it. 'We're meeting an acquaintance here in Stanleytoun,' he said, 'and after that we'll decide whether to go over the castle or motor on out to see some of the other islands'. Flaxman then bent down, picked up the wicker picnic basket and took with him. With an Hotel, a pub, restaurants and cafes in plain sight, taking a picnic basket with them struck McKinnon as odd, though not odd enough to comment upon at the time.

'Fair enough, Mr Flaxman,' he said, 'I'll no be going anywhere except maybe to get a bite to eat, so you'll find myself and Calistra here whenever it suits you.' Then he added, raising a hand and pointing a finger to the sky,

'Just remember we'll need to be leaving here around three thirty so as to be going back through the Corryvreckan by four and get you home today'.

'Understood,' replied Flaxman as he left to catch up with the other three.

After they had gone, McKinnon clambered out onto the quay and walked over towards a lifeboat; it was the Laird's, the Louisa. She was tied up near Brown's Repair Shops at the far end of the quay from Calistra. He had known the captain of the lifeboat, Sandy Grieg, all his life. But it had only been these last couple of years that he had seen more of him - ever since the Laird had bought the Louisa and Grieg had become her skipper. Grieg had been up to the RNLI station in Oban on a number of occasions to learn the many facets of the ex-Arun Class boat. He had learned well - especially on the back-up call out with his brother and some others during the great storm of 2013 when he saved a couple of lives. More than once too he had justified the Laird's purchase of her when he had got through the Corryvreckan in atrocious weather when no other vessel could have done so.

'Hi there, Sandy,' said McKinnon as he reached the Louisa. Grieg climbed down off the lifeboat, came across the quay and both shook hands warmly.

'Repairs won't come cheap on her, I'll suppose,' said McKinnon, inquisitive about one of the most expensive boats on the coast.

'Oh, nothing serious,' said Grieg, 'she'll be back in service tonight or tomorrow morning. Have you time the now for a wee dram?' he asked,

'Certainly have, and maybe I'll have time for something to eat too.' he said.

The two of them made their way towards the corner of the quay towards a small side-street that would take them to Jimmies's Bar - the locals' favourite. Just before they turned down the side street, McKinnon looked back again at the five of them, his four and the acquaintance Flaxman had said they were meeting and then followed Grieg on to Jimmies's.

As arranged, Geordie was wearing a bright yellow shirt and Flaxman and the other three had met up with him outside the Derby Arms and formally introduced each other, Geordie shaking hands with each in turn.

'I've some useful news for you,' said Geordie – addressing his remarks mainly to Flaxman. 'Ranald MacCrammond and his wife are going out mackerel fishing about two o'clock – a perfect time I would suggest, Mr Flaxman, for your wee surprise for your old friend, and I can take the other two round the Castle while you do that. How's that sound?'

Flaxman looked pleased, leant over and clapped Geordie on the back,

'Excellent plan, Geordie' he said, and then, looking down at his watch, added, 'That gives us just time for a quick lunch, do the Derby Arms do sandwiches?'

'They do,' replied Geordie, 'follow me,' and led the way into the main Bar, followed by the four.

21

Saturday, after lunch

Craithe Castle,

After their lunch with all the family, Ranald and Tatty duly set off for their boat trip to explore some of the island's coastline, with Ranald overheard by the others still trying to persuade Tatiana that she would enjoy trying the mackerel fishing as well.

On reaching the boathouse the two of them found the clinker-built dingy waiting tied up by the water gates. Earlier in the morning, Geordie had also put out the basket with the mackerel lines ready, together with nets and a bucket of water, to keep fish fresh in if they wanted to bring any of their catch back to the castle. Ranald checked the outboard and found that Geordie had failed to top up the outboard engine's fuel tank. There was a can of fuel nearby, however, so he stowed that aboard the dingy along with all the fishing gear and some waterproof clothing in case of April showers.

He helped Tatiana aboard and pushed the boat off, nimbly jumping aboard as they drifted out into the channel in front of the boathouse gates. After several energetic pulls on the outboard's starter rope, the aged engine eventually coughed into life.

With his very substantial income as Managing Director of the Towneley Vassilov Merchant Bank, Ranald could have afforded to do many things around the castle - like updating this old boat or buying a new engine for it. But whilst his father was still the Laird, he would not interfere with anything - besides there was a charm to using old, familiar things like these, many of them with memories attached to them. Tatiana had watched his efforts to start the engine and tried to imagine him doing the same thing as a little boy or even as a young man and she loved seeing him in his boyhood surroundings.

They motored a short way out from the boathouse and then turned right, to the west, parallel to the shore. Tatiana looked up to the castle above them but soon could only see the top of the South West Tower and, although somewhat fearful of small boats, she put her trust in Ranald. It had been some twenty minutes after the view of the Tower had disappeared that, without warning, the stiff breeze that had been with them since they had got out from the shore, suddenly stiffened and soon it began to rain. It started as a gentle April shower, light and warm, but soon it began to pour and the temperature dropped dramatically.

Ranald, well organised from years of experience, quickly pulled a couple of large capes from his rucksack and these they hurriedly put on. Next, from under the stern seat, he pulled out a large thin sheet of tarpaulin. He got Tatiana to rise from her seat and, after spreading the tarpaulin along the bench, they both sat back down on it and he pulled the rest of it up over their backs and then their heads. Their last defence against the sudden squall came in the form of a large gaudy golfing umbrella which he raised above them, slanted back at a sharp angle into the oncoming storm. With the anchor now holding firm and the engine switched off, the boat naturally swung slowly so that the bow of the boat behind them faced into the strengthening wind from the west.

So used to doing this kind of thing since childhood, Ranald had managed to get the weatherproofing up before they had really got wet. Now, huddled together cosily under the tarpaulin and with their backs to the strengthening wind and rain, they just needed to ride out the spring shower. Tatiana giggling a little from time to time at the novelty of the experience.

As often at this time of year, the squalls dissipated within a half hour, and in this space of time, the weather had changed back from a torrential downpour to being dry again with bright sunshine and with some warmth returning. They were left, however, with choppy water and the boat rocked quite sharply at anchor. They laughed with relief as the last clouds ran on past them heading east through the Corryvreckan and on towards the mainland.

It was then that Ranald found that not only had Geordie not topped up the outboard fuel tank, but that the spare can of fuel which he had left for them to be take out with the boat, was filled with diesel instead of a petrol mix that it ran on.

'Goddamit,' he said, 'looks as though I'm going to have to row us back unless there's someone up on the South West Tower to see us.'

'Can't you ring on your mobile phone,' suggested Tatiana

'That would be great wouldn't it,' he replied,' but unfortunately there's no signal unless one's practically sitting under a mobile phone mast on the mainland - too few people for them to bother with more phone masts out on the smaller islands and the terrain's too mountainous anyway. Some people go to the lengths of buying themselves radios to get round this problem but, other than this very moment, I've never found the need.'

They were well round the corner of the mountain beyond the castle and therefore out of sight of it, so Ranald got the rowlocks and oars up from the bottom of the boat and began to set them up. As he was in the midst of this process, to their relief, a small tourist cruising boat came round the point of the island and into view. Ranald stood up carefully so as not to rock the boat and waved energetically, shouting as he did so. They were soon spotted and the cruiser turned towards them and cut its engines as it approached. As it got nearer Ranald could at last read its name, the Calistra.

'Aha, that's good,' he said looking down at Tatiana, 'it's Neil McKinnon and some of his customers'. Having got quite close to experiencing mackerel fishing without actually doing any, and having by now had enough of the vagaries of the west coast weather, she was quite ready for something a bit more comfortable. She turned round, somewhat awkwardly, and peered at the approaching boat. She was glad to see that it had a covered cabin in which to warm up.

The Calistra came on towards them and as they were about to touch together, Ranald lifted up an oar for the large fair haired tourist to grab a hold of and pull the dingy alongside.

'Could you perhaps give us a tow back into Stanleytoun?' he asked, 'we'd be happy to carry on wherever you're going so long as we get back there at some point,'

'Sure, no problem,' said the tall man, 'come aboard and hand me the bow line,'

Ranald helped Tatiana get up into the Calistra's wide stern area, fetched the bow line and holding it firmly, climbed up after her. That was the last thing he knew for a good ten minutes, for the moment he was aboard, to Tatiana's mind-shocking horror, the tall fair-haired tourist whacked the back of Ranald's head with the butt of an automatic pistol and he crumpled to deck, to immediate appearances, lifeless.

She let out a wild scream and leapt forward and down onto him, picking up his head and cradling it in her arms. Bookie stepped forward and gently but firmly prised her away from her husband's motionless body, passing her to McKinnon. She was now sobbing, out of control and while McKinnon held her, Flaxman and Bookie man-handled MacCrammond's body down the short stairs and into the small for'ard cabin. There they threw him onto one of the bunks and returned to the wheelhouse. Shielding Tatiana from the other two, McKinnon obeyed Flaxman's gestured order and guided her down the steps and into the cabin. She sat, perched on the narrow bunk-seat, beside her husband, now sobbing quietly. McKinnon tried to comfort her by placing a hand on her shoulder and he then bent down and whispered close to her ear,

'Don't worry, Missus, we'll get you both out of this safely somehow, and at least he didn't bother to tie either of you up. You'll find pain killers in one of the cupboards in the Galley. You'll need to get them yourself later as I must get right back up on deck before they become suspicious.' He touched her gently on the shoulder, turned and hurried back past the galley and up into the wheelhouse.

'I don't want you talking to them again, do you hear?' said Flaxman and McKinnon nodded, and turned towards his white swivel seat.

'From now on, only Bookie here talks to them, is that understood?'

Again McKinnon nodded his head but this time added a barely audible 'Aye, I hear ye,'

'Right,' cried Flaxman, shouting this time, 'back to the mainland as fast as this tub will take us,'

'Aye, aye,' muttered McKinnon and he started up the motor, gently steered Calistra away from the abandoned dingy and pushing the throttles to full ahead, put her into a wide arc back east towards the Corryvreckan and the mainland.

'And keep well wide of the town as we pass, I don't want anyone to be able to see the name of the boat as we pass, is that understood?' shouted Flaxman over the noise of the engines, straining at full power. This time McKinnon simply nodded that he had got this message.

* * * * *

The lunch with Geordie at the Derby Arms Hotel was timed to fit in with Geordie's estimate of when Ranald and Tatiana would have left the boathouse and got out of sight of the castle. At this time, still convinced of Flaxman's story that he wanted to surprise his old friend Ranald, he had purposely not topped up the fuel when he had prepared the dingy for the mackerel fishing expedition. He reckoned that Ranald and Tatiana would run out of fuel after a couple of miles, making it easy for his friend Flaxman to catch up in Calistra and come to his rescue – what better surprise could there be?

He, Zaytsev and Tulloch saw Flaxman and Bookie off in Calistra, left the quay and walked back to the Derby Arms. Here they tacked themselves on behind a group of tourists who, judging from their eager chatter were bound for the castle. The group, with the three of them close behind, wound their way up the steep road till they reached the castles main gates. The road swung on to the right, past the gates, leading on round the island. The group halted and gathered together into a huddle to sort out their entrance fees between them. Geordie took his two and led them towards the small trestle table which had been set up under the massive arch of the ancient gateway. Here, where tickets were to be sold for entrance to the castle or for the gardens and grounds, Geordie quickly got out his wallet and bought tickets for his two 'guests', Zaytsev and Tulloch.

'Best to have tickets in case you're asked for them,' he said, 'I'll explain this to Ranald later on and he'll give me my money back'. The other two smiled. After what they had in mind, they rather doubted that.

Over lunch, the unsuspecting Geordie had boasted about the high-powered team of scientists who worked on something secret up in the south-east tower - so secret, indeed that the only access to the tower was now from the first floor gallery. Initially, Zaytsev allowed Geordie to take them where he wished and, eventually, he took them up to the gallery at the top of the wide, sweeping main staircase. It was at this point that Zaytsev suddenly produced his Yaragin automatic pistol from inside his bulky leather jacket and pointed it with a firm prod into Geordie's ribs.

At first Geordie thought this must be some kind of joke and let out a brief giggle. When Zaytsev prodded him a second time hard enough to almost wind him, Geordie turned pale and his face changed to an expression of one about to burst into tears.

'Take us to the south-east tower and the computer laboratory' said Zaytsev.

By now Tulloch had also produced a gun and he led on as directed by Geordie who had been told to whisper directions to him. They went along one of the corridors running off the gallery and, three quarters of the way along, entered a doorway which, in turn led to a landing with narrow stairs at the end of it.

Ahead of them they could see one of Boreyev's men guarding the entrance to the tower. As they approached, the guard recognised Geordie, smiled and held up his hand to turn him and his tourists back. Zaytsev steeped smartly forward as they neared the guard, and raised the gun he had being prodding Geordie with, pointing it directly at the guard's forehead and no more than a foot from it.

'Not a move,' he whispered in harsh, heavily accented English,

Tulloch then went round behind the guard, cuffed him with plastic ties and gagged him with a strip of cloth. He then smashed him with a vicious blow to the back of his head. The guard crumpled to the ground and Geordie let out another whimper of misery. They dragged the guard to the side of the corridor and prodding Geordie again, all three went through the door and began to mount the tower stairs. They climbed for three floors, till they reached the top and a by now tearful, Geordie pointed to a door and they gathered close together outside it.

On a nod from Zaytsev they burst into the Lab. The whole team were there, and looked back at the intruding three with a mixture of puzzlement and shock. They continued to watch, somehow transfixed, as Tulloch quietly shut the door behind him. Geordie was then roughly pushed over to join the other and in fluent English, Zaytsev began his instructions.

'As they always say in the films,' he said, looking round the Craithe team, 'don't give any trouble and no one will get hurt.' He looked at each of them, one by one, a cold stare of one who cares only for his own wishes.

'Who is head man, here?' he asked, looking straight at the Professor.

The team's defence strategy for a break-in such as this had been practiced even though it was deemed to be an almost impossible eventuality, any intruder was to be allowed to download what he or she thought was the Athena software. With all its valuable equipment and the possibility of knocking out a machine with even more valuable software on it, intruders were not to be challenged here in the Lab.

The fake software that each member of the team had been trained to download in circumstances such as these, also contained the Craithe standard self- defence package. This would ensure that when it was taken away and plugged into any other machine it would immediately attack and render that machine useless. Thus, in the same damage limitation strategy, and especially to avoid injury to any team member, attackers were to be allowed to leave the Lab either with the laptop holding Athena on it or a memory stick.

The Professor stepped slowly forward, bowed his head once in a kind of token surrender, 'I'm the senior person here,' he said, 'I presume you want a copies of the software suite we call Athena?'

'We do, but not just copies, we want you to destroy the original and all other copies, leaving us with the only copy.' said Tulloch.

'Under the circumstances, I'd be happy to comply,' said the Professor, 'but one master copy is in a bank vault in London, and some bits of different functions of our work are spread around several of these machines,' and he gave a sweep of his arm, indicating a whole array of laptops, desktops and a large mainframe.

'But we do have a concentrated copy of everything we've invented, on this laptop here,' he said picking up a small, neat machine as though ready to hand it over,'

'You think me a fool, do you?' said Zaytsev. 'I take Athena away on a laptop and no sooner am I safe distance away and you connect and wipe the hard drive of everything – or worse you lock me out of it somehow. No, I have memory stick. I take Athena on that.'

'I'm afraid Athena and other programmes that go with it some thirty Gigabytes – a lot of software – so do you have an external drive of that capacity, one with a usb connection?' said the Professor.

'I do,' said Zaytsev and handed the professor a neat external drive with a short usb lead on it. 'There's ample space on that so just get downloading Athena onto it - and be warned I'll be testing it when you've finished, so tricks, understood?'

The professor moved to the laptop he had indicated a moment before, plugged in the external drive Tulloch had passed to him, and began the download. What he was actually downloading was, a technical masterpiece of deceit – designed specifically for an eventuality such as this. On the laptops screen, a download box showed hundreds of differently named files from the Athena suite being transferred to Tulloch's external drive. In reality, what was being transferred was a huge amount of indecipherable rubbish, with just hundreds of file *names* but no actual file content. The total size of the files being downloaded also showed, falsely, to be rapidly mounting – not unlike the milometer on a motor car. Zaytsev had stepped forward and was now watching this download monitor closely, the mounting number of files the sheer volume of data, all clicking up at relentless speed. After a minute or so of this close scrutiny, he looked back at Tulloch and nodded confidently - he even let him see a glimpse of a smile.

When, after a suitably lengthy span of time to give the impression of such a large amount of software had been transferred to the external drive, the download monitor indicated that the job was complete, Zaytsev stepped forward to the laptop, pressed some keys for his hard drive to be ejected from it. He then immediately took the hard drive over to a different laptop nearby, plugged it in and keyed in for an internet connection. As soon as he had the connection, he typed in a website address and instantly on the fast fibre optic line, a website in Russian Cyrillic writing appeared on the screen.

'Just checking you have not just given me rubbish,' he said turning to look at the professor. On the Russian website there was a lot of flickering and the Professor knew that it would be trying to read and verify what had been downloaded onto the stick. Whether or not the team's false download would be spotted, would depend how good this website's electronic scrutiny programme was.

He watched, his breath shallow and faster than usual. The small red light on the website flickered away as it continued to read what was on the hard drive. It soon became clear to the Professor that their elaborate deceit was working and the Russian interrogation programme had been fooled into thinking that the rubbish-filled files contained the real Athena programme. In due course, a box popped up on the screen indicating that the process was complete and the data downloaded onto Zaytsev's memory stick appeared genuine.

The professor was relieved and wondered why an organisation such as the SVR did not have technology sophisticated enough to have detected their false programming. What he did not know was that, in Moscow, Komarov's waiting computer operative was so childlike in his excitement and eagerness at getting the long-awaited Athena software, that he had merely used his own laptop in the office to analyse the contents of the Zaytsev hard drive. The analytical programme he used was comparatively low-tech and had been unable to detect the deceit. The Professor had guessed right, had some proper SVR analytical software been used, it might well have brought up very different answer, a very uncomfortable one for the Craithe team.

'Well gentlemen,' said Zaytsev taking the external drive out of the laptop, 'the download checked out all right with my boss's website checking system. So it would appear that we have got what we came for. You say this is the only full version of Athena here in this lab and that there is only one other in a bank somewhere?''

'Yes, that's correct,' said the Professor. He was betting that, in the middle of a robbery, these two would hardly take the time to check the other machines.

Having satisfied himself that he had the real Athena, Zaytsev began to fire his automatic pistol at the laptop he had just taken Athena from, but distracted in this activity, the Professor stepped quickly forward, pressed an alarm button under the table and moved swiftly to put himself between Zaytsev and the other computers and laptops. Immediately an alarm siren went off and a red light began to flash in the ceiling and over the Lab doorway.

The shock of this had an instant effect on Zaytsev. He stopped shooting up the laptop, and looked, horrified over to Tulloch. He then gestured with the gun for the Professor to join the others,

'The key to this room, now,' he shouted and held out his hand towards the Professor, who fetched the key out of his pocket and handed it over.

With that, Zayrzev and Tulloch backed out of the room and the team could hear them the door immediately after that.

* * * * *

Down in the restaurant, three of Boreyev's men were alerted as soon as the little red light in the ceiling came on. With the general opinion that their presence here on the island was largely one of reassurance, they had been treating their job in a more relaxed manner than if they had been on duty in some trouble-spot. They had been having a late lunch and intent on their food, had heard nothing in the corridor outside earlier on – when Zaytsev, Tulloch and Geordie had slipped past on their way to the Lab.

Now they rose quickly, ran to the door peered left and right along the corridor and ran out and down till they reached a storeroom door they had left ajar earlier. The storeroom had no windows and was dark as a tomb. Both quickly entered, took out special dart-firing pistols from leg pouches, closed the door but for a slither of light from the corridor and waited. Within a minute Zaytsev and Tulloch appeared through the doorway along the corridor and walking briskly towards the storeroom, looking forward and back alternately, guns held low but ready for use.

As soon as the two of them had passed, the Boreyev's men silently swung the storeroom door open, stepped out into the corridor and fired their silenced dart-pistols at the backs of the necks of Zaytsev and Tulloch. Two tiny darts struck almost simultaneously and within no more than a second both of the thieves had dropped unconscious to the landing floor. Boreyev's men rushed forward and cuffed them both where they lay.

The two of them were dragged back along the landing, into the restaurant and then quickly tied to chairs. One of Boreyev's men ran upstairs and told the Professor that the two thieves had been captured. As they knew that Ranald was out in the boat with Tatiana, the Laird was also quickly informed what had happened and he too came to the restaurant. Boreyev himself arrived and soon as all had gathered before the two thieves, he administered an injection to each of them. Slowly both came back into consciousness as the dart antidote took effect. Their first shock was to find themselves confronted by Boreyev who immediately began questioning Zaytsev in Russian, his harsh put-on voice close to Zaytsev's ear.

'Your mission is over and it has failed,' he said, 'would you like me to tell you what happens to people who perpetrate this kind of commercial espionage in Russia?'

'Won't do you any good threatening me,' said Zaytsev in a relaxed manner, leaning back in his tilted chair, and with an arrogant smirk on his face, 'you'll have to release us soon – you'll find out why quite soon.'

Boreyev did not move his head at all, giving no sense of a reaction to this completely unexpected remark but, out of Zaytsev's line of sight, his eyes swung up to meet those of the Laird who, standing behind Zaytsev, showed his utter shock at this news. Continuing as though nothing had happened, Boreyev put his face even nearer Zaytsev's

'Bluffing will get you nowhere,' he said but he was immediately interrupted by Zaytsev. 'No bluff. Why don't you ask your man Geordie what he told my colleagues at lunchtime?'

'Your colleagues?' repeated Boreyev, glancing back up to the Laird. The other just shrugged his shoulders, not understanding either.

Boreyev quickly turned to one of his men. 'Quick as you can go up to the Lab ask them which is Geordie and bring him back down here as fast as you can – Go.'

His man ran out of the room and, after what seemed ages, returned with the quivering Geordie. Without further ado, he was positioned so that he could not see the arrogant Zaytsev's face and would therefore be less intimidated by him.

'What did you tell these people at lunchtime, Geordie?' asked Boreyev,

'All I did was tell Mr Ranald's friend, Mr Flaxman, that he and Mrs MacCrammond were going mackerel fishing…' his voice tailed off as he realised just now how he had been deceived by Flaxman's tale of being Ranald's old university friend. 'Oh God, what have I done?' he wailed,

'Start at the beginning, but as quickly as you can,' said the Laird,

Geordie, stuttered and mumbled his way through the sorry tale; the call from his cousin Hamish, these old friends of Mr Ranald's wanting to give him a nice surprise not having seen them since University – right up to his fixing of the can of fuel so that the Calistra could catch up with their marooned little boat.'

'The Laird and Boreyev exchanged looks and the Laird came over to Boreyev, exchanged a couple of words which no one else could hear.

'The rest of you stay here and keep guard on the two prisoners,' said the Laird out loud and he and Boreyev hurried out of the room. From the restaurant, they took the stairs at the end of a short corridor, climbed to the top of the stairs and opened the door which gave access to the roof of the tower. Unlocking it, they then came out onto the flat, lead-covered roof at the far end of which stood what looked like a small shed, and they hurried over to it.

The Laird undid a heavy duty clasp on the corner of the shed and then showed Boreyev that its south and east walls folded back on themselves, concertina-style, to expose a large object covered with a tarpaulin sheet tied with thin rope at its base. On undoing the rope and pulling off the tarpaulin, a large mounted telescope was revealed, similar but superior to the coin-operated ones sometimes found at notable tourist viewpoints.

The Laird quickly adjusted the eyepiece and swivelled it round to look back east.   'Yes, there we are,' he said and then beckoned Boreyev to have a look for himself.

Almost filling the whole field of view, there was a small touring motor-boat and such was the powerful magnification of the telescope that the boat's name, Calistra, could easily be read with three figures also easily discernible in the wheelhouse.

'That's the boat Geordie spoke of,' said the Laird, 'we need to get back down and see if we can trick the Russian into telling us more,' Both had another look and the Laird also focussed the view on the Corryvreckan beyond it.

After several sharp April squalls and some strong winds accompanying them, the seas around the whirlpool itself where a mass of white-topped waves, and even at this distance he could see that some of the standing waves were larger than Calistra herself. Knowing that his Louisa would not be repaired till late tonight, he quickly came to a decision on what to do now. He turned to Boreyev,

'What you don't know is that not long ago there was a kidnap and ransom incident on the west coast and the way it was mishandled by the police and their hostage negotiators resulted in the death of the young person kidnapped. I am not going to risk that with my son and our lovely Tatiana. So here's what we're going to do. First I'll ring the Oban police and tell them about the threatened theft of the Athena software. I shall tell them that I'm happy to keep the prisoners who tried to do this here until the weekend is over – and as an ex-magistrate, they'll probably be happy with that.'

Boreyev nodded agreement,

'But I'm not going to mention the kidnapping – we'll handle that ourselves. This will mean that we have to kind of lie to the police – a lie of omission. It means that you'll have to back me up when I say that we discovered the kidnapping much later – are you happy with that,'

'Of course I am,' replied Boreyev, 'but how we can fix this if Ranald and Tatiana are prisoners on that boat?'

'There's no way the Calistra will get through the Corryvreckan tonight,' said the Laird, 'and tomorrow at first light we'll have the Louisa back in operation,'

'You have an idea how that will be possible to use her in a rescue?'

'No I don't,' replied the Laird, 'but then I'm an amateur. Sandy the skipper of the Louisa is a professional and also knows Neil McKinnon the captain of the Calistra. I have absolutely no hesitation in saying that McKinnon is on our side and will know instinctively what to do with Sandy when we can somehow get the two boats into close proximity in the morning.'

'Whatever can be done, my men will do their utmost,' said Boreyev, 'they will be happy to help your skipper Sandy in any way he asks. All my men know and love Tatiana and they know what a special friend Ranald is to me, they'll do whatever is needed to get them back safely,'

'Good, let us go and see what other information we can get from our prisoners,' said the Laird, 'maybe the one who likes to brag, the Russian, maybe he can be goaded into telling us more about the men on board Calistra. Tell you what to do. Tell him that when the Corryvreckan becomes impassable to small craft, coastguard and police launches go out and patrol the area so there's no repeat of the loss of life like last year. Tell him the Calistra's been pulled in by the police – see what effect that has on him. Then I'll take over, all right?'

'Sounds good to me,' replied Boreyev.

22

Saturday evening

The Corryvreckan

On board Calistra, things were getting very uncomfortable. McKinnon had already reminded Flaxman that this was because it was now getting towards five o'clock and he had insisted this morning that they needed to pass back through the Corryvreckan by four. Flaxman could now see for himself the reason for this insistence. In addition to the time and tide factors that affect the whirlpools, additional forces had been at work during the day. There had been a number of spring squalls, one of them particularly strong and these had swept on through here at maybe fifty miles an hour, pushing the incoming tide ever faster into Scarba's underwater cliffs and stirring up the cauldron of waters and waves all the more.

Driven by his overriding need to get his two prisoners back to the mainland tonight, Flaxman had stood next to McKinnon since leaving Craithe, his unblinking gaze fixed ahead, willing Calistra on. Ahead of them, however, Flaxman could see, even from this distance of over a mile, that the waves in the Gulf were wild and white-topped. He fumed at himself and at the way things were turning out. How could he have missed factoring this weather and these seas into his otherwise careful plans? For Christ's sake, he had been told often enough about the bloody Corryvreckan, the whirlpools, the maelstrom - he could at least have given *some* credence to the accounts of its dangers, dammit. Everything else had worked so perfectly. But now, instead of it celebrating having got the young couple back to the mainland and from there just a helicopter hop back to Northern Ireland, there now looked to be a strong possibility of their being unable to get back through this bloody gulf tonight. This would throw up a whole load of additional problems. Would news of the kidnapping reach the authorities? If they postponed the trip back to mainland till the morning, would police helicopters be scouring the area by then? How would the Major contrive a rendezvous if the authorities were on the lookout for them? Worst of all, was getting the prisoners back to Northern Ireland now in jeopardy?

He was jolted out of these thoughts by the VHF ship-to-shore handset ringing. McKinnon quickly leant towards him and picked it off its stand on the bulkhead and leant to his right and put it onto the speaker system.

'Calistra? Come in Calistra', said the voice the other end,

'Aye, Calistra here,' replied McKinnon into the handheld,

'Oban Coastguard here, we've had telephone call from Craithe to say you'd been seen heading into the Corryvreckan - did you not hear the local forecast?'

'No, afraid not, missed the forecast,' he said, lying but aware that Flaxman's eyes were on him,

'The Corryvreckan up ahead of you will be impassable to a boat of your size,' continued the Coastguard, 'there was also an official announcement from us earlier to say that only the Oban RNLI lifeboat or the Louisa if she was also needed by the RNLI were to pass through the straits till further notice, did you no hear that? Yon afternoon squalls have turned her nasty an' you'll need to go back west immediately, do you hear?'

'Aye, I hear you' shouted McKinnon back into the handset, 'sorry about missing the forecast, I'll be turning back just now'. He glanced to his left, his face taut. Then he added in his native Gaelic tongue, 'a couple of gunmen have the Laird o'Craithe's son and daughter in law seized on board, will you tell the Laird?'

McKinnon saw that Flaxman was looking directly back at him, eyes narrowed at the talk in the Gaelic,

'What was that last bit you were saying,' shouted the huge man over the noise of the sea, and leaning right across to McKinnon.

'Coastguard's my cousin,' lied MacKinnon through the loudspeakers, 'just a bit of family banter in the Gaelic - I was just saying to him that I'd sooner be where he is than out here - an' he agreed with me. He warned me again that it's no safe up ahead'.

Flaxman's grimaced and let out a below [bellow] of anger.

'Well, to hell with the Coastguard,' he shouted across to McKinnon, 'we agreed that we'd get back to the mainland *today* - so that's what we're bloody-well going to do, right'.

'Would you no consider a quiet night, sheltering along the coast o' Jura, and making a run for the mainland first thing in the morning?' shouted McKinnon leaning over towards Flaxman, 'better that than going to a watery grave tonight, do you not think?'

Flaxman was appalled by this thought. Yet, at the same time the prospect of a police helicopter scouring the area tomorrow as they tried a second time to get back to the mainland was even more powerful. But, at that very moment these conflicting points were scrambling his brain, Calistra reared up onto a wave larger than herself and then quickly fell away again its far side into the next deep trough between the white-topped mountains of water. As she struck into the next oncoming wave there was a loud crack of a noise as though something had given way below decks. McKinnon knew this would just be something loose in the chain locker but, with the boat's lurch, Flaxman fell to one side smashing a hip into a large brass hook sticking out of the bulkhead on the side of the cabin. He let out a sharp curse of pain and pulling himself back up against the angle of the tipping deck by heaving on the handrail, he rubbed the hip feverishly with his other hand, muttering oaths and obscenities under his breath. McKinnon noticed that in that instant Flaxman had seemed to lose his air of invincibility as, for just a second, his huge bulk seemed to sag as though some invisible force had leaked from it.

Flaxman peered out to the left, then to the right and finally back, the way they had come. He shook his head, but still said nothing. But two more fairground-like lifts and plunges later, he looked back across to McKinnon and nodded his head. 'Okay back,' he mouthed and made a gesture with his hand and cocked thumb to confirm it.

McKinnon did not need to hear the words. Instantly, his slight, wiry frame, almost a midget compared to the huge kidnapper, relaxed and he spread his legs wider as he spun the wheel fast to starboard. The Calistra responded, turning about almost within her own length, rearing over a couple of waves like a horse being allowed to return to the stables, and began her way back the way she had come and away from the dangers of the Corryvreckan. Once fully turned, straight ahead were the mountains of Craithe once more.

'What now?' shouted Flaxman, and remembering the maps he had looked at the previous day added, 'any chance of getting back round the top of that island ?' he was looking to his right at the cliffs of Scarba.

'Nowhere near enough fuel for that,' shouted McKinnon, now well accustomed to his growing toll of lies. Then he added a spot of truth, almost as a consolation, 'there's shelter and a hill-walker's bothy a bit down the Jura coast at Glengarrisdale Bay. Anyone's free to stay there'.

'What the hell's a bothy?' asked Flaxman,

'Was a wee crofter's house till after the last war, now it's just used by hill-walkers - might be handy if we canny all of us sleep on Calistra tonight.' said McKinnon

'How will we know if' it's available?' asked Flaxman,

'We'll see when we get there. We'll tie up at the jetty an' have a look but my guess is it's too early in the season for anyone else to be it on the hills yet. Bearing in mind the amount of fuel we've got, the only other place we could go would be Craithe.'

Flaxman shook his head - no chance of *that*.

'Will this Glenthingamy place you're suggesting, will it be out of sight of anyone on Craithe?'

'Aye, aye, don't worry about that, no one will know where we are or find us in this weather,' he lied again, 'and tomorrow we'll get back to the Galley of Lorne, or anywhere else you want to go.' He had already worked out that, with this delay, there would be no going back to the Galley of Lorne itself - it would likely as not have the police expectantly waiting for them there.

Down in the for'ard cabin, riding the waves was like an out of control fairground ride. Ranald had recovered consciousness, Tatiana had already been through to the Galley and after rummaging around in some drawers, found some pain killers and got him to take them for his throbbing head. Feeling stronger by the minute, he took the trembling Tatiana in his arms and braced his strong legs against the bunk opposite to hold them both steadier. With the noise right up front of Calistra crashing every few seconds through successive waves, there was no way to speak and be heard - he could only hold Tatiana tight, trying to comfort her that way. He cursed himself for being so stubborn as to dismiss both his father's and Boreyev's cautions that, especially after the demonstration on Friday and the conference, that there was a chance that those looking for a much rumoured Athena-type cyber weapon would have found it and were now trying to steal it. In looking at his and Tatiana's present situation, he knew of course that if threats were made against her, he would buckle, give in to almost any demand – he would give no show of film-like, fantasy heroics.

Endeavouring to find a brighter way of looking at this dangerous mess he had got them into, he was heartened by just one thing – at least they had turned back from trying to go through the

Corryvreckan tonight. He also felt confident that the minor troubles with the Louisa's engines would be fixed by now and even he, nowhere near as experienced a seaman as Sandy Grieg, could imagine the Louisa being able to come up with some plan to rescue the two of them. Right now, what eluded him was *what plan* might achieve that. He gave Tatiana a squeeze as he hugged her against the boats still violent lurching – that plan would emerge, perhaps tomorrow.

23

Saturday evening

The Galley of Lorne Inn

As dusk began to creep in from the east, the Major stood on a small sharp rise in the ground just beyond Poltalloch. He had borrowed a powerful pair of binoculars from Hamish Munro - though he did not plan to return to the Galley of Lorne or meet him again. He had paid the bill in cash and was now just above the rendezvous point he had chosen for when the boats returned to the mainland, their missions accomplished. From this chosen vantage-point, he would be able to spot them easily as they came through the Gulf of Corryvreckan, and as soon as they were within range of the mainland's mobile phone masts, they were under instructions to try and speak to him on his mobile number. From here he would be able to direct them to the small bay, a hundred yards below where he now stood. The spot also had the advantage of having two escape routes in case anything went wrong and the police came searching for them.

He fidgeted nervously as he continued to scour the seas through the binoculars especially as he had been trying since early afternoon to reach either of the two groups on his mobile telephone. He cursed the poor communications of this area and wished they had made the time to buy radios for this purpose. It was only then that he remembered that all the shops were closed for the long weekend so that would not have been possible anyway.

Failing to get any response from anyone up here, he had been forced to ring Norbally House twice to tell them that the Helicopter was not needed yet. By now it was now coming up to six o'clock, long past the time when both parties should have been through the gulf and heading towards him.

The first pair due back should have been Zaytsev and Tulloch as their job of getting into the Lab and coming away with the Athena software was judged to be the quicker of the two jobs. They were to have come back in a boat, the Eileen Donan II, which had been hired specifically for their return journey. With no calls or sightings to date, the Major was sweating slightly, and his worry caused his face to twitch involuntarily just below his right eye. He was also unaware that he had just lifted his binoculars to look again at the Corryvreckan for the fourth time in less than one minute.

He looked at his watch once more, six-fifteen. He turned towards the car. Time to abandon the rendezvous spot for the night and go and check in at the Crinan Hotel - using yet another false name. He climbed into the Land rover and set off along the country lane and back onto the main Oban, Crinan road. On reaching Crinan he parked at the back of the Hotel car park, out of sight from the road and went in and asked for a room. Although the season had started today, he was lucky in getting a room with a view out towards Jura, Scarba and Craithe and hurried up there with an overnight bag. He postponed making some calls he dreaded by getting out his binoculars yet again and having another look at the Gulf, and he swept the area methodically to make sure that neither of the two boats were there. Finally he putting down the binoculars, he crossed the room to the mini-bar got out a couple of miniatures of whisky from it poured both of them into a tooth-mug from the bathroom. Taking a couple of large gulps, he sat on the bed, composed himself and made his first call - the one to Rollo.

'Ah, it's you Jock,' said Rollo as soon as the Major was through, 'I was wondering what the hell was going on – I expected news of the boats coming back and wondered when we got texts from you telling us you didn't want the helicopter yet. What's up?'

'I've been keeping an eye on the Gulf for the past two hours, and eventually gave up,' replied the Major, 'I've also moved out of the Galley of Lorne Inn and paid up. I've now staying at the Crinan Hotel. It was only when I got here that that I found out from them some more information on this bloody Corryvreckan. Apparently the hotel itself had been expecting a couple of guests coming back through it from Craithe and on checking with the coastguard, found that it's been closed to small boats till the morning. They also told me that this happens occasionally, so I'm not worrying about our two boatloads.'

'But what if the theft of the software or the kidnapping are reported to the police?' said Rollo, 'won't they come looking for you?'

'My guess is that won't happen over the Easter weekend,' replied the Major, 'anyway we don't know yet if anything's gone wrong – for all we know both might have gone off fine and are still undetected.' He knew this was highly unlikely, even as he said it, but just now he was more intent on calming everyone until the facts became known.

'Yes, suppose you're right,' conceded Rollo, 'let's just hope you're right, we've all got a hell of a lot riding on the success of both of our missions, haven't we. Have you spoken to the Russian chap yet, 'cos he's been onto me a couple of times - said he couldn't get hold of you at the Galley of Lorne,'

'That's odd, he's got my mobile number,' replied the Major, 'still, it's not worth letting him get all worked up over what's probably just a hiccup. I'll give him a call and reassure him that everything's still all right and that there's just been a delay of half a day. And you too, stop worrying, we've both been in tighter spots than this. Firstly there's no way anyone can connect our two jobs to me or to you. The moment either boat comes through the Gulf we'll be in mobile phone connection, I direct them to my rendezvous and in the time it takes for them to get me from the middle of the gulf, your man will get up here in his helicopter – so, I'll say it again, stop panicking,'

'You're right,' said Rollo, 'just get onto the Russian will you, tell him a shortened version of what you just gave me – at any rate, keep him off our backs till we've got the MacCrammond wife or both of them back here to Norbally, will you?'

'I'll do that, and I'll also speak to my friend Max Wheeler,'

His call to Wheeler was not as easy as Rollo's. As Wheeler had given Nat Matthews his word that he could put complete reliance in him to get everything sorted by Monday night. It was an embarrassment that his plan to achieve this had faltered at the first obstacle – even more embarrassing that the failure would appear to be due to the *weather*.

'Anyway,' said Wheeler at the end of some taut verbal exchanges, 'let's hope that the delay is just down to this whirlpool system and that it's calm enough again tomorrow morning. I think that you can also count yourself lucky that, for whatever reason, the police don't appear to have got involved yet – maybe that's also down to the dreadful communications up there.'

'Come to think of it', continued Wheeler, 'with all the uncertainties you've got to deal with up there, I'll take over from you and ring the Russian chap. Nat Matthews won't be bothered about details, all he's interested in is the final outcome by Monday night. In the meantime, just get the Scottish end of things finished and the software and the MacCrammonds back to Norbally House, will you?'

The Major, dispirited by today's set-backs, meekly agreed and they rang off.

* * * * *

One of the hazards of an operation such as the attacks on Craithe is that the higher one goes in the chain of command, the more demanding the people seem to get. And so it was in this venture.

With every drop in the price of oil and with each consequent slide of the Rouble against the Dollar, the President was getting both more angry and quicker at finding people to lash out at. His latest victim for a lashing was Komarov. Having made the mistake of boasting to the President that he was about to deliver the stunning new weapon with which to bargain with the West, he now looked foolish to say the least, giving excuses within days of his crowing.

It was not surprising, therefore, that he had been on the telephone to Wheeler a number of times. It was understandable too, that when Wheeler finally did ring back, the reception he got from the Moscow end was sour – and this was not helped by the fact that Komarov was in the middle of dinner which had been delayed because he had been trying to reach Wheeler.

'So you have some news for me, at last?' said Komarov, 'Here in the Federation, such inefficiencies are dealt with in a pretty forthright manner, if you get my meaning, Mr Wheeler,'

'I get your meaning all right Mr Komarov,' replied Wheeler, 'but may I remind you that I'm talking to you from London, I'm not in bloody Moscow,'

'Mr Wheeler, each of us has far too much to lose if this does not work out, so let's try and keep this civil and continue in friendly co-operation, that's surely still in both our best interests,'

Wheeler took a deep breath, this was no more than common sense.

'Of course you're right Mr Komarov . . .'

'Igor. Please . . .'

'Indeed, Igor, my name's Max, short for Maximillian,' replied Wheeler,

'Very grand name Max, anyway, you were saying?'

'Just saying that between the island of Craithe and the mainland, the seas have just been too rough for small boats. All of this not helped by the Corryvreckan whirlpools – you could look it up on Google if you have Google in Russia,' said Wheeler

'Can you spell that for me please,' said Komarov, 'and yes we do have Google here in Moscow, we're not too bad on technology as I think you've discovered,'

Duly put down, Wheeler spelt the name out for him, and then continued,

'It's only a hiccup, I assure you, Igor,' he concluded,

'Okay, Max, but let me know the moment you have better news, all right.'

'Of course I will, Igor, the moment I have any news at all.'

They rang off and Wheeler let out a sigh of relief. At least *that* was over and he was relieved that he had no need yet to ring Nat Matthews. So, now, all he had to do was wait for Flaxman to deliver the kidnapped prisoner or prisoners to the Major at some wilderness rendezvous on the rocky coast of Scotland – something over which he had no personal control whatsoever.

God, how come I pick impossible missions such as this? He thought about it as he got up from his chair and went to put on his coat. *Forget about it all for a bit,* he continued - though he did spare a thought for the Major, alone in a Crinan hotel, perhaps biting his finger-nails down to the bone with anxiety, knowing that the police might come knocking at any time.

24

Saturday evening,

Glengarrisdale, Island of Jura

After turning back from an almost inevitable fate in the Corryvreckan, McKinnon took the Calistra west and then turned south, away from Craithe and down the coast of the Island of Jura. Soon, as dusk fell, they were out of sight of Craithe and Flaxman seemed to relax – especially as there had been no sign of police boats or helicopters. He wondered why this might be so, but soon just counted his blessings and put it from his mind. In time, they eased into the bay at Glengarrisdale and as they approached a small jetty, much in need of repair, MacKinnon brought her gently alongside and Flaxman and Tulloch got onto the jetty and helped to tie her up. The MacCrammonds were then allowed up on deck but with Flaxman keeping an eye on them seated in the stern.

McKinnon brought all his remaining stores up from the drawers and lockers, and laid them out on the table in the wheelhouse. There were some tins of thick stew-like soup for when beautiful mornings degenerate into miserable wet afternoons and cold customers get tired and hungry. There was also a goodly supply of biscuits, some small cakes, some beers and several bottles of diet Coca Cola.

After a meagre supper, Flaxman and Tulloch went ashore to stretch their legs but, not trusting McKinnon and Calistra to stay tied up at the jetty if left alone, they took it in turn for this exercise. For the night, there were the two bunks down in the for'ard cabin for the MacCrammonds and benches for McKinnon, Flaxman and Tullock to stretch out on. There were blankets enough though what was not so readily available, was sleep. Each had their own particular torment to keep them tossing and turning.

Although Ranald tried to reassure Tatiana as best he could in the noise of the for'ard cabin, he could offer no evidence that things would turn out all right the next day. So her worries for little Jerry could not just be smoothed away even though he cuddled up to her and held her tight. Eventually the regular noise of the water lapping at the hull outside began to have a soporific effect and she began to sleep lightly. Ranald had recovered from the smack to his head from Flaxman's gun, and tried to put out of his mind the fact that, had he been a bit more prudent, he would never have gone out fishing in a dingy and though he knew it was futile to speculate who might be behind this kidnapping, his mind drifted back to the question time and again. The kidnap was obviously with a view to getting something in return for their release – but what was the *'something'*? Not knowing that the authorities had failed to brief Nat Matthews about using his company for the demonstration, meant that he was still unaware of Matthews's fury over the issue. Indeed, at this time he still assumed that this was only about someone getting their hands on Athena and therefore spent several hours of fitful half-sleep going over in his mind the same unanswerable question.

Flaxman was disappointed, frustrated, angry and afraid, all at the same time. His main torment was that he should have listened more to the hints about the dangers of the Corryvreckan which, had he listened, he might have taken steps to mitigate. So now he wasted several hours going over what he *might* have done. Might he not have paid more attention and planned with the Corryvreckan firmly in mind? They could easily have set off for Craithe at nine, ignoring the Major's visit to Oban. If they had set off earlier from the Galley of Lorne, they *might have* got through the Corryvreckan if they had done so by four in the afternoon. With a bit more forethought, he *might have insisted* that McKinnon top up with fuel when they arrived in Stanleytoun – that *might have* allowed them to return to the mainland round the top of Scarba. These fruitless musings on *might-have-beens* kept him from sleeping and worsened his mood as the hours passed. By around four o'clock in the morning, however, he realised that dwelling on the past achieving nothing and he began to doze off consoling himself that he had at least accomplished the most difficult part of the mission – the kidnapping.

McKinnon, lay on the bench seat in the main cabin. He envied the young kidnapper – the one who went by the odd name of Bookie. There he was, sprawled out on a bench in the stern of the boat - off to sleep almost as soon as his head had fallen onto one of McKinnon's pillows. Seemingly the one person without a worry to keep him awake. His own mind tumbled round how to foil Flaxman's plan to reach the mainland and spirit away the MacCrammond couple. Though they had not discussed it, he guessed that Sandy Grieg would have got the Louisa repaired by now. With her stability and being capable of twice the speed of Calistra he was confident that he and Sandy would manage some kind of rescue.

As a plan for the meeting of the two boats began to crystallise in his mind, keeping an eye on Flaxman and Bookie, he began to write a note to Ranald. In the morning, on the pretence that he was ensuring that all was battened down for the passage through the Corryvreckan, he would drop the note down through the plastic hatch cover so that it landed at Ranald's feet in the for'ard cabin. This plan's details would need to be refined but, with the framework for a rescue now in mind, he, like the others, began to drift off into fitful sleep.

* * * * *

The morning was cold and grey. The five of them managed to eat some breakfast, the last of McKinnon's supplies. McKinnon was keen to delay departure as long as possible so that, after more squalls in the night the Corryvreckan would be at its wildest - the wilder the seas, the more advantage the Louisa would have.

Flaxman seemed well pleased with the thought that by midday he could have got his two captives over to Northern Ireland by helicopter and handed them over to Rollo. As soon as he deemed that breakfast was over, he insisted that the time had come to get back to the mainland. Everyone was forced to gulp down their tea or instant coffee and to finish off the few remaining biscuits. McKinnon played his *Captain of the boat role* and warned them that although they would probably get through the Corryvreckan this time, it was going to be rough. Despite Flaxman's eagerness to get going, he insisted he be allowed to take the time to check round the boat. During this process, whilst making his way round the boat, checking the tightness of a rope here, or a fastening there, he glanced back at the wheelhouse to see if he was being watched. There was no one in sight. He quickly bent down, undid the latch of the plastic hatch-cover above the for'ard cabin and dropped the note he had written last night down the hatch. He saw it land on the floor in front of one of the bunks and immediately shut the hatch cover but making sure that it was not latched and could be opened easily from below when the time came for the MacCrammonds to use it for their escape. Getting up again he, checked – no one seemed to have seen him doing all of this.

Before long, with everything battened down or stowed away, McKinnon had run out of excuses to delay their departure any longer and came back into the wheelhouse. Flaxman was there pulling some lengths of fine but strong rope which he had taken from inside his picnic basket and said that he wanted Ranald and Tatiana tied up.

'It's going to be worse than yesterday in the Corryvreckan,' said McKinnon, 'so not only must they remain untied but they must also wear life jackets.' For a moment it looked as though Flaxman was going to challenge this so McKinnon added for good measure, 'it's not as though there's anywhere for them to run to, is there?'

The idea of the two of them absconding was so preposterous that even Flaxman momentarily grinned. Bookie went up onto the jetty and cast off and soon Calistra was nudging back out into the rougher waters. Flaxman and Bookie refused to wear the somewhat cumbersome life jackets, especially as Flaxman worried about agility if Ranald tried anything, but did not seem worried when the others put on theirs. Ranald and Tatiana were then bundled down into the for'ard cabin and, just before securing the door up into the wheelhouse, McKinnon saw that Ranald had bent down and picked up his note.

As soon as Bookie had cast off the mooring lines, given Calistra a push-off from the jetty and jumped aboard, McKinnon took Calistra out into the roughening waters beyond the shelter of Glengarrisdale Bay. Motoring round the point at the end of the bay towards the Corryvreckan and the mainland beyond, they came into view to the Castle on Craithe. This no longer seemed to worry Flaxman, yet even at this early hour, up on the roof of the South East Tower, Perry had uncovered the large telescope again, having volunteered for the first shift watching out for the reappearance of Calistra.

*****

The previous evening the Laird, Boreyev and Sandy Grieg had held talks up at the castle about how to attempt a rescue. They agreed that, without communications with McKinnon, he and Sandy would just have to act on instinct to bring the boats close together. The hope was that Ranald and Tatiana would take advantage of what the Louisa was built for - plucking people out of the sea. Though this meant both of them jumping into the icy cold waves of the Gulf, it was such an obvious way to effect a rescue that they hoped it would also occur to them on board Calistra.

The Louisa's repairs were completed by late evening and Sandy made her ready for the work ahead. The most important of these was the preparation of two lengths of rope with grappling irons at their ends. These would be deployed when they made contact with the Calistra. For extra support and either to take the helm or help with the rescue, he had got his younger brother Jimmy to join the trip. Three of Boreyev's men arrived down to the boat early so that the Louisa could set off for the Corryvreckan before the Calistra would be likely to leave Glengarrisdale Bay.

It was just after six o'clock in the morning that Sandy edged the Louisa out through the harbour walls and as soon as she was at sea, he powered her up to near top speed of some twenty-five knots. The tide had recently reached its peak, as she went through the narrow straits, the welling up of the waters from the deep caused the Louisa to wallow and dip as she forced her way through the six foot waves, only slowing down for the worst tide rips near the whirlpool area itself.

Sandy had thought about the outline plan a number of times and, soon after passing through the Corryvreckan, he turned south and motored a short distance along the Jura coast. On finding a good sheltered spot, he turned her back north the way they had come and put down the anchor. The Louisa now sat under the cliffs of Jura's eastern shore just near the little harbour of Kinauchdrachd, out of sight of the Corryvreckan but now within the range of the mainland mobile phone relay masts; he even moved her a couple of times to get the very best reception. It had been agreed that he would wait here till given the message to move by the castle. With the help of the Laird directing him from the top of the south-east tower, and monitoring Calistra's progress, Sandy reckoned he would be able to pick exactly where to intercept her and aimed to confront her at the most difficult point in the gulf. The Louisa's greater stability would also allow her to dominate the meeting of the two boats and allow Louisa to scoop up the young couple almost as soon as they were in the water, and although it was not certain that those aboard Calistra would hit on this plan, as a back-up, they borrowed an electrically powered ships loudhailer from Brown's yard.

Aboard the Calistra, Ranald seen McKinnon's message and had quickly picked it up a stuffed it into his belt. As soon as Calistra was well under way he sat down and read it carefully. It was starkly simple. On hearing two blasts on Calistra's horn, he and Tatiana were to climb up through the hatch cover in the roof of the cabin, and jump overboard the same side as the Louisa. He showed the note to Tatiana,

'Remember, Douchka', he said closely into her ear, 'my father's boat is a Lifeboat - she's built precisely for what for we're going to do soon - rescue people out of the water. We'll actually be in the sea for maybe a minute or two at the most. You'll see, they'll have us out of the water and into the nice warm cabin and a hot drink before you can say boo',

Tatiana smiled back up at him, grateful for his efforts to reassure her - although, in her heart, she knew this was going to be one hell of an ordeal. Ranald had one arm around her the other helping to brace them against the boats increasingly uncomfortable ride. His feet were planted firmly against the benches opposite and, with his free hand, he held onto a hand-rail that ran around the cabin at what was now head height.

As Calistra came round the western shoreline of Jura, McKinnon kept as far out from the shore as he could to be nearer to the Castle and in the wheelhouse, Flaxman once again stood forward up next to him, watching the sea changing before them as they progressed. Coming round Jura the swell had been heavy but the waves still not much more than just choppy, but as they approached the Corryvreckan, they got noticeably steeper, the boat's progress became ever more laboured and Flaxman was forced to keep a strong grip the bar in front of him.

Progressively, as the waves got to about Calistra's size, the beginnings of the Corryvreckan came into sight. Bookie stood behind Flaxman, pale, and clutching a plastic bag MacKinnon had given him.

'I thought you said the Gulf here was going to be Okay this morning,' said Flaxman, now he was peering with a worried look on his face as the waves had increased sufficiently to be throwing water up onto the glass in front of them at regular intervals.

'Never can tell just what it's going to be like till you're actually here', shouted MacKinnon back to him, and the Calistra wallowed and crashed on from wave to wave. Suddenly, Flaxman threw up his arm and pointing ahead, shouted out, 'What the hell's that?'

McKinnon, who for a second had been checking his bearing, looked back up and, right in front of them, coming at speed straight towards them, was the Louisa. She was throwing up large bow waves and through the wind chased spray, it looked as though a collision was imminent

Just as the two boats seemed to be on the very point of impact, Sandy, from his higher vantage point in the Louisa's cabin, swung his wheel sharply to starboard - the rule of the sea being that boats approaching each other from opposite directions should pass port-side to port-side... MacKinnon, taking his timing from the Louisa, also threw his wheel also sharply to starboard. Thus, travelling in opposite directions, the two boats veered off away from each other, nudging as they grazed past each other at the combined equivalent of nearly forty knots.

As soon as they were past, Sandy spun his wheel back to port and added on full power to bow propeller. Keeling over half onto her side, at an angle of some twenty or thirty degrees, the Louisa turned back round towards Calistra. As this manoeuvre was just about complete, Sandy shut off the power to the bow propeller and the Louisa finished directly astern of the Calistra, and Sandy then nudged her forward alongside and just ten feet or so away from Calistra.

Flaxman, slow to realise what was happening, quickly plunged his hand into the deep pocket of his trousers to find his gun but, in letting go of his firm grip on the cabin railing whilst doing this, fell heavily to the side and then down with the full weight of his seventeen stones right on top of Bookie. Before either of them could get up, McKinnon again spun his wheel hard to port and this time Calistra came round, beam on, that is, sideways on to the heavy seas. The huge waves, now flecked with foam, and some ten feet from trough to crest, tossed Calistra about as though she were as insignificant as an empty cardboard box. She now lurched over the top of one wave only to fall over in a great arc of more than sixty degrees, down into the next. This constant changing of the angle of the bounding deck was just about manageable for MacKinnon, who had the ship's wheel to steady him, but it was too much for Flaxman and Bookie on the deck beside him. A few seconds later McKinnon had to shift himself out of the way as both of them were thrown right across the boat. They landed in a writhing pile of arms, legs and torsos on the cabin deck behind him. Flaxman, now desperate, pulled himself clear of Bookie just as a grappling iron came flying through the air from the direction of the Louisa. It bounced off his back and then caught the boat's side-coaming piercing it and holding firm. As the broad line went taught, it pulled the hook through the glass reinforced plastic gunwale. With a breaking strain of several tons, the line held and Calistra keeled over violently. McKinnon reached up and sounded the Calistra's horn twice. Already keyed –up and waiting for it, Ranald and Tatiana clambered up out of the cabin through the for'ard hatch. Then, just as the Calistra did another sixty degree swing down into the trough of another wave, the two of them jumped together, holding hands, over the low railings and into the froth and spume of the wild seas.

As also instructed in the note, they had jumped overboard right next to the Louisa, and though there might have been a risk of them being crushed between the two boats, now perilously close to each other, one of Boreyev's men was holding the apart with a long boat-hook. Now he quickly lowered the boathook for Ranald to grab. This he reached up for, pulling himself near the Louisa as he did so.

With the other hand he pulled on the rope between himself and Tatiana and helped her as she did two last strokes of the crawl to bring her to him. The second of Boreyev's men, bent down, grabbed her by the wrist of her outstretched arm and with one powerful lift, pulled her from the water bodily and up into his arms. The first of Boreyev's men then helped Ranald aboard and as the seas brought the two boats almost crashing into each other, Ranald and Tatiana were hurried along the narrow gangway and into the safety of the cabin.

By now, with his survival more in his mind than the fate of his two former captives, Flaxman, half-kneeling, grabbed the grappling hook and its line. He waited for a moment until the line went slack as Calistra fell over the top of another wave towards the Louisa and, with all the strength he could muster, pulled the grappling iron out of the plastic coaming and threw it overboard.

His instinct to get Calistra free of the Louisa had been sensible enough but he was unlucky in his timing. The grappling iron fell down into the sea the far side from Louisa and as her stern rose up, the line passed under the keel and the iron raked along it. The next moment, as the two boats drifted apart again, the line tightened and was pulled directly into her propellers. There was an unearthly grinding noise and then the sound of metal tearing against metal as the grappling iron, the propellers and the rudder became enmeshed with each other. MacKinnon knew that any further tightening of the rope could pull Calistra over, perhaps even onto her side and, grabbing a lifejacket from under his seat, pulled himself round the side of the cabin and, a second later, jumped overboard, vanishing into the spray.

Almost immediately, as Calistra rose up the side of the next wave the grappling iron line went taught again, pulling it clear of the water. The rope went so taught, that it vibrated like a violin string. Sandy, intent on coming alongside Ranald and Tatiana to pick them up, was too slow to shout his brother or to Boreyev's men to cut the rope attached to the grappling iron and, with Calistra already precariously balanced, she was pulled further and further over by the line until, passing the tipping point, she rolled over, capsizing.

This all happened fast - in a matter of a few seconds, but to the onlookers aboard the Louisa, it appeared to happen in slow motion. One second Calistra had been riding a wave, the next she was keel-up, her entangled propellers sticking up into the sky like a raised arm with pain wracked fingers.

One of Boreyev's men seeing the danger now to the Louisa, still tied to the other upturned boat, leapt forward and with a large hunting knife which he had drawn from a scabbard on his belt, and cut through the three quarter inch line. So taught had it been that, as soon as it was severed, it recoiled away from him like a strike of lightening. This released the Louisa's pull on the upturned Calistra and she shook violently, rolling fast from one side to the other.

Between Boreyev's men and Sandy's younger brother Jimmy, they pulled McKinnon from the water. As soon as he was aboard, he too was hurried into the forward cabin for hot drinks and a change of clothes.

Sandy, now spun the wheel and put on full power to turn Louisa round almost in her own length once again. Next, with Boreyev's men and young Jimmy either side of Louisa looking out for the other two;, he cut the power again to allow gentle bouncing, wallowing and yawing progress, back towards the upturned hull of Calistra. As they approached the stricken vessel they spotted Bookie, clutching the lifebelt that he had not had time to put on properly.

Whilst Boreyev's men were busy with McKinnon's rescue and before anyone could stop him, with a line firmly attached round his waist, young Jimmy Grieg dived overboard and under Calistra. Next they spotted him surfacing again holding onto Bookie. Sandy swiftly powered the Louisa over to them and two of Boreyev's men found boathooks and ran along Louisa's side to try and keep the upturned hull of the Calistra from crashing into them.

The brave but foolhardy act of young Jimmy's had been taken on the spur of the moment and as soon as his elder brother realised what had happened he shouted for the others to pull him back up and into the boat. Dropping their boathooks back into the well in the stern, they rushed for the rope tied to Jimmy and pulled together. Some moments later a coughing and spluttering Jimmy and Bookie were heaved back on board.

Despite the Louisa slowly cruising in ever wider circles around the upturned hull for the next quarter of an hour, there was no sign of Flaxman.

25

Easter Sunday mid-morning

The Gulf of Corryvreckan

With the outgoing tide now conflicting with the strong winds coming in from the west, and with the tide race running at maybe six or seven knots, the powerful undertows and churning of the waves could drown even the strongest of swimmers. Not even the fit young folk who came here for what they call their 'extreme swimming challenge' would tackle these waters unless at slack tide and Sandy Greig had no idea if Flaxman was a strong swimmer - nor indeed if he could swim at all.

After the Louisa had circled the upturned hull of the Calistra for some while and all of those not down in the cabin, took a long last look at the sad sight of the capsized boat. It was being tossed and battered in the swirling seas and Greig feared she would be smashed on the rocky shore of Scarba long before a salvage vessel could get here, get a line onto her, and tow her back to Crinan.

At last, with a nod from the forlorn McKinnon back in the cabin, Sandy veered the Louisa off and away from the upturned boat and took the Louisa in one last slow arc round the stricken hull, taking bearings on her position. After making a guess at the speed of the boat's drift on the incoming tide, a salvage attempt could be assessed and a judgement on how fast she was drifting towards the shallower waters of the rocky shore. These positions taken, he got onto the Oban RNLI station on the VHF and gave them the standard reporting details of the loss of both the boat and one life. He also relayed Calistra's positional co-ordinates back to them, and requested that they also be passed on to the Crinan area salvage tug. This done he turned the Louisa and headed back towards Craithe.

Jimmy Greig had been asked by his brother to act as host to all the victims of the Calistra's demise and he stood near the main cabin door watching over all of them, and keeping them supplied with hot soup. He could see that of all of them that Neil McKinnon seemed to most forlorn. Like his brother Sandy he had known McKinnon almost all his life and, as a fellow seaman, knew how he must feel at the loss of his boat. He had also heard him pour out his worries to Ranald, principally his fear that his insurance would not pay out on Calistra in an event of this kind – though he seemed to brighten when Ranald promised to replace the boat with a similar. He sat near the others in the inner cabin drinking his soup, his arms resting on his knees, the cup cradled between his hands, his head hung low. He was staring at the cup and its contents, but these hardly registered with him.

Jimmy looked next at Ranald and Tatiana sitting side by side, his arm around her. She had been quietly crying and had been constantly talking about how close they had come to leaving their little boy orphaned. The gentle rolling, undulating progress of Louisa was like some great mechanised cradle, seemingly soothing away her stress and Jimmy watched as she put her head against Ranald's chest and, as she warmed, she began to doze off to sleep.

Ranald seemed only to concentrate on his still trembling wife beside him and Jimmy saw him squeezing her tightly from time to time, but saying nothing

With Flaxman gone, Bookie was clearly in a state of shock, frequently running both his hands through his hair and rubbing his face, whenever he caught Jimmie's eye he nodded as though to say thank-you again for saving his life but soon returned to his fretful signs of anguish. Jimmie wondered how such an apparently nice young man had come to be mixed up with people who had kidnaped the MacCrammonds.

These silent thoughts were interrupted by a change in the tone of the Louisa's engines. With the change of tone, her bow came down and she slowed approaching the harbour's outer walls. Above them, out in the bridge cabin, Sandy shouted down to Jimmie to get organised with Boreyev's men to tie up Louisa as they came alongside the Stanleytoun quay.

Jimmy, of an age when one feels invulnerable to danger, swiftly responded to his brother's call, apparently already oblivious to his dramatic and dangerous saving of Bookie's life or of the plight of the McKinnon or the MacCrammonds. He left the cabin and as soon as they were alongside, he leapt down onto the quay and helped tie up the Louisa.

** * * *

The news of the Calistra's loss and of a life given over to the seas spread fast - as is often the case in small communities. The Laird had needed to speak to the authorities to report all that had happened and an air sea rescue helicopter was sent out to search the area for the missing Flaxman, more in hope than expectation. The old ocean going tug that had served these past twenty years both as a salvage vessel to the Crinan area was also despatched to see if the Calistra could be saved.

Two Land Rovers, came down from the castle and the survivors were taken up to the Castle while Boreyev's men retired to the Derby Arms.

As soon as they reached the castle, Ranald and Tatiana rushed up to find Jerry. He was having another exciting day in his new surroundings and, last night, Anastasia had quickly distracted him from wondering where his parents were by showing him the first part of Brumby, one of his favourite films.

The Laird dealt with the authorities and greeted everyone back from their ordeal, while all the wet survivors were taken off to have hot baths. Clothes were found for McKinnon and Bookie, and all gathered again in the Great Hall some for tea and hot scones.

As the Laird had already decided to keep the news of the kidnap from the police, he would now be able to keep Bookie here as his guest – at least until an inquest into Flaxman's death. Right now Bookie seemed more relaxed than when he had just got off the boat and Ranald suggested to his father that, as he would prove an invaluable source of information, he should be questioned about Rollo – albeit gently and with tact.

Bookie, back from being cared for by Florence was still, understandably, shaken and, with his eyes somewhat tearful, appeared to be in a delicate emotional state, so when the elderly, softly spoken gentleman who seemed to be the 'boss' around the place, took him away into a comfortable book-lined study it was all just too much for him and he broke down in sobs of tears.

Though Rollo had taken him in from a deprived background in formerly troubled Derry, his experiences today had shattered his former unquestioning loyalty. As the reality of act of kidnapping really sank in on his mind, he recoiled in horror. The unnecessary violence, the cruelty Flaxman was intent on forcing onto Tatiana – a weeping mother pleading not to be separated from her little boy . . . Suddenly he saw the difference between the dispassionate discussions on the kidnap operation back at Norbally House, and this, he aftermath of an actual operation. His illusions broken merely no more than stark reality, had drained him of any thoughts of overpowering this kind old gentleman and trying to make his escape. The Laird had read the signs well, he planned simply to care for the young man.

'Around these parts I'm known as the Laird', said the old man seating himself down the other side of the fire. 'For a while you're to be my personal guest here at Craithe Castle. During that time you'll be in no danger from anyone - and I mean in particular your former boss, Mr Rollo, do you understand that?'

'Thank you Sir,' he managed to mutter quietly. But his embarrassment was added to as Ranald now entered the study and re-introduced himself to Bookie; he was overcome with guilt at being confronted by one of the two he had been implicit in kidnapping. He made no eye contact with Ranald and looked down as they shook hands 'You're our guest here, Bookie,' said Ranald, 'though we're not sure how long we can hold off the police wanting to take you away to ask you what part you played in both the attempted theft of our computer programmes here . . . '

'Attempted,' repeated Bookie, looking up and straight back at Ranald, 'what do you mean "attempted"?'

'I'm sorry to have to tell you that the two who came with you from the Galley of Lorne, were caught soon after they tried to steal the software – they're now in custody,'

'God, I'm the only one left,' he said, 'Rollo will kill me – literally,'

'Rollo's [not] going to get anywhere near you,' said Ranald, 'you're safe so long as you're here with us,'

'But you just said that the police will want to . . . '

Ranald put out his hand and rested it on Bookie's shoulder, as his father had done earlier.

'We'll keep the police at bay for now,' said Ranald, 'my father here's been a magistrate and I'm sure we can persuade them you're better off here than being exposed to a dangerous trip to Oban jail with a vengeful Rollo after you. In the meantime, if we can establish just how small a part you played in all of this we could try to get them to allow it to be reflected in any sentence you may be given.'

'But you don't understand,' said Bookie, looking across at Ranald, his eyes pleading, 'it's not the police I'm worried about, it's Mick Rollo, he's as vindictive as hell and . . . ' his voice tailed off as though he was thinking through what Rollo might do to him.

'Why don't you just tell me all you can about Mr Rollo and your relationship with him,' said Ranald, 'and then perhaps we can work out what to do about all of this.'

Over the next half hour Ranald managed to get most of the story out of Bookie who had come to realise that if he co-operated fully with these considerate captors, he would certainly fare better than any of the alternatives.

Ranald listened intently, intrigued, as Bookie's tale unfolded and he explained why Rollo was so dangerous – not only to Bookie but also to others. 'Trouble is,' said Bookie, 'he thinks he's invincible, immune from reprisals from the authorities',

'Immune?' repeated Ranald, 'where does he think his immunity springs from?'

'Rollo believes that he's immune from pursuit because of what he keeps on the laptop onto which I log every single job we do,' said Bookie, 'he has records going way back to the time of 'the Troubles'. These include the details of jobs done by the coverts for various Governments, dates, incidents, payments, you name it,'

'And all these details are there on the one laptop that you keep for him?'

'Yes, they are,' said Bookie, 'and apparently he has a longstanding arrangement with whomever is the Secretary to the Cabinet, that if ever he's threatened, he just picks up the 'phone and . . . '

'You mean he would expose Governments' secret dealings during the Troubles?' asked Ranald

'Good God,' said the Laird who had been silent all this time, 'and Rollo knows that you might tell someone other than the Secretary to the Cabinet what you've just told us?'

'Well, yes. I mean, though this is the first time ever, I've just told you, haven't I' said Bookie, 'so, right now, though I'm sure you'll both think me stupid, I feel like one of those mafia accountants in the films who's on the run and is being pursued by the mafia who need to kill him to keep their secrets safe,'

A flicker of a smile ran across Ranald's face,

'Let's see if we can't neutralise that fear, eh?' he said,

'How could you do that?' asked Bookie,

'Suppose we tortured you to get out of you what you've just told us,' said Ranald, 'and we then managed to get hold of all these files that Rollo uses for his protection?'

Bookie's mouth fell open, 'Torture me?'

'Of course we not going to torture you,' said Ranald, 'but if we did do you think that you could remotely access that laptop where all these files are stored?'

'Yes, I could,' said Bookie, 'it's always left that way on standby so that the files are accessible for use in an emergency,'

'What sort of an emergency?' asked Ranald,

'If Rollo was arrested, for example, and needed an excerpt from the files,' replied Bookie, 'so that he or I could print something out in that emergency to prove what it was Rollo holds against the Government.'

'Right, without the torture,' said Ranald smiling, 'what if we take Rollo's files, pretend we tortured you to get them, and that way he'll come after us and not you. In addition to that, removing a blackmail held over the Government would hugely benefit you when the authorities come to look at the part you played in all of this. Right, so as soon as the holiday weekend's over, I'll deal with the Russians and Rollo, Okay?'

It was the first time Ranald had seen Bookie smile.

* * * * *

Ranald took Bookie up to the Lab' and introduced him to Perry. After just minutes of discussion they had agreed how to remove Rollo's files from the Laptop down at Norbally House, and Rollo left the two of them to get on with it. Walking back down to the study, it took him this amount of time to think through all that he had learnt. He was still baffled why Wheeler was dealing on behalf of Nat Matthews – how the hell was Matthews involved?' It was a pity too that Bookie did not know how the Russians had got involved. But now that the kidnap had failed and the theft had been foiled, he felt it unlikely that the strange partnership between Matthews and the Russians would continue or that they would "have another go" – at least not immediately.

As he got down to the study, he decided to ring the Major who, according to Bookie, would still be unaware of the fates of the two teams and would be waiting somewhere for the two boats to come back to the mainland. Bookie had the Major's mobile number, which he would have used from the Calistra as soon as she had come within range of the mainland mobile telephone masts. He rang the Major.

'Good afternoon, Major Hunter, Ranald MacCrammond here, I'm ringing to update you on the boats you have been expecting to come back through the Corryvreckan to the mainland,'

Though there was no immediate reply, he did not have to ask if the Major was there as there was an audible gasp of breath from the other end,

'You're bluffing, Mr MacCrammond, if indeed that's really you' said the Major at last,

'It's definitely me,' replied Ranald, 'and I have to tell you that Zaytsev and Tulloch are in custody for the attempted theft of software from the Athena team. The boat, the Calistra, foundered in heavy seas in the Corryvreckan this morning. I'm also sorry to have to tell you that Mr Flaxman has been lost with the boat, drowned, and only Bookie survived that expedition.'

The Major suddenly felt sick, and found that his hands had gone clammy and he coughed involuntarily, his voice hoarse. Still, he tried to persist with his original line.

'I have no proof that you're who you say you are,' he croaked, then clearing his throat, added, 'and why should I believe such a ridiculous . . .'

'That's easy,' said Ranald cutting across him, 'you can check the apprehension of the two software thieves with the Oban Constabulary and the loss of Calistra and Mr Flaxman with the RNLI Lifeboat service, which is also in Oban,'

There was another long silence and Ranald could hear the Major's heavy breathing, 'And what would you have me do?' he said at last, 'I'm just a co-ordinator here,'

'Major Hunter,' replied Ranald, 'our sources inform us that you are a key player in organising all of this, and that not only have you known and done business with Mr Rollo for years, you also introduced Mr Wheeler to him. As for the Russians . . .'

'All right, all right,' cut in the Major, 'so what do you want from me?'

'I need you to listen carefully and do exactly what I now suggest,' replied Ranald, 'I need you to ring your fellow conspirators Mr Wheeler and Mr Rollo. You are to tell them that their plans are finished. They are to pass that message on to the Russians and to anyone else involved in this affair, is that clear?'

Again there was a silence, but this time rather shorter,

'Very well,' replied the Major, 'but, as I said, I'm just the co-ordinator, I can't tell what their responses will be,'

'I don't care if you're just the lackey,' said Ranald, 'or if you're the instigator, just get that message across or there will be dire consequences for all involved in this outrageous conspiracy, do understand *that?*'

'Conspiracy? I don't know what you mean by conspiracy,' said the Major,

'For goodness sake, man,' replied Ranald, 'you know perfectly well what I mean. A bloody conspiracy's when a bunch of schemers like you plan something underhand usually to the detriment of others. I don't know yet how many of you are involved in all of this, but I'm going to find out. And, as for underhand, I'd have thought that the events of the past few days would have...'

'Yes, yes, Mr MacCrammond, you've made your point' replied the Major, suddenly realising that to some extent his own future was in the hands of this man, 'and I'll make sure that the . . . the others understand it as well. I'll ring them both this very minute'.

'That's better,' said Ranald, 'and I and the authorities will be speaking to you later.'

He slammed the receiver down on the phone so that the Major would hear it. He now felt hopeful that the messages would indeed be passed on and tried for a moment to imagine the reactions of those who were about to get these devastating bits of news.

Disliking confrontations of this kind, Ranald sat quietly for a moment. Surely there had to be another way to get out of this mess. It was at that moment that the idea came to him. As often in times of need, inspiration can come to the rescue. He remembered that a few months back the Towneley Vassilov Bank had been offered a large packet of shares in the Matthews Finch Hedge Fund. He had brushed aside the offer in seconds – not interested in anything involved in the potentially dangerous business of algorithm trading. With all of this going on he had given it not another thought but now it occurred to him that buying these shares might lead to a solution after the weekend.

With the urgency the situation required, he rang his old friend and Stock Broker, Harry Levine.

'Harry, so sorry to disturb your weekend, guess that you've got a house full of merry revellers for Easter?' he said as soon as he got through,

'Ranald, nice to hear from you,' said Levine, 'yes I do have a few people here. But what on earth gets you to ring me on Easter Sunday?'

Ranald did not give his reasons – of course – but asked if the shares were still available and, if they were, could he buy them right now. He was assured that they were as Levine had heard of Matthews Finch's difficulties from the Bank of England conference on Friday and checked on the shares – knowing of course that they would plummet in value. There was a slight problem in that both the Towneley Vassilov Investment Bank and the Towneley Bank would probably need board approval for such a big purchase. This was soon got round when Sir Jeremy agreed to buy the shares on Ranald's behalf on his own personal account with Levine, Berkstein & Smithson. They knew, of course, that, according to Stock Exchange rules, the shares would need to be purchased in a number of separate transactions; the message could be given now, however, very soon Sir Jeremy would be a very substantial shareholder in the Matthews Finch Hedge Fund.

Ranald was naturally most grateful to Sir Jeremy for coming to the rescue as, he would be able to speak from a good negotiating position when he eventually got to speak to Paul Finch. A couple more calls indicated that he would be back from Florida on Monday afternoon or evening – but at least before the Stock Exchange and markets opened on Tuesday morning.

With these plans now well in hand, he began to feel happier with the Matthews Finch side to this nightmare and that he could therefore concentrate his efforts on Komarov. And, although he now had a good idea of how to deal with this meddling Russian and his conspiracy, his plan still contained a couple of elements over which he had no control – time to get control of them.

26

Sunday early afternoon,

The Crinan Hotel

The Major took the slamming down of the telephone as a death-knell to the project. He felt the heart go out of him and was filled at the same time, the horror of the telephone calls he now had to make. But then his sense of self-preservation took over. He went to reception, told them "something had come up" and that, having to leave right away, he needed his bill. This he paid in cash and ran upstairs and packed his belongings. Getting back downstairs in just minutes, he walked sedately through reception, out of the front door and round to the carpark. As soon as he was out of sight of the front entrance, he scurried over to the car, threw his things into it any old how, and fled the Crinan Hotel as fast as he could.

As he drove off at speed, he connected his mobile telephone and charger to the cigarette lighter port – he would risk being tracked on his mobile phone but would buy a new one as soon as he could. He had no immediate plan such as where to go but reckoned he could get lost in Glasgow. The car could just be dumped in some Hotel car park, the keys given in to reception, the car hire company notified that something unexpected had forced him to leave the country and that would be that.

On the drive south he stopped at the Stag Hotel in Lochgilphead, from where he would ring the others from here. Taking the precaution of parking out of sight of the hotel, he went to the bar as soon as he entered it; he ordered a double whisky and retired to a quiet corner from where he could keep an eye on anyone coming to look for him. Before ringing the others he looked up the numbers of the Police in Oban and the RNLI. Always good at cooking up a plausible story, he posed as a relative of Flaxman's who had just heard the rumour of his drowning, and managed to get the confirmations he feared. The Police told him that a search helicopter was out looking for a person feared drowned in a capsizing in the Corryvreckan and that they were treating as connected, the two men who were being "held for questioning regarding the attempted theft of intellectual property" on the island of Craithe. The RNLI confirmed the loss of the Calistra and one passenger but mentioned nothing about a kidnapping.

He then took a large swig of his whisky – acknowledging to himself as he did so, that it would give him only the illusion of courage – but perhaps that was enough for him as it steeled him for the first of his calls. He decided to make the easiest of these the first, the call to Mick Rollo. He knew that although Rollo had just lost one of his key men, Flaxman, he also knew there was not an iota of compassion in the man and that there would therefore be no tears. Moreover, as it was himself who had commissioned the Irish team, it was likely to stay the more business-like of the two calls.

When he got through he quickly passed on all that Ranald had told him.

'This is for real?' asked Rollo, 'This isn't some kind of dreadful joke in bad taste?'

'It's for real,' said the Major, 'I was as shocked as you and before ringing you I checked it out with the authorities in Oban – it's all true,'

'So they've also got Bookie in custody?' he said, and then abruptly he added, 'hang on a minute', and the line went silent. The

Major sat for what seemed an age but eventually Rollo came back on the line,

'Do you know what?' he said his breath coming in short gasps, 'the bastards must have got to him, because all my vital files have gone,'

'What files, what's gone?' asked the Major,

'All my files going back decades,' replied Rollo, 'my effing insurance with the UK Government, all my dealings with them and the coverts, now I've got no bloody leverage on them with the files gone. I know Bookie keeps hidden back-ups of all of it but I'm not computer-literate enough to know where those are or how to access them. God what a disaster,'

'I still don't see what that's got to do with our project', said the Major.

Rollo then explained it all to the Major and how Bookie was the 'gate-keeper' to all his treasured files,

'So if the Russian wants to have another go at those bastards on Craithe,' concluded Rollo, 'they can count me in – I've gotta get my files back and they're sure to still want Athena? So, when you speak to Komarov or Max Wheeler, you can tell them that the loss of Flaxman is like a spur to me and that I've got more top rate men ready and waiting to avenge his death.' The Major rang off after discussing a few more matters and felt strangely heartened by his call to Rollo – this made him less nervous about his call to Wheeler.

When he came to make the call, he was actually returning earlier calls from Wheeler. In these earlier calls he had implied that the delay in the boats getting back to the mainland last night had been simply the result of bad weather and had merely postponed the plan not scuppered it. When he got through, Wheeler was relieved to hear from him as, understandably, both Matthews and Komarov had been pestering him for news. His relief was short-lived,

'Let me see if I heard you right,' said Wheeler after a long silence and the Major could feel the icy tone even over the airwaves. 'What you've just told me is that Greg Flaxman has been drowned, the others are in custody and both 'effing missions have turned into complete fiascos. Have I got that about right?'

'I'm afraid that's true,' replied the Major, 'though Mick Rollo lost a man and still has enough of a grudge to want to have another go at Craithe,'

'Well, I don't know about that,' said Wheeler, 'this is a big enough cock-up for me to have to ring Nat Matthews. Difficult to say how he'll react to all of this. Let me find out what he wants to do now and I'll ring you back.' He rang off and the Major stuffed his mobile into his pocket, finished his drink and left the hotel to continue his journey down to Glasgow.

As soon as Wheeler put the 'phone down, he cupped his head in his hands for a minute. Not in his worst nightmares could he have dreamed of all their plans going so disastrously wrong or in the manner in which they had. Now, crashing in on his thoughts, was his promise to Nat Matthews that he would not let him down. Unless Rollo could quickly come up with a plan 'B', letting Nat down now seemed inevitable. However daunting it might be, he would also need to contact Komarov. Of the two, he expected to have the greatest trouble with Nat Matthews, after all, he still had the problem of opening for trading on Tuesday morning; he decided, to ring Komarov first - he might have some ideas of what to do now and so make the Matthews call easier.

Komarov had previously made a number of calls to Wheeler during the day - trying to get news; he had failed to get anything specific from any of them. In exasperation, he had left a message giving Wheeler his mobile number and telling him to ring, whatever the time of day or night – irrespective of whether or not he had any news to impart. He took a couple of deep breaths and rang the Komarov's number. Once connected, he ran right through the whole sorry tale as quickly as he could to prevent any interruptions from him.

'So there it is,' he said as he finished, 'sorry about your man Zaytsev, but these things sometimes happen.'

'Not to me they don't,' said Komarov, 'anyway Zaytsev was not my man he was my partner Silayev's. I should have known it would be better to send the 'A' team first time round. My partner told me Zaytsev was up to the job and he had the advantage of his being in London for a job at short notice. Now, this time, we'll do it properly. I'll come to London myself right now and get things properly organised. I'll be bringing someone with me and you'd better tell your man Rollo I shall also need half a dozen or so of his best men for tomorrow morning- did you get all of that?'

Wheeler was so taken aback by this, that for just a moment he hesitated before replying. 'So you don't think that the mishaps of today are the end of the matter,' he said, 'even when everyone on Craithe has been forewarned and will be prepared for anything we might consider doing now,'

'I don't care Cossack's cuss what Craithe are or are not prepared for,' said Komarov, 'and it's absolutely not the end of the matter as far as I'm concerned so unless you hear from me to the contrary, I need you meet me in the bar of the Connaught Hotel at nine this evening, yes?'

'Yes, of course,' said Wheeler, 'I'll be there at nine,' and Komarov ended the call with the sharp click of a clam-mobile phone being slammed shut.

Whether or not Wheeler had agreed with Komarov, it was clear that the Russian was go to proceed irrespective of anyone else's views. He wondered what Komarov's 'A' team might consist of – perhaps he would discover that evening.

So, at last, he came to the call he dreaded making most of his call to Nat Matthews. Their relationship had become more than just a business arrangement, with Wheeler getting the other out of difficult or embarrassing situations over the years, this venture, like some others had become personal. What made it worse ~~was that~~ was that it was today, Sunday, by which the whole thing was supposed to have been fixed. He could feel his heart pounding in his chest as he rang Matthews's number.

'I told you I didn't need to hear from you till everything was fixed,' said Matthews as soon as they were connected, 'nothing gone wrong I hope,'

There was no way of putting a good spin on it – as politicians are wont to call it. At the end of the sorry tale, however, Wheeler was surprised to hear that Matthews appeared to be resigned to the disaster.

'Well, if you'd asked me about your idea before you set out on it,' said Matthews, 'I'm not sure what I'd have said. I suppose kidnapping someone and then using the hostage to get what you want seems reasonable enough, but I'd have wondered about doing it up in the middle of nowhere. Still what's done is done – so what now? I still need to be trading normally Tuesday morning. Is it too much to hope that you have what these days they call a plan B?'

'There's the Russian I mentioned,' said Wheeler, 'he's got his own agenda and is going to pursue this matter to the bitter end, come what may. As a side-result of his plans, Craithe could be out of action tomorrow anyway, so although our first efforts failed, rest assured, we'll get you back in business for Tuesday morning.'

'Well, that's what you said first time round,' said Matthews, 'let's just hope that your faith in a collaboration with this Russian is going to work. Just let me know the moment you get some more heartening news will you?'

'Will do,' said Wheeler, and they ended the call. After a few moments reflection he felt he had got off lightly – both and Komarov or Matthews calls had turned out unexpectedly, and there was still hope that all would be well in the end.. He would now just have to hope that Komarov's new plans would also accomplish what he had promised Nat Matthews – a lot was going to hang on the meeting at the Connaught this evening.

27

Thursday afternoon,

The Dorchester Hotel, London

Guiseppe Lupo stood at the hotel suite's wide picture window. He had been admiring the view and watching the traffic seemingly floating along below them in Hyde Park, his short wiry frame, dwarfed by the size of both the size of the suite's sitting room and the window framing him.

'You chose well, Luigi,' he said, ' almost as good a view as my apartment in New York, but much lower of course since we're in little old London.'

'Glad you like it, Boss' replied Luigi, 'though I have to confess, it was Alessandro who chose it for us - hell he lives here so he ought to know. Anyway, just as well, 'cos we may be here a whiles as this thing plays out'. In contrast to his Boss, Luigi's huge two-hundred and thirty-eight pound frame, stood well back from the window, planted on the floor like some crude rock sculpture.

'Hope to God it's for real this time and that that Alessandro's right,' said Lupo, 'don't want to be missing the spring in Central Park for nothing.'

'Sure he's right and all the other signs say it's a 'go' this time, doesn't it Rocco?' replied Luigi,

Rocco, diminutive like the Boss, but overweight, giving him an air of being like a large ball, stopped rolling around only by his short fat legs one end and small, round shiny head at the other. He was seated on one of the rooms many comfortable arm chairs, a laptop open before him on a low, oblong glass coffee table. He had been studying the machine intently for some time and his answer was distracted - late in coming,

'Yeah, that's correct, all the signs are indeed *go*' he said as he tapped a couple of keys and went on peering at the laptop,

His lack of full attention to the conversation, irritated Lupo who had half-turned to see the cause of his distraction.

'What signs are you talking about, Rocco?' he asked,

At the Boss addressing him directly, Rocco looked up smartly from the laptop, took off his pebble glasses, squinted at Lupo silhouetted against the light and cleared his throat.

'Let's see now,' he said, 'and began counting off the said signs on his fingers, 'apart from all the stuff Alessandro's told us – which in itself is pretty conclusive, *number one*, Komarov's partner Silayev's man, Zaytsev, came out of hiding in the Russian Embassy the very same day as the Bank of England's Conference. They must have had confirmation of something 'cos, *number two* same day, they charter a helicopter from the London heliport and fly off to Northern Ireland – or so the charter company told us, and we have no reason to doubt their veracity. Then, there's *number three,* we hear nothing of Zaytsev for a couple of days but lots of short telephone conversations with Wheeler, the PR guy. And now, *number four,* Komarov himself books flights to London today for himself and that SVR bitch Izolda Valik.'

'Isn't she the one who did for our plans in the Ukraine?' said Lupo,

'The very same,' replied Rocco, 'so we owe her a return round in the ring so to speak,'

'But we need to be careful, Boss,' said Luigi, 'not only is she reputedly one of the SVR's very best, she's no qualms about killing people who get in the way of her missions – that's why Komarov uses her for all his really important jobs – or at least for jobs that need complete lack of any human feelings or compassion,'

'And that brings us to sign *number five*,' said Rocco, 'the fact that he's brought the bitch Valik with him. Our guess, Boss, is that Zaytsev may have screwed up. I believe that 'cos the helicopter's charter was flexible but expected to be for just a couple of days and it's still not back yet. What's even more interesting is that Komarov's people have chartered another much smaller helicopter just to take one person from London to Northern Ireland tomorrow morning, first light.'

'Good work,' said Lupo, 'have we still no idea where they're going to after they get to Northern Ireland? I mean, do we think that Athena is developed in Northern Ireland itself?'

'We don't know the answer to that,' replied Rocco, 'but actually that don't matter to us do it?'

'Why not?' Lupo asked, 'wouldn't it be nice to know where they've been hiding this new cyber weapon?'

'Well, maybe *nice,* Boss, but doesn't affect our plans one little bit,' said Rocco, 'I mean they, Valik or whoever else they use, doesn't matter to us where she gets it from, all we have to do is to track her to when she gets back with it to the London helipad, right? And we've got our plans sketched out to relieve her of Athena as she leave the heliport, simple as that,'

'And you're certain that's the way they'll bring it back, with Valik?' asked Lupo,

'Gotta be,' replied Rocco, 'most direct, safest – I mean least vulnerable to attack, and more than that, they need to return the charter helicopter.'

'Okay, and they still don't know that we've been following them since their practice attacks on banks in Manila?' asked Lupo,

'No, don't think they have a clue about that,' said Rocco, 'so there's no reason for them to bring Athena back some other way - to avoid us, for example – they don't even know we exist.'

'What if, I'm just saying, what if they *did* bring Athena back another way?' asked Lupo

'No sweat,' replied Rocco, 'Komarov's in such a dicey state with the President, that he can hardly wait to get his hands on Athena. We think his desperate need may have turned him blind to the risks of being discovered trying to get his hands on it. He's booked into the Connaught Hotel here in London, just along the road from here, so if by some chance he brings Athena in some other way, he'd still be bringing it practically to our doorstep. So just relax, Boss, enjoy London, keep an eye on your missus's shopping sorties as you always do and leave us to worry about Athena.'

28

Easter Sunday evening

The Connaught Hotel, London

Though it would have been no more than a twenty minutes' walk from his flat in Cliveden Place to the Connaught Hotel and the fresh evening air would have done him good, Wheeler was weary and decided to take a taxi. He had to walk only as far as Sloane Square to hail one and he therefore arrived early at the Connaught. Using the Mount Street entrance to get to the bar, he was going into what Paul Finch still claimed was the best hotel in London.

As he had been drinking brandy, and not being a frequenter of top cocktail bars, he took this opportunity to order a Brandy Alexander and, when it came, and he tasted it he knew why, in times gone by, nearly every block in New York had a cocktail bar and how it had been the fashion in London for so many years too. He sipped and savoured the concoction until this pleasure was interrupted by the arrival of a huge gentleman, well over six foot and built like a Russian Bear. He got up from his chair and arrived at the bar as the same time as the Bear,

'Igor, I presume,' he said

'Max, delightful to meet you at last,' replied Komarov

They ordered a drink for Komarov and then returned to the corner table where Wheeler had been sitting. Mindful of the verbal spat that he had had with Komarov earlier, Wheeler decided that on this occasion he would play the part of a willing collaborator.

To clear past history, Wheeler first told Komarov how the whole thing had started and how Matthews still needed to 'get Craithe off his company's back' so that it could trade on Tuesday morning and that failure in this would drain Matthews's company of clients faster than using an industrial extraction pump.

'This is good, Max,' said Komarov, 'I've already given my instructions to a remarkable young lady called Izolda Valik for what we are going to do next. Unable to reach you earlier, I have spoken to your friend Mr Rollo who is happy to go along with these new plans.'

'That sounds all right, but do you mind if I know what these plans are?' asked Wheeler, trying not to let his irritation show in his voice. It was galling enough for Komarov to muscle in on the Craithe project, but to now take complete control of it?

'We are going to use the helicopter for a full-on attack on the castle. They will think that the attack is an end in itself. That is to say that if it is an unqualified success and they have no defences, fine - we get our software and your Mr Matthews's company gets to be free to trade again. But if they put up defences, the attack will become a distraction and Izolda, who specialises in this kind of work, will find a way of getting into the castle to get the software on her own. Does that sound all right to you?'

'I don't understand,' said Wheeler, 'suppose she gets into the castle and gets the software which Zaytsev failed to do, how does she then get out and get away with it if they have defences and, the very worst scenario, have captured the pilot along with Rollo's people?'

'You don't need to worry about that, my friend,' replied Komarov smiling broadly.

So there it was, a *fait accompli* – take it or leave it. Wheeler was deeply suspicious but had no alternative but accept it. He knew that many Russian's played chess and suddenly he had the feeling that his inability to play the game was going to be a disadvantage here – or was that just another sign of his growing paranoia?

* * * * *

They finished their drinks, Wheeler satisfied that early tomorrow morning, there would be a raid on Craithe Castle and that his worries about failed missions would be a thing of the past. He would need to break this good news to Nat Matthews.

They parted company and Komarov went back into the main body of the hotel, from the bar through into the main entrance lobby, turned right into a small sitting-out area, and settled himself into a comfortable chair from where he could keep an eye on the hotel's main entrance. It could have been only minutes later that a smartly dressed young man entered the hotel, turned directly into the same area and came over to Komarov. He gave what looked like a small bow of recognition and Komarov waved an arm for him to sit next to him. They were soon in deep conversation - in Russian of course.

'Good to meet you, Dmitri,' said Komarov, 'how do you find living here in London?'

Dmitri launched himself into an eager summary on the wonders of the city, the numbers of Russians here in London, and Komarov soon had to stop him.

'Good, I'm glad you're enjoying it all,' said Komarov, 'what have you found out for me?'

'I'll try to be brief Mr Komarov, but there's so much and it all seems somehow interlinked,' said Dmitri. He got a piece of paper out of his pocket and showed it to Komarov. It detailed the complexities of the connections between the Towneley Bank, Ranald MacCrammond, The Towneley Vassilov Merchant Bank and The Island of Craithe; it also listed some of the many rich and famous City figures who had made donations to the Towneley Foundation. It appeared that Sir Jeremy Towneley encouraged donations to his foundation from the super-rich young traders by telling them how much good their money would do in the Foundation - infinitely preferable to buying just another picture in the Art World's rigged markets or their acquiring, say, yet another Ferrari.

Komarov looked at the piece of paper with concentrated interest. He then asked Dmitri if he could keep it,

'Just what I wanted,' he said. 'Now, another thing, did Zaytsev ring the Embassy here in London when he was allowed to make one telephone call immediately after he was captured up in Craithe Castle?'

'He did,' replied Dmitri, and delving into an inside pocket again, he produced another piece of paper. He unfolded it and smoothed it out on the table in front of them. It consisted of instructions of how to get from the main Craithe Castle entrance up to the Lab'. Komarov studied it for a few moments and asked if he could keep that too.

'You have a copy of this on your smartphone?' he asked

'I do,' replied Dmitri

'Good ', said Komarov who then produced a business card from an inside pocket and handed it to Dmitri, 'please send a copy of that page to this email address will you, please,'

Dmitri got out his smartphone, looked up the copy of the same piece of paper and sent it to the address Komarov had given him.

'That's excellent, Dmitri, thank you for your time. I assure you you've probably just done more for Mother Russia than you have in all of your career to date, well done. And please be sure to give my regards to Vasily Narinsky when you get back to the Embassy, will you?' he said. This message for the Ambassador himself was just a bit of showing-off by Komarov, but – as intended - it impressed Dmitri,

Dmitri rose, shook hands and left. Komarov, smiled to himself. 'Good, that's Izolda all set up.' he said to himself.

* * * * *

Wheeler rang Matthews from the Connaught Hotel and though Matthews urged Wheeler to tell him of the latest developments over the telephone, Wheeler said they were better to meet face to face and that it was but a short walk from the Connaught Hotel to Wilton Crescent. Reluctantly Matthews relented and as Wheeler made his way along Mount Street towards Hyde Park and then down to Wilton Crescent he was oblivious to all the evening's traffic as he rehearsed his meeting with Matthews. This was going to be his last chance to reassure his client and friend that all was about to come right after the disasters of the weekend so far.

On arriving at Wilton Crescent he was shown up to Matthews in his Drawing Room and started off by apologising once more for the fiasco of the kidnapping.

'Do you know something, I don't think I could *invent* a story of greater incompetence' said Matthews as soon as Wheeler had finished. 'Surely it's not possible to get *both* of our missions so spectacularly wrong,'

'I sympathise with your views on all of this,' replied Wheeler, 'but it's not all as bad as it might seem,'

'Not as bad as it might seem?' repeated Matthews, throwing his arms up in the air. But, then, calming himself, added, 'I'm not sure I see how it could get worse. Come Tuesday morning when the

Stock Exchange re-opens, what then, eh? We're now left with just one bloody day to fix this thing',

'And here's where my meeting this evening with the Russian comes in' said Wheeler, 'he's desperate to put matters right and will continue to help us to end MacCrammond's team's activities up there,' he said embellishing the truth. 'This Russian, says we can use the helicopter for whatever we want it for and can keep it for as long as we need it. What's more he's brought a top ex-KGB operative over with him to lend a hand.' In the worst traditions of misogyny, he purposely did not mention that it was a woman - but if Matthews, thanks to this missing detail of the KGB person's sex, got a vision of a live Russian James Bond, and was reassured by that vision, then so be it.

Perhaps Matthews *did* get the vision of Bond-like figure to the rescue for he sat up a bit and pushed himself back into his chair.

'Right, so you're telling me that the Russians are desperate to get their hands on this Athena software,' said Matthews, 'and will do anything to achieve that?'

'That's it', said Wheeler,

'Well, I've been thinking about all of this,' said Matthews, 'suppose we get over this bloody mess this time, and the company is running Okay on Tuesday morning, with the mad explosion in the numbers and sophistication of cyber hackers, who's to say this won't happen again with some other group – maybe after the company's money next time? Quite honestly I'm beginning to think it's time for a change for me. I've made a few millions with the Hedge Fund and once we've got over this current problem, maybe I'll sell up and move on to something else. Mind you, that means you still have to get over the present crisis, if things aren't back to normal by Tuesday morning, my shares in the company will be worth peanuts and I'll be trapped into staying on. So, my next questions are just how competent is this Russian who's going to help your Irish friends have another go at MacCrammond's lot?'

'The best,' said Wheeler, 'he wouldn't have survived as the President of the Russian Federation's right hand man if he wasn't.'

Matthews seemed satisfied with this – Wheeler just hoped, that for all their sakes that it was actually also true.

29

Easter Monday morning

Norbally House, Portrush, Northern Ireland

Izolda Valik was taken by small helicopter from London, direct to Norbally House. Such was the curiosity over an FSB operative, that all of Rollo's team, several of them ex-coverts, went out to the lawn to welcome her. Unlike their expectations of her, she was not built like a tank, but, at five foot five and slim, she could have passed for a young housewife – although perhaps more athletic-looking, and visibly super-fit. When one of Rollo's men went up to her and welcomed her, she replied in fluent, if slightly accented English but with a directness of gaze that quite daunted him.

. Mick Rollo came out of the house and she was more formally introduced to the team. These niceties out of the way, she and Rollo retired, just the two of them, to his office. First he briefed her about what had happened to date and the reasons for the failures of the two earlier missions or at least as much as he, himself, had been able to ascertain. As might be expected, Rollo played up the size of the waves in the Corryvreckan and the treachery of the Laird's lifeboat in 'ramming' and sinking the Calistra without 'any regard for life'.

She was more interested, however, in why Zaytsev had failed and although Rollo's account of how the two of them had been captured was second or even third hand – as relayed to Rollo from the Laird via the Major - Izolda listened to it with intensity. She was particularly interested in Rollo's description of the 'imported' Russian security people at the castle. She already knew about Boreyev and had done her research on him and his men, but she was keen to get the others' impressions of them to add to her knowledge of them.

Rollo repeated Komarov's rationale for the attack they were now going to embark upon, and although Komarov had told her every detail of both the Norbally Team's role and her own, she listened patiently as Rollo went through it.

'I don't know if he's told you or not,' said Rollo, 'but it bears repeating anyway. Your boss, Igor Komarov, thinks that the Craithe lot will simply not believe anyone will be rash enough to have another shot at stealing the Athena software so soon after the last debacle. He reckons – and I agree – that we have therefore a good element of surprise in this next venture'.

'I agree,' said Izolda, surprising Rollo that she had anything to contribute. He looked back at her but could see nothing in her large, expressionless, almost black eyes.

The team of ex Coverts, had been busily checking over their equipment. The urgency of this response to the Craithe kidnap fiasco was less to do with the death of Flaxman, it had much more to do with Rollo's keeper of his secrets, Bookie, now being held at the Castle and from the way the team was working this was what motivated them too. Rollo also knew that a bold attack now would restore his remaining team's morale.

A team of four coverts were told to get themselves into 'battle order'. This meant donning army-like camouflage uniforms together with standard black balaclavas - the usual uniform of soldiers of this kind. In addition to small arms they were to take a surface to surface rocket launcher and its missiles. Two trainee coverts were to be left at Norbally to guard it.

By the time the team were ready for inspection and briefing, it was around ten in the morning. There was a tingle of excitement - even amongst these hard men. To emphasise their former military backgrounds they stood at ease as they waited for him to come and address them but came to attention when Rollo came out into the back yard of the big house and came over to them.

'All right, at ease!' he commanded, and then followed it with 'Stand Easy!' He also had clothed himself in mock-military uniform. 'As you'll all know by now, Greg, Bookie and Shaun were prevented from completing their recent mission and Greg gallantly gave his life in trying to carry out a difficult mission. Heavily outnumbered, Bookie was captured.' said Rollo his strong voice projected out unnecessarily loud considering the small number of men present. Though this speech embellished the truth to put yesterday's fiascos into the best possible light, building morale was important for this new mission and, anyway, to hell with uncheckable 'facts'.

'Bookie is now incarcerated in the filthy dungeons of some mediaeval landowner' continued Rollo, 'and is no doubt is being tortured to disclose information of our past work here at Norbally House. These people on the island of Craithe are a serious threat to our organisation and its future. They will think nothing of distorting the truth to tarnish our reputation. Such cowardly distortion of what we do here could jeopardise everything we have built here together and I for one am not going to sit idly by and let that go unchallenged. Are you committed with me in this venture to rescue Bookie, one of our comrades in arms, and once again secure our futures together?' There was a murmur of assent in the team and he continued, 'No one up at this castle will expect such an audacious attack in broad daylight. We will catch them completely off guard. I reckon they'll submit just to the threat of our arrival. We will make a gesture of intent by firing a single missile up at the walls of the castle. I understand that the castle brochure boasts of withstanding the armies of Cromwell and the clans,' he gave a cough of derision, 'well, let's see what they make of modern weaponry and a team such as ours.'

He looked round his men, and finished his little speech in higher tempo, 'if they're stupid enough to resist, and you are called upon to fight, I know you'll give a good account of yourselves and of your rigorous training. Good luck to us all'. He raised his pistol in the air and fired a single shot.

At this point Izolda might have disclosed what she had learned of Boreyev. She might have informed the group that Boreyev was at the Castle with men to defend it, but she did not. She had her own plan to obtain the Athena software - a much more important goal than retrieving Rollo's stolen files, or even the impossible one of kidnapping the MacCrammonds a second time and even attempting them might jeopardise her mission.

They all clambered aboard the Eurocopter with Izolda first in as it had been explained that on landing, she would remain in the helicopter. One of the team rashly bet that this was to spare her any involvement in the fighting. As soon as all were aboard, the Eurocopter started up, clattered into the air and swung north.

They were soon out over the North Irish Sea and continued due north with the Mull of Kintyre already in clear view over to their right. As soon as they reached the first of the islands, however, the helicopter swung out left, to the west and flew the outer, western side of the Island of Islay and on up to Colonsay. Unknown to them of course, this was the route that Boreyev had predicted they would take – this was hardly surprising as this was the only viable approach for an undetected attack on the Castle.

The flight got them to the south end of Islay in less than four minutes; as Boreyev had predicted, not only were they still out of sight of the Castle, but the noise of the machine was also shielded from the Castle by the lower slopes of the mountains. The approach brought them round to the South-West Tower and almost immediately to the terraced lawns below the Castle's south front. It was just before coming in to land that Izolda swung herself over the back of the rear bench-seat and hid herself in the small empty luggage-well there.

Quickly drawing up, the helicopter landed on the top terrace. As soon as it was grounded, the engines were switched off and, as rehearsed, Rollo, the four men and the pilot jumped down out of the machines. All ran forward a few paces from the helicopter and crouched down onto one knee, AK47 assault weapons at the ready. Rollo then went forward and gave a signal to one of the men who had a rocket launcher over one arm. The rocket launcher was raised aimed and fired. The rocket itself covered the distance in less than two seconds and exploded into the granite wall of the tower. A deafening smack of the impact and explosion rattled and echoed round the castle walls. For all the noise of the impact, it left just a four foot star shaped circle where it had blasted the surface off the granite.

Less than a couple of seconds later, as the balaclava-hooded man began to lower his the rocket launcher to reload it, there was a sound of two dull thuds as mortars were fired from behind the low walls on either side of the terraced lawns. Two arcs of smoke traced the fired canisters through the air. As soon as they were directly over the helicopter, both canisters exploded with as much noise as the rocket moments earlier and two huge umbrellas of dark grey rain-like material spread out in wide circles from each of them – like grim, dark star-bursts from some sinister firework display. These wide charcoal- coloured umbrellas of rain then fell towards the ground, landing on and covering the helicopter rotors and then the helicopter itself and, all the while, the constituent parts of the umbrellas seemed to be coalescing into a fine net, droplet merging with droplet.

The men beneath this spreading net that had been thrown over them, looked up in stunned silence. They seemed frozen by the effect of the extraordinary weapon that had been unleashed over them. Seconds later, just as the first 'rain' was reaching the men themselves, two more mortars were fired at slightly different angles from the first two. Further umbrella- shaped nets of the fine rain also fell over the machine and the men below.

Within another two or three seconds the helicopter and men were coated in a cold, dark grey gunge which was quickly setting like some epoxy glue. Like dark-grey honey in texture to start with, it quickly set thicker and, if pulled, it stretched apart stickily, a little as would any glue if pulled before it has set. The men were now struggling with it, arms sticking to sides, hands to weapons, fingers to fingers. The more they struggled, the more the myriad fine stings [strings] of pulled glue-like substance stuck a hand to a thigh, or a weapon to a knee. In a matter of seconds the whole area looked as though it were coated in some weird Spanish moss with the immobilised men entrapped within it.

Boreyev and his six men, along with Ranald, Sir Jeremy, and the Laird walked slowly out to the men from behind the hedges bordering the terraces. All but two of the attackers had by now given up struggling. These two were still valiantly trying to fire their weapons - now in self-defence. At first they found the sticky glue-like substance caused their fingers to slip off safety catches but, within seconds, with the glue set, it rendered them powerless to do anything.

All six from the helicopter, Rollo, the pilot and the four coverts, were now gently handcuffed with plastic pull through handcuffs by the castle group wandering around between them. All were relieved of their weapons which were collected up into a pile and taken to one side, well away from the helicopter and the men. Sir Jeremy, now able to touch the set glue, helped Rollo to his feet. The latter was red in the face and seemed in danger of heart failure, excepting for the stream of quiet, vituperative, cursing pouring out of him.

The two men stood there facing each other were, for a second or two, as sharp a contrast between each other in appearance as they were in character. The tall Sir Jeremy, looking frail in comparison to the well-built slightly shorter Rollo. Sir Jeremy smiling, but not unkindly, Rollo now reduced to an almost speechless, gunge-covered statue.

'Don't suppose you were expecting that reception, were you Mr Rollo?' said Sir Jeremy.

Rollo did not reply immediately. He looked down at the ground for a moment and then looking back up at the other simply said, 'what in God's name is this stuff?'

'It came with some friends of my nephew's,' replied Sir Jeremy, not very helpfully. Then he added, as though to complete the answer, 'comes the whole way from Russia - quite effective don't you think. It's only been used for mob control to date but it seems to have worked quite well for this too?'

As he spoke the set glue-like substance began to turn white and then, quite quickly, to degenerate into fine white powder. This released the bonds and all those formerly entrapped in the glue-netting, and they all became progressively freer to move - apart from the handcuffs of course.

"That's been a problem with this new weapon,' said Boreyev smiling as he brought a couple of Rollo's men with him up to stand next to Sir Jeremy and Rollo, 'We're working on that. In crowd control we have had to work fast before the degeneration has released everyone, because of course those formerly entrapped can run off as soon as the glue turns to powder.'

Soon all the ex-coverts and the pilot had been brought over and stood there in a group near Sir Jeremy and Rollo. As though no one but Sir Jeremy was present, Boreyev continued with his explanation of the failings of this new weapon of his.

'When we were in the Ukraine the other day, in order to retain the power of crowd control over the mobs, we had to keep firing more canisters until we'd got them all tied up - very expensive.'

This aside made Rollo even more enraged than before.

'And what do you propose to do with us now, might I ask?' he said in a whisper of fury.

'We'll answer all your questions in due course, but for now, we just need to get you all locked up until the authorities get here,' replied Sir Jeremy.

The group was then turned and moved up the steps and across the gravel towards the great oak doors. As one of the doors was unlocked from inside, Sir Jeremy turned again to Rollo who was being led in just behind him.

'Firstly, of course, you've done rather more than just trespass onto Crown Dependency property' he said. 'This means that you've broken International Law as well as several laws of the Isle of Man and the Isles.'

Rollo's sullen response was just a grunt of 'so what', as he ran over in his mind the implications of this debacle.

'I shall also be informing Her Majesty's Government of this shortly' continued Sir Jeremy, 'and no doubt they would like to talk to you some more regarding work you used to do for them during 'the Troubles',

'I'll have you all for the theft of my property as soon as your bloody authorities get here,' swore Rollo.

By now they had all filed into the cavernous outer hall and from there back through the kitchens areas, across an inner courtyard and put into an outhouse full of stacked piles of logs and firewood. There were a number of redundant old benches and chairs, long past normal use which would one day feed the fires in the castle and the prisoners were told to sit on these.

'As you may imagine, the Laird has very extensive dungeons here in the castle,' said Sir Jeremy, 'but the tourists looking round the castle like to see those –but empty - so I'm afraid you'll have to manage in these sheds until the Police Launch is able to get here. You'll no doubt be happy to hear that should be in not much more than a few hours or so.'

With that, Boreyev's men, Ranald, the Laird and Sir Jeremy left them, locking the stout door firmly behind them.

Almost as soon as the Prisoners had been gathered together and taken up to the Castle – indeed even before they were fully out of sight through the front door, Izolda, who had kept low in the well behind the rear seats when Boreyev's man had checked it out from the ground, now climbed over the bench-seat. Peering at the disappearing captors and prisoners, she scrambled forward and jumped down out of the helicopter. Then she ran over to a group of tourists who were just coming round the side of the castle, through the great arch near the south west tower and joined in behind them. They had not seen Rollo's arrival – though they had heard it. But they had not seen the attack or the counter attack, and, even if they had, with the helicopter now sitting there, they might well have wondered why a film was being rehearsed without any cameras in sight.

As the group in front of Izolda were shepherded in through the main front doors and into the entrance hall, they had not noticed as she tagged herself on behind them.

Having memorised the castle diagram and descriptions that Komarov had emailed to her smartphone yesterday, as the group went towards the main dining room, she veered off to the right and ran up the stairs, holding a satchel-like bag on a strap round her neck close to her side. She hoped that most, if not all of Boreyev's men had been involved in the helicopter attack and she had seen none since, but she now held in front of her, her neat little Yaragin pistol with its silencer, down by her side but ready for instant use. Running silently up the stairs, she counted floors as she went. On reaching the floor of the Lab she slowed down and listened. There was just the faintest sound of someone speaking inside, but that was all. She quickly entered the pistol in front of her. There, in front of her, was just the

Professor, Perry and Kim. Perry, to whom Kim had spoken so often from the Isle of Man, had been showing her round the Lab. The three of them froze in horror on the appearance of Izolda, now holding her pistol out in front of her.

She now faced the dilemma she had earlier wrestled with. Boreyev, his men, along with Sir Jeremy and the Laird would probably not take long settling their prisoners in wherever it was they were to be held. After that they would be coming back into the castle and most likely checking around that all was now well. This now meant that she did not have the time for another lengthy download of Athena. With the integrity of the download of Athena the very crux of the mission, she had arrived at the point of decision. She opted to ask for the hard drive that Zaytsev had checked out but had been taken back from him.

'I am here for the external Hard Drive that my colleague Mr Zaytsev had taken from him,' she said, pointing the pistol directly at the professor.

He seemed to hesitate, as though not sure she would use the weapon. Naturally, she noticed this and, in a single smooth, but lightning-fast move she swung the gun to her right, aimed at an exposed lightbulb the far end of the room and shattered it with one shot. She then levelled the gun back at the Professor. As she did so, she took a step closer towards him and lowered the aim of the gun.

'If you want to go on walking into old age,' she said quietly, 'you'll find that external hard drive right now, is that clear enough for you?,'

The Professor knew that it still only contained the faked up copy of the Athena software they had downloaded for Zaytsev yesterday. He stepped gently forward to the trestle table, picked out from behind one of the laptops there and handed it over to her.

'Put it into one of these drives, bring up "properties" and then stand back so that I can verify a second time what's on it,' she said

The Professor did as she asked and plugged the drive into the laptop. Perry had written a programme which just listed all the files that *should make up the real software* but here only listed them without their contents. As this deceit was an invention of the Craithe Team's, no amount of training or experience could have prepared her for it. Izolda's was therefore taken in by it – especially as Zaytsev had not mentioned anything about it in his call after he had been captured. Now she just nodded her head.

'You,' she then said, waving the gun at Kim, 'over here next to me, and the two of you,' she continued looking back at the professor and Perry, 'your mobile telephones please, put them on the table there.' She then looked around and seeing one other picked that up too and pulled the telephone wires out of the wall socket. She put the mobiles and the external drive in the bag strung around her neck and, with the gun still trained on the two men, threw two small plastic ring handcuffs over to the professor.

'Put those round your ankles, both of you and do them up tightly – I assure you that you will not want it to be me checking them or tightening them if I think they're slack,' she said. As soon as they had done this, she came round behind the two of them, at the same time glancing back at the trembling Kim. 'Hands behind your backs and turn round and get down on your knees,' she said and as she did so, she bound the wrists of both of them with more plastic cuffs.

Leaving the two men kneeling near the trestle table, she then waved Kim to the door and cuffed her hands behind her back. Next, with Kim immediately in front of her and the gun in her back, the two left the room. Izolda practiced a couple of different holds on Kim as they walked down the corridor and then the stairs, By the time they had got to the Gallery at the top of the main stairway, she had got it to look as though the two of them were merely close friends walking arm in arm. In a leisurely manner, they descended the stairs looking as though in conversation – though, in reality, Izolda was giving Kim instructions as to where to go next and warning her against any false moves.

'Remember, that if I have to shoot you for what I think is a false move,' she whispered harshly in her ear, 'I will do so and leave you lying where you fall. I was last year's Moscow's over twenty-fives two-hundred metres champion and I won't mind at all leaving you like that as I run for the helicopter. Do you understood that?' Kim, moist eyed, just nodded her head.

A minute or so after Kim and the young woman had gone, the Professor was able to get to his feet, hop along the bench, leaning on it from time to time until he arrived at a window. He was just in time to see the helicopter rotors start up and soon it lifted and, when some twenty feet or so off the ground, it swung quickly away down over the terraced lawns, south and out to sea.

30

Easter Monday, lunchtime

The London Heliport, Battersea

    Izolda flew the Eurocopter south towards London with Kim sitting beside her. She had warned Kim again about trying anything stupid and although Kim was probably amongst the best of PAs Ranald could ever have found for himself, she was not from a mould for heroes; she sat silent and meek during the entire journey. Flying over the sea initially, she followed the route she had come. She needed to refuel at Belfast, and as she called in there, as the arrangements had already been agreed, getting it paid for by the Charter Company proved easy. From Belfast, she crossed the Irish Sea and flew along the coast of Wales, round to Cardiff, across to the River Thames, following the river after that right to the London Heliport on the south bank.

    On landing, Izolda went in with its papers, explained that the pilot had been taken ill and was in the care of Sir James MacCrammond at Craithe Castle. She explained that she was fully certificated on Eurocopters, and her whole demeanour and the speed with which she rattled all of this off in perfect English, left the girl at reception so taken aback, that, when she was asked to get them a taxi, she got one for them immediately and without question.

While waiting for the Taxi to arrive, Kim asked if she could borrow Izolda's mobile phone to ring or text that she was all right.

'No, not until I've discussed your positon with Mr Komarov,' said Izolda, 'and now that you've come this far with me, he may have plans for you,'

As soon as they had set off for the Russian Embassy, Izolda sent a text message to Komarov to tell him that if he wished to contact them, they would be at the Embassy shortly. She also asked the taxi driver if he would mind going along the river, and he soon turned off York road, and up a side street. Inexplicably for her – as she later regretfully recalled – she had not noticed that, as soon as they had left the heliport, they had been tailed by a large black SUV. It was no more than a couple of hundred yards further on that another large SUV pulled out of a side-street and came to an abrupt halt in front of the taxi blocking its path. Within seconds there was a gun at the open window of the taxi.

'Not a move, or I'll blow your head off,' said an American accent. Another gun waving man, also in dark glasses had appeared on Kim's side of the taxi and the two of them were ordered out. Then, with no warning, as she was getting out of the taxi with her hands held empty out in front of her, as soon as Izolda's head cleared the taxi, it received a vicious blow at its base. She crumpled towards the ground but was caught by another large man who had come round beside the one with the gun. As though she were just a rag doll, she was carried to the rear SUV and Kim was ordered into the same vehicle. The doors were slammed shut and both the unconscious Izolda and Kim were blindfolded.

Kim next felt the sharp acceleration of the SUV and was thrown from side to side on the rear seat as it was driven at speed round corners. Minutes later she was thrown forward as the car came to a sharp stop. She was helped out of the car and, as she could hear the heavy breathing of someone nearby exerting themselves, she sensed that Izolda was being carried next to her. She was helped up several flights of stairs, and along a couple of corridors. They were then both taken into a room where their blindfolds were removed. It was a small room with just one window looking out across a narrow space onto the back of another building covered in white ceramic tiles. There were only two pieces of furniture in the room – a chair and a bunk-bed and the overall it had the feel of unlet property – bare, unpainted walls, plain concrete floor and ceiling.

As soon as their captors had left the room she heard the door being locked just as Izolda began to regain consciousness. Kim got up quickly from her chair and crossed to the bunk-bed on which they had lain Izolda; she helped her as began to struggle to get upright. As soon as she had managed this, Izolda got up from the bed and wandered around the room shaking her head from side to side and round in circles. Then, quite suddenly, she came back to the bed, sat down and turned to Kim,

'I'm sorry this had to happen to you,' she said unexpectedly in English, 'though there was always a risk this might happen, it was not part of my . . . my, how you say?'

'Plan?' suggested Kim in Russian,

'Yes, it's good that you speak Russian?' said Izolda, 'it might yet prove useful. But, as I was saying to you earlier, I took you with me when we were in the castle simply in case we met someone before we got into the helicopter. I did not mean it about killing you – but you know that I...'

'Had to say it nevertheless,' said Kim finishing her sentence for her in Russian,

'It's now time for us to make our escape,' said Izolda,

'Make our escape, how the hell are we going to manage that?' asked Kim.

In the next instant, before Kim realised what was happening, Izolda made some movements like a circus contortionist, and got her bound hands from behind her back to out in front of her – it was so unexpected and happened so fast that Kim had only the vaguest idea how she had done it – slipping her feet through between her bound hands once these had been brought through to the front.

Izolda now put her finger up to her lips and made the gesture for silence. She went over to the door, lay down and, putting her face to the floor, looked under it, shifting her head a couple of times to get views in different directions. She got up again and listened with her ear pressed against the door. Next, she turned away from what Kim, and thrust her still bound hands down her front and deep into her underwear where she squirmed and delved around for a second or so. A moment later she took her hands out again and Kim could see that they now held a small pouch. This she brought over to the bed, sat down and, holding one end of the pouch in her mouth, she managed to undo the smallest zip that Kim had ever seen, spilling the pouch's contents out onto the bed. She selected a tiny blade from an array of the smallest and strangest assortment of 'things' Kim had ever seen – even mentally she labelled them 'things' as she had no idea what some of them were.

'Turn round', she said and severed the plastic cuff around Kim's wrists.

'Now me', she said handing the blade to Kim and holding her hands out in front of her. All of this happened so fast that, under the guise of making their escape together, it had never occurred to Kim to try and escape from Izolda. As soon as they were both free, she took Kim by the shoulders looking intently into her eyes.

'I want you to listen very carefully to what I'm now going to tell you,' she said, 'We're now going to make our escape and I need you to do *exactly* what I tell you to do. Can you manage that?'

'Depends what that is, but I'll have a go at anything to get out of here,'

'Good,' said Izolda. 'Just one minute while I prepare, then I want you to lie down on the floor over there so that you're the first thing that anyone sees on coming into the room, Okay?'

'Yes, I can do that'

'I'm going to call for help and I want you to writhe around on the floor, not too theatrical, but just enough to gain attention,' continued Izolda,

'But won't whoever it is that comes in suspect that it's a trick?'

'Almost certainly they will. But, as you are about to see that won't matter,' said Izolda, 'and as soon as I say the word '*now*', I want you to get up as fast as you can and get behind me. Got that?'

'Yes, just get up as fast as I can, ignore everything else that's happening and just concentrate on getting behind you the moment you say '*now*',' said Kim,

'That's good, are you ready now for our escape?'

For a second Kim did not know how to answer as she could practically hear her heart beating in her throat and feel it in her chest, wondering at the same time what the hell was going to happen next, but she nodded her assent.

'This will take just a second,' said Izolda and from the bed she picked up what looked like a small white hair-band but soon saw it fitted over a thumb and finger to form a tiny catapult. She then picked out a tiny object which she somehow twiddled for a moment, turning it into a minute dart,

'Okay, now lie down over here,' she said, leading Kim to the right spot and lie down in the foetal position, 'facing this way so that you can see what's happening,' she continued, and as soon as I fire this dart, that's when I'll say '*now*', and she indicated the catapult and the tiny dart, 'and that's the moment you get up and rush round behind me, all right?'

'Yes,' said Kim, so hoarsely that only a whisper came out,

'And from that moment on you just follow me, as fast or as slow as I go, exactly as though you are my shadow, yes?'

This time Kim just nodded 'yes' as Izolda helped her to lie down as instructed.

What happened next happened at such speed that, later trying to recall it, Kim had concentrate hard to remember - so many happenings in so few seconds.

As soon as Kim was lying down Izolda carefully positioned herself so that she would be just behind the door when it was pushed about half-way open. She then got herself down on the floor next to Kim, making a surprising amount of noise as she did so. Instantly she was back up onto her feet and positioned where she had been in her practice. She began shouting for help before she was even up. A moment later there was the noise of the door being unlocked and then it swung open quickly. The huge man entered and saw Kim lying on the floor. Kim watched spellbound at what happened next. Izolda said 'Hi' and as she did so raised her catapult to the man's eye-level just as he spun round to face her. At that second, she fired the dart which, the moment it hit the gunman's left eye, sprang alight – like a lighted match. As he yelled out in shock and pain, he dropped his gun and rushed both hands up to his burning eye. Izolda caught the falling gun before it even hit the ground and shouted *'now'*. At the same moment she struck the gunman a savage blow with the gun and he collapsed like a felled tree as Kim leapt up and got behind Izolda. No sooner this than a second gunman came racing round the corner of the corridor and Izolda put an almost silent bullet smack between his eyes. Almost as though all were but one movement, she laid the first gun on the floor as she grabbed up the gun from the second gunman. Both had silencers on them, so, instead of having to choose between them, she picked up the first and stuffed it into her trousers. She next checked the second and ensuring it was loaded, cocked and also ensured that the safety catch was off. Beckoning for Kim to follow her, she then moved out of the room and along the corridor towards the corner. She was just nearing it when a third gunman, came running round a corner shouting out, asking if everything was all right. For him it was not. As soon as he was out of sight of anyone behind him, Izolda put a bullet neatly into his left temple. The next two gun men that came running round the corner were also felled from the side and landed almost like fish on a fishmonger's slab, side-by-side next to their earlier companion. Then there was silence.

Izolda peered cautiously round the corner and across from it could see into a room where the five of them had been playing cards. There was an eerie silence and slowly, gun held in front of her but pointing first this way then that as they crept forward, they moved towards the doorway of their guardians' room. On reaching it, she looked round it following the point of her gun as she did so. The room was empty. She stepped over the threshold looked round the room more carefully - searching for something. Eventually she spotted it – the small hard drive with the Athena programme on it. She crossed the room, picked it up along with the bag she had had round her neck earlier which was lying nearby; the two of them retired back into the corridor.

'Right, just wait here a moment,' said Izolda, and she went back, collected up the other guns, bound the unconscious first gunman with plastic cuffs she had found in his pocket and did a quick search of pockets of all the dead men. She found several things which seemed to interest her, put them into her bag and hurried back to Kim.

'You, Okay?' she asked, smiling for the first time since they had met in the Lab at Craithe,

'As well as can be expected – no, I'm sorry - I mean fine,' said Kim,

'Good, let's get the hell out of here before anyone else appears, ' said Izolda, ' and whilst we're here in the building continue to follow me like a shadow again, doing exactly what I do. As soon as we get out into the street, pretend we're just a couple of friends, arm in arm, out for a gentle stroll. I've got one of their mobile phones, so let's find a café and get the Embassy to collect us this time, enough chases for one day eh?'

'Yes,' agreed Kim,

'Then we'll have to think what the hell we're going to do with you, aren't we?' she said.

31

Easter Monday late morning

Craithe Castle

As soon as he was able, Perry, knocked a telephone off its hook so that it fell over onto the desk and Morag, who, in addition to her work on the team, also ran a switchboard for the Castle, came on the line.

'Morag? it's Perry here,'

'Hi, Perry, what can I…'

'Morag, just listen, the Lab has just been attacked and robbed again and the thief has also taken Kim, you know, Ranald's PA, she's been taken hostage, they're heading back to the…'

'Good, God,' shouted Morag, interrupting him, 'I'll get Ranald, I'll try ringing him down in the hall, hang on there,' and left Perry hanging onto then silent telephone.

Perry's call coincided almost exactly with Ranald and Boreyev coming back into the front of the castle after locking away the invaders. The sound of the helicopter starting up drowned out the noise of the telephone ringing in the hall, but as Ranald and Boreyev raced through towards the front door, Ranald just heard it and picked up the remote's hand-piece while still running out of the door. He and Boreyev were just in time to see the helicopter rising and swinging away down over the terraces, towards the sea, south towards Northern Ireland. As the two of them stood on the gravel in front of the great door, Ranald answered the telephone and Morag passed on Perry's message. Running back into the hall, he slammed the telephone back on its stand and beckoned Boreyev,

'Up to the Lab, quick,' he said, 'someone's taken Kim, and stolen Athena again.'

'Oh, God no,' cried Boreyev and threw his hand up into his mouth, biting into the soft flesh below his thumb.

Both ran as fast as they could up the main stairs and then up the south-east tower stairway and into the Lab. Desperate to hear what had happened, they first untied the Professor and then Perry, both of whom scrambled over to chairs and sank onto them.

'From her accent,' said the Professor, 'I think that it was another Russian – a young woman this time – God knows where she came from, just appeared in the Lab with a gun in her hand. She took the external drive we got back off the first Russian yesterday – the one containing the fake Athena suite of programmes. But, when she'd got what she came for, she also took Kim with her as a hostage. When they'd gone, I managed to sidle over to the window and was just in time to see Kim being dragged into the helicopter at gun-point,'

'Right Perry, here's what I want you to do,' said Ranald. 'I want you to do some fast targeted hacking. We need to make some educated guesses as to where they're heading and then hack into any CCTV cameras around where we think they might go. With luck we might spot them. Can you do that right away?'

'Sure, Ranald,' said Perry and seeming to get a new source of energy from nowhere, leapt to his feet and hurried over to one of the laptops.

'My first guess,' said Ranald, 'is that they'll take the helicopter back to the place they got it – they wouldn't want to alienate the charter company and get them calling in police to help them find an overdue charter helicopter. Rollo just told us that the helicopter came from the London Heliport. Perry can you hack into them and see what they've got by way of CCTV?'

'Doing that right now,' said Perry typing fast on the keyboard.

Boreyev, was still wiping his mouth with the back of his hand, and he, the Professor and Ranald, crowded round Perry as he did his searches on the laptop.

'I'll put this up on the big screen so that you can see better,' said Perry. The other three moved from standing over him and went to near the big screen. Soon up came some images.

'These are from the heliport,' said Perry as he began to increase the number of pictures on the screen, different angles showing the entrance to the building, the lobby, and the heliport apron outside. 'These will do for a couple of hour's time or so.'

'Is there anywhere else they might fly to?' asked Ranald, almost to himself,

'No, they need to get back as near to the Russian Embassy as they can,' said the Professor, 'and I think you're right, this girl whose got Kim certainly appears to know what she's doing, she won't want to be caught out in the open with a hostage at gun-point,'

'True,' agreed Ranald, 'let's try and calculate how long it will take them to get down there from Craithe.'

He went over to one of the laptops which was already up and running but just on standby.

'Boris, what kind of helicopter was it? Eurocopter of some kind?' he asked as he brought up the London Heliport website to see what charter companies resided there and what equipment they chartered out.

'Don't worry too much the type of Eurocopter,' Boreyev suggested, 'how far to London from here, I'll do the rest of the calculations, I know Eurocopters well,'

'She won't risk going direct, over busy places in the Midlands,' said Ranald, 'so if she skirts round them, or maybe just keeps over water the whole way down the Irish Sea and then cuts across and pick the River Thames, equally she might go back the way she came, past Norbally House. We don't know about her fuel situation.' He paused doing some calculations, 'I'd say whichever route she takes it will be well over four hundred miles. But we don't have to be too accurate, as we don't know if she'll have to stop on the way all we're trying to do is make a sensible guess at her arrival time at the helicopter pad,'

Boreyev had taken out his smartphone and done some calculations based on Ranald's guess of four hundred miles,

'She'll get there in between two and a half hours and three hours,' said Boreyev eventually, 'depending of course on the factors we've been talking about,'

'Right,' said Ranald, 'Perry keep an eye on the CCTV cameras down there at the heliport and concentrate on everything from two hours from now. If you get anything at all, find me wherever I am and let me know.' Then turning to address them all, he added, 'Borislav myself and some of his men will get down to London as quickly as we can. Perry, you Okay with what you have to do?'

'I am,' said Perry,

'Borislav, you come with me,' said Ranald and they ran back downstairs and through to the Laird's office. He found both his father and Sir Jeremy there, told them what had happened including, of course, the kidnap of Kim.

'After these people's fiascos of the past twenty-four hours,' said Ranald, 'God knows what they might do to her. One thing's for certain, they'll use her as a bargaining chip.'

'Have you a plan to deal with this?' asked Sir Jeremy,

'First, Borislav and some of his men need to come with me right now. We need to get down to London as fast as possible,' replied Ranald, 'and, Father,' he said turning to the Laird, 'you deal often with the Helicopter charter people at Glasgow Airport, could you get us the fastest they've got available that will take, six of us and some equipment down to London – the City Airport,'

'Of course I'll do that right away,' replied the Laird, 'but from your discussions a moment ago you said that this Russian Girl will be heading for the Russian Embassy, that's Kensington Palace Gardens isn't it?'

'Yes, Father, you're right but we haven't the time to stop that happening,' said Ranald, 'so I've something else in mind. I'll tell you about that shortly but getting the helicopter for us is current top priority,'

'Of course it is,' said the Laird, 'I'll do that right now,' and he got up from his chair and round to his desk to get on with organising it.

Ranald turned to Boreyev.

'I'm going to try and get them to do a deal with us,' he said, 'maybe even offer him a usable version of Athena in exchange for Kim,'

'You're not going to give him your software, surely,' said Boreyev looking shocked,

'Of course I'm not,' replied Ranald, 'but I've thought of a way round that too. First I need to get them to bring Kim to a place we know well, somewhere I can appear to be giving them the real Athena – the Newby Centre in Tower Hamlets. But before I do that I've got to get Wheeler and his lot away from trying to get revenge on us. Once we've got them pacified, we can concentrate on dealing with Komarov; I hope he still has control of the Russian girl who's holding Kim hostage.'

'I understand that,' said Boreyev, 'You want me and some of my men and some equipment – I'll go and get it organised. You said your father would get the helicopter here in half an hour – I'll be sure to be ready with my men by then.'

As Boreyev left, Ranald turned to Sir Jeremy.

'Sorry this has spoilt things,' he said, 'I was hoping for a quieter weekend than this – I hope it's not been too much for you, with your…'

'Rubbish,' cut in Sir Jeremy, 'is there anything I can do? Everyone else seems to be contributing,'

'You agreed to fix the purchase of the shares earlier,' said Ranald, 'I'm about put that great contribution you've already made to very good use, but if you want something else to do, could you break the news of all of this to Tatty and Florence and help them to take it calmly – we don't want to spoil everything for Anastasia and Jerry, do we?'

'Consider it done,' said Sir Jeremy, 'by the time I've … what do they call it these days? … Put a nice spin on it? They'll be fine – in fact I'll go and do that now so that they're prepared for another helicopter arriving here – that might even distract Jerry, eh?'

He rose slowly from his chair, helped by Ranald, smiled and left the room.

Thanks to Bookie's comprehensive files – now safely on one of Perry's computers – Ranald had access to Wheeler's numerous telephone numbers and rang him - finally getting him on his mobile. He guessed that Wheeler would still be in a state of shock from the disasters of the weekend so decided to treat him gently, to turn him into an ally if possible.

'Mr MacCrammond,' said Wheeler, 'I don't quite know what to say …I, er …'

'Mr Wheeler, may I suggest we put the events of the weekend to one side for the moment, as I have some suggestions to make which I hope you will see as the basis for a new start for all of us,'

'A new start would be wonderful, of course, but…'

'As I just said, Mr Wheeler, let's not go back over what's happened these past few days, I've something I need to tell you which I hope will change everything; sorry to rush you but we have an emergency up here and my time is short,'

With Wheeler just finished dealing with Nat Matthews, this call from Ranald was not only unexpected, it was very embarrassing.

'I understand that Mr Matthews was furious when he discovered that his company had been tampered with,' said Ranald, 'and, worse that it was then used publicly to show how poor everyone's cyber defences were; no doubt he felt it showed Matthews Finch in a poor light,'

'That's right,' said Wheeler, 'and he was still trying to get back at your team for doing that, in fact right up until that too failed,'

'Yes, I'm sorry about that,' said Ranald, 'but I hope that you realise that we had nothing to do with the choice of Matthews Finch for that demonstration,'

There was silence for a moment, then Wheeler cleared his throat, 'What do you mean, you had nothing to do with the choice, you…'

'The choice of company,' cut in Ranald, 'was made entirely by the Bank of England's regulatory bodies, we were not even informed which of the two regulatory bodies was responsible – this was done so that no personal animus would arise from it,'

'Good God,' said Wheeler, 'we had no idea.'

There was a silence on the line for quite a few seconds, then Wheeler continued,

'That means that Nat's vendetta against you was based on wrong assumptions,' he said, 'but that's appalling, I don't know quite what to say – yet again, I, er …'

'Even so,' said Ranald, 'I felt I owed Mr Matthews something for his loss of prestige; I hope he also knows that the Bank of England will pay for any financial losses incurred?'

'Oh, this is getting really too embarrassing for words,' said Wheeler, 'we never knew that either,'

Ranald then went on to tell Wheeler that he had thought of a way to help repair matters – to inject some Towneley Bank money into the company, add the prestige of the Towneley name and publicly praise the Matthews Finch Hedge Fund for so selflessly offering themselves as guinea pigs to make the very important demonstration message possible. He told Wheeler that The Towneley Bank would soon own just under thirty percent of the hedge fund. What he was saying in effect was that this would be a complete game-changer.

To say that conversation had been surreal would have been endorsed by Wheeler, in the space of a few minutes, his view of the whole sorry saga had been completely up-ended – from disaster to a future full of possibilities.

'Mr MacCrammond, frankly I'm dumfounded,' said Wheeler at last. I need to contact Nat Matthews right away, of course and his partner, Paul Finch – he's due back from the States this evening. He, poor man, doesn't know anything at all of the disasters of the weekend. I shudder to think how he's going to react to this when I go through it all with him – maybe he'll think I made it up as a bad joke.'

Ranald felt sorry for Wheeler having to deal with this unenviable task and his final words to him that he would be in London in a couple of hours if he could be of further help.

It did not take long for a top PR man to realise the potential of what he had just heard, He could see that Ranald's proposal would probably set the new company off on a track of undreamed-of success. He would need to give the news the pizzazz it deserved. He even began to feel elated at the prospects ahead.

For his part, Ranald hoped that this would turn out right, for if it did, all that remained was to deal with Komarov. Already he had a plan forming in his mind would fix that too. While thinking about this he absent-mindedly brushed an imaginary fly away from the small scar just above his eyebrow – just near his left temple.

32

Monday early afternoon

The Towneley Foundation, Newby Centre

It was fortunate that Albion Helicopters, the charter company at Glasgow Airport, had just one machine left, but it met the needs of Ranald, Boreyev and his team. It got to Craithe Castle terraces within half an hour of the Laird's call and, with everyone ready and waiting for it, everyone's baggage and Boreyev's equipment were quickly loaded aboard; after farewells and good wishes Ranald, Boreyev and his men climbed aboard and were watched by the family as the helicopter took off and swung away south, London bound.

The flight was comfortable of course but tension ran through the helicopter as each realised how much was at stake in this – hopefully the last mission and an end to the weekend's dramas. As soon as they landed at the City of London Airport around three in the afternoon, the car waiting there for just Ranald and Boreyev, sped them to The Towneley Foundation's Newby Centre in Tower Hamlets. A minibus took Boreyev's men and equipment to an hotel near the Centre. These two moves were spaced a quarter of an hour apart in case Komarov had anyone watching out for a retaliation from Ranald.

As soon as Ranald and Boreyev got to the Centre they dumped what they had brought with them in the main computer training room and Ranald showed Boreyev around so they could begin to put practical details to Ranald's outline plan. They retraced their steps to the main entrance, turned and with their backs to the set of double (of) glass doors of the entrance; Ranald then started to outline his plan.

'When we entice Komarov here with his Russian SVR Operative – or whatever she is, the one whose holding Kim - they'll arrive here at the main entrance,' said Ranald, as he gestured and Boreyev looked on intently, one arm folded across his chest, the other hand stroking his chin in concentration. He was formulating defence and counter-attack strategies as Ranald spoke.

'Once through into the large reception area here,' continued Ranald, 'we'll put the Russian girl and Kim into the classroom beyond reception on the right there and take Komarov into the computer room with us. Because of the glass panel walls throughout the Centre, we'll be able to keep an eye on everything; we must presume that the Russian girl will have Kim threatened with a gun.

'I'm sure Komarov will want me to transfer his money to somewhere like Russia. Next, I have no doubt that I'll then give him a clean copy of the Athena software,' Ranald smiled as he saw Boreyev's sullen expression, mouth turned down at the corners.

'But, I'll have a surprise for him.' He added and Boreyev seemed to brighten. 'And I think that what I have in mind will persuade him to tell the Russian girl to release Kim.'

'Don't suppose you're going to tell me what the surprise is?' said Boreyev,

'Not now,' replied Ranald, 'wouldn't want to spoil the pleasant surprise you also will get – anyway I've still to set that up.'

'But, no doubt you'd like me to position my three men in such a way that they can intervene if anything goes wrong. Let's face it,

Komarov's the sort of man who will try to have his cake and eat it as you say here in the West.'

'Yes, he will, though this time he's going to go hungry,' said Ranald, 'Anyway, I've got to set up my treat for him now, so would you like to have a good look round and work out where you and your men want to position yourselves?'

'Will do,' replied Boreyev and the two went their separate ways; for a moment as Ranald went back into the main computer room and Boreyev went towards the back of the building to check out access points and places Komarov might position any backup he might bring to the party.

Ranald chose a large trestle table on which to lay out papers and was soon joined again by Boreyev; between them they set up a six-by-six foot screen which they would use when they got to the stage of dealing with Komarov. The next step was to establish a link between the Centre and Perry's computers in Craithe Castle. This link needed to allow for anyone connected to the Centre by, say a Skype conversation, to be seen, large as life on the six-foot screen. Ranald also wanted the team at Craithe to see everything happening down here in the computer room. It took about half an hour and a number of telephone conversations with Perry – these took place on the telephone, over the internet and, lastly on Skype. By the end of the setup session they had everything just as they wanted it.

'I'd better explain what we're about to attempt to do, hadn't I,' said Ranald,

'Would be nice,' replied Boreyev,

'Some while back I was looking at getting myself some insurance for Athena,' said Ranald, 'ways in which I could protect it in different parts of the world. Perry and I discovered that within the Russian Federation, the President keeps all the minutes, notes and telephone conversations of his innermost circle hidden away but recorded. We found where he keeps all these files and using Athena's special talent for breaking through any digital encryption on the

Planet, we hacked into his hiding place. It's now all set-up and the message to the President is that if we have found all his secrets once, we'll be able to do it again, no matter where he hides them,'

'Good God,' said Boreyev, 'a permanent grip on the Russian President? You expect to get away with baiting this man like him? You've surely heard of what happens to people who cross him?'

'Yes, I am aware – of all the accusations anyway,' replied Ranald, 'but, even if they're true, he's not likely to do anything to me when he knows what I or my team could do to him – he's hardly likely to risk my publishing his darkest secrets on the internet, is he?'

'He could always deny they're his,' said Boreyev,

'Not if I leave his real files and secrets where they are and tell the rest of the world how to find them. They could just compare the two' said Ranald,

For a moment Boreyev just looked back at his old friend, his mouth half-open in astonishment,

Ranald just smiled back at Boreyev, picked up the telephone and rang Perry. He was not in the Lab at that moment, and while Morag tracked him down, he said to Boreyev, 'don't worry, after my discussions with the President or whoever else he speaks to me through, they'll all be eating out of my hand.'

Morag came back on the line and said that Perry was just coming,

'Perry,' said Ranald as soon as the other was there, 'The discussions we've had about the Russian President's inner circle of friends, is that actually set that up and how soon could we implement it?'

'All the software's written and been tested,' replied Perry, 'so last minute hacking processes and the theft itself could be done within a few minutes, I would think. Why, are you thinking of doing it soon?'

'Right now, if you can manage that,' said Ranald, 'and once you have the stolen files, can you put them up onto that new Athena Services Website we also discussed?'

'Sure,' replied Perry, 'but, do you remember, so that the President's files can't be seen by all the world the moment we steal them, we need to do this job through our VPN,'

'Sorry, our what?' said Ranald

'You know, we've discussed this when I set it up,' replied Perry, 'our Virtual Private Network. But this is getting highly political, can I hand you over to the Proff, he's standing right here next to me'

Professor Hapsley came on the line and reminded Ranald of the technicalities of this risky operation and how the President could be assured that it was just a temporary measure – a means to an end.

'That way we avoid trace routes,' continued Professor Hapsley, 'and we simply put the all of the President's stuff into an encrypted folder and onto the website and it'll just sit there – a bit like Wikileaks. Only difference is that we've put in place special security measures. Firstly so that the President's IT people can't get into the new website and destroy what we've taken, and secondly so that we can't be accused of threatening the security of the State of the Russian Federation and get counter-threats that what we're doing amounts to an Act of War or any nonsense like that,'

'Ah, yes, of course, I remember the process now, thanks Proff,' replied Ranald, 'so will you all go ahead now as fast as you can, and soon as you have it all safely up onto the new website, can you ring me back and let me know?'

'Right away,' said Perry, a note of excitement in his voice. 'We're not going to start World War Three doing this are we?' he asked as an afterthought.

'We'll get started right away,' replied Hapsley, 'shouldn't take long, so I be ringing back soon.'

'Oh, and one last thing,' said Ranald, 'not a word to anyone about this - my father, Sir Jeremy for instance - till we're actually going to use it on the President or his spokesman, all right?'

'Of course,' replied Hapsley, 'though with us making a move of this gravity, I suspect we're going to have to have another chat soon about moving Athena to a new location – though I admit that's a whole new game for another day.'

'You're right,' agreed Ranald, 'when you lot got us into this mess by going on and developing the Athena to the level it's got to today, relying on the remoteness of Craithe was never going to be secure enough was it?'

'So you're blaming us now are you?' laughed Hapsley, 'bit late for that, what would you have us do about it?'

'Uninvent it,' said Ranald, 'and while you're about it, uninvent nuclear weapons too.'

They both laughed and put their 'phones down.

Shortly after that Professor Hapsley rang back.

'All done,' he said, 'the last two months files, documents, notes, emails and telephone conversations all copied to the new website, we've just called it "Athena Services" and I've given it the password 'meanstoanend', all right?'

'Good,' said Ranald, 'On a separate laptop can you get through to me here on Skype and then leave that open – that would leave the big screen here free for something else I need it for.'

There was a pause while the Skype link was set up and Ranald could see Perry and the professor standing there in the Lab.

'That's looking good, I expect to be using it later this evening,' said Ranald, 'or earlier if I can entice Mr Komarov here before that. So it looks as though we're already. I'll now contact my father in law, whose been waiting for me – he should be able to get us quick access to the President. I'll keep you informed as things develop.'

Ranald rang Mikhail Vassilov.

'Mikhail, we're on,' said Ranald as soon as they were connected. 'There's only one further complication to what we've been discussing. That man Komarov's still got Kim and as his operative whose actually guarding her is either an SVR or an FSB agent, chances are that the President will already know about all of this,'

'Damn it, that man Komarov's a real pain,' said Vassilov, 'I met Kim many times on my visits to the bank on the Isle of Man, she's a lovely girl and if her life is at risk from Komarov, you're right, I wouldn't trust him an inch . But don't be surprised if the President thinks it's you that's the nutter. I've been thinking of the best approach to this whole matter and I'm going to take a new direction to win his confidence. By the time I've finished telling him why he needs to ring you he'll ~~will~~ think it's you whose the one who's nuts. Another thing, don't be surprised if he does all of this through one of his close circle, he never likes doing any of his dirty work personally.'

'I'm really grateful, Mikhail,' said Ranald, 'and, just so you know, I don't care what the President thinks of me,'

They laughed and Mikhail rang off to make his call to the President.

When Mikhail Vassilov's name was given as calling to speak on a personal matter to the President, he was put through to one of the Kremlin's most senior security man, General Andrei Yolkov of the FSB. As a personal friend of both Mikhail and the President, he was the ideal person to assuage the President's permanent paranoia about all callers.

'Mikhail, nice to hear from you,' he said as Vassilov was put through to him, 'we don't see enough of you at our receptions – we must put that right soon. I hear you have a *delicate matter* of which you wish to warn the President. He's entertaining someone at the moment – if you get my meaning – but as you said this was of the utmost urgency and it's you ringing, I thought I should take the call,'

'I'm grateful Andrei, though this is also extremely embarrassing for me,' said Vassilov, 'and it's partly because I'm so worried for my daughter Tatiana that I have decided I cannot remain silent.'

'That sounds very melodramatic, Mikhail,' said Yolkov, 'tell me more,'

'My Tatiana's husband has a team which has developed a new super cyber weapon,' said Vassilov, 'it's called Athena and it's the same weapon that Igor Komarov has been boasting about stealing for the President,'

'Yes, Komarov's been boasting that he has finally almost got this weapon,' said Yolkov, 'in fact he's been boasting about it for so long now, the President's getting sick of him. But you say he's now actually got it and it was your *son-in-law* he stole it from?'

'Yes, that's right, but that's not why I'm ringing,' went on Vassilov, 'my son in law is called Ranald MacCrammond and he has gone literally berserk as a result of this theft. He thinks that the President ordered Komarov to steal it and has done something horrendous in revenge – I mean horrendous for the President.'

'Something horrendous for the President? Did I hear that right?' said Yolkov,

'Yes, that's right,' said Vassilov, 'So before anything happens as a result I'm begging you to tell the President that it was me who brought this shocking act of revenge to your attention before it can do any harm – I need to try and protect my Tatiana, and despite our differences in the past, I wouldn't want anything to happen to the President either.'

'I understand perfectly, Mikhail,' said Yolkov, 'I'm sure that the President will bear that in mind. But, why don't you tell me what this horrendous act of revenge is, then we can see what we can do about it,'

Vassilov then carefully spelled out the details of the website that had been set up and that it now contained the President's most private and probably also incriminating secrets – all the dealings of his most inner circle. He gave Yolkov the Website address and password so that he could check it out for himself. He added that a boastful Ranald had given him the access information so that he could see that he was telling the truth,'

'My God, Mikhail,' said Yolkov, 'this is dynamite, I'll try and deal with it myself – even before it gets to the President. I'm most grateful for your loyalty to the Mother Russia and to the President, even if it may doom your son in law. Let's just keep this to ourselves for now whilst I ring your son-in-law and deal with him.'

'I suggest you humour him to start with,' said Vassilov, 'that way he'll tell you all this himself,'

'I'll do that, Mikhail,' said Yolkov, 'and, again, thank you for telling me all this – am so glad we should be able to fix it before the President gets involved.'

The moment the call from General Yolkov came in to the Newby Centre, Ranald breathed a sigh of relief – the ploy had worked and he instantly felt more confident that Kim could now be delivered unharmed.

As soon as they were connected, Ranald smiled to himself as the General began to pour verbal honey down the line.

'Mr MacCrammond, on such a wonderful day as your wedding,' said Yolkov, 'and all those hundreds of people, you could not possibly be expected to remember me, but I had kindly been invited by Mikhail and, I must say what a great event it was.'

'You're right, I don't remember, General,' replied Ranald,

'Anyway, I've had a look at your Website, "Athena Services",' continued Yolkov and Ranald tried to picture him at the other end of the line - was he relaxed as he sounded, or had this ploy got him sitting on a sharp knife's edge?

'I have to say that this Athena of yours seems to be all that Komarov said it was, quite a feat to lift the President's personal files – steal them to be more precise,'

'And?' said Ranald,

'And I have to compliment you on a degree of bravery in carrying out such a ... such an act of vandalism,'

'And?' repeated Ranald,

'I was wondering why you would risk so much to do this, the penalties being potentially so enormous.'

'Oh, I've only borrowed your President's files for an hour or two,' said Ranald, 'after he – or even you – have done what I am about to ask of you. If you do just one simple thing for me, I will give the President's IT people another password which will enable them to delete the entire contents of the website themselves.'

There was a silence for several seconds and Ranald was sure that he heard Yolkov whispering to someone near him.

'Ranald, if I may call you that,' said Yolkov after clearing his throat a couple of times, 'this is just plain and simple blackmail, but blackmail of one of the most powerful men on the Planet. Before commenting further, I just need to hear from you what it is you want us to do. For I have to tell you we need destroy the website's contents as soon as possible – before we have a truly dangerous situation on our hands.'

'There have already been deaths involved in the theft of Athena by Komarov,' said Ranald deliberately slowly, 'he also has my Personal Assistant and close friend, Miss Kim Bradley taken as a hostage. I expect Komarov to be here at this place at around seven o'clock GMT with my PA Miss Bradley in his custody. I will give you the ability to destroy the website and guarantee that no one else gets to see any of its contents on just two simple conditions.'

'And they are?' asked Yolkov,

'One, that you order Komarov to immediately hand over to me Miss Bradley unharmed,' said Ranald, 'and two, that you announce publicly that Komarov is now a persona non-grata with the President, that he is denounced for the outrageous manner in which he stole Athena, and is to hand over the memory stick containing Athena to my PA as she is released. That's it. You and I can talk about Athena and the President's understandable desire for it once this mess is out of the way. I also want this to be done over a visible internet link which my people can set up with yours – be that Skype or direct video link – that way Komarov, who will be standing next to me, will believe his fate.'

Again there was a pause and this time Ranald did hear whispering going on.

'I'm sure that for the complete destruction of your website,' said Yolkov, 'that I can get the President to agree to disown and castigate Komarov and demand the release of your PA with the memory stick and Athena on it. Nice talking to you, Ranald, and I hope we can do business over Athena as soon as this mess is out of the way. I'm happy for your people and mine to fix up the video link when we've finished talking and I look forward to seeing you again around seven GMT tonight.'

Ranald then got Yolkov to arrange for his IT people to set-up the video link between Newby and The Kremlin and he then transferred the call to Perry to do his end of this set-up.

'Right,' said Ranald, turning to Boreyev and giving him a mock-punch on the shoulder, 'let's ring Komarov at the Russian Embassy, and get this thing done.'

33

Monday afternoon

The Russian Federation Embassy,

Izolda and Kim had no idea where they had been taken after their kidnapping. And although Izolda had taken one of their captor's mobile telephones after she had killed all but one of them, it did not have an application on it to tell them their location. Soon they came to a small café and Izolda asked the owner where they were. They rang the Russian Federation Embassy in Kensington Palace Gardens, and Izolda spoke to one of the senior members of staff she knew there. They gave little information in case the mobile she had taken from the gunman was bugged or had a trace on it, and persuaded the Embassy to send a car to collect them.

On getting to the Embassy, Izolda immediately rang Komarov on his mobile phone,

'What a relief to hear from you,' he said as soon as he heard it was her, 'I found out from the Heliport that you had landed there safely and had taken a taxi to the Embassy. Then silence, what happened?'

'I'll tell you all that when I see you?' she said, 'more importantly, I have Athena on an external hard-drive, and I also have

Mr MacCrammond's Personal Assistant as a hostage. What would you like me to do with them both?'

'Fantastic,' shouted Komarov down into his mobile, 'don't do a thing with either until I get there, from the Connaught Hotel to the Embassy is but a hop in a taxi – I'll be there in minutes'.

As soon as Komarov was taken to the room where Izolda and Kim had been waiting for him, he burst into it,

'Congratulations again,' he said, 'the President will be delighted with your great work. Come with me both of you. On my way up here I've arranged for the Embassy's top IT man to take a look at the memory stick, just to confirm that we have the real thing – not that I doubt you for one minute of course,' he added, smiling broadly.

At this he nodded to the young man who had brought him up to the room and they followed him off to the Embassy's IT department. On reaching it, the young man introduced the three of them to the head IT man, by the name of Anton Dudko.

Izolda handed over the external hard-drive to Dudko who carefully plugged it into a laptop on one of his worktops. Almost as soon as it was in the laptop, its little in-built light began to flicker at speed, then, with no warning the laptop's screen went blank and the machine itself went silent as though it had been switched off.

For a moment, Dudko frowned at the machine but then stepped forward and pressed the start button on the rear of the keyboard. Still nothing happened. Just in case the battery had suddenly decided, coincidentally, to die at that very moment, he plugged a mains power lead into the machine and pressed the start button again. Nothing.

'Strange,' said Dudko, stating the obvious. He took the external hard-drive out of the dead machine and took it over to a much larger, mainframe computer.

'This should be Okay' he said, as he plugged the memory stick into one of the machines ports. Almost instantly the same thing happened – except that it was rather more dramatic. The little memory stick immediately began to flash its in-built light as before, but soon after that, rather spectacularly, all the monitors being run off this bigger machine suddenly closed down simultaneously. In just a couple of seconds, all systems were dead and a secretary came in from the room next door demanding to know what had happened to her screen.

Reverentially this time, Dudko took the memory stick out of the dead machine, shaking his head slowly from side to side.

'Where did you get this?' he said to Izolda,

'Why do you ask?' she replied somewhat fatuously,

'Because it has an extremely sophisticated self-defence mechanism built into it,' replied Dudko, 'one that's even going deny me the opportunity to see what is on it.'

'Have you seen this kind of thing before?' asked Komarov,

'Only once read about something like this in the UK, as it so happens,' said Dudko, 'but I'm sorry to have to tell you that I'll need a bit more time to do some more work on this and be sure I've got it right can you give me a couple of hours?'

'A couple of hours,' echoed Komarov, then he paused, 'OKAYAY we've waited this long and don't want to damage what's on there. 'Let me know as soon as you're finished with it.'

In around an hour and three quarters, Dudko contacted Komarov and with Izolda and Kim, he hurried back to the IT department. He explained that his first guess had been right. The memory stick could only be opened by a computer it recognised or one that identified itself as belonging to the same family.

'That's why I asked where you got it,' said Dudko, 'because it looks to me that the only place it will open is if it's plugged into a machine which is in the same family as the people who gave it to you. Sorry but that's all I can suggest.'

'What's this 'family' thing you talk about, said Komarov, 'I don't fully understand?

'If the people you got this download from get themselves a new machine, 'said Dudko, 'they add a small programme which brings it into the 'family' as all the other machines owned by them. In this case all the machines owned by Athena carry this 'family' recognition programme. So, you plug your hard drive into any of their family of machines and you'll have no problem with it.'

'Bastards', said Komarov and stormed out of the room.

Once Komarov had recovered from his outburst, he began to plan. As soon as he felt he had it all worked out he set about tracking down Ranald and eventually reached him at the Newby Centre.

'I must say that I'm disappointed that you let my people leave Craithe Castle with what is effectively a useless external hard-drive' he said as soon as they were connected,

'Just before we get embroiled in all of that,' said Ranald, 'I trust that you have my PA Kim with you and that she has been properly looked after,'

'Very well, if you wish to discuss that first,' said Komarov, 'may I say that I hope that you value her highly as in passing her back to you, I have some things I want in return,'

'Some things?'

'Yes, for example I would like you to transfer my thirty million Euros to my bank in Moscow,' said Komarov, 'and, almost needlessly to say, but I'll need to have proof of that transfer before we discuss anything else at all,'

'I can do that quite easily,' said Ranald, 'and the other things you said you wanted in return for my PA?'

'As I said at the beginning of our conversation,' said Komarov, 'I've been told that the external hard-drive will not work on anything but one of your 'family' of computers,'

'Yes, that's right, your people worked that out obviously,' replied Ranald, 'and there's a very good reason for that. As you will know by now, Athena is so powerful that it could be disastrous for the world if it found its way into the wrong hands. So our computers automatically add a defensive programme onto Athena if it's copied at all. If the copy is going onto another of our own machines, it will be recognised and will not go into defensive mode, but if it's stolen then the defence mechanism will prevent it being used – quite simple really, helps protect the world from terrorism'

'If you want your PA back alive and well,' said Komarov, 'I need to get a copy of Athena which I can take away with me and actually use?'

'You have to come to an Athena-friendly 'family machine first of all,' said Ranald, 'the nearest of those is where I am now, at the Towneley Foundation's Newby Centre, in Tower Hamlets. If you are here by seven o'clock this evening, bringing with you Kim in good health and spirits, we can then get on with settling these matters, all right?'

'We'll be there by seven,' said Komarov, 'and I suggest that for the sake of your very pretty little PA, that you do not set any traps or try to go back on what we've just agreed,'

'Rest assured, Mr Komarov,' said Ranald, 'I shall be concentrating entirely on the safety and wellbeing of my PA and will not do anything to jeopardise that. Furthermore, Mr Komarov, should you try and act clever by turning up here without my PA, you will suffer consequences you cannot even imagine.'

'There's no need for you to threaten me further, Mr MacCrammond, I have come too close to getting what I want and have no wish to jeopardise my money. You have my word, therefore, that I will bring her with me, though her continued safety will be in your hands.' said Komarov.

'Understood,' said Ranald,

'See you at seven, then', said Komarov.

Having already made himself highly unpopular with the President by promising Athena before he had it in his hands, Komarov did not want to risk yet another false dawn; he now steeled himself to wait until the evening when he would finally be able to broadcast the good news. Kim was informed of events and, inwardly felt a frisson of excitement wondering what Ranald would get up to at the Newby Centre. In her own mind, she was certain, of just two things ; one, whatever he did, Ranald would not risk her life and, two, there was no way in which he would let Komarov walk away with a copy of Athena,

Ranald felt confident that the secrets he held of the President's would ensure that Komarov was denounced and that he would realise that his career was at an end. He guessed it might cause all hell to break loose when Komarov was faced with the reality of his position. He therefore set about looking at the battle-ground in which this would be played out. If Komarov brought with him secret backup, for example, he and Boreyev's team would need to be ready for them.

34

Monday, afternoon

The Dorchester Hotel

The events of the morning had left Guiseppe Lupo in a state of shock. He stood, motionless except for almost imperceptible swaying to the rhythm of one of his favourite Italian songs wafting through his mind as he tried to blot out the horrors of the morning.

But, as he stood at the suite's panoramic window looking down towards the traffic speeding through Hyde Park below him, he hardly saw it, the music was not working; Goddamit, four of his men brutally slaughtered in what should have been a humdrum task of guarding a couple of hostages. The blow to his ego was crushing. As one of New York's most notorious – indeed, celebrated – mafia kings, it was humbling to have suffered such ignominy. Just one deranged gun-happy assassin had gunned down his men. How had such a thing been possible? They should have disarmed her, there were five of them against just her with her hostage. The whole thing beggared belief.

At least he still had Luigi and Rocco. The two of them, about as devoid of compassion as anyone can be, watched in silence as the Boss got himself mentally back into shape, Soon they would expect him to make some counter moves. Rocco, the brains of Lupo's connections worldwide and his team in New York, was quietly confident – and, without consulting the Boss, had already put out calls to cousins and other connections here in London, back in New York and elsewhere. Right now, all he needed was a new, totally dependable London team, and his contacts might make suggestions as to how to achieve that – well, anyway, that was Rocco's justification if later challenged.

Over an hour after Rocco had rung her, Mina must have got his message at last, and rang him back,

'Cousin Guiseppe, I didn't know you were in London,' she said, 'you should have given me more notice,'

'This isn't Guiseppe, this is his right-hand man, Rocco,'

'Ah, Rocco, Hi,' said Mina, 'your message seemed urgent– is everything all right?'

Rocco quickly gave her a run-down of the day's happenings and Lupo's involvement in the hunt for Athena. He also had to relate the sorry state in which they now found themselves. He finished by saying, 'Why don't you speak now to your mother's cousin, he's right here?'

By now, Lupo had heard that it was Mina, had turned away from the window and come across to the sofa. He took the phone from Rocco and forced a smile,

'Mina, bambina,' he said loudly, perhaps a little unnecessarily loudly, for he had wished not to appear too traumatised by the disaster that had overtaken him, 'I hear from your mother great things of your progress,'

'Well that's nice,' replied Mina, 'I think I've got London quite well sewn-up by now, so, yes, London's good. Sorry to hear of your set-backs, anything I can help with?'

'I was thinking of getting in touch with the Favero family, they used to be associates of our family in days gone by. I know old

Guido died, but do you know any of them by any chance? I'd like an opinion from family such as you and I'll ask Alessandro too,'

'I understand,' replied Mina, 'and, I can think of no one better to contact than the Faveros... I could certainly have a word with my ex-boyfriend's father – I'm sure that if the rewards are right he'd be happy to help you out,'

'Is he the Capo?'

'He is,' said Mina, 'and his name is also Guido. Shall I try and get hold of him for you and get him to ring you at the Dorchester,'

'Good girl, Mina,' said Lupo, 'talk to you again as soon as we've sorted all of this out and I'd like to meet you and see if we can't strengthen family bonds again.'

Guido Favero rang Lupo back almost immediately and, although their conversation started edgily, like boxers weaving round a ring sizing each other up, they soon began to reminisce about former family co-operation and ties. Soon Lupo got really enthusiastic as he explained the huge potential for using Athena for blackmail, *'on a majestic scale'* he had added.

Had he not suffered the shocks of the morning, had his mind been at its peak, he might have noticed that Guido Favero was strangely silent whilst he was eulogising about Athena and what they could achieve with it. Still, when Lupo got to the crunch and asked Favero if he wanted to join in this evenings 'action' to get Athena back from Komarov, the answer he got seemed positive enough. It was finally agreed that he would come to Lupo at the Dorchester as soon as possible with a couple of young supporters who *'know how to handle themselves'* as he put it.

'By the time it takes your lads to get kitted up and get over here to the Dorchester,' said Lupo finally, 'I hope to have tracked down Komarov and company - and we'll be ready to go.'

They rang off with Lupo's spirits much recovered and his pulse racing at the prospect of being back in the hunt for such a valuable prize.

By the time Guido and the two young Favero brothers arrived at the Dorchester half an hour later, it had been easy for Lupo to ascertain that Izolda and her prisoner were in the Russian Embassy. Lupo, Luigi and the Favero threesome set off right away, and finalised their plans in the back of the taxi on the way. After the short journey from the Dorchester to the top of Kensington Palace Gardens – sometimes referred to as Millionaire's Row – the group decided to split up and only Lupo went into the Embassy. He said he was a client of Izolda's and could see her on a matter of some urgency. She was apparently out with 'another young lady' but the receptionist kindly volunteered that the Embassy's young IT man, Dubko, had been with them much of the morning and, as he had gone out with them to give them directions, he might well know where they had gone. Dubko was duly sent for and when he arrived, volunteered to show Lupo where he had told the young ladies to go. As soon as Dubko was out towards the gates out of the Gardens, Lupo, thrust a gun forcibly into his ribs, causing him to cry out in pain.

'Just walk,' said Lupo and pushed the terrified Dubko along beside him, This group of three walked a few yards before being joined by the massive Luigi and the three Favero. By Dubko had realised that whatever was on the external hard-drive he had been looking at this morning, what was going on now showed it was way beyond anything he, a mere IT geek in the Embassy, should be involved in. He was soon pushed left, down into the Palace Gardens mews and as soon as they were a bit away from the main thoroughfare of Bayswater, he was pushed up against a wall and surrounded by the others. He quickly made it clear he was no hero, and asked them what they wanted.

As Dubko had told Komarov that they needed to plug the hard drive into a 'family-friendly' computer he had also heard Komarov and planning to do that at the Towneley Foundation's Newby Centre in Tower Hamlets at seven. He now readily passed this information over to Lupo.

Leaving Dubko in the mews, the group went back up to Bayswater and hailed a couple of taxis to take them through to the City and on to the Tower Hamlets area of London. The Towneley Foundation Centre was well-known to many near the north entrance to the Blackwall Tunnel but they asked the taxi-driver to drop them a couple of blocks away from it.

Being a Bank Holiday weekend, the centre was closed but the group soon found a café from which to watch the place. Despite this, figures could be seen inside but none of those they had seen were large enough to be Komarov. They decided wait until Komarov arrived.

35

Monday, 4.30pm

The Newby Centre, Tower Hamlets

From late afternoon, following Ranald's talk with General Yolkov, Ranald at the Newby Centre and Perry in the Lab' in Craithe Castle had checked through their systems. They had brought another large screen into the main computer classroom and linked it to the Castle's mainframe. This would mean that, at the click of a mouse, either of them could bring up onto the screen a number of sources – for example, at one point Ranald was going to want to show Komarov that his money had been transferred to his bank in Moscow. At another time, he would like to show whomever it was that was talking to them from the Kremlin in Moscow.

On the occasions that Ranald had had dealings with Komarov, he had seemed to be polite, even urbane – certainly not prone to rages or even outbursts of petulant behaviour. Today, however, he was going to be robbed of his connection with the President – at least in the public's eye. So, if Komarov was ever going to lose his temper or react violently, it was likely to be today. As for the transfer of Kim to the safety beside Ranald in the computer room, Ranald was hoping this would go smoothly but, if it turned nasty, Boreyev and his men would be able to take care of it.

In the time left before what Ranald hoped would be the last act of a play already far too long, he had some other unfinished business he needed to attend to. As he wanted no distractions when concluding matters to do with Komarov, he needed to deal with the mess that still lingered around the Matthews Finch Hedge Fund.

From earlier discussions with Wheeler, he had Paul Finch's home number and just hoped that, as anticipated, Paul Finch would be back from the States. He rang the number, and after ringing for a dishearteningly long time, it was eventually answered,

'Paul Finch', said a tired voice – almost as though he had been woken from a deep sleep.

'Mr Finch? It's Ranald MacCrammond here, is this a good time to call?'

There was a long pause, absolute silence, long enough for Ranald to say again,

'Is it convenient to speak to you now Mr Finch?'

'Mr MacCrammond . . .' started Finch hesitating, 'I'm so sorry but I have my PR consultant Mr Wheeler here with me and he has just finished telling me the quite unbelievable happenings of the weekend. So you may imagine that you would be the last person I would expect a call from. And, what's worse of course is what has happened to you personally at the indirect instigation of my partner, Nat Matthews.'

'Is Nat Matthews there with you also?' asked Ranald

'No Nat Matthews won't be involved with me again except to tidy up matters between us. He says he's had enough and wants to be bought out. Considering everything that's happened I can't say I'm that surprised,' said Finch.

'And you've heard, have you, that I've bought a large shareholding in your hedge fund?' asked Ranald,

Again there was a long silence and Ranald could hear Finch talking – presumably to Wheeler – but with his hand not very effectively covering the telephone. Eventually he returned,

'I'm so sorry Mr MacCrammond,' he said, 'but I've had so much to take in that my head's in a bit of a spin, To answer your question, yes, Mr Wheeler has told me that fantastic news and mentioned that you thought that Sir Jeremy would not mind if we used his prestigious bank's name to the company launch a new company. May I put the telephone on speaker I think Mr Wheeler has something to say?'

'By all means, good afternoon Mr Wheeler,' said Ranald

'Good afternoon, Mr MacCrammond,' said Wheeler, 'since we last spoke I've had a chance to evaluate all you told me. I've not really had a chance to explain to Paul here what a fantastic opportunity this is for the company; but, putting on my PR hat I would have told him that by the time I've polished the press releases I have drafted, the new Towneley Finch Hedge Fund should take off like a rocket. Should I get those ideas over to you or Sir Jeremy for your approval?'

'No Mr Wheeler,' replied Ranald, 'why don't you and Mr Finch just use your rechannelled talents to get those press releases out yourselves. We can discuss the exciting possibilities of a future together at some other time. I'd also look closely at what needs to be done regarding any police matters that might arise out of the weekend's activities. For what it's worth, my wife and I will not be pursuing any complaints about our short-lived kidnapping.'

There was another long silence before Wheeler spoke again,

'I can't tell you how relieved and grateful I am,' said Wheeler in a hoarse voice, 'I shall do whatever I can to make it up to both yourself and Mrs MacCrammond,'

'I am afraid that I still have some urgent dealings with Mr Komarov and I imagine that your dealings with him are now at an end,' said Ranald.

'They certainly are,' said Wheeler, 'I felt really uncomfortable doing business with him at all.'

'Goodbye to both of you for now, then,' said Ranald, and he heard muttered answers to this as he put the telephone down.

Ranald noted down for later some other outstanding matters, not least of which was the purchase of a new boat for McKinnon and the ordering of a new engine for the dingy which had let them down – albeit with Georgie's connivance.

With a heavy sigh but a smile, he finally ended the last call. His mind now clear of all the clutter of the tumultuous weekend, he could now give his undivided attention to the demise of Igor Komarov.

36

Monday, 4.30pm

The Newby Centre, Tower Hamlets

Rather before seven pm GMT, Komarov, Izolda and Kim arrived at the Centre. As directed by Boreyev, Izolda took Kim at gunpoint into the small glass sided classrooms the opposite side of the corridor from the computer classroom. As these two had glass walls above about four feet, the whole arena in which the great denouement was to be played out was almost completely open and visible, with just the occasional structural pillar to obstruct the clear views. Komarov felt happier with this arrangement than having them too near himself, and having heard the detail of Izolda's exploits with Lupo's thugs, he was confident that his bargaining position was in good hands.

Komarov came into the computer room and gave a slight bow but did not offer to shake hands. As all spoke Russian – and Ranald knew that the Kremlin was coming online around seven, he too spoke in Russian.

'Shall we get over the easy bit first,' said Komarov, 'moving my money from the Isle of Man to Moscow?'

'Certainly,' replied Ranald, 'I just need your bank details in Moscow,'

Komarov handed him a piece of paper with the details on it and Ranald turned to the big screen and read them out to Perry. As soon as he had them, those in the Centre could see Perry on one of the large screens; he went over to one of the larger desktop computers and after a fair amount of keying, turned back to face the camera.

'If I now switch screens you can see the whole transaction,' said Perry, and his own image was replaced by a screen-shot of the completed transaction.

'In addition to seeing the transaction like that, you're welcome to use one of the laptops here to check your bank account in Moscow,' said Ranald.

'Thank you,' replied Komarov, 'I will if I may.' He crossed the room to a laptop, went onto the internet and using a small piece of paper with notes scribbled on it, and logged into his Moscow Bank account. Up came a screen of the account he had called for and it showed the new very substantial balance.

'Excellent, that's that out of the way' he said as he logged off his bank.

'Now if you wouldn't mind having Kim, my PA brought in here,' said Ranald,

'Ah, just a minute, change of plan,' said Komarov, 'because you see I'm not sure that you will honour our agreement and let me have Athena on a proper usable memory stick of external hard drive,'

'So, not being sure whether or not I'll keep *my side* of what we agreed earlier,' said Ranald, 'you're now, unilaterally, going to break you word on *your side* of it, is that a fair analysis?'

'Afraid so,' said Komarov, smiling,

'In that case' said Ranald, nodding pointedly to Boreyev, 'it would seem that it was just as well that we did not trust you with Athena.'

As Ranald was speaking, Boreyev had picked up telephone and had dialled a number. On the big screen there was a sound of the number ringing out and seconds later the figure of the seated General Andrei Yolkov appeared on the screen. He was seated in a huge guilt and heavy brocade arm chair – almost large enough to qualify as a throne. Behind him the backdrop was of one of the Kremlin's magnificent smaller reception rooms with great swathes of gilded baroque plasterwork on both walls and what could be seen of the ceiling and heavy red curtains on what must have been fifteen to twenty foot windows.

There was an audible gasp from Komarov who moved sideways and leaned heavily on one of the desks near him. 'Andrei?' was all he managed to say.

'Good evening General,' said Ranald, 'I hope that this timing suits you as I know it's around ten in Moscow,'

'It's absolutely fine,' replied the General, smiling broadly,

'In our earlier conversation you had something to say about the two attempts to steal the Athena programme from Craithe Castle – one of them being successful,' said Ranald,

'I did indeed,' replied the General, 'and I have had a chance to speak to him since then; he has commanded me repeat our apologies on behalf of the Russian Federation for these outrageous and completely unsanctioned invasions of your Castle on a Crown Dependency island. I said I also hoped that you would convey our heartfelt apologies to Her Majesty, your Queen. When we catch up with Mr Komarov, you may rest assured that he and the other culprits will pay a due price for their effrontery. And as Mr Komarov is presently in London, you might ask him to contact me personally right away, I need to tell him that when he returns to Moscow, he is not to go back to his old offices. Mr Pavel Rostov will be taking over all his former connections and duties.'

Ranald found it quite hard not to smile at this over-the-top yet splendid performance for, although he had discussed what was needed to get the message across to Komarov, he had made any suggestions on what to say.

Komarov had already turned pale but after this brief speech he put a hand up to his forehead and was now gently massaging it, preferring to look no longer at his old friend, General Yolkov.

'Thank you for making that so clear for us, General' said Ranald,

'Our pleasure,' replied the General, as he gave a sidelong look to his right to someone just outside the camera's frame, 'and I hope shortly that we may meet and do some business over your Athena programmes' he added.

During the latter part of the General's speech, Ranald had made a sign to Perry up on Craithe who had acknowledged the pre-arranged signal,

'I'm also pleased to tell you General,' said Ranald, 'that my people have just sent the password for the website you were interested in. If you care to look at your mobile phone – the number which you gave me earlier - perhaps you can check that it has reached you,'

The general pulled his mobile out of an inside pocket, fiddled about with it for a moment and then looked up at the camera again,

'It has indeed arrived,' he said,

'Good,' said Ranald, 'I hope you have fun doing whatever you wish to do with it,'

The General just waved and then must have switched off the camera because his image faded from the big screen.

Ranald turned to speak to a now ashen-faced Komarov,

'I thought the General put our position on Athena rather well, didn't you?' but before Komarov could reply a fusillade of shots rang out from the main hall just outside the computer room. All of them

311

in the computer training room ducked out of sight below the level of the glass as the next shot shattered one of the classroom panels and they were showered with broken glass. Ranald squirmed towards the door trying to see across and into the small room where Izolda was guarding Kim. He saw that they too had come under fire and that Izolda, crouching by the classroom door, was retuning fire. He also looked back to the reception area where the new intruders seemed to be. He saw one figure get up and go back out of the Centre's main entrance; maybe going round for an attack a different way; not a moment to lose.

Boreyev had pulled himself across the floor and was rummaging around in a five foot long, black canvas bag. He pulled out a mortar and some of his canisters of crowd-control gunge and pulled himself over to the doorway past Ranald. Rolling over onto his back he prepared the mortar and put two canisters on the floor right next him. When he was ready, he nodded to Ranald, knelt up to peer over the partition wall and through the gap of the broken glass panel, and gave covering fire with the AK47 which Boreyev had passed him for this purpose. As soon as Ranald laid down an arc of fire, Boreyev swung himself up onto his knees, pushed the mortar into the doorway, and angling it as best he could, he dropped one of the canisters into the tube. As soon as it hit the firing pin at the bottom of the tube, it fired the canister and a swirl of smoke traced a shallow arc over the reception area where the new intruders were still firing towards Izolda and Kim.

The first canister burst, like a firework and a wide umbrella of thick charcoal-grey gunge shot out in every direction, spattering the windows and temporarily blocking Boreyev's view. On the assumption that he could not see them, they could not see him he squirmed further out of the door, and fired two more canisters in rapid succession but in different directions. The gunge flowed down the door beside him for a few seconds, and then the droplets began to gel and form into the same netting that had covered Rollo's men and the helicopter on the terraces at Craithe. At this moment the gunfire ceased and was replaced by cursing and the noises of struggling gunmen. Ranald had already leapt to his feet and ran through to the room where Izolda and Kim had been under a hail of fire for several minutes.

Izolda was lying, covered with blood, her body twisted into an awkward shape, her head in Kim's lap, her eyes looking up into Kim's. As he got closer to the two of them, he was just in time to see Izolda smile faintly and say something to Kim who was looking back down at her, gently pushing away the blood matted hair from Izolda's forehead.

Boreyev had followed Ranald out of the computer room, taking with him a number of sets of plastic hand-cuffs and both ran forward half crouching towards the main reception desk, being careful not to slip on the now almost set netting of gunge. On getting to the desk, Boreyev rose slowly from behind its cover and could see three of intruders struggling in the meshes of the setting gunge. As fast as he could Boreyev ran to each in turn, cuffing first their wrists behind their backs and then their ankles. As a final precaution, he then put a third cuff on each binding their wrists to their ankles. The three of them could now hardly move at all, looking somewhat like game trussed for the oven. Two other men lay dead over towards the Centre's entrance, presumably shot by Izolda in the early exchanges of fire.

Ranald knelt down and comforted the quietly crying Kim and laid a hand on Izolda's neck searching for a pulse. There was none and on looking again he could see that Izolda's eyes were staring, unblinking, up to the ceiling. She was dead.

As though suddenly remembering something left burning in the oven, Ranald leapt to his feet and reassuring himself that Kim was all right, ran back towards the computer room. He was joined by two of Boreyev's men who had now emerged from just beyond Izolda and Kim classroom, and tucked their guns into the backs of their trousers.

The three of them quickly but carefully approached the computer room where the smoke from the firing of the canisters was now clearing, As they entered it, even a cursory look was enough to tell them that is was empty – in the smoke, gunfire, canister firing and confusion, Komarov must have made his escape.

With the intruders trussed and the gunge now turning to white powder, Boreyev cut the plastic cuffs binding their wrists to their ankles and those round their ankles too and ordered the three of them at gunpoint to move to a row of chairs against the wall opposite the main reception desk. As soon as they were seated, new cuffs were put on them, tying their ankles to one of their chair-legs.

Ranald took Kim into the computer room, sat her down in one of the more comfortable chairs from in front of one of the consoles, drew up a chair next to her and sat down.

'How are you doing?' he said softly, 'this has all been one hell of an ordeal for you.'

Kim straightened up, and brushed smudges of drying tears away from her cheeks, then to Ranald's surprise, she smiled and even gave a brief laugh,

'You know, one never remembers the worst bits,' she said, 'and some of it was really exciting. Looking back, all I can say is, thank God I was kidnapped by someone as unbelievably good at her job as Izolda,'

Ranald smiled back at her, puzzled for now as he did not know how Izolda had extricated the two of them from the clutches of Lupo – and he would later be horrified by the story of that ordeal.

'Look, I've got to go back and find out who the hell these other intruders are, and see if it's not too late to find Komarov' he said gently and then added, 'are you sure you're all right?'

'I'm fine, really,' said Kim and getting up from her chair at the same time as Ranald, added, 'and if you'll point me in the right direction I could go and see if I can make cups of tea for everyone,'

Considering that an activity of this kind would be good for distracting her for a spell, Ranald pointed out for her how to get to the canteen and kitchen behind it.

Returning to the main reception hall, he found Boreyev watching over the prisoners,

'I've sent my two off to look around and see if they can find any trace of Komarov,' he said, 'though I suspect that he's used all the confusion to get the hell out of here and may be well away by now,'

'Well, by now, as you put it' said Ranald, 'I'll bet he's well on his way to the Connaught to pay his bill and get himself out of the UK. It'll be interesting how that develops because, of course, General Yolkov would have said anything to get our website destroyed and, with it, all the President's secret files. For all we know he may secretly welcome Komarov back into the arms of the President - who knows?'

'I doubt that,' said Boreyev, 'the President's persona is one of great importance to him. Anyone who taints that persona – such as Komarov being caught stealing something as high profile as Athena from another sovereign state, is unlikely to be soon forgiven. Anyway, that's my *Russian opinion,*' said Boreyev,

Ranald then turned to face the three remaining intruders. They sat there, shock and bewilderment on their faces.

'Before calling the Police and handing you over to them,' he said, 'you have just five minutes to explain what this is all about. If you think that all you have to fear is what the Police can do to you, think again. For starters, ballistics will soon establish which of you is up for murder – the other two will be accessories to murder – take your pick'

The eldest-looking of the three raised his hands a bit off his lap, as though to raise a hand in class.

'I'm Alfredo Favero,' he said, 'Mr Lupo who's lying over there dead, next to my father, rang us only today. His family used to be friends with ours. As he was over staying at the Dorchester Hotel, he said he would like to meet some old family friends. Our father and the two of us went over to the Dorchester to represent the rest of the family and as an act of British hospitality. When we got there Mr Lupo quickly persuaded my father that, we were honour-bound to join him in something he was involved in. He said it was an old association, but still very much alive. We know how important our family's word used to be so we went along with him. We had no idea it would involve any of . . . er . . . this'

He paused and looked pleadingly from Ranald to Boreyev and back again. Then he went on,

'Mr Lupo gave us guns but said he was being persecuted by some Russian and that they were only for protection – he said there would be no violence. Beyond that we know nothing of what he was involved in.'

Ranald smiled back at him,

'Though there may be a few elements of truth in some of that,' he said, 'I think we'll just let the police deal with you – though I will be giving my views on this matter to them – especially after we've delved a little further into your family friend, Mr Lupo,'

He turned, nodded for Boreyev to continue watching over the three, and went back to the computer room to ring for the Police. There he found Kim had brought back a tray of tea and was handing some of it to Boreyev's two men,

'You all right now?' said Ranald putting a hand on her shoulder,

'Fine,' she said, 'just fine now', she replied

Ranald rang the police, gave a basic run down of the scene and happenings at the centre and then went to one of the laptops. On it he dialled up Perry on Skype, and when Perry answered, told him what had happened at the centre and asked if all was well at Craithe.

'Everything's fine here,' replied Perry, 'in fact as quiet as a graveyard,'

Whilst waiting for the police to arrive and deal with Izolda's, Lupo's and Favero's bodies and take away the remaining three intruders, he got Perry to find Tatiana up in the Castle so that he could have a talk with her on Skype.

Just as he finished this his mobile phone, buzzed and vibrated in his pocket. He took it out and scrolled through to new messages where one, just arrived, was flashing. He opened it and read it and then read it again.

'I am most unhappy at the way you, single-handedly, destroyed my name, my credibility and my long-held position and favour with the President. You have not heard the end of this nor of me'. It was signed Komarov.

The Police and forensics arrived, took away the three bound intruders and the bodies of Lupo, Favero and Izolda. DI Morgan, in charge of the investigating team spent some time with Ranald, Boreyev and Kim getting their stories and took statements from Boreyev's two men as well.

As a result of Ranald's persistent pleading, Morgan promised to let Ranald know of any developments still not obvious right now – well, at least developments that did not break the 'ongoing investigation' rules of confidentiality.

Ranald, got on with tidying up from the fall-out of the Easter weekend's quite extraordinary happenings and Kim helped him with all of it, learning the full story as well.

'Well, I must say Boss,' she said at one point, 'I have to take my hat off to you as they say,'

'What on earth for?'

'The sheer cunning of your ploy with Komarov,' she replied, 'that was far more the pirate's blood in you than the royal name you also carry,'

'I don't understand,' said Ranald,

'Remember when we had all just arrived in Craithe and you showed me the big book and the family tree, Bonnie Prince Charlie and the pirate chap?'

'Oh, yes, of course, yes bad Jack Black' said Ranald smiling, 'fancy you thinking of that, maybe you're right.'

Although Boreyev's men returned to Moscow after a short holiday sightseeing in London, Boreyev stayed on to help Ranald find a suitable new, secret home for Athena in London – and were successful in finding just such a spot above a busy Italian restaurant in the West End where comings and goings of people connected with the further development of Athena would go unnoticed amongst the busy restaurant's human traffic.

Though the team had been happy in the wilds of Scotland these past couple of years, Ranald persuaded them all to move to London as soon as the new centre could be made ready and, with the help of the conglomerate's deep pockets, also helped very generously with relocation and expensive London housing costs for all of the team.

It was some two weeks after the shoot-out at the Newby Centre that DI Morgan telephoned Ranald.

'I thought you might be interested,' he said, 'a completely unexpected finding from one of the bodies from the Newby Centre shooting,'

'Unexpected,' repeated Ranald, 'in what way?'

'The unexpected bit is to do with the shootings of Mr Lupo and Mr Favero,' said Morgan, 'we found that both had been wounded by shots from Izolda Valik's gun but what killed them both were shots fired from a gun not even found at the Centre,'

'I don't understand,' said Ranald, 'how's that possible?'

'Must have been fired by someone who was with the group before you clobbered them with the sticky stuff,' said Morgan, 'someone who fired the shots that killed both Lupo and Favero, but left *before* the gunge was fired. Oh, and another strange thing, in both of them the shots that actually killed them were shots in their backs. We've managed to trace the gun to who it's registered to – an Alessandro Scaalay, originally of Sicilian origin, was involved in a mugging a couple of years back but was stolen from a police lock-up. Does that name, Scaalay mean anything to you?'

'Scaalay? No I don't think so,' said Ranald, How's it spelt?'

'S-c-a-l-e,' repeated Morgan, 'as I said, Sicilian, Italian in origin,'

'And his Christian name?' asked Ranald,

'Alessandro, as in Alexander,' said Morgan,

Ranald suddenly noticed his heart-beat in his chest, but did not immediately mention a number of quite extraordinary things that had suddenly stormed into his mind. *Need to think about this a bit more,* he thought.

'Sorry, nothing at the moment,' said Ranald, biting his lower lip,

'Well, we'll carry on following that up, especially the Sicilian connection as both the Lupo and Favero families were not only originally from near Palermo in Sicily, they were also Mafia,' said Morgan, 'but if anything occurs to you, give us a bell, will you?'

'Of course,' said Ranald and they rang off.

'Good, God,' thought Ranald, 'Alessandro Scaalay, Italian pronunciation, could that be the same as Sandy Scale, head of the City of London cyber police?'

Wondering if he was allowing his imagination run away with him, he took a deep breath. *Still, there was a possibility of that being right was there not? He was in on the whole saga from the moment he was told of the Manila bank attacks. He kept popping up at odd moments, the conference in particular. And what was there to prevent him being head of the City of London's Cyber Crime Unit as a cover for what might be called 'the family business?'*

He needed to find if there was a logical way in which this could be tackled – check out a Scale connection to the Mafia, rule out a connection between Sandy Scale and Alessandro Scale. But where to start?

In sudden inspiration, he picked up his iPad, went to the 'maps app'. He typed in *'Palermo, Sicily'*, enlarged the map that came up and began his search,

Suddenly, he felt that heart-beat in his chest again, stronger than before, because there it was on the Google map, on the outskirts of Palermo, to the south-west, the village of Scale. He enlarged the map further. And there, east and slightly south of Scale, past Rigolizia, was the village of Fontana Lupo – the wolf's fountain. This was absolutely *not* evidence, it was what the police would call mere conjecture – still what a hell of a coincidence.

He rang Morgan, and after exchanging brief pleasantries, Ranald said,

'I was thinking about the question of Scale, the Mafia, Palermo and all that, and I looked the names up on the map and found Scale and Lupo near each other just outside Palermo. I know that Lupo means wolf so is common enough for that to be purely coincidental. The only Scale I know, pronounces his name the English way to rhyme with *pale* and he's the highly respectable

Sandy Scale head of the City of London Cyber Police – so what you might call a dead end. But he would know everything about Athena and is probably very computer savvy, it would clear my conscience if you could do the kind of checks you usually do in such circumstances and rule him out of this for me.'

'Thank you for that,' said Morgan, 'every little snippet of information helps. I'll let you know if that comes to anything – come to think of it, I'll ring you even if your connection Sandy Scale does turn out to be nothing to do with all of this.'

'Many thanks, Detective Inspector Morgan,' said Ranald and rang off.

It was a shock therefore, two weeks later, when Morgan rang back to say that they had arrested Sandy Scale for the murder of both Guiseppe Lupo and Guido Favero. It appeared that Scale had been in on the hunt for Athena from the start and had soon found that cousinly Mafia from New York, the Lupos, were coming at Athena from a different starting point and were going to ruin his own plans by bringing in the Faveros. Scale's operation included a cousin of the American lot who he used to keep tabs on them – her name is Mina – short for Giacomina and her surname - Falcone.

'Scale was going to allow them to do his dirty work for him' said Morgan, 'and was planning to take over the theft of Athena from Komarov with his own team waiting nearby. Your people put an end to that, however, with your quite extraordinary weapon in those canisters. Scale has confessed to all of it. As soon he saw that a simple theft of Athena from Komarov was not going to happen, he wanted to erase any connections with the whole thing; he couldn't risk anyone knowing of his involvement and so disposed of the only two people who knew of it, namely Lupo and Favero. Incidentally we'd like to know more about that sticky stuff in the canisters.'

'I'm afraid that won't be possible, the canisters were supplied from Moscow I believe and have gone back there with the security people I hired briefly. Still, that was quite an investigation of yours – my congratulations,' said Ranald, 'and it sets my mind at ease so thanks for ringing,'

'Let's hope that's an end to it all, then,' said Morgan, and, with that, was gone.

An end to it all, thought Ranald. Well, yes, apart from a very rich and vengeful Komarov still on the loose.

Printed in Great Britain
by Amazon.co.uk, Ltd.,
Marston Gate.